Carol...
Writing contemp...
readers. Walks by the sea with coffee/ic...
thrown in! Torrential rain. Sunshine in sp...
What Caroline hates: losing her pets. Fighting with
her family. Cold weather. Hot weather. Computers.
Clothes shopping. Caroline's plans: keep smiling and
writing!

Alison Roberts is a New Zealander, currently lucky
enough to be living in the South of France. She is also
lucky enough to write for the Mills & Boon Medical
Romance line. A primary school teacher in a former
life, she is now a qualified paramedic. She loves to
travel and dance, drink champagne, and spend time
with her daughter and her friends.

FROM HEARTACHE TO FOREVER

CAROLINE ANDERSON

MELTING THE TRAUMA DOC'S HEART

ALISON ROBERTS

MILLS & BOON

First Published in Great Britain 2019
by Mills & Boon, an imprint of HarperCollins*Publishers*
1 London Bridge Street, London, SE1 9GF

From Heartache to Forever © 2019 by Caroline Anderson

Melting the Trauma Doc's Heart © 2019 by Alison Roberts

ISBN: 978-0-263-26990-1

MIX
Paper from
responsible sources
FSC® C007454

This book is produced from independently certified FSC™ paper
to ensure responsible forest management.
For more information visit www.harpercollins.co.uk/green.

Printed and bound in Spain
by CPI, Barcelona

FROM HEARTACHE
TO FOREVER

CAROLINE ANDERSON

MILLS & BOON

CHAPTER ONE

'Ah, Beth, just the person. I've got a favour to ask you.'

Her heart sank. *Again?*

'How did I know that was coming, right at the end of my shift?'

She turned towards James with a wry smile and then everything ground to a halt, because the man standing beside the ED's clinical lead was painfully, gut-wrenchingly familiar.

His strangely piercing ice blue eyes locked on hers, his mouth opening as if to speak, but James was still talking, oblivious to the tension running between them.

'Beth, this is Ryan McKenna, our new locum consultant. Ryan, this is—'

'Hello, Beth.'

Her name was a gentle murmur, his eyes softening as he took a step forward and gathered her up against his chest in a hug so warm, so welcome that it brought tears to her eyes.

'Oh, Ry—'

He let her go long before she was ready, stared down into her eyes and feathered a kiss on her cheek.

'OK. So I'm guessing you two know each other already, or this is love at first sight,' James said drily, and Ryan laughed a little off kilter, taking a step back and giving her some much-needed space to drag herself together.

'Yeah, we know each other,' Ryan said, his voice oddly gruff. 'We—er—we worked together, before I went abroad. Best scrub nurse I've ever had the privilege of working with.'

There was a whole world left unsaid, but James just nodded, still unaware of the turmoil going on under his nose.

'Well, it's good to know you got on—we rely on teamwork. Beth, I was going to ask you if you could be a star and give Ryan the once-over of the department and then take him for a coffee? They really need me in Resus, and I'm sure you'd like to catch up?'

'What, now?' she asked, feeling a flicker of something that could have been panic.

'If you can spare the time. I'd be really grateful and they do need me.'

She met Ryan's eyes, one eyebrow raised a fraction. 'Are you OK with this?' he murmured.

As if James had left her with a choice…

'It's fine, Ry. I don't have to be anywhere,' she said quietly, surrendering to the inevitable, and she turned back to James. 'Go. You're right, they could really use you. Sam's tearing his hair out and Livvy's rushed off her feet. We'll be fine.'

He nodded, his face relieved. 'Thanks, Beth. You're a star. And while you're at it, if you could convince him to apply for the permanent post, you'll have my undying gratitude.'

Her heart thudded, the flicker threatening to turn into a full-on panic attack.

'I thought the application window was closed?'

'It's been extended. So—if you could twist his arm?'

He was smiling, but his meaning was clear, and they were desperate for another consultant, but simply seeing Ryan again had sent her emotions into freefall and her hard-won status quo felt suddenly threatened. A locum post was one thing, but she didn't know if she could cope with him here on a permanent basis, not when she was finally putting her life and her heart back together after the last two agonising years.

Not that it, or she, would ever be the same again…

Anyway, it wasn't relevant, because he was committed to Medicine For All, the aid organisation he'd been working with for the past two years, and she knew how strongly he felt about that. He'd walked away from Katie because she didn't understand, so there was no way he'd be looking for a permanent job and he obviously hadn't been clear enough with James.

'Leave it with me,' she said, which wasn't a yes but it was the best she could do, because she was oddly torn between wanting to run away and wanting to talk to him, to find out how he was.

Because something had changed him, she could see that at a glance. He was thinner, his face slightly drawn, shadows lurking in the back of his eyes. The same shadows that lurked in hers after all that had happened between them? Or other shadows, from the things he'd seen in those two years? Both, probably.

'Sure?' James asked, maybe finally picking up on the tension running between them, and she nodded.

'I'm sure. Go. Leave it to me.'

'Thank you. I know you'll do your best. I'll see you on Monday, Ryan. I'm really pleased you've agreed to join us.'

'So am I. I'll look forward to working with you.'

They shook hands and she watched James go, then Ryan turned back to her with a wry smile that touched her heart.

'Forget the guided tour. Is there somewhere quiet we can go and get a coffee?'

She felt a wave of relief and nodded. 'Yes. There's a café that opens onto the park. We can sit outside.'

The café was busy, but they found a little bistro table bathed in April sunshine and tucked out of the way so they could talk without being overheard, and he settled opposite her and met her eyes, his searching.

'So, how are you?'

Her heart thumped. 'Oh—you know.' She tried to smile. 'Getting there, bit by bit. You?'

That wry, sad smile again, flickering for an instant and then gone. 'I'm OK.'

She wasn't sure she believed him, but there was something else…

'So, how come you're here, in Yoxburgh? Is that de-liberate?' she asked, needing to know if he'd sought her out or just stumbled on her by accident, but he nod-ded slowly.

'Yoxburgh? Yes, sort of. I needed a job, there was one here, and I know it's a lovely place. But I didn't know you were here, if that's what you're asking, not until I saw you.'

'Would you have applied if you'd known?'

He shrugged. 'Not without talking to you first to see if you were OK with it.'

'Why? If you needed a job—'

'There are plenty of jobs.'

'But not here.'

'No. Not here, and I wanted to be here, but now— well, that depends.'

Her heart hiccupped. 'On?'

'You, of course. If you're working in the ED, we'll probably be working together. I'm OK with that, we worked well together before, but us—you and me— that's different. Much more complicated, and the last thing I want is to make things difficult for you, so I need to know if you're going to be OK with me being underfoot all the time.'

Was she?

'Just so long as you don't expect to pick up where we left off. Well, not that, obviously, but—you know. Before…'

He frowned, his eyes raw. 'I don't expect anything, Beth. The way we left things, I've got no right to expect anything. For all I know you might be back with Rick.'

'Rick?' It startled a laugh out of her because after everything that had happened Rick was so far off her radar it was almost funny. 'No way. He was a lying cheat, why would I be back with him, any more than you'd be back with Katie?'

He gave a startled laugh. 'OK, I can see that, but—someone?'

'No. It's just me, and I'm happy that way. You?'

He laughed again. 'Me? I haven't had time to breathe, never mind get involved with anyone. Anyway, people get expectations and then it all gets messy.'

'Not everyone's like Katie.'

'No. They're not.' He studied her, his eyes stroking tenderly over her face. She could almost feel their touch, but then he closed them and shook his head with a little laugh. 'I can't believe you're in the ED. What brought that on? I thought Theatre was your life.'

'You can talk. I thought surgery was *your* life.'

He shrugged. 'People change. I was facing a lifetime of increasing specialisation, and I didn't want to spend every day doing the same thing over and over again until I'd perfected it. I wanted a change, and MFA provided me with that, and over the course of my time with them I realised I like trauma work. I like the variety, the pace, but you...'

'I wanted a change, too.' Needed a change, because everywhere she'd looked there'd been reminders of what she'd lost, and she'd found working in Theatre with anyone but him just plain wrong. 'So, when did you get back?'

'Two weeks ago. I've been back a few times on leave, picked up a bit of locum work here and there to refill the coffers and keep my registration up to date, but this time it's for good.'

For good?

She felt her eyes widen, and her heart thumped. 'Really?'

His smile was sad. 'Yes, really. I've seen enough horror, lost some good friends, seen way too many dead chil—'

She flinched, and he gave a quiet groan.

'Sorry. I didn't…'

'It's OK,' she lied. 'And I can only begin to imagine what it must have been like. So, was it after you lost your friends you decided to come back?'

He gave a wry laugh. 'No. Oddly, that was when I decided to stay on longer, to carry on the work they were doing because it was so necessary, but there'll always be others waiting to take my place and it was time to come home because I'm just as needed here in many ways. My grandparents are frail and my mother's shouldering the whole burden on her own, and it just seemed like it was time. Time to move on with my life, to get back to the day job, as it were. Back to the future.'

With her?

He'd said it was time to move on with his life, but he was the one who didn't do relationships. Not after Katie had tried to get pregnant to stop him going away.

But what if he'd changed now, got MFA out of his system and was ready to settle down? It sounded like it, and maybe he wanted to try again with her? Maybe a bit more seriously this time—although it could hardly have been more serious than the way it had turned out. But if he did?

She wasn't sure she was ready for that, not yet. She

was still working through life day by day, hour by hour, step by step. She stared down into her coffee, stirring the froth mindlessly.

'So that's me,' he murmured. 'How about you? Are you happy here, in Yoxburgh?'

Happy? She could hardly remember what that felt like.

'As happy as I can be anywhere,' she said honestly. 'It's a lovely place, and that weekend we spent here—it was really special, the walks, the feel of the sea air—we said then what an amazing place it would be to live, and then a job came up here and I thought, why not? I was sick of working in an inner city, the noise and the dirt and the chaos, and I wanted to get away from all the reminders. I just needed peace.'

Peace to heal, to reconcile herself, to learn to live again, and where better than here, where it all began—

She sucked in a breath and looked up again. 'So how come you applied for the locum job?'

He shrugged. 'Same reason, I guess. I loved it here, the peace, the tranquillity of the coast and the country-side, and I needed that, after all I've seen. And there were the memories. I know we were only here for a weekend, but it was hugely significant.'

He looked away, his brow creased in a thoughtful frown, then he looked back and met her eyes. 'If I'd known you were pregnant, Beth, I wouldn't have gone away—not then, at least. I would have found a way out of it, delayed it or something. Not that it would have changed anything, but at least I could have been there for you. And I did try when I knew, but you didn't seem to want me there, and I couldn't really do anything anyway, nothing constructive, so I left and I tried to airbrush you out of my life, out of my thoughts, but I couldn't. I realised that, the moment I got back when all I could think about was seeing you again, making sure you were all right.'

He'd tried to airbrush her out of his thoughts? And failed? Well, that made two of them. Even so…

'Why didn't you act on it? You've been back two weeks and you haven't contacted me.'

'You've changed your phone number.'

She felt a twinge of guilt. 'I know. I'm sorry, I suppose I should have told you. But you could have found me if you'd really wanted to. You know enough people.'

He nodded. 'You're right, and I was going to as soon as I knew what I was doing, where I was going to be, but whatever, I've found you now, I'm here, I'm back for good, and at least I know you're all right. Well, as all right as you can be, I guess.'

Their eyes locked, his heavy with understanding, and she felt her heart quiver.

'I've missed you,' she said, the admission wrung from her without her consent, and he smiled sadly.

'I've missed you, too. I didn't realise how much, until I saw you again. All that airbrushing just didn't work.'

Her eyes welled, and she blinked the tears away.

'Ry, I'm not the person I was. I've changed.'

'I'm sure you have. So have I. Don't worry, I don't expect anything, Beth, but it is good to see you again and I'm so sorry I let you down. I wish I could undo it.'

She nodded, looking away from those all-seeing

eyes, turning her attention back to the froth on her coffee. She poked the last bit of froth with the spoon, then looked up again.

'So if you really are done with MFA, are you going for the permanent post? James was groaning the other day about the calibre of the applicants so they've obviously had to extend the closing date, and it sounds like he wants you to apply.'

He looked thoughtful. 'That depends.'

'On?'

'You, again, of course.' He shrugged again. 'I don't want to do something that you don't want, Beth. If you don't want me here, I won't apply, especially since we'll be working together. I know I've accepted the locum job, but if that's an issue, too, I can always pull out. I haven't signed anything yet.'

She frowned at him. 'But you've said you'll do it! You'd never go back on your word.'

'I would if it would hurt you. The last thing I want is to hurt you again.'

She shook her head. 'You didn't hurt me, not like Rick hurt me. You didn't lie and cheat and sleep with my best friend and then pretend it was over when it wasn't. Your only failing was your commitment to Medicine For All, but I got that. I understood, and I admired you for it.'

'Katie didn't.'

'I know, but I'm not Katie, and you're not Rick, and you've never hurt me. And you were there for me when it mattered, and you stayed until it was over. That meant so much.'

'I could have stayed longer. *Should* have stayed longer.'

'No. I didn't want you to, Ryan. You needed to go back, to fulfil your commitments, and I needed to be on my own. You were right, you couldn't do anything constructive to help me, and there were people in other parts of the world who really did need you. Don't feel guilty.'

'But I do.'

'Well, don't. I don't need your guilt, I've got enough burdens. You did the right thing.'

She straightened up and smiled at him, pushing back the shadows. 'Why don't I give you that guided tour James was talking about, and introduce you to some of the others? And then you can decide if you want to apply.'

'You don't mind? I might get it. You have to be sure.'

She shrugged. 'Ryan, we're in desperate need of another consultant and I can't stand in the way of that, but I can't promise you a future with me, not in any way, so if you're thinking of applying because of that—'

'I'm not. I've told you, I don't expect anything from you.'

'Good. Let's go and do this, then.'

The department was much as expected—modern, well equipped, but ridiculously busy, and he could see why he was needed.

And they had a permanent post going. It would be a great job, a perfect place to settle down—with Beth?

No. She'd warned him off, said she'd changed, and so had he, and yet he'd still felt his heart slam against his chest at the sight of her, felt a surge of something utterly unexpected when he'd pulled her into his arms and hugged her.

Love?

Of course not. He didn't do love, not any more, and anyway, it wouldn't work. She wanted other things from life, things he didn't want, things that didn't include him, but they could still be friends. They could work on that, and it was still a great hospital in a beautiful part of England. What more could a man want? And anyway, it was only a temporary post at the moment. It wasn't like he was committed. If they couldn't work together, he could always leave it at that and move on.

'Seen enough?'

He met her soft grey-green eyes, so bad at hiding her feelings, and he could tell she wanted to get away.

'Yes. Thank you, Beth. I need to get on, anyway, I've got to find somewhere to live by Monday. Any idea who to ask?'

'Hang on, Livvy Henderson might know.' She stuck her head back into Resus. 'Livvy, do you know if anyone's moved into the house you were renting? Ryan's looking for somewhere.'

'Ah, no, Ben's got a new tenant.' She flashed him a smile. 'Sorry I can't help. I hope you find something, Ryan.'

'I'm sure I will. Never mind. Thanks.' He turned back to Beth. 'So—any other ideas?'

'Baldwins? They've got a few properties near me advertised to let. Might be worth asking them. They've got an office on the High Street. It depends what you want.'

He laughed, thinking of some of the places he'd slept in over the past two years, and shook his head. 'I'm not fussy. Just so long as it has a garden. I need to be able to get outside. And somewhere to park would be handy.'

'Go and see them. I'm sure they'll have something.'

He nodded. 'I will. Thank you. I was thinking I'd check into a hotel and maybe look at some places to-morrow.'

Something flickered in her eyes and then was gone, as if she'd changed her mind. 'Good idea,' she said, but nothing more, and he wondered what she'd been going to say. Whatever, she'd thought better of it, and he realised he had some serious work to do to rebuild their friendship.

Baby steps, he thought, and then felt a stab of pain.

'Right. Well, I'll see you on Monday.'

The eyes flickered again, and he could see the mo-ment she changed her mind. 'Give me a call, tell me how you get on.'

'I don't have your number, remember.' And nobody changed their number unless they wanted to hide, so from whom? Rick? Him? Or from the others, the well-meaning friends who hadn't quite known what to say to her? He could understand that. He'd blocked quite a few numbers.

He pulled out his phone and found her entry. 'OK, give it to me?' Then he rang her, and heard her phone buzz in her pocket.

'OK. I'll let you know how I get on with—Bald-wins?'

'Yup. Good luck.'

* * *

Was it those words, or was it just that the fates had finished playing Russian roulette with him?

Whatever, the agent showed him a whole bunch of stuff, none of which appealed, and then said, very carefully, 'There is something else. It was for sale but it didn't shift, so the owner got tenants in and they've done a runner and left it in a state, but he's disabled and can't afford to pay someone to sort it out, so if you didn't mind rolling up your sleeves I'm sure I could negotiate a discount. It's a great place, or it could be. It's a three-bed bungalow on Ferry Lane, overlooking the marshes and the harbour, and you can see the boats on the river in the distance.'

The river? He could feel his pulse pick up. 'Does it have a drive?'

'Oh, yes, and a double garage and a big garden. They had a dog so the house smells a bit, but with a good clean and a tidy-up…'

'Can I see it?' he asked, impatient now, because it sounded perfect, doggy or not, and he'd grown up with dogs.

The agent glanced at his watch. 'I can't take you today, I'm on my own here, and I'm out of the office until eleven tomorrow, but I can give you the key. I take it you're trustworthy?'

Ryan laughed. 'I think so. After all, what can I do to it that the tenants haven't? Apart from clean it?'

'Good point. Here. And take my card and give me a call.'

'I will. Thanks.'

He hefted the key in his hand, slid it into his pocket and headed back to the car, cruising slowly along the clifftop before turning onto Ferry Lane and checking out the numbers. And there it was, a tired-looking bungalow set back at the top of a long concrete drive with weeds growing in the cracks.

Uninspiring, to say the least, and it didn't get better as he went up the drive, but as he got out of the car he caught sight of the view and felt peace steal over him.

He slid the key into the lock, went through the front door and was confronted by multi-coloured chaos.

The agent was right, it did smell of dog, the kitchen and bathroom were filthy, and the garden was a jungle, but every time he looked out of a window and saw the river in the distance his heart beat a little faster.

It might be awful now, but with a good scrub, the carpets cleaned and the grass cut, it would be transformed. Oh, and about a vat and a half of white paint to cover the lurid walls and calm it all down. All he had to do was roll up his sleeves and get stuck in.

He pulled out his phone and rang the agent.

'I'll take it,' he said, and the man laughed.

'I thought you might. Your eyes lit up when I mentioned the river.'

'Yup.' He laughed. 'So, where do we go from here? It's just that I am in quite a hurry, I start work on Monday. Is there any danger we can sort it by then?'

'Yes, we can do it today. We're open until seven tonight. If you come in at six, that'll give me time to get it all sorted.'

So he rang Beth, although he hadn't meant to, and told her about it.

'Where is it?'

'Just up Ferry Lane on the left. It's number eleven.'

'Are you still there?'

'Yes—why?'

'Can I come? I'm only round the corner and I have to see this.'

He laughed. 'Sure. You'll be shocked, it's pretty dire, but I'll get my body weight in cleaning materials and paint and it'll be fine.'

'It can't be that bad.'

He just laughed again, and went outside to wait for her.

'Oh, my word...'

'Yeah. Great, isn't it? You've got to love the shocking pink. But look.'

He wrapped her shoulders in his warm, firm hands and turned her gently towards the window, and she felt her breath catch. 'Oh—you can see the river! It's where we walked that day—'

The day he'd lifted her off the stile and into his arms and kissed her, and she'd fallen a little bit in love with him. The day it had all begun...

'I know,' he murmured, his voice a little gruff. 'It's beautiful down there, and the thought of having it on my doorstep, being able to look at it all the time, is just amazing.' He dropped his hands and stepped away from her, but she could still feel the echo of his fingers, the warmth that had radiated off his body.

'Come and see the rest. He said it's got three bed-rooms but I only got as far as the first one and gave up.'

She could see why. The place was dirty and untidy, as if the tenants had picked up their things and walked away without a backward glance, and there was a per-vading odour of dog. There was a lot to do before it was a home.

They walked through it, examining all the rooms, finding the third bedroom at the opposite end to the other two, tucked away beyond the kitchen with a patio door to the garden. It even had an en suite shower room.

'So will you make this your bedroom?'

He shook his head. 'No. I'll use it as a study because of the door to the garden. Do you know what, the house is actually in pretty good condition under all the dirt. I don't think it'll take a lot to turn it around.'

She eyed the grubby carpets, the faded curtains, the filthy bathroom. 'If you say so.'

'It's only dirt. I'll get on it in the morning. I've got to go down to the office now to sign something, then I need to eat and find a bed for the night. Any sugges-tions?'

Why? Why did she say it? She had no idea, but with-out her consent her mouth opened.

'I've got a spare room, and a casserole in the slow cooker that's enough for three meals so that should do us, so we can eat after you've done the paperwork and then come back here and make a start if you like? I'm on early tomorrow but I can help you now, and again after my shift. Bear in mind it's Friday tomorrow, so you've only got three days before you start work and I guess you've got other stuff to do first. Like find some furniture, for starters.'

He laughed. 'Furniture would be handy.' His smile faded as he searched her eyes, his own unreadable. 'Beth, are you sure? That's a lot to ask.'

Sure? She wasn't in the slightest bit sure, but it seemed the sensible thing to do, the most practical, and she was nothing if not practical.

'I'm sure,' she lied. 'And anyway, you didn't ask, I offered.'

She just hoped it wasn't a huge mistake.

It was just as well she'd agreed to help, because the house was worse than he'd thought.

After they'd eaten he changed into jeans, rolled up his sleeves and they went straight back to tackle the mess, armed with the contents of her cleaning cupboard. She hit the kitchen while he tore up the bedroom carpets, and by the time he'd done that it looked a whole lot better. Then he studied the sitting room carpet.

Was it salvageable? Doubtful, but with a clean…

He turned back the corner to see what was underneath, and blinked. Seriously? An original wood block floor? He pulled back more, then more, and started to laugh because it was so unexpected and wonderful.

'Hey, come and see this,' he called, and Beth went into the sitting room, clad in shocking pink rubber gloves that matched the awful walls, a streak of dirt on her cheek, and his heart crashed against his ribs.

How could she look so sexy?

'Wow! That's amazing. It's gorgeous!'

It wasn't alone. He dragged his eyes off her, look-ing way more appealing than she had any right to look with dirt on her face and her hair all sweaty, and stud-ied the floor. 'Well, I don't know about gorgeous, but it knocks spots off the carpet and it'll save me money. I wonder if the hall's the same?'

It was, so was the dining room, and he was stunned.

'It's incredible. I love it. I think you're right, a bit of polish and it will be gorgeous. Right, let's go. It's late, you're working tomorrow and I could kill for a cup of tea.'

'Me, too. It might wash the dust out of my throat.'

He chuckled, and her eyes softened with her smile. Without thinking, he pulled her into his arms and hugged her, burying his face in her hair and breathing in dust and bleach and something else, something fa-miliar that made his heart ache.

'Thank you. Thank you so much for all you've done. You've been amazing and I wouldn't have got nearly as far without you.'

She eased away, leaving him feeling a little awk-ward and a bit bereft. 'Yeah, you would, because you wouldn't have stopped. Right, time to go.'

'Tea or coffee?'

'Tea would be lovely, thank you. Want a hand?'

'No, you're fine. Go and relax, I won't be long.'

Relax? He was too wired for that, and stiffening up nicely after all the heaving and bending. He was going to hurt in the morning. Ah, well. At least they'd made a start.

He flexed his shoulders and strolled over to the shelves in the corner of her sitting room beside the fireplace, where a silver trinket box had caught his eye. It was a heart, he discovered, smooth and rounded, incredibly simple but somehow beautiful, and crying out to be touched.

He picked it up, and it settled neatly into the palm of his hand as if it belonged there, the metal cool against his palm, the surface so smooth it felt like silk. There was something written on it, he realised, and he traced it with his fingertip, his heart starting to pound as he read the tiny inscription.

A date. A date he recognised, a date he could never forget because it was carved on his heart, too.

He heard her footsteps behind him.

'Tea,' she said, her voice sounding far away, the clink of the mugs as she put them down oddly loud in the silence. He turned slowly towards her, the heart still nestled in the palm of his hand.

'What's this?' he asked gruffly, knowing the answer, and her smile nearly broke his heart.

'Her ashes.'

Her face blurred, and he bent his head and lifted the tiny urn to his lips, his eyes squeezed tightly shut to trap the tears inside.

'You kept them,' he said, when he could speak.

'Of course. I didn't know what else to do. You weren't there by the time I picked them up, and I didn't want to stay where we were because of all the reminders and I knew if they were there I'd feel tied, so I had to keep her with me until we could decide together what to do.'

He looked up, blinking so he could see her face, and her smile cracked.

'Oh, Beth...'

He reached out his free arm and pulled her against his side, and she laid her hand over the delicate little urn in his hand, her fingers curling round over his as she rested her head on his shoulder.

'Grace didn't suffer, Ry. At least we know that.'

He nodded, and she lifted the little heart gently out of his hand, kissed it and put it back on the shelf, next to a pretty cardboard box. She touched it fleetingly.

'That's her memory box,' she said softly. 'The midwives gave it to me in the hospital. Would you like to see it?'

He shook his head, mentally backing away from it, unable to face it. 'No. Not tonight. I'm too tired, Beth. I think I might head up to bed. I've got another long day tomorrow and you're working.'

Her smile was understanding, as if she'd seen straight through him.

'When you're ready,' she said gently, but he'd spent two long years running away from it and he wasn't sure he'd ever be ready for what he knew must be in that memory box.

Time to stop running? Maybe, but not now. Not tonight.

Not yet...

CHAPTER TWO

'ARE YOU OK?'

Ryan propped himself against the doorframe of his newly acquired home and gave her a slightly crooked smile.

'Yeah, I'm fine.'

'Are you sure? Because you didn't look it last night.'

He hadn't felt it, and between the memories that the little heart had dragged up out of their hiding place and the knowledge that Beth was just on the other side of the wall, he'd hardly slept at all. And then seeing this place in daylight, realising the enormity of the task, had made him wonder what on earth he was doing.

So, yeah, one way and another, he was very far from fine.

He scrubbed a hand through his hair and shrugged away from the doorframe, stepping back into the hall to let her in. 'I was tired. And, yes, OK, I was—uh—I was a bit emotional. It was just holding it, you know? Knowing Grace was in there.'

She nodded. 'I know.' Her smile faltered, and she

sucked in a breath and looked around, then blinked. 'Oh—wow! What happened to the pink?'

He laughed. 'Three coats of white paint happened to it.'

'Three? Already? What are you, Superman?'

'It's been a nice breezy day and I've had all the windows open so the paint's dried quickly and it really doesn't take that long. I've done the sitting room, as well. Have a look.'

He pushed the door open and followed her in, and she gasped.

'Oh! It looks so much bigger. And brighter.'

He chuckled. 'That wouldn't be hard. Cup of tea?'

'That would be lovely. I haven't had a lot to drink today. I've brought scruffy clothes.'

He frowned at her. 'You've been working all day.'

'So? It was the sensible Friday shift. The late shift won't have it so easy.'

He headed for the kitchen. 'Tea or coffee? I bought a kettle and some mugs and stuff.'

'Tea, please.'

He felt her watching him dunking tea bags, pouring milk, his hands covered in paint. There was some in his hair, too, he'd noticed. He was going to have to do some serious scrubbing to get it off by Monday.

'So how was work?' he asked, handing her the mug. 'Anything interesting?'

'Not really, a few sporting and gardening injuries, the odd fall, but nothing nasty, just busy.'

He thought of his average day with MFA and laughed. 'I'll take that.'

'I guessed you would. Bit of a change from what you've been doing.'

'Yeah.' He put away the memories and conjured up a smile. 'Here—let's go in the garden. I found a bench. It's a bit wobbly, but it should be OK if we sit down carefully.'

He scooped up a packet of biscuits and she followed him through the dining room and the tired conservatory into the garden.

She eyed the bench dubiously as it creaked under his weight. 'I think I'll sit here,' she said, taking a biscuit and perching on the edge of the steps that led up to the garden from the patio. Well, patio was a bit of a stretch. Some uneven crazy paving, but it was somewhere to put a table and chairs.

'It's a pretty garden.'

He snorted, but she stuck to her guns. 'It is! Look at the perennials in the border.'

'I see them. I also see the weeds, and the foot-high grass, and the fence that's making a bid for freedom. I don't think this place has had any maintenance in living memory but hey, it'll give me something to do in my time off. That'll be a bit of a luxury.'

'Time off?'

He nodded. 'Yeah, you don't get a lot of that in the field. You only do three months at a time, but it's pretty full on.' He fell silent, his thoughts obviously miles away, and she wondered what he was seeing. Probably just as well not to know.

'Here, have another biscuit before I eat them all.'

He got up to hand her the packet, and as he pushed himself up the bench creaked again and slid over sideways into a heap.

She laughed. She tried not to, but his face was a picture and she dissolved into giggles.

'How is that funny?' he asked, but his lips were twitching and seconds later he was sitting beside her on the steps, clutching his stomach and laughing just as helplessly as her.

'Maybe you need to invest in some new garden furniture,' she suggested when she could speak again, and he nodded.

'Maybe. Or I can sit here and study the windows. They really need replacing.'

'Buy a new bench. It's cheaper than the windows and you don't own the house.'

'No, I don't. Not yet.'

Yet? She turned and met his eyes.

'Yet?'

'It's possibly for sale.'

'But—you're a locum! Why would you buy it?'

'Well, I wouldn't, unless I was going to be living here long term.' He paused, looked away, then looked back, his eyes searching hers. 'I think I want to apply for the permanent job.'

She wasn't expecting that, not so soon, not before he'd even started work there, but realistically what was there to know? He'd met James and a few of the others, he knew her, he knew he loved the town—what more was there?

Nothing—except her, and her feelings, and if he'd

asked her what they were she'd be hard pushed to tell him, because after seeing him with Grace's heart last night they were even more confused. She looked away.

'I'd give it a few days before you decide. You might hate it.'

'Unlikely, and I can always withdraw my application if I want to.'

'Withdraw it?' She laughed. 'You seriously think James wouldn't talk you out of doing that?'

'I know he wouldn't. Not if I don't want to be talked out of it. If you don't want me here, Beth, I'll go, no matter how much James wants me to stay.'

She searched his eyes, read the sincerity in them, the concern for her welfare. And then she thought of the little silver heart that had fitted so perfectly in the palm of his hand...

She wanted him to stay.

It was the last thing she'd expected to feel and she had no idea where it had come from, but it hit like a lightning bolt, and she sucked in a breath and got to her feet.

'Let's just see,' she said, tipping out the dregs of her tea onto the weedy grass behind her. 'So—what's next?'

'My bedroom. I'm picking up my clothes and other stuff from my mother's on Sunday, and I can borrow her airbed.'

'Airbed?' She turned and stared at him. 'Ry, there's no hurry. You can stay with me as long as you want.'

He shook his head. 'No. I've put you out quite enough, Beth. I'll stay tonight and tomorrow, but then I'll be here.'

'But—you've got no furniture. It's a bit basic,' she murmured, but he just laughed.

'Basic? Having a roof is a luxury in some of the places I've been. Trust me, this is a palace. I've got a new bed and sofa coming on Monday evening. I'll be fine.'

'If you say so.' She shrugged, not quite believing him, and headed back into the house, wondering if she should feel hurt that he didn't want to stay, and telling herself not to be stupid. He'd always been independent and she wasn't going to change him. 'How about I get stuck in and clean the rest while you do the bedroom, then?'

They stopped at eight because the light was failing and they were both tired, but his bedroom was painted and the kitchen, cloakroom and both bathrooms were gleaming and she'd started on the windows.

He waited till she'd finished the pane she was working on, then took the cloth out of her hand. 'Come on, it's late, and you're working tomorrow. Why don't we pick up a takeaway?'

She gave him a tired smile. 'That sounds great. How does the bedroom look?'

'Bigger, and it's got that amazing view.'

'Just as well, as you don't have any curtains. Right, come on, we've got another long day tomorrow.'

'Are you sure you don't mind? I feel like I'm taking advantage of your good nature.'

'Don't be silly. I wouldn't offer if I wasn't happy.'

He wasn't sure about that. Beth had a heart of gold,

a heart that he'd broken, even if only indirectly, by not making sure she couldn't get pregnant.

'You're a star,' he said, echoing James, and she shook her head.

'No, Ryan, I'm a friend,' she said simply, and her words brought a lump to his throat because while it was true, in a strange way she meant so much more than that to him and he didn't have the words to say so.

He didn't even think there *was* a word for what they were to each other, he just knew she was an indelible part of his life and always would be.

By the end of Saturday the place was transformed.

Once the paint was dry he'd pulled up the carpet in the sitting room, dining room and hall, and together they mopped and polished the wood block floor and stood back to admire it.

'Wow. You were right, Beth, it is gorgeous. Stunning.'

'I thought it would be. How about pots and pans and things, if you insist on moving in so quickly? And bedroom curtains, come to that.'

'Oh, I'm sure Mum's got some I can borrow. I don't need much for the kitchen, and there's a box in the pantry. There might be something in there worth salvaging.'

They went and had a look, and the answer was a maybe.

'I'll take the box home, sort through it and put anything worth having through my dishwasher and bring it back tomorrow, if you give me a key,' she said, so he loaded it into her car, locked the house and went back to hers for the third and final night.

Not that he'd have a real bed until Monday, but as he'd said, a roof was more than he'd had at times, and he'd be fine—and maybe better than fine. He might even sleep if she wasn't lying there in the next room, just on the other side of the wall...

'Morning!'

Beth turned and met his eyes with a smile, her heart skipping a beat at the sound of his voice.

'Morning. All ready for your first shift?'

'Yes, absolutely. It'll make a refreshing change from painting. That's just mind-numbing.'

She felt her mouth twitch and bit her lip. 'Be careful what you wish for. Did you get on OK yesterday? And did you sleep last night?'

He laughed softly and propped himself up against the central desk. 'Like a log, but I'm looking forward to my new bed. I'm all done with sleeping bags.'

'You could have stayed at mine again,' she reminded him.

'I know, but I didn't want to outstay my welcome and I know you well enough to realise you wouldn't tell me if I had. Thanks for the card and the house plant. The place looks almost civilised in a rather empty way.'

'You're welcome,' she murmured. 'I thought it needed cheering up a bit. I put the kitchen stuff in the pantry, too. It might come in handy. Here—your spare key. And talking of keys, has anyone given you a locker or anything?'

He slid the key into his pocket. 'No, and I could do with some scrubs, if you could point me in the right direction?'

She nodded, and spent the next ten minutes sorting him out. 'Right, is that everything you need?'

'Pretty much. Thank you. I'd better go and find James.'

'He's in Resus.'

He nodded, and she went back to work and left him to find his feet, but it wasn't long before they were in Resus together, working on a patient who'd been brought in after being knocked off his motorbike by a driver who hadn't seen him.

His left leg had an open fracture and the paramedics has splinted it, but it didn't look good and he was clearly in a lot of pain and his blood pressure was low.

'Right, someone cut his clothes off so we can have a good look please,' Ryan said swiftly. 'Can I have the FAST scanner, and a gram of TXA in an infusion, and I want X-rays of the skull and that leg. Leave the collar and helmet on for now. Hi, I'm Ryan, and I'm a doctor. Can you tell me what happened, Jim?'

While he spoke to Jim and the radiographer took the X-rays, Beth set up the tranexamic acid infusion to slow the bleeding while Ryan's gentle fingers checked the man's ribs, abdomen and pelvis.

His leg was tinged blue below the fracture, and Beth checked the pulses in his foot.

'No pedal pulse,' she told Ryan, and he nodded.

'OK. Jim, there's a problem with the blood supply to your foot, so I'm going to have to pull your leg straight to sort that out. I'm sorry, it's going to hurt for a moment but it should feel better afterwards. OK, are you ready, Beth? On three.'

He pulled it straight, checked the pulse and then left her to deal with splinting it while he went back to the abdomen, a frown on his face as he ran the ultrasound wand below the man's ribs.

'There's a shadow. I think he might have an encapsulated bleed.'

'Spleen?'

He shook his head. 'No. Left kidney, maybe. There's a lot of bruising on this side, so I suspect a blunt force injury. Give him another gram of TXA as a bolus and let's get an X-ray of these ribs, and can we catheterise him, please, and check the urine for blood?'

She was already on it, and it proved his diagnosis right. The blood was obvious, and their patient was starting to deteriorate, so he was whisked away to Interventional Radiology for embolisation of the bleeding vessels before the orthopaedic surgeon could deal with his leg fracture.

They watched him go, and Ryan shook his head, a slightly bemused expression on his face as he stripped off his gloves and apron and headed for the sink.

'It feels odd not to finish the job. I would have had to deal with both of those injuries in the field, but at least we got the pulse back to his foot and he hasn't got a skull fracture, so it's all good.'

'You almost sound as if you wanted to do it all yourself,' she said, but he laughed and shook his head.

'No way. I'm happy to hand him over. I've had

enough of juggling too many balls. They get dropped, and anyway, it's nice to have time for coffee occasionally. And that'll teach me to say the *c* word,' he said, and she looked up and saw the next patient already being wheeled in.

It set the tone of the day, one case piling on top of another, but he worked fast and thoroughly, and it was a joy to her to be working alongside him again. It gave her a chance to study him, to remember all the little things she'd forgotten, like the way he frowned when he was concentrating, the way his brow cleared the second it was all under control, the quirk of a brow, the brief nod when he was happy with something.

'Right, go for lunch, both of you,' James said, and she realised it was after two. She'd been working alongside him since before eight, and they hadn't stopped for breath.

'Sandwich and a coffee?' she suggested, and he nodded.

'That would be great. I'm starving. Breakfast was a long, long time ago.'

But yet again it wasn't to be. Another patient came through the doors, one of three from a nasty RTC, but Jenny, her line manager, came in and relieved her, so she went to the café and picked up lunch for both of them and he ate his in a snatched quiet moment a while later, washed down by the now tepid coffee she'd brought back for him.

'I can see why I was needed,' he said with a wry laugh.

'Oh, you're certainly needed. Still think it's better than painting your house?'

His chuckle was dry and a little rueful. 'It's certainly more mentally challenging.'

'Oh, well, you've only got another three hours to go. What time's your furniture being delivered?'

'I said not before six, and I can't see me getting away before then so hopefully it'll be eight or something. Whatever. They said they'd let me know. Right, I'd better go back and reassess my patient. I'll see you later.'

Not much later, as it turned out.

He was in Resus with another emergency, gloved up and trying to assess a nasty scalp wound with an arterial bleed when his phone jiggled in his pocket.

'Could someone get my phone, please?' he asked, and one of the nurses delved in his scrub top pocket and held it up to him.

Damn. He stared at it and groaned. 'Can someone find Beth, please, if she's still here? I need to ask her a favour.'

'I think she is,' Jenny said. 'Although she shouldn't be.'

'No, I know that, but I saw her walk past ten minutes ago so she might still be around.'

The nurse who'd delved in his pocket came back with Beth a moment later, and she tipped her head on one side.

'Problem?'

'Just a bit. I need another favour. I've had a message from the delivery team. They've said they'll be there at five and there's no way I can leave before six and if it goes on like this I won't get away then. Is there any way you could let them in?'

'Sure. I should have gone off an hour ago anyway.'

'I know.' He sighed. 'I keep asking you favours—'

'Don't be ridiculous.' She held out her hand. 'Key?'

Damn. It was still where he'd put it a few hours ago.

'Right trouser pocket.'

Their eyes locked, and she looked hastily away and squirmed her hand under his plastic apron and into his pocket, groping for the keys while he tried really, really hard to keep his mind in check.

Not to mention his body—

'These them?'

'No. The loose one, the one you gave me back,' he said, and gritted his teeth again while she went back in and rummaged again, then returned the others.

'Do you want me to check everything's OK?'

'No. Just let them in, sign for it as unchecked, that's all. Well, unless it's obviously trashed in transit.' He gave her a rueful smile. 'Thank you, Beth. I owe you, big-time.'

'You do. Don't worry, I'm keeping a tab.'

He grunted, and she gave him a cheeky grin and left him to the spurting artery and his mounting guilt.

She'd spent days helping him, and now she was heading back to his house, waiting in for the furniture. And he was clock-watching, dividing his guilt between his new job and his old friend.

If that was what you could call her, the woman you'd had a brief affair with, who'd ended up giving birth to a baby whose heart was so compromised she'd been doomed from the moment of conception.

There had to be a better word than 'friend.' It was what she'd called herself when he'd thanked her for all her help, but she was so much more than that, their relationship so complicated, and he knew they'd be bound together for ever by the heartbreaking loss of their tiny daughter.

His chest squeezed, and he focused his attention on his patient and put Beth, their baby and his guilt out of his mind.

It was after eight before she heard the scrunch of tyres, and she gave the bedding a last swipe with her hand to straighten it, then opened the door.

'Beth, I can't believe you're still here!' he said instantly, his face hugely apologetic. 'I'm so sorry. I thought you'd be gone ages ago. Have they not come yet?'

'Yes, of course they have, they came at five. I've just been pottering and waiting for you. Jenny rang me so I knew you'd be late.'

'I didn't. Not this late, anyway, and there was no way I could leave.'

'No, I gather you had another really nasty RTC with multiple casualties. Nice, gentle introduction on your first day.'

He snorted softly. 'Tell me about it. At least I was working with you, which made it significantly easier. So I assume everything was OK with the furniture?'

'Fine—lovely. Come and have a look.'

She opened the bedroom door, and he stopped in his tracks.

'They built the bed?'

'No, I did, because I didn't think you'd want to do it after such a hectic shift.'

He stared at her. '*You* did it? Wow. I didn't for a moment expect you to do that, Beth. Thank you.'

'It was easy,' she said, lying slightly because another pair of hands would have been hugely useful. 'Eight bolts and a few screws.' She waggled an Allen key at him. 'They even provided the technology.'

He gave a soft laugh, and hugged her.

'Thank you so much. I really wasn't expecting—'

She put her hand over his mouth, cutting him off. 'Hush. You've spent your life looking after people. I thought it was time someone looked after you a bit.'

He reached up and caught her hand, pressing a kiss into her palm before threading his fingers through hers.

'Thank you.'

His eyes were filled with a host of conflicting emotions, and she guessed he was just as confused as she was. And it really didn't help that there was a massive bed right beside them...

She retrieved her hand gently and stepped out of reach, ignoring the tingling in her palm. 'I hope I used the right bedding. It was new, but it was all I could find that would fit.'

'No, that's great, it's all there is,' he said, his voice unexpectedly gruff. 'Did the sofa come?'

'Yes, they unpacked it and the coffee table and took all the packaging away. It looks really good. Go and see.'

She followed him into the sitting room with a silent sigh of relief, and he sat down on the sofa, then swung his legs up and groaned contentedly. 'Wow. An actual sofa, long enough to lie on—and it's comfy. That's such a luxury.' He looked around and laughed softly. 'It looks almost homely, in a rather bare sort of way. And the floor's beautiful.'

He got to his feet, staring down into her eyes searchingly. 'Look, I could do with a shower, but I'm hungry, and if you haven't eaten yet, how about going out for something? Nothing fancy, just a pub—or we can go posh, if you like. Up to you.'

Her stomach rumbled, and she gave him a wry smile. 'Food's probably a good idea. I haven't even given it a thought but there's not a lot in my fridge. I was going shopping after work but I got slightly side-tracked.'

'Then I'm definitely buying you dinner,' he said firmly, the guilt back in his eyes. 'Go home, get changed while I shower, and I'll pick you up in half an hour. And work out where you want to go.'

She nodded, then on impulse went up on tiptoe and kissed his cheek. The brush of stubble against her lips sent a shockwave through her body, and she dropped back onto her heels and headed for the door, more confused than ever.

'See you in half an hour, then,' she said lightly, and walked out, letting out a quiet rush of breath.

Clearly her body hadn't forgotten him, then...

'Where to?'

'I thought the Harbour Inn?'

Really? He glanced at her, then away again quickly before she could read his expression. Of all the places to choose…

'If you like. It's nice and close.'

He headed down towards the little yacht harbour, to the pub where they'd had lunch nearly two and a half years ago, just before he'd kissed her for the first time and set the ball rolling.

He'd split up with Katie when he'd realised she was trying to get pregnant to stop him joining MFA, and Beth had been right there at the time, working along-side him in Theatre, intriguing him, tempting him—but when after a few weeks he'd asked her out she'd said no, holding him at arm's length because she didn't want a relationship.

Well, neither did he, not so soon after Katie, and maybe not for years, but that didn't make him a monk, and after a week when everyone in the Midlands seemed hell-bent on injuring themselves and they'd been trapped together in Theatre for countless hours, the tension simmering between them had reached break-ing point.

He'd needed to get away, get out of the city and away from Beth, but by sheer coincidence they'd both been scheduled for a long weekend off, so he'd put his cards on the table and asked her to go away with him. No strings, no commitment, no relationship, just a few days of adult fun by the seaside after the week from hell, and with any luck it'd get it out of his system.

If she'd said no it would have made life awkward,

but frankly it had been awkward enough, so he'd had nothing to lose.

She hadn't. To his astonishment she'd said yes, so he'd booked a room in a posh spa hotel in Yoxburgh and picked her up on the Saturday morning with a tingling sense of anticipation. They'd been too early to check in, so they'd driven down to the harbour, found the little pub and had lunch, then gone for a stroll along the riverbank to kill time.

And then he'd lifted her down off the stile and kissed her.

She hadn't held him at arm's length then, and they'd spent most of the next two days in bed having the hottest sex he'd ever had in his life.

He parked the car, slammed the door on his thoughts and headed into the pub with Beth.

'It hasn't changed at all,' he murmured.

'No. I doubt if it's changed for decades. All part of its charm, I guess. So, what are we having?'

'Fish and chips.'

She laughed at him. 'Well, that's healthy.'

'I don't care. You can have whatever you like, but after a day like today I need comfort food and calories.'

She gave a low chuckle, the sound running over his nerves like teasing fingertips, and his body leapt to life.

'I might have the baked cod with a salad,' she said, and then she tilted her head and looked at him. 'How's Jim? Any news?'

'Yeah, he's OK. They took out his left kidney, and

he's got an ex-fix on his leg, but he's doing all right. He's alive, anyway.'

'Good. How about the RTC that held you up this evening?'

'Well, they all made it, which is a relief. It's never good to lose a patient on your first day.'

She chuckled again, and he gave her an answering smile, but hers faded and she studied him thoughtfully.

'It was good working together again,' she said, and he nodded slowly.

'Yes. Yes, it was. I'd almost forgotten how intuitive we are together. It was like you knew what I'd want without me asking, but then you always could read my mind.'

'Or maybe I'm just a good nurse and know my stuff.'

He arched a brow, and she pretended to scowl at him, her mouth puckering and making him want to kiss it.

He put his hands in the air, giving up the fight to hold back his smile. 'Sorry, sorry. You are a good nurse. Best I've ever worked with. Is that better?'

'Yes. Thank you.' Her smile was back, playing around her mouth and softening her eyes, and for a moment he had an overwhelming urge to lean over and kiss her—

'Fish and chips?'

He sat back, took a long, slow breath and looked up at their server.

'Yeah, that's mine.' And in the nick of time...

'Coffee? Unless you want to get back to your lovely new bed?'

He hesitated, then gave in, knowing it was foolish, knowing he was on a knife edge but unable to walk away.

'It'll keep another half hour. Coffee would be lovely.' He cut the engine and followed her into her house. 'Anything I can do?'

'No, you're fine, go and sit down, I'll bring it through.'

So while she put the kettle on he wandered into the sitting room and closed the curtains, then sat down to wait for her, his eyes seeking out the little silver box as they always did, his heart heavy.

If they'd known before that weekend what was to follow, none of this would have happened, but of course they hadn't. They'd spent the next two months together in blissful ignorance, and then in late January MFA had sent him on his first posting.

No strings, he'd said, so he'd had no contact with her, which had been fine because he'd been too busy to think about anything else, but then he'd come back on leave in early May, and he'd discovered she was pregnant.

It was his worst nightmare, the last thing he'd ever wanted to hear, and his first instinct was anger because he thought she'd done it on purpose, but then she told him their baby girl had such hugely complex congenital heart defects that she was unlikely to make it to term, and his world fell apart.

He was still reeling with shock when they lost her at twenty-seven weeks, the child he hadn't even known about until the week before. The child he hadn't wanted—or hadn't known he wanted until it was too late. The child he would never have the chance to get to know because her little heart had given up the unequal struggle and stopped beating before he could meet her and tell her how much he loved her.

He'd spent two years trying to forget, but he knew now he never would.

He walked over to the little silver box and picked it up with infinite tenderness, nestling it in his palm, his other hand stroking it, needing to touch it, to touch her, to hold her again.

His poor, perfect, broken baby girl.

Why?

'Ry?'

He put the heart down gently, as if not to wake her, and walked into Beth's open arms.

'I'm so sorry,' he murmured gruffly, his voice a little ragged. 'Why did it happen, Beth? Did they ever find out?'

'No. They have no idea. They didn't find anything in the tests—no chromosomal abnormalities, no genetic links, nothing to indicate it was anything other than a fault in her embryonic development. Just a glitch. One of those things.'

She eased out of his arms and sat down, patting the sofa beside her.

'Come on, sit down and drink your coffee.'

He sat, but his eyes kept going back to the little heart and the pretty box beside it. Pandora's box…

She put her mug down and looked at him, her eyes searching.

'Do you want to look at it now?'

Could she read his mind? Maybe.

'I don't know.'

She got up again and went over to the box, bringing it back and putting it down on the coffee table, just out of reach. He could feel his heart beating, feel every thud against his ribs, taste the fear.

But fear of what? The contents of the box, or his own feelings? Maybe it was time to face them both.

He put his mug down and reached out, picking up the box and resting it gently on his knees. Like Pandora's box, once opened, things could never go back to how they'd been. Could he risk that?

He swallowed, sucked in a long, slow breath and lifted the lid.

CHAPTER THREE

IT WAS THE letter that finished him.

He was expecting the rest. The beautiful little box contained all the poignant things he'd tried to blank out, like the tiny, precious footprints the midwife had made for them, the photographs she'd taken of them together holding Grace, the blanket they'd wrapped her in as they'd held her for hours in their arms before they said goodbye.

But at the bottom of the box was a single folded sheet of paper, and he lifted it out and unfolded it, totally unprepared for what it was.

A letter, from Beth to her baby daughter.

My darling Grace
I can't tell you how much I love you, how much I miss you every single day, with all my heart. But you'll always be part of me, and you're with me wherever I go.
Carrying you in my body for your short life, giving birth to you, holding you in my arms, was

*an honour and a privilege I will never forget, and
I'm so grateful I had that chance.*

*You are the best part of me, and I will trea-
sure you forever.*

Sleep tight, my darling.

Mummy xxx

The words swam in front of him, and she took the
letter gently from his nerveless fingers and replaced it
in the box with all the other precious things, then gathered him in her arms and held him while the racking
sobs tore him apart.

She said nothing, just held him and rocked him, and
gradually the pain subsided, leaving him feeling oddly
cleansed, as if he'd been wiped clean.

Except not, because Grace's name, her footprints,
her photo, and the memories they'd made that day were
engraved on his heart, an indelible part of him just as
they were of Beth, and it felt right.

She handed him tissues, then said gently, 'I guess
that's been a long time coming.'

He gave a ragged, fractured laugh and met her eyes,
tender with understanding. 'I guess so. I'm sorry.'

'Don't be. It's OK to cry. I can't begin to tell you how
much I've cried for her.'

He swiped the tears off his cheeks again with the
palms of his hands and shook his head to clear it. 'I
haven't, though. I haven't let myself. That's why I didn't
want to see. I suppose I've been in denial, really, ignoring it, but it didn't work, because it's always been there,
deep inside, gnawing away at me like acid. It's odd. It

doesn't feel like that any more. I'm sad, of course I'm sad, and I guess I always will be, but it's like a weight's lifted—does that make sense?'

She nodded. 'It makes absolute sense. It's acceptance, Ry. It takes a while to get there, but it makes it easier. You'll still have bad days, though, times when things bring it all back and it catches you on your blind side.'

He nodded and leant back, wrapping an arm around her shoulders and holding her as they sat there quietly together. They didn't speak, but for the first time he let himself think about the events of that day, the day their daughter had been born.

He thought about her delivery, how hard it had been all night knowing that at the end of it they would have nothing but memories. They'd induced her, because Beth didn't want to wait, and she'd refused all pain relief, wanting to feel every last moment of it because it was the last thing she could do for her daughter, so he'd been there for her, supporting her as well as he could while his heart felt as if it had been locked in ice.

It had been a long night, and then as the first fingers of dawn crept over the horizon and touched the sky with gold, the midwife lifted Grace's tiny body tenderly into Beth's waiting arms.

He'd stood there helpless in the deafening silence, the silence that should have been filled with a baby's cries, feeling as if he had no place there, no role in the tragedy, no way of making it better, but he'd been unable to leave them and so he'd stayed, eyes dry and gritty with exhaustion, his body as tight as a bowstring, his heart numb while Beth wept silent tears and spoke softly to her daughter.

And then she'd placed the baby in his arms, and his heart had cracked in two. It was the first and last time he'd cried for her, until tonight, and even then he hadn't really let go.

A week later they'd gone together to register her birth and death, and then they'd held a quiet funeral service for her. Three days later he'd been recalled for his next posting by MFA and she'd told him to go, so he'd gone, relieved to be able to escape the all-consuming grief and get on and do something useful that would help someone somewhere, even though he couldn't help her or himself.

Except of course there had been no escape, just a fierce suppression of his emotions until he'd become so used to it he'd thought he was over it.

Apparently not. Not by a long way.

He broke the silence at last, needing to acknowledge what she'd been through and his guilt for leaving her to deal with it alone. 'I'm so sorry I wasn't more help. I don't know how you did it—how you were so strong, so brave, through all of it.'

'I wasn't brave, Ry, not at all. I was just doing what had to be done, and then once it was done I just felt empty.'

'I shouldn't have left you.'

She took his hand and kissed it, then held it in her hands, warm and firm and kind, Beth all over.

'I sent you away, Ryan. I couldn't deal with your grief as well as mine, and that was wrong. We should have grieved together for our daughter, but we didn't know each other well enough. We still don't, but we're learning, day by day, and we'll get there.'

He nodded slowly. 'Yeah, I suppose so.' He glanced at his phone and sighed. 'Beth, I'm sorry, I need to go. It's after eleven and I'm sure tomorrow will be just as long as today.'

She chuckled softly. 'No doubt. I'm on a late, but you need to get to bed. You've had a hectic few days, you must be exhausted.'

'I am. I tell you what, that bed had better be comfortable,' he said wryly. 'Did you try it?'

'No, I didn't have time, but if it isn't there's always the sofa. At least you know that's comfy.' She cocked her head on one side, her eyes searching his. 'Are you all right, Ry?'

He laughed softly and nodded. 'Yes, Beth. I'm all right. You?'

Her smile was sad. 'I'm all right. I'm used to it now. It's the new normal.'

He nodded, wondering how long it would take him to reach that point. He got to his feet, pulled her up and into his arms and hugged her gently.

'Thank you. Thank you so much, for everything. You've been amazing, ever since I got here. You've always been amazing.'

'Don't be silly.'

'I'm not. I mean it. You're the strongest person I know, Beth, and the kindest, and I don't deserve you. Thank you.'

She hugged him back, then let him go. 'You're welcome. I hope you sleep well.'

He laughed. 'I'm sure I will.'

She walked him to the door and he turned and kissed her, just the slightest brush of his lips on hers, and let himself out and drove home, then paused a moment on the drive, staring up at the stars twinkling in the clear, dark night, just as he had everywhere he'd been sent by MFA.

He loved the stars. They never changed, untouched by all the madness around him, the one constant in a changing world, and they never failed to centre him and put everything back into perspective.

How small and insignificant we are...

He let himself in, checked his email and looked at the bed—his new bed, carefully put together by Beth to save him the trouble because that was the kind of person she was—and felt another wave of guilt for leaving her alone when she'd been so sad and lost and torn with grief.

She would never have left him. He knew that, but at the time she'd been adamant that she didn't need him. Only now it turned out she had needed him, but she'd been unable to cope with his grief, too, because they didn't know each other well enough to grieve together.

Well enough to make a baby, but not well enough to lose one. Maybe, given time, they would find that closeness and with it some closure. He hoped so.

He looked at the bed again, but tired though he was he wasn't ready, so he made himself a cup of chamomile tea and went out into the garden, sitting on the steps where they'd sat together only a couple of days ago, Beth's letter to Grace echoing in his head.

Should he do the same? Write down his thoughts about his tiny daughter, the child he hadn't known he wanted, and add them to hers? All the milestones they'd miss, the tears, the tantrums, the laughter? Her first smile, her first tooth, her first step—

He heard a noise behind him, a slight scrabbling, rustling noise. A hedgehog, probably, or a fox. They were on the edge of farmland, so it wasn't unlikely.

And then he heard a whimper, and turned to see something creeping towards him across the grass. Something large, much bigger than a hedgehog, less shy than a fox.

A dog?

'Hello, sweetie. What are you doing here?' he asked softly, and it moved closer.

A dog. Definitely a dog, and not a small one, its tail wagging tentatively, black nose gleaming in the moonlight. He held out his hand, careful not to meet its eyes so it didn't feel threatened, and the dog crept closer, flicking out its tongue to lick his fingers. He turned his hand over and scratched its chin, and it wriggled closer—close enough for him to smell it.

Dog, river mud and who knew what else.

It whined, and he stroked the tangled, scruffy head that pressed into his hand, its ears scarcely visible under the matted hair.

'Oh, poppet. What a mess you're in. Who are you? What are you doing here?'

It crept closer still, until it was resting up against his

hip, its head heavy on his lap, and his hand slid down and felt ribs sticking out, and the bumps of its spine. It must be starving. 'Are you hungry? Is that the matter?'

The dog got to its feet, tail wagging, and he got up and headed inside, the dog running ahead through the sitting room door to leap onto his brand new sofa.

'Hey! No! Get off that!'

It wagged its tail, tongue lolling, still on the sofa as if it owned it, and everything fell into place.

He let out a rueful laugh. 'You live here, don't you? This is your house.'

The tail thumped, and he shook his head.

'Get off my sofa. I don't care how cute you are, you stink and you're covered in mud. Come here, let's find you some food and then work out what to do with you.' He headed into the kitchen, and the dog followed, standing up on its back legs and peering at the worktop hopefully, tail lashing.

'Dog! You have absolutely no manners! Sit!'

Paws dropped to the floor, and the dog sat and whined at him pitifully. He tried hard not to laugh, and pulled open the pantry to find the things he'd raided from his mother yesterday.

'Right, what have we got here? Tuna. Do you like tuna? I guess you like anything. Tuna sandwich? Yup? Just don't tell the vet.'

He drained the spring water off the tuna and mashed it between two slices of wholemeal bread, and then chopped them roughly, put them in a bowl Beth had found in the box and dumped it on the floor.

'Well, that went down OK,' he said with a chuckle,

and shook his head slowly. 'Dog, you need a bath, and a serious haircut. You're the scruffiest thing I've ever seen.'

He put some water down in another bowl, but after a couple of slurps it gave up and came back to him, wuffing hopefully.

Still hungry. He had some ridiculously expensive peanut butter with no added anything, so he smeared a little dollop on another bit of bread and gave it to him. Her? He didn't even know, but that was the least of his worries.

The smell, however…

He called Beth.

'I'm sorry to disturb you. Are you still up?'

'Yes. What's the matter? Is the bed awful? Don't tell me it fell to pieces—'

'I haven't got that far. Do you have any very mild shampoo and conditioner? And a brush you don't care about, and a pair of scissors with blunt ends? Oh, and a hair dryer. And old towels. Lots of them.'

He heard a slightly choked noise, like a strangled laugh. 'OK, what's going on?'

'You know the house smelt of dog? Well, it's come back.'

'The smell?'

'No—well, yes, but on the dog. The dog came back, I have no idea where from, but whoever it belongs to, it's in urgent need of a bath. I think it's been in the river.'

She chuckled. 'I'll be right round.'

'I'm glad you think it's funny. Wear something scruffy.'

He heard another laugh as the line went dead, and he

slid his phone into his pocket with a smile on his face
and turned back to the dog, just in time to see it sneak-
ing back onto the sofa, a stolen banana in its mouth...

'Oh, my word.'

'You have a habit of walking in here and saying that,'
he said drily, and she chuckled and eyed him up and
down.

'Well, you are covered in mud. So where is it?'

'In the conservatory. I had to banish it. It jumped on
the sofa with a banana it stole off the side in the kitchen.'

She felt her eyes widen. 'Your new sofa, that you
haven't even sat on for more than ten seconds?'

His mouth quirked. 'That's the one.'

She bit her lips, trying really, really hard not to laugh.
'Oh, dear. Good job it's leather, at least it'll wipe clean.
Well, let's see this thing, then.'

'This thing' turned out to be a clump of tangled, matted fur on gangly legs, but one swipe of its tongue on
her outstretched hand and she was smitten.

'Oh, dear. You are really, really muddy, poppet. I
wonder what colour you are?'

'Goodness knows. I have no idea where to start.'

She laughed and shoved up her sleeves. 'Water, I
think. A lot of water. Have you got a plastic jug or bowl
or something we can mix the shampoo in?'

It took an hour, but finally the dog was bathed, then
bathed again, and it turned out to be a dull, creamy grey,
although that might have been the remnants of the river

mud. They cut the matted hair away around its ears and neck, and then turned their attention to its body.

'Well, little lady, you're a girl,' he said softly, clipping clumps off carefully around her armpits as she lolled on her back in the kitchen, tongue hanging out and all but grinning at him. 'I wonder what your name is, you tatty old thing?'

He sat back on his heels, studied the dog for a moment and grinned. 'Tatty. Perfect. And we can always call you Tatiana if we're trying to be posh.'

We? Where had that come from?

'You don't need to name her, Ryan. You don't even know whose she is,' Beth pointed out gently, and he felt a sudden sense of anti-climax.

'No. No, you're right, I don't,' he said, coming down to earth with a bump. 'I wonder if she's microchipped?'

'The neighbours might recognise her. Have you met any of them yet?'

'No, not yet,' he said, looking up from his clipping to meet her eyes. 'I haven't really had a chance.' He looked down into the dog's trusting eyes and sighed. 'And you're right, I don't need to give her a name because I can't keep her, can I? Even if she does think I've bought a new sofa especially for her.'

It was an odd thought, and he wasn't sure he liked it, but he had to be realistic. How could he keep her? He worked ridiculous hours and he lived alone. It simply wasn't fair.

But then she licked his hand, and his heart wrenched.

'You can't, Ry.'

He looked up at the softly voiced words. 'Can't what?'

'Keep her. You can't keep her.'

He stroked the damp head with its appalling haircut, looked into the melting dark eyes and felt like a traitor.

'Let's worry about that tomorrow,' he said hastily. 'For now, I have to find her somewhere to sleep, and you need to go home.'

He got to his feet, walked her to the door and hugged her hard.

'Thank you so much,' he mumbled into hair that smelt vaguely of river mud. 'I couldn't have done that on my own.'

'Don't thank me. It's not like it's your dog.'

That pang again.

'Yeah, you're right, although I'd stake my life she belongs to the tenants. She needs to go to the vet to see if she's microchipped. Goodness knows when I'll fit that in.'

'I can do it. I don't start work until tomorrow lunchtime. If you give me the key again I can pick her up and take her.'

'I don't know any vets. I don't know any anything here. I wouldn't know where to start.'

'I'll ask Annie Shackleton. They've got a dog, she'll tell me everything I need to know.'

He shook his head, then gave in, because something needed to be done with the dog, whatever. 'Here—the spare key. You might as well keep it,' he said, suppressing the thought that it felt vaguely symbolic. 'I'll leave her in the conservatory when I go, so if you could put her back there afterwards that would be great. There's nothing there she can trash. You'll need a collar and lead to take her, though, if your friend's got one.'

'I'll sort it. Get to bed. We'll be fine. I'll see you at twelve when my shift starts, and tell you what the vet said.'

He searched her eyes, then nodded and bent his head to kiss her, just as she came up on tiptoe to do the same to him. Their lips clashed, held, and he felt fire shoot through his body. The kiss deepened, changed from an accidental clash to a very deliberate but tender caress that came out of nowhere and didn't seem to want to end.

He wasn't sure who backed away first, but she turned and opened the door and let herself out hurriedly with a little wave, and he watched her go, his emotions in turmoil, his body screaming in protest.

The dog whined at his side, and he dropped his hand down and found her head. 'She's gone, sweetheart,' he said regretfully. 'It's time for bed. Come on, Tatty. Let's find you a bed and put you away for the night. I need some sleep because I've got to be at work in five hours.'

Haha.

Between the kiss and the dog howling and whining in the conservatory there was no way he was going to sleep, so after two hours he relented and let her in, spread one of his new bath towels on the floor beside the bed and pointed firmly at it.

'Down!'

She gave him a baleful look, curled up on it and stayed there, to his relief, and he finally managed to drop off.

For a while, at least, but when his alarm dragged him up to the surface at six she was there, lying up against him on the bed, her head next to his on the pillow.

He turned his head and glared at her. 'Tatty, you can't do this! Off!'

No chance. She grinned and licked his face, and he wondered just exactly when, if ever, she'd been wormed. He threw the covers off and got up, heading for the bathroom with the dog at his heels.

'You need the vet, and I need a shower and some clothes that don't smell of you, because I have to go to work. Do you want breakfast first? Probably.'

She polished off the rest of his loaf of bread, mostly while his back was turned, and she didn't even have the grace to look guilty.

He put her back in the conservatory and went to work hungry.

Poor Ryan.

The look on his face when he'd realised he couldn't keep her. Still, maybe by this morning he'd thought better of it. He'd probably thought better of their goodnight kiss, at least. She certainly had—hadn't she?

Liar.

She got up, showered and washed her hair to get rid of the occasional whiff of river mud that was coming from somewhere, dressed in jeans and a top that didn't matter, and headed for Annie and Ed Shackleton's house.

They lived just round the corner on the seafront, and it was the school holidays so hopefully they'd be in. She pulled up outside their house just as Annie was walking back with their dog, Molly, and she got out of the car with a smile.

'Morning, Annie. That was perfect timing!'

'Hi, Beth. Are you OK? What can I do for you?'

Ten minutes later, armed with a collar and lead and an appointment with the Shackletons' vet, Beth collected Tatty from Ryan's conservatory and was about to load her into the car when a voice came from behind her.

'She came back, then. I did wonder if she might.'

Beth turned round and saw an elderly man peering through the hedge. 'Oh—hi. Do you know her?'

'Yes, she belonged to the tenants. Said they were re-homing her but they looked a bit shifty about it. Did a runner in the middle of the night, too. Packed up a van and went. I reckon they owed rent again. So, you and your young man have taken it on, have you?'

For a moment she wasn't sure if he was talking about the house or the dog, but then she realised he was looking at the house. 'Yes—well, Ryan has. He's not my young man, he's just a friend.'

Why did that feel like a lie?

The man pushed his way through a gap in the hedge, and stuck his hand out. 'I'm Reg, by the way.'

She freed a hand from the lead and shook his. 'I'm Beth.'

Reg stooped and patted the dog. 'He's brave taking it on. They left it in a right old state.'

'Yes, they did, but it's better now. Reg, I'm sorry, I don't want to be rude but I've got an appointment with the vet.'

'Better not hold you up then, young lady. Nice to meet you. And tell your Ryan if there's anything he needs, just ask.'

'I will.'

He gave the dog a last pat and she watched him wrestle his way back through the gap in the hedge, then she opened the boot and gave Tatty a little tug. She sat down and whined, and Beth eyed her thoughtfully.

She was NOT a small dog. The boot was barely big enough. Did she *really* need to wrestle with her?

'Please, Tatty. Come on. Good girl,' she wheedled, and to her astonishment the dog jumped in, licked her hand and sat down.

Phew. She got behind the wheel and drove carefully to the practice, one eye on the rear-view mirror, but the dog just sat there, giving the odd whine. Presumably her last journey had ended in her being evicted from the car and dumped in the middle of nowhere—unless she genuinely had been rehomed and had simply run away?

'Poor Tatty,' she said softly, and the dog whined again.

'Well? Do we know who she is?'

'Sort of. No microchip, as expected, but I met your neighbour, Reg. She was the tenants' dog.'

He nodded. 'I was pretty sure she was. She made herself at home last night, anyway. She ended up on my bed.'

Beth's eyes widened, and he laughed.

'Don't look surprised. She's very persuasive when

she's howling at three in the morning and I didn't want to be kicked out by the landlord.'

'I don't think that's going to happen. After the last lot, he's going to be only too happy to have you there. Reg said if there's anything you need, just ask, by the way. He seemed to think we were a couple. I told him you were just a friend.'

That word again. Even less right after their kiss last night. He grunted. 'I'll go and introduce myself when I get home. So did he say what the dog's name was?'

'No, but I didn't ask, and the vet didn't recognise her, but apparently she's possibly some kind of retriever cross, she's young, and there's something else you need to know. She's about four or five weeks pregnant.'

He felt his jaw drop, and sighed and rolled his eyes. 'Seriously? Oh, Beth. What the hell do we do now?'

'We?' She laughed and walked away. 'Your dog, McKenna. It's nothing to do with me. I suggest you try and contact the owners.'

Over his dead body.

But realistically, did he have a choice? He rang the letting agent, told him the dog had come back and asked if he had a forwarding address for the previous tenants, but of course he didn't. They owed two months' rent. Why would they give anyone their address?

Which left him with the need to rehome her some-how. He found a rescue centre on the internet, and the moment he got home he rang them.

They were full, but they said they'd take her as soon as they had a space.

'Don't hold your breath, though,' the receptionist said. 'It could be a while. Are you able to keep her in the meantime?'

He said he could, trying to work out why the feeling in his chest felt remarkably like relief, then gave her his details and went into the kitchen and found a note from Beth, propped up against the kettle.

Dry food's in the pantry. She's twenty-five kilos but add twenty per cent more food because she's pregnant. Couldn't find scales, but she's had lunch and didn't seem to mind! Chart on the side of the food bag. Divide by three—obvs. And keep the door shut!

He sighed, went into the pantry with Tatty at his side, and examined the chart with a bit of enthusiastic assistance. Beth hadn't been able to find the scales because there weren't any, but he made an educated guess.

That would do, for now. He'd give her a bit more later and buy scales tomorrow. Assuming he'd still have her. Sounded like it.

He put her dry food into the bowl Beth had left him, ate a tin of baked beans cold out of the can with a fork, and looked at the clock on the cooker.

Quarter to eight. Still time for a quick walk before dusk, if they didn't hang about. He put Tatty—no, the dog—on the borrowed lead and took her down to the river and along the river wall. She didn't seem keen on the lead, but she seemed happy enough by his side and soon got used to it, and they walked until the light was fading and got home just before nine.

He was still hungry, but of course she'd eaten the bread that morning so he couldn't even make a sandwich, so he had a bowl of cereal and gave the dog another handful of kibble, then made a coffee and headed for the sitting room, the dog in tow.

All he wanted was to sit down quietly on the sofa with his phone, check his emails and do a little research into dog pregnancy and rehoming—although if he was rehoming her, the pregnancy research was irrelevant.

Assuming he got a chance to do it anyway, because Tatty had gone in the garden and come back victorious with a muddy ball in her mouth, and dropped it at his feet.

Of course. Somewhere in her ancestry was a retriever. And all they wanted to do, like all the gun dog breeds, was just exactly that. So he rolled the ball, and she fetched it, and he rolled it, she fetched it, over and over again until finally he hid it behind his back.

'No. It's gone. Lie down.'

She whined, gave a resigned sigh and hopped onto the sofa, curled up and went to sleep. Well, almost. One eye was still slightly open, just in case...

He grunted and turned his attention back to his dog-rehoming research.

CHAPTER FOUR

'How's Tatty?'

'The *dog* is clingy. And needy. And playful. Endlessly playful. Not to mention greedy in the bedroom. I bought a six-foot-wide bed because I like space, and she's claimed at least half of it.'

Beth suppressed a smile. 'You could buy her a basket.'

He made a noise somewhere between a grunt and a snort, and rolled his head on his neck. It crunched and made her wince.

'Ouch.'

'Oh, it doesn't hurt, it's just stiff from hanging off the edge of the bed half the night. I met Ed Shackleton, by the way. We were out on the river wall by six this morning, and so was he, and he recognised her. He stopped me and introduced himself and asked how she was, so I told him. He laughed.'

He said it deadpan, but his lips were twitching and she had to bite hers. 'He laughed?'

'Yes. Apparently he thinks it's funny. She and Molly made friends.'

'Did you let her off the lead?'

A definite snort this time. 'No. I have better things to do with my early morning than look for a dog that's messed off and won't come back.'

'I thought she was clingy?'

'Would you rely on that? Anyway, Ed said Annie could pick the dog up on her walk with Molly and take them both, and give her some lunch, so I gave him the key to the back door. At least I don't have to worry about that today. So, what's going on this morning?' he asked, turning his attention back to the day job, and she ran through the weirdly short list of patients on the whiteboard.

'That looks pretty quiet. Excellent. I might sneak off for a proper, decent coffee. I haven't got my coffee-maker out of store yet—'

'Adult trauma call, five minutes. Paediatric trauma call, five minutes.'

He tilted his head and glared at the speaker on the wall.

'Seriously? I need a coffee first!'

She grinned at him. 'Poor baby. You can get one later. Come on. Last one in Resus buys lunch.'

Lunch? What was that again?

He ignored his whinging stomach, and finally, some-time after three, there was a gap. An actual, time-for-a-break gap.

Hallelujah! He grinned at Beth.

'Coming for lunch?'

'Absolutely. And you're buying.'

'My pleasure. Let's just get out of here before the red phone bursts into life again. Are you always this short-staffed?'

'No, it's the Easter holidays. Andy Gallagher's technically only part-time, but he's picked up a lot of the slack until you arrived and they've got five children, so he's having time off in lieu now, and Sam Ryder's wife's sick so he's off with the kids, and when Andy comes back James is off for a week. And two of the nurses with kids are off as well, so it's worse than usual.'

'I'm glad to hear it. I can't imagine what it's like at Christmas.'

She gave a slightly hysterical laugh and pushed open the café door.

'Trust me, you don't want to know.'

He picked up a tray and slid it along the counter, peering at the range of salads on offer. He really, really needed to do an internet food order—

'So have you applied for the job yet?'

He rolled his eyes. '*Et tu, Brute?* I've had James on my case all morning.'

'So, are you going to?'

He picked up a bowl of mixed salad, added a dollop of coronation chicken and dumped it on the tray with a bread roll and a banana. 'I guess—if I ever have a minute. The dog's taking up a lot of my time.'

She put her salad down on the tray beside his. 'I thought you were going to rehome her?'

'They're full. All of them. I did some ringing round.'

'Ah.'

'Indeed. Black Americano, please, with an extra shot. Beth?'

'Oh—skinny cappuccino, please. So what are you going to do?'

He stared blankly at the back of the barista. 'Honestly? I don't know. Technically, she's not my problem.'

'But?'

He laughed softly, took the coffees, picked up the tray and paid, then headed out into the park to find a table.

'But?' she repeated. She raised an eyebrow at him and waited, and he gave a resigned sigh.

'What can I do? Dammit, Beth, the dog's pregnant! I can't just kick her out. That would make me no better than them. Oh, she was called Dolly, by the way.'

'Dolly?'

He laughed. 'Exactly my reaction. Anyone less like a doll... Tatty suits her a lot better, but according to Reg, the kids used to carry her around in their arms when she was a puppy.'

Her face crumpled slightly. 'Oh, they must miss her.'

'Yeah. I reckon she misses them, too. She keeps going into the other bedroom as if she's looking for them. Whatever. I'm sure the rescue centre can find her a good family, when they've got room.'

He took a mouthful of food, but it stuck in his throat, lodged on top of a strange lump that had appeared. He swallowed hard, took a gulp of coffee and burnt his mouth.

Livvy Henderson smiled at them and walked past, waving at a man sitting at a table beyond them. He'd

met the ED registrar last week when Beth had asked
her about the house she'd rented, and he'd worked with
her a couple of times since. He followed her with his
eyes as she bent over and kissed the man, then sat beside him as he put his arm around her.

'Who's that with Livvy?' he asked, pretending interest to change the subject.

'Matt Hunter, consultant trauma surgeon. You're
bound to meet him. He's her fiancé. They're getting
married in a few weeks—at our hotel, actually.'

His eyes flicked back to hers, then away again, his
heart pounding as his mind was dragged back to their
weekend.

'Good venue,' he said calmly. *So much for changing
the subject. Be careful what you wish for...*

'Yes, it is. Actually, there's something I want to ask
you. I've got an invitation to the evening do. I don't suppose you fancy being my plus one? I don't really want
to go on my own, and I know you aren't going to get
any ideas if I ask you.'

He stifled a snort. He wasn't so sure about that, especially not in the hotel that had so many X-rated memories. And besides, he thought most weddings were
outrageously lavish, absurdly expensive and he'd never
understood the need to squander that much money on
what amounted to a party.

Not that Katie had agreed about that, but then it
turned out that they hadn't agreed on much. He'd been
very clear that he didn't want to get married or have
children any time soon because he really wanted to
work with Medicine For All, and he thought she'd un-

derstood. When he realised she'd stopped taking her contraception and was quietly planning a wedding, he'd put his foot down, and it had finally dawned on her that he wasn't just saying it and she couldn't talk him round, or talk him out of his plans to sign up with MFA.

She'd had a screaming fit, said she wouldn't stay with him unless he backed down, so he said fine, told her to go and walked out.

Cue all kinds of fallout, underpinned by a certain amount of guilt, a tinge of regret and a huge sense of relief on his part when it turned out that she wasn't yet pregnant. That was just before he'd started working with Beth, and why he'd wanted a no-strings non-relationship with her, something light-hearted and physical and without any kind of commitment from either of them.

So much for light-hearted, given their fated pregnancy and the emotional turmoil it had left in its wake. After his initial furious reaction that she'd done it on purpose, the way Katie had tried to, came the gut-wrenching knowledge that their baby was dying, which had tapped into something deep inside him, a paternal urge he hadn't even known existed. Something he still, even now, couldn't really understand and wasn't sure he was ready for.

And going back to the hotel where it had all started wasn't in any way on his agenda. Emotions aside, he was finding working with her distracting enough and his libido was running riot.

'Are you sure there isn't someone else you could go with? You know I don't really do weddings.'

'I take it that's a no, then?' she said, her voice light

but her eyes guarded, with a tinge of hurt lurking in their depths.

Dammit. He gave up fighting. 'When is it?'

'Four and a bit weeks. The eleventh of May,' she added softly, and he felt as if a bucket of ice had been tipped over him. 'It's—'

'I know what day it is,' he said gruffly.

Exactly two years to the day since Grace's heart had stopped beating, and she'd been born the next day, the date engraved on the little silver heart. And on his, and Beth's, too, he had no doubt.

Such bitter irony, that the wedding should be on that day, of all days, and in that venue, of all the venues they could have chosen.

How could he not go, just because he *didn't do weddings*? Not even he was that selfish and self-centred.

He nodded. 'OK. I'll come. What's the dress code?'

Not that it mattered a jot. He'd go in a bin bag if necessary, because there was no way he'd leave her alone on Grace's anniversary, no matter how little he wanted to be there.

'Black tie. Livvy wanted black tie because she said Matt looks so good in a DJ.'

He grunted, searching in his head for where the hell he might have stored his DJ. His mother's wardrobe? There was still some stuff there. Or he could buy a new one. He was thinner now, the old one might not fit any more. Whatever, he had a month to sort it out.

'Problem?' she asked, her eyes troubled, and he smiled at her and shook his head.

'No, Beth. It's not a problem. I just can't remember

where I've put my DJ, but that's fine. I've got time to sort it. Unlike the dog. I don't know what to do about her. I can't leave her alone and unfed all day while I'm at work, but I just feel stuck with her.'

'I have an idea. Why don't you ask Reg if he could pop in at lunchtimes and let her out and feed her, just until the rehoming place can take her? He seemed to have a bit of a soft spot for her.'

He looked at her thoughtfully. 'Do you think he would?'

She shrugged. 'I don't know. He might. You could ask. And then you could stop worrying about her all day.'

'I don't.'

'Liar.'

Could she actually see straight through him?

He ate his salad, drank his coffee and met her eyes again. 'We need to get on.'

'We do. What are you doing later?'

He laughed. 'Walking the dog?'

'Can I come?'

On the river path, over the stile where he'd kissed her that time? His heart crashed against his ribs in anticipation.

'Yes, of course.' Only this time he'd keep his hands to himself...

Beth put jeans and boots on, and drove round to Ryan's. She could have walked, it was only about five minutes away, but she knew he'd be in a hurry, and when she pulled up on the drive they were already there waiting. And Tatty seemed ridiculously excited to see her again.

'Hello, sweetie,' she crooned gently, rubbing Tatty's chest and earning herself a happy, doggy smile, and they set off across the lane through a gap in the hedge and along a footpath that led over the marshes to the river.

She fell into step beside him, their arms brushing as they walked. And somehow, she wasn't sure how, her hand ended up firmly wrapped in his. She knew how it had got there—she'd slipped on some mud, and he'd grabbed her—but then he hadn't let go, so they'd walked on, her fingers curled around his, his thumb over the top of hers, and every now and then it moved, a gentle, rhythmic stroke, or a little squeeze that made her feel warm inside.

They reached the river and went left, heading up-river for a while, then turned back towards the harbour nestled in the river mouth, retracing their steps as they had all that time ago.

He had to let go of her hand to steer Tatty round the stile, but then as she climbed over after him he held out his hand again, and their eyes met and held.

'This is where you first kissed me,' she said softly, and something hot and wild and a little dangerous to her peace of mind flickered in his eyes and was gone.

'I know.'

And then he let her go, and turned on his heel and walked on, Tatty hanging back to wait for her as she jumped down off the stile and caught them up, her heart fizzing in her chest.

It was still there, whatever *it* was, simmering between them like molten lava, and she felt a sudden surge of regret for asking him to go with her to the wedding. It was bound to be unashamedly romantic and inevitably they'd be expected to dance, and that would only complicate things, although how they could get more complicated it was difficult to see. Maybe he'd pull out, because right now he couldn't seem to get away from her fast enough.

He turned his head and looked at her, his expression neutral now. 'Fancy going to the pub again for supper?' he asked, and her eyes widened in surprise. She'd thought he was desperate to get home, but for some reason he wasn't. Had she read him wrong?

'What about Tatty? Will she behave?'

He shrugged. 'We could give it a try. Ed said they're dog-friendly, and I've got nothing at home because I still haven't done an internet order and lunch seems like a long time ago.'

It did, and she didn't have much food in her house, either. That had been a job for her way home, only her agenda had been hijacked again, by herself this time.

'Sounds lovely,' she said, summoning up a smile and wishing it didn't feel like a date. Too complicating. Too much, too soon.

But it wasn't a date and anyway she'd said yes now, so she followed him in, and they found a little table in the dog-friendly end of the bar, and Tatty lay down with her head on her paws and went to sleep.

'She's tired. I ought to take her to the vet and talk about this pregnancy.'

'I thought you were going to rehome her?'

He shrugged, his mouth pulling down at the corners in a wry grimace. 'I will, when I can. But in the meantime I need to know what to do for her.'

'What, apart from letting her sleep on your bed and dominate your every waking moment?'

The wry grin turned into a chuckle. 'That's the one. Still, I talked to Reg when I got home and he seems happy to let her out and feed her in the middle of the day, so it's not as urgent any more. Right, I'm starving. What are we going to eat?'

'Coming in for coffee?'

Beth hesitated, but he had a slightly guilty look in his eyes, as if he had an ulterior motive.

'I'd like your help,' he added when she didn't answer. 'Again.'

'With?'

'My job application. The closing date's Friday, and it's already Wednesday, and it needs some serious work. I haven't updated my CV recently, and—well, a lot's changed. There's all my aid stuff, and I've only got a basic CV for locum work. It's not nearly adequate for a consultancy.'

'So what do I know about it? It's James you need to talk to. He's so keen to have you he'll probably write your application letter for you if you ask him.'

She knew there was no way he'd ask him, but she left it hanging, and he shrugged.

'I think I can manage without doing that,' he said drily. 'And don't worry if you'd rather not, I'll be fine,' he added, obviously reading the reluctance in her eyes, but she relented and smiled at him.

'It's all right, I'll help you. You've bought me lunch and supper today, so it's the least I can do—and anyway, I haven't got anything else planned.'

'Thank you.' He returned her smile, opened the door and headed for the kitchen. 'I need to feed the dog, then I'll make some coffee.'

'I thought you didn't have coffee?'

He grinned at her. 'I don't, not bean to cup, at least, but I have got a cafetière and some ground coffee so I'm not entirely deprived.'

He disappeared into the pantry. 'Stick the kettle on,' he added over his shoulder, but she was already at the tap with it in her hand, staring across the marshes to the river path in the distance. She could just about make out the stile. Did he stand here looking at it like that?

Wondering how it had all happened, how something that was meant to be harmless fun had gone so wrong?

She put the kettle on its stand, her eyes drawn back to the stile, picked out on the horizon by the setting sun. There'd been a strange expression in his eyes today as he'd looked up at her on the stile, as if his feelings had bubbled close to the surface. She wondered what would happen if he set them free, and felt a shiver of anticipation.

'Tatty, sit.'

She dragged her eyes off the stile and turned to see the dog obediently sitting, her eyes fixed on the bowl, tail lashing back and forth across the worn-out tiles.

'Good girl,' he said, putting it down and giving the

dog a little pat, and then he straightened up and met her eyes.

'What?'

Beth shrugged, suppressing a smile. 'Nothing.'

'I'm not going to be mean to her just because I can't keep her.'

'If you say so.'

He made that grunty, snorty noise that was becoming all too familiar as a punctuation point in their conversations, and then reached down two mugs and the cafetière, spooned coffee into the jug and poured water on it, releasing the aroma.

'Oh, that smells good. It'll probably keep me awake all night, though.'

'Want to change your mind?'

'No, I'll just hate you all night instead.'

'I'll get some decaf for you,' he promised with a chuckle, and picking up his coffee, he headed for the sitting room with Tatty in hot pursuit. He threw her off the sofa, sat down on one side and patted the other for Beth, pushed Tatty off again and opened his laptop.

'Right. Let's nail this CV.'

'I've got an interview on Tuesday.'

Beth glanced up from her patient notes and grinned at him. 'Well, there's a surprise. Did you get a letter?'

He shook his head. 'No. James just told me. They gave it a few days longer, but there's only been one other serious applicant and James thinks he's looking for a nice quiet seaside town to wind down into retirement.'

She felt her eyes widen. 'He told you that?'

'Off the record. Apparently he's got more experience than me—well, on paper he has, I'm sure, as he's older, but I've done a lot so maybe that'll balance it.'

He had. She'd seen his CV—she'd practically written it for him a week ago—and it was packed with a huge variety of things he'd seen and done. He might not have great depth of experience, but he certainly had breadth.

Which meant he was in with a good chance of getting the consultancy.

Which meant she was in with a good chance of having him here, in Yoxburgh, for the foreseeable.

Did she want that? Even now, not quite two weeks into their new—no, not relationship. That sounded like something else, something they definitely didn't have. Friendship, then. Two weeks into their new friendship, she still wasn't sure if she could live with him so near. So near and yet so far?

No. Friendship didn't say enough. They'd been friends before, but this—this was different. This was life after Grace, and that changed everything, every aspect of their interaction with each other.

It was broader than a friendship, deeper than a physical relationship, more complicated than an ex-relationship but without its depth. Although they'd certainly plumbed the depths in their grief, if not together. And then there was that kiss last week, and the sizzling look he'd given her last week by the stile—

'Beth? Are you OK?'

She found a smile, contemplated lying and gave up. 'I was just trying to work out what we are to each other.'

His answering smile was wry, with a wealth of sadness that made her want to weep. 'I gave up trying to work that out days ago. I don't think there is an accurate definition, but at the very least, we're friends. Well, I hope we are.'

'Of course we are.'

'Good.' He gave her a gentle hug, then let her go, leaving a tidal wave of emotions in his wake. 'I'm needed in Resus. James had to do a thoracotomy in a field. Literally. A car overshot the junction, ripped through a barrier and cartwheeled down into a field. I gather it wasn't pretty.'

She winced. 'It doesn't sound pretty. How on earth did that happen in broad daylight?'

'I don't know. The driver was dead at the scene. He might have had a heart attack or a stroke—who knows. I think this is the front seat passenger coming in. I'll let you know more when I find out.'

'Good luck with it. I'm off to sort out an ingrowing toenail.'

'Sure you don't want to delegate and come and help me?'

She smiled and gave him a push towards Resus. 'Quite sure. I had enough of Resus at the weekend. Go on, shoo. I'll see you later.'

'Dinner at mine after a dog walk?'

She hesitated, and he frowned.

'Tatty misses you. She hasn't seen you for days.'

'Three days. I saw her on Sunday evening.'

He smiled coaxingly. 'That's a long time in a short life and you're on nights all over this coming weekend, so she'll hardly see you then. If I've even still got her,' he added in a blatant attempt at emotional blackmail, and she rolled her eyes.

'Oh, all right, I'll come for a dog walk and dinner—now go!' He grinned, blew her a kiss and strode off, leaving her wondering how she'd given in so easily. And she'd been trying to keep him at a little more distance, too.

'Weak.'

'Who's weak?'

'Oh, hi, Livvy. Nobody. I'm just trying to work out how long I have to get an outfit for your wedding.'

'More than a week! Try three and a half.'

'Are you ready for it?'

She laughed. 'Emotionally, yes. Are all my ducks in a row? Probably not! Still, I've got Mum on the case. She'll pick up the slack, she always does. She throws the best parties. Did you want me to have a look at this ingrowing toenail? I hear it's pretty horrendous.'

His furniture arrived that weekend, delivered from the storage unit where it had all been lurking for over two years, but he'd given up trying to manage without it, even though he'd only been offered an interview for the permanent post and might well not get it. Still, previous or not, he needed some of the things he'd had in store, and in between shifts he spent the entire weekend trying to work out where to put it all. Not that he was going to unpack everything. Not yet.

His study was the last thing he needed to worry about, because he'd need bookshelves for all the endless boxes of books and notes and paperwork, so he stashed all study-related stuff in that room together with other things that he simply didn't need yet, if at all, and shut the door on it and tackled the rest.

That in itself was quite enough, and it was made worse by the fact that Beth had been working all weekend on nights, so he hadn't even been able to enlist her help.

Not that that was fair. He'd asked enough of her as it was and she'd been more than generous, and anyway, he was beginning to think he was just using the house as an excuse to spend time with her, so he ploughed on alone. Safer that way, because working with her was becoming a bit of a minefield, the tension starting to build again as it had before, but sorting the house alone was getting very, very dull.

He was contemplating the mess and tearing his hair out when she breezed in early on Monday afternoon, all smiles and bearing a carrier bag. She delved into it and pulled out a cake, and suddenly everything seemed doable.

'Oh, I love you,' he said fervently, and all but snatched the cake out of her hands.

'Hey! Where are you going with that?'

'The top shelf of the pantry until we get round to it. I'll make coffee first. My bean-to-cup machine arrived.'

'I can see that. Are you assuming it still works after being in storage?'

He laughed again, ridiculously pleased to see her. 'Are you kidding? It was the first thing I unpacked. It works—I've nearly worn it out in the last two days. So, what's it to be? Cappuccino?'

She smiled, her eyes crinkling at the corners and making him want to kiss her. 'Definitely. Oh, and while I think about it, you'd better put this in the fridge for later.'

She delved into the bag again and pulled out a bottle of something fizzy. 'I figured as you were properly moving in now and claiming it, at least for a while, we ought to christen it.'

'Ah, Beth, you're a sweetheart. Thank you! We'll definitely have it later.'

He took it from her, stashed it in the fridge and pulled her into his arms for a brief hug, but she settled against his chest as if she belonged there, and it was a real struggle to let her go, because it just felt so *right*.

No. Don't go there. Too messy, and you've done enough damage, and anyway, she doesn't want you. He dropped his arms and stepped back.

'Right. Coffee and cake in the garden, then I've got a job for you.'

'You have? What a surprise. Go on, then, hit me with it.'

But she was smiling, so he relaxed and smiled back.

'Pictures. I'm going to put my old bed together for the spare room so my mother can come and visit me sometime, and I want you to look through the pictures and work out where they need to go. Not all of them, just the odd one here and there to make it feel like home. But first, cake.'

He didn't have a huge number of pictures, but there were a few she remembered, including one of a wild, rugged landscape that had hung over his bed, and it made her body tingle just to look at it.

How many times had they made love on the bed beneath it? Dozens, every one of them memorable. She put it to one side and sorted through the others, the less contentious ones. Or less evocative, at least, of their past, the pre-Grace period before he'd gone away for the first time, when their lovemaking was smoking hot and nothing else was taken seriously.

He'd made her laugh, made her gasp with ecstasy and weep with frustration, but always, always, he'd set her on fire. It had been the perfect antidote to Rick's cheating and lying ways, and just what she'd needed. Intensely passionate, and yet light and frivolous—or it would have been if things hadn't turned out the way they had, but the heat, the passion, was still there smouldering under the surface, and it was getting harder and harder to ignore.

'I like this one,' she said, turning her head when she heard him behind her, and he nodded, coming right up close to look over her shoulder at the painting.

'I got it in a gallery in Cumbria when I was visiting my uncle shortly before he died, and I've never got round to hanging it. I just love the miles of flat sand and the distant sea. It all looks so harmless and peaceful, but look at the menace in the sky, and when that tide comes in...'

Like their relationship, which had seemed harmless enough, and would have been, if tragedy hadn't intervened. She sucked in a breath and looked away.

'Where do you want it?'

He shrugged. 'I don't know. On that wall, opposite the sofa?'

'Go and hold it up, then, let me look at it.'

She sat on the sofa, instantly joined by Tatty, and her hand found the dog's head and lay on it while she gave him directions.

'Right a bit—down—OK, hold it there. Have you got a pencil?'

'No. Come and take it from me and hold it here, and I'll find one.'

She squeezed under his arm and took it from him, all too aware of his body against her back, the closeness of his head to hers, the soft whisper of his breath against her hair.

'Stand back and have a look at it while you're at it, but be quick, it's heavy,' she said over her shoulder.

'Perfect. Right, keep still,' he said, and leant in against her, his arm coming round her to mark the bottom of the picture.

The back of his hand brushed against her breast and she jerked, the frame knocking the pencil so it slid a little on the wall.

'Sorry—lost my grip,' she muttered, which wasn't far from the truth, although only in a metaphorical sense, and he backed away with a chuckle as she put the picture down.

'I wasn't trying to grope you, Beth.'

Pity...

'I didn't say you were. Want to try again?'

His eyebrows shot up, and she struggled to keep a straight face.

'Not that, idiot. The picture.'

His chuckle was infectious, and she got the giggles in spite of herself.

'Sorry,' she said, when she could speak again, but he just shook his head and pulled her into his arms and hugged her.

'Don't be. It's lovely to see you laugh, Beth. I've missed it.'

'I've missed it, too.' Missed him, missed his arms around her, missed his body entwined with hers. Missed lying in his arms afterwards, listening to his heart beat as she fell asleep. Missed all of it.

She smiled, a wonky little smile by the feel of it, and eased away from him. 'So, the picture.'

He looked at the mark on the wall and shrugged.

'That's good enough. I can hang it a fraction lower to cover it,' he said, his voice suddenly gruff, and she backed away, her legs like jelly, because the air was suddenly full of something wild and dangerous and totally not on her agenda. Or it shouldn't be.

He measured the wall, marked the centre, measured the height for the hook and banged it into the wall. Firmly.

'Right, how's that?' he asked, settling it on the hook.

'Good. Great,' she said without giving it a glance. 'So what else is there?'

'More coffee?' he asked, heading for the kitchen, and she followed him, her body still reeling from that accidental touch.

Stupid. It happened all the time at work when they

were reaching round each other to get to the patient, so why did it feel so different now?

Because we're alone, playing house, and it's all getting a bit real...

'I fancy another bit of cake—going to join me?' she asked, and hoped her voice sounded normal, because the rest of her body certainly wasn't. It was clamouring for that wild and dangerous something she'd seen in his eyes, and she put the slice of cake on his plate and slid it towards him, picked up her own and retreated to the window, standing with her back to him while her body screamed at her to turn round, walk into his arms and forget every scrap of common sense she had left.

She stayed firmly where she was...

CHAPTER FIVE

THEY HUNG A few more pictures, but this time he held
them and she made the pencil mark, on the grounds that
he was, as he put it, less likely to lose his grip.

She didn't argue. Frankly, ducking under his arm
and being that close was complicated enough, especially when they were standing on his bed hanging the
picture right over it.

The one that had hung over his bed before, the one
that brought back memories that did nothing for her already compromised peace of mind.

'How's that?'

'Perfect.' If you wanted to be tortured...

She made the mark, he banged the nail in, hung it
and stood back.

'Good. Right, that'll do. I've got my interview tomorrow and I need to check my suit and iron a shirt.'

She stifled a sigh of relief and walked out of the
room. 'I'll head home,' she said quickly, wanting to get
away before he said or did anything that might under-
mine her resolve, because the bed was much too close

and far too inviting and she had a feeling they were standing on the edge of a precipice.

'Fizz first,' he said, heading for the kitchen. 'Well, unless you're driving?'

'No, I walked,' she said, unable to lie about it because he'd realise as soon as she opened the front door that there wasn't a car there apart from his.

She heard the soft pop of the cork, the fizzing of the glasses being filled, and he handed her one.

'Here.'

'Thank you.' She took it, vowing to go the moment it was finished, and clinked it gently on his. 'Here's to your new house—well, for now, at least. Maybe here's to a proper roof over your head and your own things around you.'

'I'll drink to that.' He smiled and clinked back. 'And here's to you, for all you've done to help me in the last few weeks, not least with the dog.'

'Where is she, by the way?' she asked, picking up a scuffing sound. They found her in the pantry, chasing a paper plate around the floor with her tongue. The paper plate that had held the cake.

'Tatty!' he yelled, and she scooted out of the pantry looking guilty and a teeny bit smug.

'Oh, Ryan, that's my fault, I left it on the side! Will it hurt her?'

He shook his head. 'No. It wasn't a fruit cake or a chocolate cake. Lemon drizzle should be fine—well, fine for her, not so fine for me.' He sighed. 'I was looking forward to the rest of that.'

'When did you feed her? Because you haven't done it since I got here, I don't think.'

A look of guilty horror crossed his face, and he smacked his forehead with his palm. 'Lunchtime! Tatty, come here, sweetheart. I'm sorry. Are you a hungry girl?'

'That's so not your dog,' she said drily, and drained her glass, but she was trying not to laugh and the wine dribbled round the side of her mouth and down her front, and he put the bowl on the floor and walked back to her with a tissue in his hand.

'That'll teach you to laugh at me,' he said, his lips twitching, and he blotted her gently dry, lingering a little too long on the corner of her mouth.

She put the glass down, and he lowered the tissue and stared down into her eyes, his lips parting slightly, his eyes searching hers and finding—what?

She looked away hastily, slipping out from between him and the worktop and heading for the door while she still could.

'It's time I went home,' she said, her voice all over the place, and he followed her to the door.

'I'll bring Tatty and come with you, she could do with a little walk before bed,' he said, trashing her escape plan. It only took five minutes to walk her home, maybe a little more with Tatty sniffing every blade of grass to check it out, but then they were there, and she slid her key into the lock and turned back to him.

'Before you ask, I won't come in,' he said, and she

nodded, trying not to look relieved because the air between them was still humming with whatever it was.

'Good luck tomorrow. I hope your interview goes well.'

He held her eyes. 'Are you sure you want me to go for it?'

Was she? She nodded, hoping he hadn't noticed her hesitation, because it wasn't really hesitation, she was just checking up on herself, making sure she could do this because after the sizzling tension between them this evening she really *wasn't* sure, because she had no idea where it was taking them.

Although it wasn't all about her, and they desperately needed another consultant…

'Yes, I'm sure. Thanks for seeing me home, Ry.'

'You're welcome,' he said softly, and cradled her face in his warm, gentle hands. 'Thank you again. For everything. I'll see you tomorrow.'

His lips brushed hers, just the lightest touch that lingered a moment, but fire scorched through her and she was ready to reach for him when he dropped his hands and turned away, and she let herself inside and closed the door, her legs suddenly like rubber.

Her fingers found her lips, pressing gently where his had touched hers, and she wanted to cry because his kiss had been so sweet, so tender, so unlike the raging passion they'd felt before two and a half years ago, or the kiss on the night he'd found Tatty, two weeks ago. So unlike the feelings she'd had when his hand had brushed her breast earlier today.

It had hardly been a kiss at all, and yet, as fleeting as

it had been, she could still feel the rivers of fire flickering through her veins and reaching every part of her, and she'd been so close to inviting him in.

Thank goodness for Tatty, because he couldn't have stayed anyway and it might have been embarrassing.

She watched him walking away down the road in the dusk, Tatty at his side looking up at him devotedly, and she found herself smiling. Crazy man. He was deluding himself if he thought he'd rehome her.

She waited until they were out of sight, then turned and looked at the little silver heart sitting on its shelf. The heart that bound them together, no matter what else the future held, no matter where life took them.

She picked it up, cradling it in her hand, the dog forgotten.

'Your daddy's got an interview tomorrow,' she told Grace softly. 'He might be going to live near us permanently. I wonder how that will feel?'

She had no idea. No idea at all, of how she'd feel or what the implications might be, and she felt horribly unsettled and confused.

Shaking her head, she pressed a goodnight kiss to the little heart, picked up a glass of water from the kitchen and headed upstairs for an early night, but sleep was a long time coming and she woke to the lingering fragments of a weird, disturbing dream that didn't make any sense but left her feeling even more unsettled.

She looked at the clock. It was only ten to six, and she was on a late so technically she could be having a lie-in, but she was wide awake after her run of nights and she felt suddenly unaccountably nervous for Ryan.

And for herself?

Because of course what happened today had massive implications for her, as well as him.

Would he get the job?

Did she even really want him to?

Yes—but what if he didn't get it? What if the other candidate was better after all? Or if there was another one who'd applied out of nowhere?

He'd leave if he didn't get it, but would that be the end for them? Probably. Let's face it, he'd made no attempt to keep in touch while he was with the aid organisation, so why would now be any different?

He had said he'd tried to phone her, and as she'd changed her number she couldn't blame him for that, although if he'd really wanted to he could have found her. Only he said he'd tried to airbrush her out of his life because he'd found it all too hard to deal with, so why would he have tried? And if he didn't get the job, he might well go back to MFA and do a better job with the airbrushing this time.

But if he got the job, then what? What would it mean for them as a couple? If they even were a couple...

They certainly weren't at the moment, and they'd never talked about that, never considered it, never mentioned the future. Was the future even in his mind, or was he simply looking for a job, loved the town and was happy to have her there as a friend?

Ugh. That word again, which covered everything from a slight acquaintance to—them? Maybe, as things stood. But would that be enough for her? She had a horrible feeling after yesterday that it wouldn't be, but on the other hand she wasn't sure what else there might be on offer apart from an affair, and she knew she didn't want that, or at least not in isolation, because her heart simply couldn't remain that detached.

It would need to be more than that, but how much more?

They hadn't lived together before, but maybe he would want them to this time, and where would that lead? If they fell in love, then maybe to marriage?

A family?

Her heart thumped against her ribs. Would he ask that of her? He'd said over and over again that he didn't want children, and he and Katie had split up because she'd tried to get pregnant without discussing it with him when she knew he was going away with MFA, possibly for several years.

But what if he'd changed his mind? What if it was only that he hadn't wanted to be an absent father? He'd said it was time for him to settle down now, to go back to the future. Did he mean with her, and if so, did he mean as a family, and if so, could she do it?

Only if he loved her, but she had no idea whether he did or not, except as a friend. She already knew she loved him, but enough for that?

Did she even dare to consider another pregnancy? Her body yearned for a child, her arms ached to cradle a baby, but she was so scared. Would she be brave enough to try again?

Her heart thumped, even the thought making her mouth go dry.

Don't go there. It's all theoretical—and anyway, it

might never happen. He probably isn't even thinking about it.

And even if he was, there were so many unknowns. His interview, the job, their future together—only time would tell how their relationship would pan out, but she'd never been patient.

One step at a time. Get the interview over, see if he gets a job offer, go from there.

She threw back the covers, pulled on her clothes and went downstairs, made a cup of tea and took it outside, perching on the edge of the damp bench and staring at the garden in dismay.

It was ages since she'd done anything out here; she'd been so busy helping Ryan with Tatty or the house or both, and in that time spring had definitely sprung. Oh, well. She had all morning, and as soon as it was a civilised hour she'd cut the lawn, but until then she could do some weeding and tidy up around the edges and refill the bird feeders.

Anything rather than sit there with her nerves strung so tight she thought they'd snap…

'How did it go?'

Ryan gave a soft huff of laughter and tugged off his tie before it strangled him. 'I have no idea, Beth. OK, I suppose. I answered all the questions, but it was pretty tough. James didn't cut me any slack, but that was fine, I didn't expect him to, and he wasn't alone. The others were just as thorough.'

'What kind of questions?'

'Oh, I don't know, medical stuff and personnel management, mentoring, being a team player, that kind of thing, but also loads of ethical scenarios. What do you do if someone comes in in a coma and the person with them isn't down as their next of kin but is obviously very involved with them? The rights of children, the absence of a DNAR statement and the relatives saying don't resuscitate, they don't want it—all the usual stuff which gets handed up the food chain to the most senior person in the department at the time. How do you deal with staff members who've broken the rules? Do you cover your ass or do the right thing kind of questions.'

She bit her lip and he could see laughter sparkling in her eyes. 'I'm guessing you're not a cover your ass kind of person,' she said drily.

He chuckled. 'No. I'm not. So it might have lost me the job because I'd bet my life the other guy is.'

'Did you meet him?'

'Yes, but he had to leave suddenly. Cited family reasons, apparently, so they've postponed his interview for a week and he's coming back then.'

'So what was he like?'

He laughed again, wondering how to phrase it. 'Let's just say he seemed pretty confident.'

'Arrogant, then.'

He felt his lips twitch, and Beth chuckled. 'Oh, dear. That won't have gone down well with James. He's got no time for arrogance.'

'Ah, but, if he's good, if he comes over better than me in the interview—he's got a lot of experience, Beth, he's been a consultant for several years, and I'm pretty sure he thought they were only interviewing me because I was on site and they didn't have to pay travel expenses. He asked me where I'd been working, so I told him, and he then implied I'd been out of it for a while, which in a way I have, but not in a trauma sense. I'm sure I've covered far more in the last two years than he has. I don't think he had the slightest idea of how much I had to deal with. One minute you're fighting to contain an outbreak of Ebola, the next minute you're in a war zone and being shot at, then it's an earthquake and you're dragging people out of rubble during the aftershocks—it's crazy, and you pack more into every day than you ever would working here, busy though it is. And he wouldn't have lasted ten seconds, I don't think. I could be wrong.'

'I doubt it. It takes a special kind of person, I would imagine. I don't know how *you* did it.'

He huffed softly, seeing things he'd rather forget. Things that haunted his sleep. 'I didn't, always. I lost it a few times. Kids, mostly. That's what gets to you. The kids. You never forget their faces.'

'You never talk about it.'

'No. No, I don't.'

'More airbrushing?' she asked quietly, and he tried to smile.

'Probably.' He dragged in a breath and put the memories away. 'So, anyway, I've got to wait at least another week before I have the answer, so it's back to the day job for now. Want to fill me in?'

Her eyes were gentle, as if she could see what he could see, but her voice was quiet and steady and matter-of-fact, and he was grateful for that.

'The usual mayhem, I gather, not made better by you and James being out all morning, I don't suppose. I don't really know, I haven't been here long, I'm on a late today. I walked Tatty before I came in, by the way, and because one of Annie's boys isn't feeling well, I took Molly, too.'

'Oh, thanks. I was worrying about that. Amongst other things.'

'I thought you might be. I told Reg I'd walked her and fed her, but he's going to pop in a bit later anyway. I think he's enjoying it. Breaks up the day for him. I think he's been lonely since his wife died last year.'

He felt a pang of guilt for not knowing that. 'I didn't realise it was so recent, but I expect you're right, he will be lonely. What are you doing later?'

'What, like nine o'clock tonight later?' she said with a laugh. 'Nothing.'

'Good. Come round and I'll cook you dinner and we can celebrate me surviving my interview if nothing else. So what should I do now? Where do they need me?'

'I don't know. Sam's back, he's in Resus and he could probably do with a hand, he's only got Livvy and they're busy.'

'OK. I'll go and change. Tell them I'm on my way.'

She didn't get to his house until well after nine, and she couldn't get an answer, which was odd.

His car was there, but it was getting dark and she was pretty sure he wouldn't still be out with Tatty, so she let herself in and called his name, but he didn't answer and there was no sign of the dog and no lights on. Maybe they were still out?

She could smell something delicious cooking, though, so she went and investigated and found a fragrant casserole bubbling away a little too fast. She turned it down, stirred it and put the lid back on, and then realised the dining room doors were open to the garden, so she went out, her footsteps all but silent.

He was sitting on the steps, his elbows on his knees, his head hanging, and she knew instantly that something was wrong.

'Ryan?'

He looked up, and even in the dusk she could see he looked upset, and her heart stalled.

'Ry, what is it? What's happened? Where's Tatty?'

'Gone,' he said, his voice uneven, and she felt sick. 'The rescue centre rang. They had space in a foster home. I've just handed her over. The carer's going to keep her until she's had the pups, and then they'll re-home them all. They said they'd easily find her a new family, she's got such a lovely nature—'

His voice cracked, and she went over to him, sat down beside him and put her arms round him. 'Oh, Ry, I'm so sorry. I know how much you loved her.'

'I didn't love her,' he said angrily, his body stiff and resistant. 'She was a liability, and the last thing I needed! I'm well rid of her.'

'If you say so.'

'I do—and I don't want to talk about it.' He straightened up and shrugged out of her arms. 'I cooked a tagine.'

'I saw. I turned it down, it was starting to catch on the bottom of the pan.'

He groaned and met her eyes for the first time. 'Is it all right?'

'I think so. It's certainly cooked. It smells lovely.'

'Good. Let's go and eat it.'

He got to his feet and headed inside, but it was only when they got into the house she realised his eyes were red rimmed.

Poor Ry. Such a kind heart, and so much love to give...

'Can I do anything?'

He shook his head. 'No. I've just got to make some couscous. There's some of that fizz left. I recorked it—I found a gadget in my kitchen stuff. You could pour us some.'

'I've got the car here.'

'You can have one glass. Or you could stay.'

Their eyes clashed and held, and she looked away, her heart pounding. Stay, as in stay with him? Sleep with him? Make love, like they had before? What, to distract him from losing Tatty? She'd need a better reason than that.

'I don't think that's a good idea,' she said, her voice a little uneven, and he laughed, a sad, bitter, broken laugh that wrenched her heart.

'No, you're right. Pour the wine, Beth. I can always walk you home again.'

She only had one glass, so he didn't need to walk her home, in the end, and he was glad he didn't, because it was only last night he'd done it with Tatty, and it would have felt weird without her.

Weird and wrong and sad—

Stupid. She was just a dog, for heaven's sake!

But all night, in the huge bed with more room than he could ever need just for himself, he worried about her, about how she'd be coping in unfamiliar surroundings, if the people would let her sleep on the bed with them or if she'd be banished to a shed—

No. Surely not a shed. He was being ridiculous. He rolled over, thumped the pillow and shut his eyes firmly, but he slept only fitfully for the rest of the night, and the following morning he was in work by seven.

So was Beth, and she gave him a searching look.

'Are you OK?'

'Of course I'm OK,' he said brusquely. 'Why wouldn't I be?'

She arched a brow and stood her ground. 'Have you had a coffee yet?'

'I've had about four. Why?'

She shrugged and propped herself against the wall. 'I thought a coffee might improve your temper. Obviously not.'

He sighed heavily and rammed a hand through his hair. 'Sorry. I'm being an idiot. I know she'll be fine.'

'She will. Really, Ry. She loves everyone—and everyone loves her.'

Including him?

Her hand on his arm was warm and comforting, but he shrugged it off. He didn't want to be comforted, he wanted to be left alone. 'So, what can I do for you, Beth?'

That eyebrow again. 'There's a patient due in Resus in a few minutes. You might be needed, so if you're not up for it, go and occupy yourself in Minors and I'll make an excuse for you.'

'I'm fine.'

She looked over his shoulder, and shrugged away from the wall. 'Good, because we're on. Are you coming?'

It was another busy week, but that was fine. He didn't want thinking time, not about anything and most particularly not about the dog, and events played into his hands, but then at three on Friday afternoon there was a sudden lull and everything stopped, so he took a break and headed off to the café, taking a coffee outside and sitting alone on a bench under a tree.

And there was a dog, a golden retriever who reminded him a little of Tatty, and he felt a lump in his throat.

What if she wasn't happy? What if she wouldn't settle?

He was being ridiculous. Of course she'd settle. All she needed was food and a sofa and she'd be fine.

Wouldn't she?

He pulled his phone out, hesitated, then rang the rescue centre and got put through to Zoe, the person he'd dealt with.

'Zoe, it's Ryan McKenna. I don't know if you remember me, I brought Tatty in to you on Tuesday.'

'Of course I remember you, Ryan. What can I do for you?' she asked, and he felt suddenly foolish.

'Probably nothing,' he admitted. 'I know you can't tell me anything, because she's not my dog and I hardly know her and I've handed her over to you so I've got no rights, but I'm just wondering if you can tell me how she is, if she's settled, you know—just to put my mind at rest?'

There was a sigh, and a few 'should I, shan't I' noises, and then she said, 'I can't lie to you. The person who's looking after her is worried. Tatty won't eat anything, she's hardly drinking, she's cried constantly and we're really concerned, but there's nothing you can do, I know that, and I'm sure she'll settle, given time.'

'But—what about her puppies? If she's not eating…'

'I know. And my foster lady's experienced, too. She's tried everything—even hand-feeding her boiled chicken, but she just takes a mouthful and then turns her head away.'

He felt the lump in his throat swell, and he swallowed and blinked hard.

'What if I had her back, just until after the puppies are born?' he said, wondering what he'd done with his brains but—how could he leave her there like that? Even if she was just a dog and it was really none of his business?

'Could you?' Zoe said, sounding doubtful. 'Would you be able to? What about your work commitments?'

'I can work round it. I've got a friend who helps me out—' assuming he hadn't upset her so much this week that she'd never speak to him again '—and my neighbour's been feeding her at lunchtime, so we can manage, I'm sure. I can't let her suffer. It's not fair. Not with the pups.'

There was a long silence, then Zoe sighed again. 'Can I call you back? I'll talk to the foster lady again, and my manager, see what they say, and I'll let you know.'

'OK. I'm at work so leave a message if you have to, I'll get back to you as soon as I'm free.'

He looked at his watch. Three eighteen. Another two hours and forty two minutes till he finished his shift. Assuming he finished on time, which was a big assumption. And then, maybe, he would be picking Tatty up.

Or not…

Time to get back. He swallowed his coffee, threw the cup in the bin and headed back to the ED, but the phone rang before he was even halfway there.

He glanced at the screen. Zoe. He answered, his heart in his mouth.

'What did she say?'

'No change. She thinks if you can manage it, she'd be relieved. She's even had the vet out because she was so worried about her puppies.'

He felt the air go out of him like a punctured balloon. 'OK. I'm still at work now but I can get her later. Just tell me when and where.'

Beth stared at him. 'You're doing *what*?'

'Picking her up at seven from the foster person. Beth, I have to. She hasn't eaten since Tuesday and she's crying constantly and they're worried. It's only till she has the pups.'

'Yeah, right. And you'll be able to give her up then?'

'Yes! Of course! This is just for the sake of the puppies and it's not for long,' he said, and she wondered who he was lying to, her or himself. 'The vet said she's probably due in two or three weeks. It's hard to say, apparently, and they can't tell how many puppies there are without an X-ray but she doesn't think it's a huge litter. Whatever, I can't let her suffer. Yes, it's a pain, but needs must.'

She eyed him sceptically. A pain? She didn't think so. Not for a moment. He looked relieved. And at least his horrible mood had lifted, because he'd been vile all week.

'Well, I'm glad to see you're happier. You might not be such a grump to work with now,' she said a little bluntly.

'Sorry.' His smile was rueful. 'I don't suppose you're around later, are you?'

'What, as a welcoming committee for the dog you don't intend to keep?' she teased, and the shutters came down again.

'Forget it. I just thought you might—'

'I'm sorry, I'm sorry. Yes, I'm around,' she said quickly. 'Of course I'm around. Do you want me to cook? I finish soon so I've got time. I can bring something over.'

'Could you? I've got to dive into the vets' to get some food for her on my way to pick her up, so I won't have time to shop, again! Are you OK with that?'

'Sure. I could do with picking up a few things.'

She detoured via the supermarket on the way home, made a chicken curry for them and poached some of the chicken in a little water for Tatty, because the dog's plight had pulled at her heartstrings and although she'd teased Ryan, she was fully behind his decision to have her back, whatever his motives.

Was it purely the dog? Or was it, in some subliminal way, to atone for his guilt for not being there for her after Grace? A determination not to let Tatty down the way he felt he'd let her down?

Whatever, she was sure both he and Tatty would be happier as a result, even if, inevitably, it would put some of the responsibility on her, but she didn't mind that and she'd been as worried as him all week.

He was back when she got to his house just after seven, and the dog ran to her for a quick cuddle before rushing back to her hero, and the look on his face said it all.

'I've made us a curry, and I cooked her some chicken,' she said, and he smiled at her properly for the first time in days.

'Thank you. I've got some dry puppy food from the vet for her. They said little and often, just till she's eating again normally. Why don't we mix it? Bit of each, just to tempt her?'

'I've made us lots of plain boiled rice, so she can have some of that, too.'

'Good idea.'

Tatty thought so, and while she ate, Beth dished up their curry and took it through to the dining room, and

Ryan followed her, Tatty at his side, and sat down to eat nearly as hungrily as the dog, who was now lying on his feet. She wondered if he'd been eating, either. Maybe not. The man was riddled with guilt.

'She's clingy, isn't she? Even worse than before.'

He nodded. 'She is. Not surprising, really. At least she's eaten, though, so I can stop worrying about that. The curry was delicious, by the way. Thank you.'

'You're welcome.' She looked down at Tatty and smiled. 'Do you think she'd like it if we moved to the sofa?'

He laughed softly, but she thought she heard a tiny catch in his throat. 'I'm sure she would. Come on, Tatty.'

He got up, and she glued herself to his side and licked his hand continuously until he sat down, then jumped up beside him and settled with her head and shoulders on his lap.

His hand went down automatically to her side, and Beth saw him wince as he stroked her gently.

'She's so thin—she's back to square one. I'll give her more food in a while. They said little and often at first to give her stomach time to adjust, but she's just ravenous. Silly, silly girl, aren't you?'

'I can't believe she didn't eat all week.'

'Well, she certainly has now I've got her home.'

The word made her heart squeeze in her chest. Was it home? His, and the dog's? Did she even dare dream it might be theirs, down the line?

Yes, for now, but what if he didn't get the job? Although James had said something yesterday that she still hadn't had a chance to tell him.

She should, because until he knew about the job he was in limbo, putting one step in front of the other, day by day, with no idea where he was going. Well, at least not until he heard.

What if he didn't get it? Would he take Tatty with him wherever he went? And where would he go? He couldn't take her if he went back to MFA, although he'd said he wouldn't do that.

And what about her? What about them?

Was there a 'them'?

She had no idea about that, either, but it was time she did, so she took a deep breath and tackled it head on.

'Ryan, we need to talk.'

CHAPTER SIX

HE SWITCHED OFF the television he'd just put on and turned to look at her, searching her eyes for clues, but there were none.

'That sounds serious.'

'Not necessarily serious, but there's something I haven't had a chance to tell you. I don't know if it was significant, but I bumped into James yesterday as I was leaving work and he was asking me about you.'

'I thought he was on holiday?'

'He is, but he said he'd popped in for something. He wanted to know how I'd feel if they offered you the job.'

He felt his eyes widen. 'Are they going to? They haven't even interviewed the other guy yet, unless something's changed.'

'No, I think he was just sounding me out.'

'Why? I thought he didn't know about us? Unless you've told him?'

She shook her head. 'No, of course not. I haven't said anything to anyone, but he knows we know each other pretty well, and he may have put two and two together and come up with something which is obviously not even going to scratch the surface, but I wasn't about to put him right.'

'So what did you say?'

She looked away. 'I told him I'd be delighted for you if you got it, because I felt you deserved it, you're a brilliant doctor and would be an asset to the department, you love the town and I thought you'd be very happy here.'

He studied her carefully. 'Is that true?'

She looked confused for a second. 'Well—yes. Wouldn't you be happy here? And if not, then why *are* you here and why did you apply for the permanent post? And scrolling back, why did you apply for the locum job in the first place?'

'Because I needed a job. I told you that, and yes, I think I would be happy here. I *am* happy here. It's a lovely place, with a great hospital and the added bonus that you're here, so why wouldn't I be? That's not what I was asking, though. You said you'd be delighted if I got it, which rather implies you want me here.'

She looked confused again. 'I didn't say that. I said I'd be delighted *for you*. Not for me.'

'Or us?'

'Is there an "us"? Is there, Ry? I don't know. I don't even know if you want there to be an "us". Unless that's why you're here, after all.'

She cocked her head on one side and searched his face, her eyes suddenly filled with doubt. 'Are you *sure* you didn't know I was here?' she asked carefully, and he stared at her, slightly stunned.

'Absolutely. You know that. The fact that you're here

was nothing to do with it because I didn't have a clue. I told you that weeks ago. I saw the locum job advertised, I needed something short-term until I worked out what I was doing with my life, and then you were here, but I had no idea you were, Beth. For heaven's sake, I'm not stalking you! Is that what you think?'

'No—no, of course not, but I'm still not sure why you applied for the permanent job—not really.'

He gave a little huff of laughter, feeling lost in this circular conversation that didn't seem to be getting anywhere. 'Because it's a great place, and I love working here, and you said you were fine with it—are you not fine with it? Have you got a problem with it now?'

'I don't know,' she said, searching his eyes again, her own troubled. 'I honestly don't know, because I don't know where we stand, what we are to each other, where we go from here, if anywhere, because I don't even know you well enough to know if you're telling me the truth.'

He was shocked at that, a sick feeling in the pit of his stomach, and he stabbed his hand through his hair and stared at her.

'Why would I lie to you? It was sheer coincidence, I promise. I can't believe you'd think that of me. I'm not Rick!'

'I know you're not Rick. It's not that, it's nothing to do with him. He was a lying, cheating love rat and I know you're not that, but…'

'But?' he prompted, still smarting, and she shrugged.

'I just know we see things differently.'

'Such as?'

That little shrug again, touched with despair. 'I know you don't trust me, either. You don't trust anybody. When I told you I was pregnant…'

He let out a shuddering breath. 'Don't. I reacted badly. I know. I should never have accused you of getting pregnant on purpose. I know you're not like Katie, and you were hugely supportive of my decision to join MFA, but a bit of me wondered if you were just looking for an absent father, a convenient sperm donor. It's not unheard of.'

She looked stunned. 'Why would I want that? I'd just split up with Rick, I was bruised and battered emotionally, he'd been sleeping with my best friend and I'd lost them both—why would I suddenly decide to have a child on my own?'

'I don't know. You're right, we didn't know each other, we probably still don't, but I was wrong to jump to conclusions, and I'm sorry. And when I realised how serious things were with the pregnancy, I was gutted and I did what I could to help you, but it doesn't excuse how I was with you. But, no, you're right, I don't trust easily, any more than you do. I guess we're both wary, trying to protect ourselves, and sometimes that hurts other people.'

She nodded. 'Yes, it does. So—will you do that again, if it gets tough? And what if I trust you, and let myself fall in love with you, and then we start having the difficult conversations?'

'Such as?'

She shrugged. 'I don't know—about starting a family, maybe—something I know you don't want to do.'

'I haven't said that.'

She stared at him blankly. 'You've said it over and over again!'

'To Katie, and about Katie and my relationship with her, because I was signing up with the aid organisation for the next few years and I had no intention of being an absent father! That doesn't mean I don't want children in the future. I'd love them.'

'With me?'

It was his turn to shrug, the question too close to home. 'Maybe, if that's the way this goes, but we don't know each other well enough yet to say that, Beth. We've shared a colossal history, in a way, and yet we're still strangers. We haven't reached a point in our relationship where we can see the future panning out, and that's one reason why I want this job, so we have time to see where it's going. If I don't get it and I have to move away, then we might find a long-distance relationship too much of a challenge, and I couldn't expect you to uproot yourself to come with me until we were both sure.'

'So you're just buying time?'

Was he? 'Maybe. I've made enough mistakes, hurt enough people, been hurt myself. I want to do it right this time, for you, for me, for us. And that means giving us time.'

'And you'll want children?'

He nodded. 'If it works between us, then yes, probably, I would, but not if you didn't feel you could do that. After Grace—I don't know. It must be hard.'

'It is. I do want children, desperately, but frankly I'm too scared to even consider it because I don't know if I can go through that again. And if I get pregnant by accident, would you blame me again? Say I've done it on purpose? What if I *can't* get pregnant again? What if we can never have a child? What if I'm just not brave enough?'

He stared at her, wondering how they'd got to this conversation when so far he'd hardly kissed her! Although it wasn't because he didn't want to.

He shook his head slowly. 'Why are we talking about this now?'

'Because I need to know how you feel so I don't end up letting myself fall in love with someone I know might break my heart! I can't be hurt like that again, Ry.'

'You said I hadn't ever hurt you.'

'You haven't—not yet. Well, maybe when you accused me of getting pregnant on purpose, but you didn't hurt me like Rick did, no. But this time, you might, because this time it's different. We're not starting from the same place. Before, we had total freedom and a lack of commitment, a relationship based purely on sex. It was all about fun, and it *was* fun, but we can't do that now, we can't go back to that and I wouldn't want to. Not after Grace. It would just feel wrong, as if we were trying to turn the clock back, but we can't. Grace died, and we can't change that, but I don't know how we move on from it. Who was it said you can't go back and make a new beginning?'

'C.S. Lewis,' he said quietly, his mind grappling with all the things she'd said. 'Well, it's been attributed to C.S. Lewis but that's been questioned. The actual quote is "You can't go back and change the beginning, but you can start where you are and change the ending". Maybe that's what we should be aiming for, because for us, where we left off, our ending was just heartbreaking, and maybe it's time to rewrite that, to make it the middle and not the end, and give ourselves a better ending.'

'Together?'

He shrugged. 'I don't know, Beth. That depends on so many things, some of which we have no control over. I just know we owe it to each other to leave ourselves in a better place than we were in. I don't want to hurt you, I never want to hurt you, but I don't know if I can give you what you want, what you need, and I don't know if you can give me that. I don't even know what it is I need and it doesn't sound like you do, either. All we can do is try. Try to understand, try to trust, try to care.'

'And if we fail?'

He searched her eyes, and tried to smile, but it was hard. 'Then at least we know we've done our best to heal each other,' he said quietly, and she closed her eyes and nodded.

'Yes.'

'So what do we do now, Beth?' he asked softly, and held his breath. What would she say? A light-hearted relationship, like they'd had before but without the disastrous consequences? No, she'd already ruled that out. A solid, straightforward friendship? Or something else, something deeper that would involve a greater commitment?

It felt like he'd tossed a coin and he'd only know what he wanted when it landed, but she shrugged again, a tiny shift of her shoulders, as if she didn't know what she wanted any more than he did.

'I don't know. I like you. I more than like you, much more, but—Ry, I don't know if I'm brave enough to test us. I don't know how strong we'd be together, how much we could lean on each other if life got tough. We couldn't before. Why would now be any better? If that was even what you wanted. I have no idea. You give nothing away—nothing at all, and I have no idea what you're thinking or feeling.'

'I can't tell you that, because I don't know,' he said after a long pause. 'I just know I want to see if we can make it work this time. We're not the same people we were. We've both changed.'

'But does that make us more compatible?'

'Not necessarily, but maybe more compassionate. I didn't stay with you when I should have done. I let you down, I know that. I wouldn't do it again.'

'But I didn't want you there, Ryan. I didn't want your pity, and I don't want it now.'

'No, I'm sure you don't. I wasn't offering it, then or now. But I don't know what you do want now, and if I'm honest I haven't got a clue what I want, either. Well, you. I want you, that hasn't changed, but I don't know if it's just physical still or if there's more than that, and if it's more I don't know how much more. Not now, not since Grace, because it's changed us both, tied us together in a way we'd never expected, and I don't know how we move forward from that. I just know that, one way or another, I'd like to have you in my life. I *need* to have you in my life, and if that means we have to test our relationship, to give it a try, then I'd like to do that to see if we've got what it takes, because I can't imagine living without you in my life in some form or other and I'm sick of living in limbo, too.'

'And what if we can't make it work?'

He shrugged. 'I don't know. Maybe we'd just have to try harder, because I can't imagine that I'll ever have a relationship with anyone else that comes near to being as profound and life-changing as what I've shared with you. And I don't know if losing Grace will be the thing that keeps us together, or drives us apart, but I just know it would be there in any other relationship I had with anyone else, and that getting past it would be unimaginably difficult. It'll be hard enough doing it with you.'

She nodded slowly, and a sad little smile flickered on her lips for a moment and then was gone.

'So what happens if you don't get the job?'

Her words hung in the air, and he felt the breath sucked out of him.

'I don't know, because it has all sorts of implications. But I certainly don't want to lose you.'

'And Tatty?'

'Tatty's going to be rehomed,' he said firmly, and hearing her name, she looked up at him and licked his hand.

'Yes, of course she is,' Beth said drily, and he swallowed hard and looked away.

'She is! Beth, if I don't get this job I won't have a choice, because I'll have to move on, I have no idea where, or how long for, so until I hear about it, I can't make any kind of commitment to her—or to you, come to that, because I'll have to get another job and it could take me anywhere. Anywhere at all.'

'I could maybe come with you. If you wanted me?'

That stunned him. He turned his head and met her eyes again. 'You'd do that?' he asked, slightly incredulous. 'You'd be prepared to uproot yourself again and follow me? What if it was somewhere you didn't want to go? And besides, it's only three weeks since you told me not to expect us to pick up where we left off.'

'I know. And I'm not sure how I'd feel about following you, but if our relationship was strong enough and the need arose, I should be prepared to. I guess there's only one way to find out. We need to try and open up more, talk to each other about our feelings. We need to give ourselves a chance.'

She held out her hand, and he stared at it for a moment, then slowly lifted his and threaded his fingers through hers, palm to palm.

'I guess so.'

He pressed a gentle kiss to her fingers, then laid their hands down again on Tatty's back. She turned her head and licked them both, then got off the sofa, stretched and lay down at his feet.

'Come here,' he said softly, turning towards Beth and giving her hand a little tug, and she shifted towards him. He slid his arm around her, tilting her face up to his with the tip of his finger, and then his mouth found hers in a kiss that lingered endlessly.

It would be so easy to take it all the way, to scoop her up and carry her into the bedroom, but they weren't ready for that yet, not emotionally, at any rate, and he didn't want to hurt her, so he eased away, turned the TV on again and settled back, Beth's head on his shoulder and the dog at his feet.

He could get so used to that...

'I should go home,' she said a while later.

Ryan met her eyes, and nodded slowly.

'Yes, you probably should. We don't want to rush this.'

'No. And it's not as if we don't know that the sex works,' she said with a wry smile, and instantly regretted it because she saw the heat flare in his eyes.

'Now why did you say that?' he murmured, lifting a lock of her hair back from her face, his fingertips skating lightly over her skin and making her shiver with need.

It would be so easy to reach up and kiss him, but it would never end with a kiss, so she pulled away and got to her feet and headed for the front door, and he followed, Tatty in tow as if she didn't trust him out of her sight. When they reached the door he drew her into his arms and hugged her gently, and she wrapped her arms around him and absorbed his warmth, wishing she could stay, wishing it wasn't such a bad idea.

Wondering where life would take them now.

'Drive carefully,' he murmured.

'It's just round the corner!'

'Yeah.' She could hear the smile in his voice. 'I know that, but it's Friday night and there are idiots about.'

She felt his fingers tunnel through her hair, and then he tilted her head and touched his lips to hers, warm and firm and so, so good. They clung, motionless, and then he groaned and deepened the kiss, nipping, biting, licking, parting her lips and delving until she whimpered.

He backed her against the wall, his knee nudging between her legs, rocking against her as he plundered her mouth. One hand was anchored in her hair, the other sliding under her top, his fingers splaying over her breast, and she arched into him, her body on fire, her hands on his back urging him closer.

'Ry...'

He swore softly and eased away, resting his forehead against hers as his breathing steadied, then he slid his hand round her back and pulled her close again and held her, his palm against her skin, cradling her head against his shoulder with his other hand so she could hear the echo of his heart thundering under her ear, his fingers toying with her hair for a moment before he straightened up and stared down into her eyes.

'Go home, Beth,' he murmured raggedly. 'We don't want to do something we could both regret.'

She nodded, went up on tiptoe and kissed his cheek, the stubble making her lips tingle all over again, and then with a pat for Tatty she opened the door and let herself out on legs that didn't quite work.

'Call me when you're home,' he said.

'What, so we can prolong the agony with phone sex?' she threw over her shoulder, and his eyes flared again, simmering with frustration.

'Just—call me,' he said through gritted teeth, so she did, the moment she got home.

'I'm safe. I survived the drunks and the idiots on the road. Are you happy?'

'No. Obviously I'm happy you're safe home, but if I'm honest I'd be happier if you were here finishing what we started.'

She swallowed, the teasing long gone, replaced by a deep ache overlaid by common sense. 'I would be, too, but if we're in this for the long haul there has to be more to our relationship.'

'I know. I still want you, though. That bed's awfully big.'

'I'm not sure Tatty would like sharing it.'

She heard him laugh and say something to the dog, then he was back. 'I need to feed her. She's hungry again, then I need to take her out for a little walk. Do you have any plans for tomorrow?'

'What, apart from working? I'm on a late.'

'Breakfast at the pub, and a dog walk?'

She smiled. 'Sounds good. Can we make it nine and walk her first? I start at twelve and I've got a twelve-hour shift, so a nice big breakfast at ten thirty would be good.'

'Sure. We'll walk round and pick you up. At least in daylight we're likely to behave ourselves. OK, Tatty, I'm coming. Sleep well, Beth. I'll see you tomorrow.'

'You, too.'

Sleep well?

In his dreams.

He had Tatty crushed up against him, as if she was making certain he was still there, and every time he moved she shifted back up against him again until he was clinging to the edge.

He didn't care. She was back, and anyway, he had plenty to think about while she kept him awake, starting and ending with Beth.

Did he love her? It certainly felt like love, or what he imagined it felt like. Not the white-hot physical craziness they had before, although that was still certainly there, but something much deeper and more profound, born of what they'd been through together.

Except they hadn't really been together, they'd just both been there, trapped on the same rollercoaster. The togetherness had been sadly lacking, but they'd been too wrapped up in shock and grief to forge a closer bond, and then he'd gone, leaving her to deal with it alone.

Could they make it work this time? Forge that bond now, two years later?

He hoped so. He knew he'd bust every sinew to give it a chance, but it wasn't just him, and she'd had more to deal with than he had.

Well, with Grace, anyway. He'd had all the MFA stuff, and some of the things he'd seen were pretty damaging. He wasn't quite unscathed, he knew that. The nightmares were a constant reminder, as were the scars, but it had to be worse for Beth.

He thought about her, about all the little ways she'd shown him kindness since he'd arrived in Yoxburgh. Would she have done that if she didn't care? He doubted it. Certainly no one else would, unless they were a better person than him—but then she was, he knew that.

There was no way she'd have left him the way he'd left her—except she'd told him she didn't need him and all but sent him away. Had she really meant it, or just said it to free him of his obligations? Probably.

Whatever, he'd gone, without a backward glance.

Well, he was back now, and it seemed they might have another chance, but only time would tell if it would work, and as for them having children—no, that was too far down the line to think about.

He rolled to his side, shoving Tatty out of the way, and finally he drifted off to sleep, only to wake from one of the many recurring nightmares to find the dog standing over him whining and licking his face.

He struggled up and propped himself against the headboard, turning on the light, and she lay on him, still washing any part of him that she could reach, as if to comfort him.

'It's OK, Tatty. I'm all right,' he murmured, and she rested her head down on his chest and watched him with soulful eyes.

He glanced at the clock. Four thirty. Too early to get up, and probably too late to go back to sleep again properly, but he ought to try.

He heaved her out of the way, turned off the light and lay down again, and she flumped back against him with a grunt.

'You're going to have to learn to share me,' he warned her, but he wasn't sure how that would work. Ah, well, Tatty would be gone soon, and until then maybe they'd find a way…

* * *

They had a lovely morning.

The weather was glorious, a beautiful spring day with everything bursting into life, and for a change they wandered through the little housing development she lived on, taking the footpath that cut behind all the gardens, with the cherry trees in bloom sprinkling them with confetti and the last of the daffodils and crocuses bobbing their heads in the grass verges. They crossed to the cliff top, following it to the steps and coming back along the beach, and Tatty was tugging at the lead.

'You could let her off.'

He raised an eyebrow and snorted, but then shrugged and took off the lead, and Tatty rushed into the sea, leapt back out and shook all over them.

'Got any more good ideas?' he asked, swiping water off his face with his hand, but she was too busy laughing at him to answer.

'Sorry.'

'I should think so,' he muttered, but he must have forgiven her because he took her hand in his and they strolled along the sand, with Tatty playing at the edge of the water.

He put her back on the lead when she soaked him again, but she'd got the tickles out of her toes and she trotted along peacefully beside them all the way to the pub.

They ate breakfast outside with her lying at their feet, smoked salmon eggs Benedict with wilted spinach and lashings of Hollandaise, washed down with copious coffee and followed up with a pastry just because why not, then she looked at her watch and sighed.

Was that really the time?

'I have to go. I've got a twelve-hour shift ahead of me, but at least I'm off then till Monday.'

'Lucky you. I'm on call from eight tomorrow morning until midnight, and then I'm working Monday, too. It's going to be gorgeous, I can hardly wait.'

She frowned at him. 'What about Tatty?'

He stared at the dog, lying asleep at his feet, and swore. 'Good point. She wasn't here when I said I could do it so it wasn't an issue, so I haven't even thought about it. If it's really busy, I might not get home. Damn.'

She waited, knowing what was coming, more than ready for it, and she heard him sigh.

'Yes,' she said, and he looked up and met her eyes.

'Yes?'

'Yes, I'll look after Tatty, and I can stay over tomorrow night if necessary—in the spare room,' she added, just so he knew. 'Then you can come and go if you have to, without worrying about her.'

He hesitated for an age, then nodded slowly. 'If you're sure...?'

'I'm sure. Are you done? I need to go. Duty calls.'

It was odd in the house without him the next day.

She spent a while with Tatty in the morning, then took her back to her own house and introduced her to it, picked up a few overnight things and the book she'd been trying to read for weeks, and walked back, her rucksack slung over her shoulder. And of course she met Reg on the drive, beaming at her through the gap in the hedge.

'Morning, Reg,' she said with a smile, and he gave her a nod.

'Morning. I see she's back, then.'

Tatty strained to get to him, and he eased through the hedge and gave her a little scratch on her head. 'Didn't think I'd see her again. I thought he'd sent her to the dog rescue?'

'He did, but she wasn't eating, so he went and picked her up on Friday. It's just until she has the puppies—or so he says, but he's a bit of a softy.'

'I can see that, just how he is with her. I was surprised when he said he'd taken her. I didn't think he would.'

'No, nor did I, but whatever, she's back for now, and I'm dog-sitting until tomorrow because he's at work.'

He tilted his head on one side. 'I can look after her, if you like? You know, while the two of you are at work. She's good company. I don't mind at all, any time.'

He looked so hopeful, so desperately lonely, and she knew how that felt, from the yawning void after Grace had died when nobody knew what to say to her so said nothing or just plain avoided her.

'You'll have to talk to him, but I'm sure he won't say no. He's very grateful for your help.' She hesitated, then stifled her selfish urge to curl up with a book and went on, 'Reg, what are you doing this afternoon? It's just that Ryan's garden is a bit of a mess, and I thought I might have a go at it but I'm not sure what's what, really, and your garden's immaculate, so I thought you might be able to give me some pointers.'

All of which was a lie, because she hadn't had any intention of working in the garden, Ryan had already done quite a lot of tidying, and she knew exactly what was what down to the last perennial poking its head out of the earth. But the old man's eyes lit up, and he nodded.

'I'll just get myself a bit of lunch, and I'll be over. Leave the gate unlocked, I'll come round the side.'

That was odd. He could hear laughter coming from the garden, Beth's and someone else's. He let himself in and walked through the house, to find her sitting on the garden steps, Reg beside her with a mug in his hand and Tatty lying on the floor at their feet, dismantling a supposedly indestructible dog toy.

'Hi, all,' he said, and Tatty thumped her tail as he crouched down and gave her a tickle.

Beth smiled at him. 'Hi. Good day?'

'So-so. It won't last. What have you three been up to?'

'We've been gardening. Reg kindly offered to lend me a hand and show me which were the weeds and which weren't,' she said, staring pointedly at him, and he stifled the smile.

'That's kind. Thanks, Reg. Horticulture's not my strong point and I'm not sure it's Beth's, either.'

'Ah, well, she asked the right person, then. I was a nurseryman for fifty years. Only gave up when Queenie got sick, so if there's anything you need to know, you only have to ask.'

'Thank you. That's very kind. I'll bear it in mind.'

Reg gave the dog a pat and got stiffly to his feet. 'Well, I'd better be going then,' he said.

'You're welcome to stay,' he heard Beth say. 'I was going to make a salad, there's plenty.'

'Ah, now, that's very kind, my dear, but salad doesn't agree with me, and I've got a nice piece of fish from the hut down by the harbour, freshly caught this morning. I'll make a bit of batter later and pop it in my fryer. Won't be as good as my Queenie's, but it'll do. I might have a nap first.'

He gave Tatty a little pat, then Ryan showed him out, thanked him again and went back to Beth.

'Show you what's a weed and what's not? Really?' he murmured, and she smiled, but her eyes were filled with sadness.

'Yeah, I know, but he was so lonely, Ry. He loves looking after Tatty, he says she's good company. I think he might be spending most of the day here, you know, while you're at work. It must be so lonely for him without Queenie. They were married for sixty-five years, and she only died last July. She had Alzheimer's and she didn't know him any more, but he kept her at home right to the end, and I think he's just lost now. It's so sad.'

Poor Reg. Trust Beth to get him to open up. It was her all over.

'You're a good person, do you know that?' he murmured softly.

'I just felt so sorry for him. That awful empty ache...'

An ache she must know only too well.

'Oh, Beth.'

He pulled her into his arms and hugged her, resting his cheek against her hair and breathing her in, fresh air and sunshine and Beth, and it felt so good coming home to her.

Fingers crossed their fledgling relationship might stand a chance of flourishing into something that could stand the test of time, like Reg and Queenie's had.

He could only hope.

'Right, I haven't got long but it was quiet so I thought I'd make a break for it for a while, so can we eat? I haven't had anything apart from a biscuit since this morning.'

'Sure, it won't take a minute.'

She went up on tiptoe and kissed him, and it would have been so easy to take it further, but he was still on call and he didn't want to start something he might not be able to finish, so he eased away, hugged her again and led her back into the house.

CHAPTER SEVEN

TATTY WAS FUSSING.

Beth had no idea why. She'd had a walk, been fed, been out in the garden again, and Beth wondered if she was going into labour.

No, surely it was too early? The vet had said another two to three weeks. But she'd kept running to the door and whining, and now she was barking, so Beth got up to let her out again, this time following her into the garden.

'What is it, Tatty?'

She couldn't see or smell anything, but then Tatty barked again, standing and facing Reg's bungalow. She went up the steps to get a better look, and to her horror saw flames in his kitchen.

Dear God...

'Oh, Reg... Tatty, come here.'

She called the dog back in, grabbed her phone and keys, and ran out of the front of the house, through the hedge, banging on Reg's front door while she dialled 999.

No answer, and it was locked, of course.

Back gate. Please be open...

She ran round to the side, pushed the gate and it opened, and she gave the address to the emergency services, asked for fire and ambulance and tried the back door.

Eureka. She was in, and she shoved her phone in her pocket and turned off the gas ring. The pan was still burning but she knew better than to touch it, so she ran through into the hall, closing the door behind her to try and stop the smoke from spreading.

'Reg? Reg, where are you?' she asked, but the air was filled with smoke so she opened the front door wide and to her relief heard the sound of sirens.

'Reg! Reg, it's Beth. Where are you?'

A nap. He'd said he was going to have a nap, but not necessarily in bed.

Be systematic.

She started with the room beside the kitchen, but it was empty, so she went to the next, and there he was, sitting in his chair clutching his chest, his eyes wide with fear.

'Beth—the chip pan—can't breathe—'

'It's OK, Reg. The fire brigade are here now—see the flashing blue lights? And there's an ambulance, in case you need it. They'll take you to hospital to get checked over, but I need to get you out—'

'I can't leave—Queenie. She's on the mantelpiece. I can't leave her, Beth...'

'It's OK,' she promised. 'I won't leave her, Reg, but you need to get out now.'

He nodded, just as the fire officer ran in and assessed the situation at a glance.

'Fire's in the kitchen. I've turned the gas ring off but it's still burning,' she told him.

'That's all right, we're dealing with it, but you need to leave the house now.'

'We will. Reg, can you manage to walk to the ambulance?'

He nodded, but he was shaking like a leaf so the fire officer scooped him up in his arms and carried him into the front garden, and she scooped up Queenie and ran out after them.

'Queenie,' he coughed, but she shook her head.

'It's OK. I've got her here, Reg.'

'If I go, bury me with her—'

'You're going nowhere but the hospital,' she said firmly, 'and I'm going to follow you in my car, and ring Ryan and tell him to expect you. If you think for a moment he's going to let you die then you're underestimating him.'

She turned to the paramedics. 'Look after him. I've just got to put his wife's ashes next door and lock up and I'll follow you, but if you get there first, tell them to get Ryan McKenna.'

'Beth?'

He got to his feet, abandoning the notes he was writing up because her face had black smudges on it and something was clearly wrong.

'Are you OK? What's going on? What are you doing here?'

'I've come in with Reg. He had a chip pan fire in the kitchen.'

'Is he all right?' He sniffed. 'Beth, you stink of smoke. Tell me you didn't go in?'

'I had to. I wasn't going to leave him, Ryan. It hadn't spread so I turned off the gas and shut the door and found him—'

'You what? Beth—'

He swore, hauled her into his arms and hugged her hard, his heart hammering. 'What were you thinking? You should have called the fire brigade!'

'I did, and the ambulance, but I wasn't going to wait and watch his house go up in smoke. He was worried about Queenie. He wouldn't leave her ashes. I had to make him come here, and the only way I could get him out was to bring her, too, so her ashes are in your study. I hope that's OK.'

'Of course it's OK. So how is he?'

'Respiratory distress, maybe from smoke inhalation? I don't know, there wasn't that much, it could just be shock. He couldn't walk, but there wasn't really any smoke in the sitting room where he was. His breathing was awful, though, so I don't know how much of it was panic.'

'What kind of smoke was it?'

'Oh, it was only the oil, the kitchen hadn't caught fire, but it was pretty stinky. I think they put it out really fast, though.'

'Oh, well, that's all right then,' he said wryly, rolling his eyes. 'Although of course you didn't know that when you went in. Right, we'll get you both checked over.'

'I'm fine. I'm not stupid, Ryan, I didn't inhale it. You

need to worry about Reg. I promised him you wouldn't let him die but his heart was misfiring a bit.'

He grunted. 'Great. Has he got atrial fibrillation?'

She shrugged. 'I don't know. Possibly. He had a triple bypass last year, apparently, but he was very shaken. It would be easy to say he's a tough old bird, but—he said if anything happened, bury him with Queenie, but I'd rather he didn't get to that point.'

Ryan nodded. 'Yeah, me, too. Have they got children? Anyone we need to contact?'

'I don't know. He didn't mention children, but I didn't get his entire life story this afternoon,' she said with a smile, and he wiped the smuts off her cheek and kissed her, frowning at the frizzled ends on a lock of her hair. Jeez…

'Let's hope we don't have to worry about it,' he murmured, letting it go for now, and they went to find Reg.

It was nearly eleven before she got home, leaving Reg safely tucked up in bed on a ward with a heart monitor just to be on the safe side and Ryan more or less happy that she wasn't about to die of smoke inhalation.

He'd given her another lecture, though, about not waiting for the fire brigade before she went in, but she'd ignored it, knowing full well he'd have done exactly the same thing.

The fire engine was gone but the response car was still outside, to her surprise. Maybe it had been worse than she thought, but at least Reg's home hadn't burned to the ground. If she'd gone to bed, or ignored Tatty…

She went up the drive and knocked on the open door,

and the firefighter who'd carried Reg out appeared. 'How is he?'

'He's OK. He's staying in overnight. I promised I'd come and get some stuff to take in to him, but I'll do that tomorrow. I'm surprised you're still here. Is the house OK?'

'Yes, it's fine. I was just filling in the paperwork before I leave, but the kitchen needs a deep clean to remove the smoke residue.'

'I'm sure we can sort that out. He was all for coming home tonight but I talked him out of it.'

'He was lucky you were here. Was it you who raised the alarm?'

She nodded. 'Yes—I was next door. The dog started fussing, so I went out in the garden to find out why, and I saw the flames.'

The man eyed her thoughtfully. 'He's lucky you did. You saved his life, there was no way he was getting out and it would have gone up. And well done for not trying to put the fire out, although you could have had serious burns even just turning off the gas.'

She smiled a little wryly. 'Oh, I know. I'm a nurse in the ED. I've seen what can happen with a chip pan fire, and it isn't pretty, especially if they put water on it. I give the "call the fire brigade and get out" message over and over again, so I wasn't going to forget, and I was very careful.'

'Good, but don't do it again. Right, I'm ready to go, so if I could give you the keys?'

'Yes, of course. And thank you so much for all you've done.'

'All part of the job, my love. You know that as well as I do.'

He locked the door, handed her the keys and headed down the drive, and she went through the hedge and let herself in to a rapturous welcome from Tatty.

'It's all right, sweetheart,' she crooned. 'Come on, come and have something to eat, and then I need a shower because I stink.'

She'd just got out of the shower and wrapped herself in a towel when she heard a car, and Ryan appeared in the doorway behind her.

'Are you OK?'

Was she? Maybe, maybe not.

She felt herself well up, and walked into his arms, suddenly desperate for a hug.

'He wouldn't leave Queenie, Ry,' she said tearfully. 'He was going to stay there and die rather than leave her. If I hadn't been here, if Tatty hadn't warned me—'

'Don't.' His arms tightened around her, one hand cradling the back of her head and pressing it hard against his shoulder, the other firmly round her waist. 'He's OK, and so are you, but all I've been able to think about is what would have happened if anything had gone wrong. I could have lost you, Beth. You could have died, or been horribly burnt—'

His voice cracked, and she tilted her head and cradled his cheek in her hand.

'I'm fine, Ry. I'm OK. Nothing happened.'

'This time. But don't ever—ever—do that kind of thing again, OK?'

'You would have done it, too, you know you would. You've probably done far worse.'

'Yes, I have, but that's no excuse, and it wasn't a good idea. You were lucky, Beth. So lucky. Your hair's singed, for God's sake. You could have died. I could have lost you...'

His grip slackened, and he cupped her face in his hands, staring intently into her eyes, and then his mouth found hers in a desperate and yet tender kiss that turned her legs to jelly and her heart to mush.

She felt the towel fall away, dropping to the floor and leaving her naked in his arms, and he stared down at her, his eyes a little wild.

'I want you, Beth,' he grated. 'I need you. When I think about what could have happened...'

She nodded. 'I need you, too,' she said, her voice uneven. 'I didn't even think about it until afterwards, and then—'

She broke off, and he kissed her again, his whole body trembling, then he took a step back and stripped off his clothes and hauled her up against him as his lips found hers again, their legs meshing, the tension that had wound tighter and tighter finally snapping as their bodies came together.

There was no finesse, no foreplay, no tenderness, just a terrible urgency, a raging need to hold and be held, to be as close together as they could be until she couldn't tell where she ended and he began.

'Wait.'

He let go of her, yanked open the bathroom cabinet and pulled out a condom, his fingers shaking.

'Let me.'

'No. I'm too close.'

And then he was back, lifting her against the tiles and driving into her with a ragged groan. The spring coiled tighter inside her with every thrust, every touch, every heartbeat, and then she felt it shatter and she clung to him, sobbing his name as he slammed into her one last time.

He caught her cry in his mouth, his body stiffening, and then he slumped against her, chest heaving, his head on her shoulder, breath rasping in her ear, and then he lifted his head and stared down into her eyes.

'I'm sorry...'

'Don't be. I think we both needed that.'

He laughed softly and lowered her until her feet touched the floor, then eased away, turning to deal with the condom, and she frowned.

'Ry?'

She ran her hand lightly down his back, feeling the sweat-slicked skin, the strong columns of muscle, the— scars?

It wasn't a good idea.

Was that what he'd meant when she'd said he'd probably done far worse?

'What happened to you, Ry? What did you mean just now when you said it wasn't a good idea?'

He turned back to her, his mouth tipped into a smile, if you could call it that.

'There was a shell. I shouldn't have been where I was, but I was trying to get back into the hospital. It had been bombed, and my friends were in there trying to salvage what they could, and I wanted to get them out, to warn them that it wasn't safe, and there was another one.'

He looked away. 'I was the only one who made it out, and only just. As I said, not a good idea.'

'Are these the friends you said you'd lost? The ones whose death made you decide to stay and carry on their work?'

He nodded, his eyes meeting hers again. 'Yes. But I was careful after that—well, when they let me out of hospital. I was hit by shrapnel.'

'Shrapnel?' She looked down at his body, searching it for signs, but then he turned his back to her again and she saw the other scars, peppering his back and legs. She reached out and touched them. So many of them, some so small she could hardly see them, others bigger, as if the holes had been enlarged. Those were the ones she'd seen, the ones she'd felt.

'Did they get it all out?'

He turned back towards her, his mouth tilted into a wry smile. 'Mostly, but let's just say it wouldn't be a good idea to put me in an MRI scanner.'

She winced. 'Well, it would get all the last bits out, I suppose,' she said drily, and he chuckled and pulled her back into his arms.

'You have such a bad sense of humour,' he murmured, and kissed her again, tenderly this time, his hand stroking her damp, tangled hair. 'You need to deal with this or it's going to dry in knots, and I probably should go and talk to the whining dog. Have another shower, and I'll follow you.'

He kissed her again and let her go, and she stood in the shower and rewashed her hair, this time using the conditioner that she'd taken over there for Tatty, and she was almost done when she felt his hands on her, turning her into his arms as he stepped into the shower behind her.

'Are you OK? I was a bit rough, but I couldn't think about anything but getting close to you, so close I could feel your heartbeat so I knew you were still alive.'

'Don't you think you're being a bit dramatic?' she said softly, but he shook his head.

'No. If you'd seen what I've seen…'

'Tell me.'

'No. There are things you don't need to know, things I don't need to remember.'

He rested his head against hers. 'I still can't believe you went in there,' he said, his voice unsteady, and she hugged him hard, feeling the tension in his body.

'I'm fine, Ryan. I know it was stupid, looking back on it, but at the time it was no big deal and I'd probably do it again. I couldn't have let him burn to death, I couldn't have lived with myself.'

'No, I get that, I do. You just scared the spit out of me.'

'I'm sorry. How is he, by the way?'

'OK. He might have AF. They're monitoring him. How did you know he'd had a triple bypass?'

'I saw the scar when they were doing the ECG, and I asked him. He only had it done last year, after Queenie died. He wouldn't do it before. He's such a good man.'

'He is, and I'm glad you saved his life.' He let her go,

stared down into her eyes and then bent his head and kissed her again, with a touch of desperation. 'Even so, don't ever do anything like that again, please,' he muttered gruffly against her mouth.

She stroked her fingers lightly over his cheek. 'I'm fine, Ry. You look shattered. You need to go to bed.'

'Come with me. I still need to hold you.'

'Tatty might have a view.'

'Tough. She can find herself somewhere else to sleep.'

'Unlikely. I'll come and join you both. You finish your shower and sort the dog out, and I'll dry my hair and see you in a minute.'

She was more than a minute, but not much, and he was lying in the middle of his bed, with Tatty beside him. She got in on his other side, and he pulled her into his arms, cradling her face against his shoulder.

'OK?'

She nodded and yawned. 'I feel exhausted. It's so late—what time is it?'

'Nearly one. Go to sleep, my love. I've got you.'

She tilted her head and kissed him fleetingly, then settled against him, comforted by his warmth and the strong, steady beat of his heart as she fell asleep in his arms.

He couldn't sleep. All he could think was that he could have lost her.

If the chip pan had exploded, or the gas line to the cooker, or any one of a dozen other things, he could have lost her.

It must have taken such courage to go in there. Courage and humanity, things Beth had in spades, it seemed.

She'd even rescued Queenie's ashes to put Reg's mind at rest.

God, he loved her. He hoped he'd get the job, so they could stay here and make this their home, start a new life together, but there was the other candidate to consider. He had his interview tomorrow—no, today. It was today.

He hoped he didn't run into him. He might be tempted to sabotage him.

Beth whimpered in her sleep, and Tatty got up, walked over him and lay down beside her. He shifted slightly to give them both more room, and Beth snuggled closer in her sleep.

It felt so good to hold her. Really good...

He fell asleep with a smile on his face.

She woke to a kiss, and she opened her eyes and smiled up at him.

'Morning.'

'Mmm. It is, and I have to go to work, but first...'

He kissed her again, his touch tender this time, lingering and full of promise.

'Do you have to go?' she asked as he pulled away, and he gave a wry chuckle.

'Sadly I think I do, especially if I want the job. The other guy's got his interview today and shirking doesn't look good.'

She smiled at that. 'Probably not. Go on, then. I'll see

you later. I start at twelve again, but just till nine so it's a bit more civilised. You can cook for me, if you like?'

'Or we could go out for dinner?'

She shook her head. 'No. Let's stay in. Reg won't be here so we need to spend time with Tatty. I'll take her for a quick walk soon, then again before I come in, but I've got to take some things in for Reg as well, so I might do that mid-morning. Want to grab a coffee then?'

'If there's time. Come and tell me how he is.'

'OK. I'll see you later.'

He kissed her again and left, and she spent a few more minutes coming to, listening to the sound of Tatty chasing her bowl around the kitchen floor, then she threw back the covers and went into the bathroom and caught sight of herself in the mirror.

Her hair was dishevelled, her eyes had smudges under them, but she was smiling, and she realised that for the first time in a very long while she felt happy.

Not just content, but genuinely, truly happy.

Humming under her breath, she washed and dressed, glad she'd brought clean clothes because the ones she'd had on yesterday really did smell awful, and then after she'd walked Tatty she let herself into Reg's house.

The smell was still lingering in the air, and she guessed it would take a while to shift. She found him some wash things in the bathroom, and had a hunt for some clothes because the ones he'd been wearing would smell of smoke, but the first cupboard she opened was full of women's clothes, like a giant memory box for Queenie.

She fingered the sleeve of a pretty blouse, and felt her eyes fill. Poor Reg…

Core business.

She opened the next cupboard and found what she was looking for, pulled out trousers, a shirt, some underwear and pyjamas, and left for the hospital.

He was sitting out in the chair when she arrived, and she perched on the bed beside him with a smile.

'You're up bright and early,' she said, and he nodded.

'I couldn't settle. I was worried about the house.'

'No need to worry, Reg. The house is fine. They were still there when I got back last night, but the kitchen isn't damaged, and it's all locked up, though it's a bit smelly, I'm afraid.'

He nodded. 'I thought as much. But the rest is all right?'

'Yes. It'll be fine, I'm sure. But how are you, that's the main thing?'

'Oh, I'm all right, Beth. Don't know why I'm here, really. I'd rather be at home.'

She took his hand and squeezed it. 'I'm sure they won't keep you in any longer than they think is necessary. We were a bit worried about your heart and your breathing.'

'Oh, I've always been a bit wheezy. I'm best outdoors, really. I always have the windows open, even in the winter. I guess that's how you smelt the fire.'

'The dog warned me. She was fussing.'

'Was she? Bless her. I was so pleased to see you last night, Beth. I thought I was going to die in there…'

His eyes filled, and he patted her hand with his other one, and she clasped it.

'But you didn't. Why didn't you go outside? Come round to me and raise the alarm? Was it because of Queenie?'

He nodded, and she felt her own eyes well.

'Oh, Reg. She's safe. She's in Ryan's study, waiting for you to come home. Do you have any family we can contact for you?'

He shook his head. 'No. We were never blessed with children, and all the rest of my family have died. That's what happens when you get old, girl.'

She nodded, then glanced at her watch and sighed. 'I'm sorry, I'm going to have to go, I've got to walk Tatty again and give her lunch and I start work at twelve, but I've brought you in some clothes. I have no idea if they're the right ones, but if not I can go back to get some others. And I've brought some wash things. I'll be back later to see you. I'll just go and tell Ryan how you are.'

She kissed his grizzled cheek and eased her hands away from his, and he let her go with obvious reluctance.

Ryan was just coming out of Resus when she got down there, and she caught him up with Reg's progress.

'His breathing's much better now. They might discharge him later today, but he hasn't got any family so goodness knows where he'll go.'

'We'll keep an eye on him, don't worry. As you said he spends most of his time with Tatty, and we're in and out. Got time for coffee?'

'Probably. What about you?'

'Probably not, but the other candidate's having a guided tour so to be honest I'd rather make myself scarce for a bit.'

'You don't want to show off?'

He snorted. 'I did have a childish urge, but it's quiet—'

'Adult trauma call, five minutes. Paediatric trauma call, five minutes.'

She laughed at the dirty look he gave the tannoy speaker. 'Here's your chance, McKenna. I'll leave you to it. Knock their socks off.'

His chuckle followed her as she walked away, and she couldn't stop the smile on her face.

CHAPTER EIGHT

THE NEXT FEW days were hectic, but luckily Reg was back home by Monday evening, a little shaken still but seemingly unscathed, and when Ryan suggested that they could juggle their shifts so he didn't need to worry about helping out with the dog, Reg looked so crest-fallen that he relented.

In return, though, he cleaned and repainted the old man's kitchen on his day off, and gave him a lecture on safety and an electric chip fryer that only used a teaspoon of oil, and they juggled the odd shift without telling him.

The upside was that Tatty was spending lots of time with Reg in the run-up to her puppies, which as far as they were concerned was a win-win, because it kept both the dog and the old man happy, and one or other of them would walk her before and after work. And since she seemed to be spending most nights with Ryan, Beth moved some of her things there. First a toothbrush, then some underwear and a couple of tops, her trainers for dog walking, then some work clothes...

She wasn't there every night, but the nights she

was—those nights were everything she'd remembered, and more.

She'd forgotten just how in tune their bodies were, how responsive she was to every touch, and their love-making now had an extra edge that it hadn't had before, an exquisite tenderness that left her feeling cherished. Because he loved her? Or at least she supposed he did, although he hadn't said it yet in so many words.

She wished he would, not least because it was on the tip of her tongue all the time, but she guessed he was holding back until he was certain how he felt. After all, it wasn't just her who'd been affected by Grace's death, and he'd had all the aid stuff to deal with. The fallout from that must have been pretty devastating at times, although he hadn't said a lot. Not that he ever did, but she was getting to know him now, and she knew there was no way he'd tell her anything until he was ready.

Then at the end of the week a woman and child were brought in from an RTC. The fire crew had cut them out of the car, and although the mother seemed unin-jured, the child was struggling to breathe and she re-fused to leave him.

'Right, let's get the clothes off and have a look,' Ryan said, reaching for his stethoscope. 'We need CXR, echo and let's get him on one hundred per cent oxygen. Can you tell me what happened?' he asked the mother, and Beth looked at her and frowned.

She looked OK, and yet there was something...

'I—I swerved. There was a dog. I must have hit the kerb, and the car just rolled over and over. I wasn't even going fast. Don't make me go. I can't leave him.'

'It's OK, you don't have to,' Beth said softly, putting an arm round her. 'He's in good hands. Come and sit down over here and give Emma all your details, and let us do our job. We'll make sure you know what's going on.'

'Don't let him die—'

'Not my plan,' Ryan said, but his face was oddly expressionless and Beth's pulse hiked. 'Beth, I need you, please. I think we've got a tamponade.'

He was listening to the chest, looking at the little boy's neck, checking the monitor.

Low blood pressure, she noticed, but only slightly, and he was tachycardic. 'Are you sure?' she murmured, out of the mother's earshot.

'No, but I want an echo. Can I have the FAST scanner, please? And where's the radiographer?'

'I'm here,' Sue said, coming in, and moments later they had a picture of his chest on the screen, confirming the FAST scanner's findings.

'Increased cardiac silhouette, so he'll need pericardiocentesis,' Ryan said, and then the monitor began to bleep and he said something under his breath and met her eyes. 'Someone call cardiology, please, and, Beth, can you talk Mum through pericardiocentesis and then give me a hand, please? I'll get him prepped.'

Great. Tell a worried mother someone was going to stick a huge needle into the boy's chest and suck blood out from around his heart before it killed him. She sat down beside her and took her hand.

'Mrs Gray—'

'Louise, please. What's he doing to Tim?'

'It looks like he's got fluid around his heart, under the pericardium, the membrane that surrounds it, and that's pressing on the heart muscle and stopping it from doing its job, so what we need to do is put a needle in, very carefully, and draw off the fluid.'

'What kind of fluid?'

'Blood, most likely. It looks as if he might have a bleed in there, possibly from the collision.'

She shook her head. 'But there wasn't really a collision. I don't understand. Was it the seat belt? He's in a five-point harness—it can't be that.'

'There's an old bruise on his chest,' Ryan said, turning his head. 'Has he fallen recently, in the last week or so?'

'Um—yes, a couple of days ago. More, maybe. He fell downstairs and landed on a toy. He was only halfway up, but he was being silly. He's always silly, he's a boy—'

She pressed her hand over her mouth, and shook her head. 'He seemed fine, and then today he was tired and didn't seem to want to do anything. I was going to take him to the doctor if he wasn't better tomorrow, but it's the weekend. I should have gone today—'

'Well, you're here now,' Beth said, 'and maybe it wasn't that, but at least you're here and you're in the best place. I need to go and help, but Emma will stay with you.'

She nodded, her face contorted with fear for her son, and Beth went over to Ryan, who was already gowned and gloved.

'Cardiology can't spare anyone fast enough so I want you to help me,' he said quietly.

'What do you need?'

'A twenty-one-gauge spinal needle with the trocar removed, a five mil and thirty mil syringe, a three-way tap and T connector.'

'OK.'

By the time she was ready he was poised with the needle just under the bottom of Tim's sternum, aiming for his left shoulder and advancing the needle in little jerks, under the guidance of the FAST scanner wand she was holding, until the syringe suddenly began to fill with blood.

'OK, I'm in. Let's get the T connector and tap on it, and get this fluid off.'

He was still drawing off the fluid when the boy's respiration rate and heart rate slowed, his blood pressure picked up and his breathing steadied.

'Well done,' she said softly, and he looked up, his eyes suddenly bright.

'Yeah. I didn't want to lose this one.'

This one?

She straightened up and smiled at Louise across the room.

'He's looking better already,' she said, and Louise put her hand over her mouth and stifled a sob. Her other hand, Beth noticed, was lying against her abdomen, almost cradling it...

'Are you done with me?' she asked Ryan quietly. 'I've got a bad feeling about Louise.'

He glanced over his shoulder and nodded. 'You go. He's fine. We'll ship him up to PICU shortly, they can continue to monitor him but I think we've done enough for now.'

She went over to Louise and sat down again, taking her hand. 'Louise, I think I need to have a look at you. You might have been hurt by the seat belt.'

Her eyes flared wider, and she sucked in a breath. 'My baby,' she whispered. 'Oh, no—Beth, I'm pregnant. I can't lose it.'

Please, no...

'Let's get a look at you,' she murmured. 'Come and lie down here on this other bed and I'll get the ultrasound and we'll have a look, OK? How many weeks are you?'

'Sixteen—no, seventeen. I don't know.'

About what she'd been when she'd found out she was pregnant with Grace, when she'd put her tight clothes down to comfort eating after Ryan had gone away...

'Can I borrow the FAST scanner, please?' she said, and Emma brought it over to her and handed her the gel as Louise pulled her trousers down over her little bump. She could see the mark of the seat belt over her hips. Was the baby high enough to have escaped injury?

Please let it be all right...

A nice, steady heartbeat filled the room, and Ryan lifted his head and met her eyes, his expression startled.

'Baby's fine,' she said to Louise, choking back tears, and Ryan's shoulders dropped and he went back to dealing with the boy.

* * *

'Are you OK?'

She didn't pretend not to understand.

'Yes, Ry, I'm OK. The baby was fine, Louise is in the antenatal ward under observation, Tim's doing well in PICU, and her husband's trying to split himself in half. I'm happy with that.' She cocked her head on one side and searched his eyes. 'What about you?' she asked softly.

He shrugged and turned away, busying himself with his fancy coffee machine. 'Just another day at the office,' he said lightly, reaching for a mug, but she shook her head.

'No, it wasn't. What did you mean by "I didn't want to lose this one"?'

He shrugged again, but she wasn't having it and she turned him gently to face her. 'Ry, talk to me.'

He let his breath out on a huff, put the mug down and folded his arms across his chest.

'He was called Raoul. He was six, and he used to hang around the medical centre hoping for food. One day he got caught in an explosion, and a small lump of concrete hit him in the chest. I didn't get to see him in time, and by then it was too late. There was too much blood under the pericardium and his heart gave up and I couldn't get it going again. And then I had to tell his mother. It's a sound you never get used to, the wail of a mother who's lost their child—'

He tilted his head back, but she could see the tears he refused to shed, and she wrapped her arms around him and held him close.

'I'm sorry.'

His arms went round her, his head resting against hers, and they stood like that for a long time.

'There were too many children like Raoul,' he said eventually. 'Babies, little kids, all caught in the fallout, and then the teenagers, the ones who'd joined a militia movement and got themselves shot. Kids who died of diseases we can cure so easily. Malaria, bilharzia, and things like Ebola which are much harder and wipe out whole families. It's just endlessly heartbreaking.'

'Is that why you came home?'

He nodded slowly. 'I had burnout, I think, or if I didn't, I was getting dangerously close to it. That's why I wanted to be here, why I wanted the job, not another one in an inner city fighting to stem the tide of gang violence and drug culture. I just wanted to be normal, Beth. I wanted to feel safe. Is that so wrong?'

'No. No, it's not wrong, Ryan. It's human—and you're still a great doctor, and you're needed here. Without you and the rest of the team, little Tim could have died today, but he didn't, because you spotted it, even though it wasn't that obvious at first.'

'No. He's got Raoul to thank for that, so maybe his death wasn't in vain.' He dropped his arms and stepped away, letting his breath out on a long, slow sigh, then he met her eyes and smiled gently. 'Are you sure you're OK?'

She nodded. 'Yes. Yes, I'm fine. Fancy something to eat?'

'That would be good. I'll take Tatty out while you sort it. And then an early night, I think.' His eyes were warm and tender, and she smiled up at him, and went up on tiptoe and kissed his cheek.

'Sounds perfect,' she said softly.

It was the following Monday and she was walking the dog when her phone rang. Ryan.

'Where are you?' he said brusquely.

'By the river, with Tatty. Why? Where are you?'

'On my way home. I'll come and join you.'

'OK. We'll wait for you outside the pub. Can you bring the car? Tatty's a bit tired.'

'OK. See you shortly.'

The phone went dead, and she stared at it, puzzled. He'd sounded—weird? Very short, which wasn't like him.

'Are you OK, Tatty? Let's go and sit down and wait for Ry, shall we?'

She wagged her tail, but she'd lost the spring in her step and Beth wondered how soon she'd go into labour. If they only knew exactly when the pups were due.

They walked slowly back to the Harbour Inn and found a table outside the front, and Tatty lay down with a sigh at her feet while Beth kept an eye out for his car, her nerves on edge.

What was going on? Had the other guy got the job? Please, no. Not that. Anything but that, but it had been a week now since his interview, two weeks since Ryan's, although they'd been trying not to think about it. Surely they'd decided by now?

His car turned into the car park, and he slotted it

into a space, slammed the door and strode over to her, his face tense.

Oh, no. She stood up and took a step towards him, and he stopped.

'I've got a second interview this Thursday,' he said, his voice strangely tight. 'We both have.'

'Why?'

He shrugged. 'They couldn't decide. The panel were divided, apparently. James couldn't say a lot, but he was obviously on my side from the few things he did say. I don't know. I hoped it would be over, but it goes on.'

She hugged him, and he hugged her back, his head resting against hers as he sighed.

'I hate interviews,' he mumbled. 'The last one was vile, and this one—well. Who knows? I can only do my best, and I'm sure there'll be other jobs. Just not here. Ah, well. Fancy eating here?'

'Not really,' she said quietly, feeling crushed for him and gutted that he still didn't know, that they still didn't know, when she'd finally realised how very important it was to him to stay here in this place that meant so much to them. 'Tatty's quite tired. Let's just go home.'

Or home for now, at least.

Please let him get the job...

If he'd thought the first interview was gruelling, the second was much worse, the questions designed to challenge even the strongest candidate, but he knew what they were doing. Piling on the stress to see how he coped.

Well, he could do stress. He'd lived on a knife edge

for over two years and kept his head, and he kept it now, making sure he addressed his answers not only to the person who'd asked the question but to the others as well, and when it was over he went back to work, resigned to another week or so of torment.

And then the following afternoon James came and found him and put him out of his misery.

She heard the scrunch of tyres while she was in the kitchen, and she met him in the hall. He was early—and he was never early. Why?

'I got it,' he said, looking slightly shocked. 'I got the job. I actually got the job!'

'Oh, Ry!' Her eyes welled, and she threw herself at him and he picked her up and swung her round, his laugh echoing in her ears, and then put her down, cradled her face and kissed her senseless.

She could feel his smile against her mouth, and she pulled away and looked up at him, searching his eyes and finding nothing but relief.

'How did you find out?'

'James told me. He said the panel were still divided, but much less so. Apparently I interviewed really well yesterday and I was much more convincing, but it's gone on so long now I'd begun to think I didn't stand a chance.'

She frowned. 'Why? The other candidate is much older than you, and I thought James felt he was ready to wind down.'

'He did. He still does, but some of the others felt he was a safer pair of hands, and it's my first consultancy and I haven't exactly had a conventional career path in the last few years.'

'So what swayed it in the end?'

He shrugged. 'My interview yesterday, I think. The CEO had the casting vote, so it was his decision.' He laughed. 'Looking at it cynically from his point of view, I'm cheaper, and I'm already here, so they don't have to wait six months for him to work his notice. That's got to help. And James was pretty adamant, I think, from what he said—plus he seems to have realised something's going on with us and I don't think he wanted to lose you, too.'

She narrowed her eyes. 'Have you said anything to him?'

His mouth twitched. 'I might have let something slip.'

'You are so naughty.'

'Yeah, but you love me,' he said.

There was a breathless silence, and then she smiled.

'Yes, I do,' she said softly, and went up on tiptoe and kissed him again. Just a fleeting kiss, and then she sank back on her heels and looked into his eyes.

They were suddenly bright, and he swallowed hard, his hand coming up to cradle her cheek.

'It's been so hard waiting, not knowing what was going to happen, but now…'

'Now we have a future here?' she suggested, holding her breath, and he shrugged.

'I hope so—or at least a shot at it. That's up to you. If it's what you want—'

'Of course it's what I want!'

'Good. I'd better ring James, then, and tell him I'll take it.'

She felt her jaw drop. 'You haven't told him?'

'No. Not till I'd spoken to you.'

'Why?'

His shoulders lifted in a tiny shrug. 'I didn't do things right with Katie. I told her I was signing up with MFA, I told her what it meant to me, that I'd be away maybe for years, that I didn't want kids any time soon if at all—I thought she understood, but I never asked her what she wanted, I just assumed she'd be fine with it, but it turned out she wasn't, and so she tried to manipulate me by getting pregnant. And yes, she didn't handle it well, but nor did I and we both got hurt. I don't want to make the same mistake again.'

'I'm not Katie, Ryan, and you're not the man you were then. Phone James, tell him you want the job, if you really do, but don't do it for me. Do it for yourself. This has to be right for you, and if it's not what you want, then don't take it. I don't want you turning round to me in six months' or three years' time and accusing me of making you do something you didn't want to do.'

He kissed her gently. 'You're not. And I do want it.'

'So ring him. Ring him now, and while you're doing that I'll finish getting supper. Oh, and is your DJ OK? You've got to wear it tomorrow for the wedding.'

'It's fine, it's all ready. I'll ring James now.'

He kissed her again, then pulled out his phone and she went back to the kitchen and stared out of the window at the river in the distance.

It was happening. He was staying, and maybe he'd

buy this house and they'd live here together, with that beautiful view in front of them.

With a family?

Her heart thumped. Too soon to think about that. She wasn't ready, and just to be certain, she'd gone back on the Pill. Not that it had worked for them last time, but that was because she'd failed to take it on time in the hectic week leading up to their weekend. She'd be more careful this time, and in the meantime Ryan was being meticulous.

But—maybe one day?

Or maybe not. She frowned. He still hadn't said he loved her. She'd given him the perfect chance, and he hadn't taken it. Why not? And now she knew he'd want children in the future, maybe he was holding back until he was sure she was ready for that. And she wasn't sure she was, or would ever be. It was only two years ago that she'd lost Grace. It seemed like yesterday, but in another lifetime.

Was she ever going to be brave enough to try again?

'All done. He said he'll see us tomorrow at the wedding. So, my clothes are sorted. What are you wearing?'

She pasted on a smile and turned to face him. 'I don't know yet. I'm sure I've got something. I'll have a look tomorrow.'

'You're on duty from seven to five. You changed your shift, remember, so you didn't have to work on Sunday?'

She clapped a hand over her mouth. 'I'd forgotten. I'd better have a look tonight, and I might as well stay at home if I'm at work for seven. Is that OK?'

'Of course it's OK. We're not joined at the hip, Beth. You can do whatever you like.'

Did she imagine it, or did that sound like he didn't care?

No. He might not have said he loved her, but she knew he cared about her. Just maybe not enough...

'What?'

'Hmm?'

'You've got a strange look on your face, as if I just said something weird.'

'No. Just—"do what you like" sounded a bit...'

'Like I don't own you?' He laughed softly and pulled her into his arms, staring down into her eyes with a smile. 'I simply meant you don't need my permission to do something. It would be nice if you let me know you aren't going to be around just so I'm not worried about you, but you can do whatever you want, of course you can.'

'Are you sure? Because really, I could do with spending this evening at home. I've got so much to do, I haven't done my washing for days and—I don't know, Tatty's beginning to look a bit imminent and if I need to be here I could do with sorting out some clothes and also working out what I'm wearing tomorrow. Would you mind if I go as soon as we eat?'

'Of course I don't mind.'

'Are you sure? Because we probably should be celebrating your new job, and I'm going to take myself off.'

He laughed and hugged her. 'Of course I don't mind. I've got to write a formal letter of acceptance, anyway, and I could do with settling Tatty in whatever place she wants to have her pups. Any ideas?'

'She keeps hanging out in the spare room, at the end of the wardrobe. There's a space there, a bit tucked away? I've found her there a couple of times in the last few days.'

'Yes, so've I. OK. I'll make her a bed. So, what are you cooking? It smells good. Anything I can do to help?'

She smiled up at him, kissed his cheek and handed him the vegetable knife.

It felt odd being back in her own house for the first time in days. Odd, and a bit lonely, but she had plenty to do, starting with putting on a load of washing and then finding a dress for the wedding.

Easier said than done, but it was too late now to worry about it, and she had a few options, one of which was a dress she'd worn the only other time she'd been to the hotel. She'd been going to wear it for dinner, but she'd put it on and they hadn't made it through the door.

She pulled it out and looked at it critically. It was certainly smart enough, a midnight blue velvet dress with a scoop neck front and back, gently figure-hugging with a straight cut and a subtle slit up the back to just below the knee. Discreet, simple, elegant—and he'd taken one look at her in it, peeled it off her and made love to her slowly and systematically, kissing every inch of her and taking her to the brink over and over again until she'd been begging him to finish it.

Would he remember?

She wriggled into it—a little tighter than it had been,

but then she'd been reeling from Rick's lying, cheating betrayal and she hadn't been eating a lot. But it still fitted, better now if anything, and it was the best thing in her wardrobe.

She found earrings and a necklace that were perfect with it, nude heels that weren't so high she couldn't dance in them, and a nude wrap in case it got chilly if they went out into the courtyard, because it was only early May.

She closed her eyes briefly, then put the dress on its hanger and went downstairs, picking up the little heart. This time two years ago, their baby had still been alive. They'd been lonely and heartbreaking years, but now there might be light at the end of that long, dark tunnel.

'Your daddy got the job, my darling,' she told Grace softly. 'He's going to be here, and maybe we're going to be with him, if it all goes well.' She smiled sadly. 'I think you'd like him. I'm so sorry you'll never get to meet him, but I think he loves you. We'll be thinking about you tomorrow, my love.'

She kissed the little heart, then carried it upstairs and packed it in the bag of things she'd got ready to take to Ryan's. She was going to drop it off on her way to work in the morning then come back here after her shift to get ready, and he was picking her up in a taxi at twenty past seven.

And she was already getting nervous, wondering if she was reading too much into their relationship, hoping she wasn't investing too much of herself in him.

Her phone rang, and it was Ryan.

'You OK?'

'Yes—I've got a dress, so I'm all good. How's Tatty?'

'She seems to like that corner. I found a cardboard box in the garage left over from the pictures, so I've cut it down and put a blanket in there for her, and she seems perfectly happy. I think she's getting close.'

'I think so. Are you OK? Coming down off cloud nine?'

He chuckled. 'Yes, I'm fine. Tired. I think the suspense got to me. I might have an early night. You take care, and I'll see you tomorrow evening.'

'You, too. Let me know if anything changes with Tatty.'

'I will. Sleep tight. It'll be odd without you.'

'It's only one night. I'll be with you tomorrow.'

'Good. I'm looking forward to it.'

He hung up, and she put the phone down, the words 'I love you' still hovering on her lips, but he'd gone before she'd had a chance to say them. Just as well, maybe.

CHAPTER NINE

HE WAS WALKING down her path looking drop-dead gorgeous in his DJ when she opened the door, and he stopped in his tracks.

'Is that the dress…?'

The butterflies were having a field day inside her, and the look in his eyes did nothing to settle them down.

'I wasn't sure if you'd remember it.'

He laughed, a slightly strangled sound, and ran his finger round his collar. 'Yeah, I remember it. Even though you only had it on for—oh, maybe thirty seconds?'

And then he smiled, a tender smile full of promise. 'I might let you wear it a little longer tonight, so I can enjoy it. You look beautiful, Beth. Absolutely beautiful.'

He took her hand and met her eyes. 'Are you OK?' he asked, his eyes sober now, and she nodded.

'Yes. I am now. It's been a bit of a funny day.'

'I'm sure.' They were silent for a moment, Grace in both their thoughts, and then he sucked in a breath and straightened up, holding out his arm. 'Shall we go?'

He held the taxi door for her, then went round and

got in the other side. 'So,' he said, turning to face her and deftly changing the subject, 'who's going to be there that I might know?'

'Oh, Ed and Annie, definitely. Ed and Matt were at school together. And James and Connie, and Sam and Kate, Jenny, my line manager, and her husband. I think he's called Peter. Matt and Livvy, obviously. You've worked with both of them. Otherwise I have no idea. I only know her from work and I think they've got lots of friends and family, but it should be a lovely wedding. He's got two little children, a girl and a boy, and his wife died of a brain haemorrhage when they were tiny. That was the same year as Grace, so not long ago. And Livvy's had breast cancer, so it's been pretty emotional for them all.'

'Wow. I had no idea. They never give the impression of being sad.'

She gave a tiny huff of laughter. 'Do we?'

He reached out and took her hand, squeezing it gently. 'I guess not. Are you really OK?'

She smiled at him, not willing to lie and yet wanting to enjoy this evening with him.

'Yes, Ryan. I'm OK. Grace isn't far from my thoughts, but then she never is, and I want to enjoy tonight. Can we do that?'

'I'm sure we can,' he murmured.

The taxi pulled up outside the hotel, and he asked the driver if he could do the return trip. 'What time is it winding up, Beth?'

'I don't know, but I don't want to be late. Can we leave at half ten?'

'That's fine. I don't want to be late, either. Tatty was a bit restless.'

He spoke to the taxi driver again, paid him, and then offered her his arm as they walked towards the hotel, the place where it had all begun.

Strangely fitting, and yet oddly she hardly remembered anything about it once they were inside. They'd either been in their room, or in the dining room, or out and about in the town, strolling by the sea, walking by the river, listening to the sound of the surf and the keening of the gulls, and as far as the hotel was concerned, they could have been anywhere.

They were ushered into a large and beautiful function room, and Matt and Livvy were standing there greeting their guests, looking ridiculously happy and utterly in love.

'Congratulations, Livvy,' she said softly, giving her a gentle hug. 'I'm so happy for you both.'

'Thank you. And thank you for coming. It's so lovely to have you here, and I'm really glad you brought Ryan. I hope things work for you.'

She smiled at the innocent remark, because like everyone else, Livvy only knew that they'd once worked together and that they were seeing each other now. Nothing more, but that was fine. She wasn't sure she knew much more than that herself.

'Thank you,' she said, and hugged Livvy again before turning to Matt and hugging him, too.

And then Ryan was at her side again, his hand resting on her waist as they looked around.

'Matt says there's a bar over there, so shall we?'

She pasted on a bright smile. 'I think that would be a great idea. Maybe we can find something fizzy to celebrate your job.'

'Good plan.'

Her dress was going to kill him.

There was live music playing quietly in the background, and the hubbub of voices from the colourful throng, but his eyes kept being drawn back to Beth. She was radiantly beautiful tonight, and yet when he looked deep in her eyes there was that lingering sorrow that never quite left them.

They mixed and mingled, chatting to the people he'd worked with over the past five weeks, people who might become friends, and they seemed genuinely delighted that he'd joined the department. They were a similar age to him and Beth, a little older but not much, and he could see why James might have been wary of an older consultant coming in.

'I'm so glad it's you,' his new clinical lead said to him in a slightly indiscreet moment. 'That stuffed shirt would have driven me insane.'

Ryan laughed. 'Yeah, me, too. Just a few minutes in his company was enough.'

'Tell me about it. I'm absolutely sure he's a great doctor, mind, but he's so pompous. It never would have worked. You, on the other hand—I can mould you.'

Ryan laughed. 'You can try. Many people have. But to be fair, I think we work in a very similar way.'

'Nah. You're more like Sam. He's a bit of a wild one. Ex-army. Bit like you, seen it, done it, knows how to fix it. He may not be entirely orthodox, but he saves lives and that's what it's about.'

'Maybe you needed your box ticker.'

'No, thank you. You're fine. Have another drink.'

'What was that about?'

Ryan smiled at her a little wickedly. 'Oh, just our clinical lead being a little indiscreet.' He looked across the room, then back to her. 'I think the dancing might be about to start. I can see Matt and Livvy over there by the band. Want to go and watch?'

'Oh, I do. She's been making him practise, apparently.'

Their dance was beautiful, the song outrageously romantic, and once it was over the guests headed onto the dance floor to join them.

The tempo picked up at that point, the music morphing into the classic cheesy wedding songs that everyone knew, and Ryan turned to her, held out his hand and smiled. 'Dance with me?'

'Sure. Why not?'

She took his hand and let him lead her into the throng, wondering what kind of a dancer he would be.

Good, was the answer, and he seemed to enjoy it, which was great news as she loved dancing, so she relaxed and threw herself into it, and he shot her a grin, twirled her into his arms and they had a ball.

'Oh, I can't, I need to stop, I've got a stitch,' she said, breathing hard and clutching her side, and he chuckled and led her off the dance floor.

They went to the bar and got some fizzy water, and she rolled the ice-cold glass against her face and sighed.

'Oh, that's good. I haven't danced like that for years.'

'No, nor me. Out of practice.'

'You didn't look out of practice.'

Their eyes locked, and then the music slowed and he put down his glass and held out his hand.

'Dance with me again,' he said softly, and she let him lead her to the dance floor, turned into his arms and settled against him as if they were made for each other. She could feel his hands resting lightly in the small of her back, and she slid her arms around his waist and rested her head on his shoulder.

It felt so good. So right. If only she was sure he loved her...

She shut off that train of thought, and as they swayed together to the music she closed her eyes, stopped thinking and let herself feel.

'It's nearly ten thirty,' he murmured, and she lifted her head, dragged back to reality.

'We need to go. The taxi will be here.'

'Matt and Livvy are over there. Let's go and say goodbye.'

Two minutes later they were standing outside waiting for their taxi, and she shivered.

'I forgot my wrap.'

'Here, borrow my jacket,' he murmured, shrugging it off and draping it round her shoulders.

'So chivalrous.'

'Of course. Not to mention warm. It got quite hot in there.'

It had, in all sorts of ways, but she was cold now, counting down the time.

The taxi pulled up at his house, and they went in and the first thing he did was check Tatty.

She was in her box, and she lifted her head and licked his hand, then got awkwardly to her feet and headed for the door.

'I'll just take her outside.'

'Is she all right?'

'I think so.'

He went with her into the garden, and she wandered round a little, then bopped down for a wee and came back to him, tail waving gently, and pressed her head against his leg.

'Are you OK, little lady?' he asked her softly, but she just headed back inside to her box, and he went to look for Beth.

He found her in his bedroom, sitting on the bed holding the little silver heart in her hands, and when she looked up there were tears on her face.

He crouched down in front of her and rested his hands over hers.

'Are you OK? Would you rather be alone?'

She shook her head. 'No. Sit with me.'

So he sat beside her, his arm around her shoulders, and remembered Grace.

It could have been yesterday, it was so clear.

He was on duty that night and still at the hospital when she rang him.

'It feels weird. Something's different. I'm coming in,' she'd said, and he met her in Maternity reception.

They were taken to a side room, and she was put on a monitor and they watched as Grace's heart slowed, the beats fading to nothing.

He'd never forget Beth's anguished cry, or the howl of pain inside him that had been so unexpected. He'd heard that cry so many times during his aid work, the wail of a parent when a child died.

'Ry?'

He felt her fingers on his cheek now, wiping away tears he hadn't known he'd shed, and he blinked them away and met her eyes.

They were dry now, as if the moment had passed and she was at peace, and she lifted the little heart to her lips, then gave it to him.

'We need to put her somewhere safe,' she said, and he nodded and got to his feet, his daughter's ashes cradled carefully in his hand.

'How about the study?'

She nodded, and he went in there and placed the little heart on his desk, then kissed his finger and touched it to the cool metal. 'Sleep tight, my precious girl,' he murmured, and then went back to Beth.

She was standing waiting for him by the bed, and she cradled his face and wiped away his tears.

'Make love to me, Ry.'

He let his breath out on a huff. 'Are you sure?'

She nodded. 'Yes. Yes, I'm sure. I need you.'

He stared down at her for the longest time, his eyes searching, then gently lowered his head and took her mouth in the sweetest, tenderest kiss.

She felt the moment it changed. It was still tender, and there was no urgency, but she felt the passion welling in him, the need to be close. He stepped away, stripped off his clothes and came back to her, then with a wry and gentle smile he took hold of the hem of her dress and peeled it off over her head, closing the gap between them with a groan.

Still holding her, he led her to the bed and threw back the covers. She lay down and held out her arms to him, and he followed her down, gathering her up against his chest, his mouth finding hers again.

He took his time, his touch gentle and sure, and when it was over he cradled her in his arms as she drifted off to sleep.

He heard a sound.

Nothing much, just a tiny whimper, and he eased his arm out from under Beth's head and went out into the hall.

A definite whimper, from Tatty. He went into the other bedroom and found her circling restlessly in her bed, and he went back into his bedroom.

'Beth? Beth, wake up. I think Tatty's in labour. Mind your eyes, I need to put the light on.'

She propped herself up on one elbow, blinking slightly, and he pulled on clean clothes and went back to the dog, kneeling down beside her.

'Are you OK, sweetheart?' he asked softly, and she pressed her head into his hand and gave a little groan.

Definitely in labour. He dredged up a memory from his youth, of sitting on the kitchen floor in the semi-darkness, watching his father's black lab giving birth to a litter of eight fat little puppies.

Please God not eight. Two or three, maybe four, even, but not eight. And, more importantly, please let them be all right. He couldn't bear it if they weren't, not today, of all days.

Beth came quietly into the room and stood behind him.

'How is she?'

'Uncomfortable, I think. No puppies yet, but she's working on it.'

'Cup of tea?'

He smiled up at her in the dim light. 'That would be amazing.'

He shifted so that he was sitting near her box, leaning against the bed so he could watch her without crowding her, and Beth brought the tea in and sat down beside him.

'I know nothing about this,' she murmured. 'Well, not from a dog perspective.'

'I don't suppose it's a lot different,' he said, hoping the outcome would be, at least, and his heart squeezed. 'Hopefully she'll know what's going on and will instinctively do the right thing, but I don't think we should leave her. The vet didn't think she'd ever had a litter, she's too young and her nipples didn't look as if she'd lactated.'

'Reg would have known if she'd had puppies and he would have mentioned it,' Beth said, and then added thoughtfully, 'I wonder what they'll look like? We have no idea who the father is. They could be a bit weird.'

He chuckled quietly. 'They could. Let's just hope he wasn't huge. A couple of nice little puppies would be perfect.'

'I think you'll get what you're given, Ry. I'd settle for them all being OK,' she said philosophically, and sipped her tea, then rested her head on his shoulder with a quiet sigh.

He turned his head and pressed his lips to her hair, wondering what was going through her mind. Probably the same as his—

Tatty moved, stretching out her back legs with a tiny grunt, then turning and licking herself, and he peered at her.

'Are you OK, Tatty?' he murmured softly, but she ignored him, concentrating on whatever she was doing.

Licking a puppy?

He leant forwards, and saw two black paws and a black nose, then with another grunt the puppy slithered out, and she licked it furiously, pushing it almost roughly until they heard a tiny squeak.

'Oh! It's alive!' Beth said, and he could hear the joy in her voice.

'Looks like it. And she seems to know what to do.'

They watched her, spellbound, as she nosed the puppy until it was lying by her teats, then it started to suckle and she lay down again, resting but keeping an eye on it until she became distracted.

'I think there's another one coming,' he murmured.

'Will the first one be all right or will it be in her way?'

'We can move it if we have to. She'll probably be OK.'

Beth turned her head and looked at him. 'Have you seen this before?'

He nodded. 'Once. Our dog had puppies. I was probably about seven or eight? That's when I decided I wanted to be a vet.'

'A vet? Am I missing something?' she asked softly, her voice slightly incredulous.

He gave a low chuckle and shook his head, then his smile faded. 'No. I changed my mind when my father was dying. I was twelve when he was diagnosed with cancer, fifteen when he died. I wanted to be able to do something, and of course I couldn't, but I spent a lot of time visiting him in hospital off and on, and it sort of rubbed off on me. Here we go,' he added, leaning forwards again to watch closely, but this time there was a problem.

'It's breech,' he said tightly. 'All tail and bottom, no feet. She might struggle. I'll give her a moment, then I might have to help.'

'How?'

'Gentle traction. If that doesn't work, then the vet.'

Nothing happened, and Tatty was clearly struggling, so he shook his head, picked up a towel he'd put ready and gently grasped the puppy's hindquarters and eased it down and out with her next contraction.

'There we go,' he said, his fingers clearing the membranes away from its face, but it didn't breathe, despite Tatty licking it furiously, so he picked it up, held it in his hand as he'd seen his father do and swung it down to drain the fluid from its lungs.

Nothing. He did it again, and again, and again, and then finally there was a tiny cough, and he grabbed the towel and rubbed it gently, and it squeaked.

'Oh, Ry,' Beth said, and he swallowed hard and put the squeaking puppy back with its anxious mother. She washed it firmly, tumbling it around by her teats, and then nosed it up to lie beside its sibling.

It latched on after a moment, and he gave a sigh of relief and slumped back against the bed, and Beth tucked her arm through his and hugged it. 'Well done,' she said, her voice choked, and he turned his head and kissed her wordlessly.

No choice. He couldn't have spoken if he'd tried, but the pup was OK, Tatty was OK, and all they could do now was watch and wait.

The next two puppies arrived without event, and then after washing them all again and giving them time to feed, Tatty got carefully to her feet and stepped out of the box, looking at them expectantly.

'I imagine she needs to go out,' Ryan said, and left Beth there with the puppies while he took her in the garden.

She shuffled over to them and looked at them closely. Two black, one a pale cream, the other, the smallest and the one who'd had problems, a darker gold, all fat little butterballs with Tatty's black nose.

They came back, and she got up and moved out of the way so Ryan could clean out the box and give them fresh bedding.

'Here, cuddle the puppies,' he said, handing them to her, and she sat on the bed and cradled them in her lap while Tatty sniffed them and wagged her tail.

'You're a clever girl,' she said fondly, and looked up at Ryan. 'Four's nice.'

He laughed and looked at her over his shoulder. 'I wonder if we'll still be thinking that when they're tumbling round the kitchen causing havoc,' he said, and spread out fresh newspaper in the bottom of the box.

'There you go, Tatty. In you get.'

He scooped up her babies and put them back in the box, and she stepped carefully over them and lay down again with a quiet sigh, the puppies snuggling up to her in a sleepy heap.

He straightened up with a smile, and held out his hand. 'Come on. Let's go and have some breakfast. I'm starving. I didn't eat a lot last night.'

'No, nor did I. What time is it?'

'Quarter to six.'

She swallowed. Two years ago she'd been lying in a side room in the maternity unit cradling her daughter, her world in pieces, and now, all thanks to Tatty and Ryan, the date had a new, happier memory.

She reached up her hand and took his, and he pulled her to her feet, and as if he understood he put his arm around her and walked with her out to the garden.

'How do you fancy a bacon sandwich?'

'Amazing,' she said, conjuring up a smile, and he kissed her gently.

'Sit here in the sunshine. I'll bring you some coffee while the bacon's cooking.'

She perched on the wall and hugged herself, rubbing her arms. It was a bit chilly, but the sun was just coming over the roof of the bungalow and she could feel the warmth of its rays on her head and shoulders. It wouldn't be long before it was summer, she realised. Just another few weeks. By the time the puppies were ready for rehoming, it would be glorious out here.

'You need a new bench,' she said as he emerged with her coffee.

'I do. I also need to talk to the agent about the house.'

'Are you going to buy it?'

'I don't know. I think I'd like to. I love it here. It's so peaceful, and anyway, it's Tatty's home so I sort of have to,' he added with a grin. 'Why? What do you think?'

'What do I think? I think I thought she was going to the rescue centre.'

He pulled a face. 'Yeah. I've been having second thoughts about that, and I don't think Reg would ever speak to me again. I meant the house, by the way. What do you think about the house?'

'I like it,' she said simply. 'You're right, it's lovely and peaceful here, and it's got a beautiful view. And it's Tatty's home, of course.'

He grunted, handed her the coffee and walked away, leaving her smiling.

'I knew you wouldn't rehome her,' she murmured, and wrapped her hands around the mug, the smile lingering.

* * *

The puppies were gorgeous, and they'd grown like weeds.

It wasn't long before they were bumbling around the kitchen where he'd moved them to. He'd rigged up a bedroom for them all in the passage that led to the garage, and every now and then they were let out to play, collapsing soon into a heap back in their bed or just falling asleep on their feet and keeling over where they were, usually underfoot.

He and Beth were sharing their care; she'd more or less moved in, and they'd fixed their shifts so that one or other of them was about most of the time, and of course Reg was almost a permanent fixture, turning up every afternoon just after lunch and sitting with the pups in the garden while they tumbled on the lawn.

And because Tatty had been feeding them until they were fully weaned, he and Beth had the luxury of the enormous bed all to themselves, and they were taking full advantage of it.

Life was good, and once the pups were rehomed in three weeks it would be even better, because they'd be working together again, and he missed that, but for now it worked for them, and it wouldn't be long.

Beth was exhausted.

She wasn't sure why. Yes, the puppies had been full on, but she was used to being busy, and work hadn't been any harder than normal. OK, it was summer and there was a small influx of visitors to the town getting into trouble, but that didn't explain it.

Maybe it was the lack of sleep? They'd certainly been staying up late so Tatty could have a last feed before they put her away for the night with the pups, but even allowing for the fact that without fail they'd make love before they went to sleep, she was still getting a solid six or seven hours.

Whatever, she was too tired to eat, not interested in food, and she found her eyelids drooping in the middle of every afternoon regardless of what she was doing.

It was almost as if she was pregnant—

No. She couldn't be. She was back on the Pill, taking it meticulously on time, and until it had kicked in Ryan had been just as meticulous about birth control, so how?

No. She couldn't be—could she? It was either that or something worse, and there was an easy way to find out. Numb, feeling chilled to the bone despite the lovely day, she shut the puppies away with their mum, got in her car and drove to the nearest supermarket, bought a pregnancy test and drove home, then sat in the bathroom for half an hour summoning up the courage to do the test.

And when she finally did, it was positive.

She felt sick. Sick with fear and dread and horror at what this would mean for them, what it would mean to Ryan, because he'd still not said he wanted children yet, or that he wanted a permanent relationship with her, and he still, despite everything, hadn't told her that he loved her.

Because he didn't?

Maybe living together for the last few weeks had made him realise it wasn't what he wanted? Maybe he regretted taking that step and had only done it out of guilt because of Grace?

How was she going to tell him?

She heard his key in the lock, and quickly grabbed the test wand and the box and stuffed them into her washbag in the cupboard as he walked in.

'Sorry, I didn't realise you were in here—are you OK?' he added, tipping his head on one side and searching her face.

'I'm fine. Why wouldn't I be?' she lied, and pushed past him. 'Are you going to take Tatty for a walk?'

'Yes, in a second. I just need—'

He broke off, and she held her breath as he walked out of the bathroom after her, a sheet of printed paper in his hand.

The instructions for the pregnancy test.

He looked up, his eyes shocked, then looked down at it again, dropping it as if it was red hot.

'You're pregnant,' he said, his voice hollow. It wasn't a question. Her face had probably given her away.

He swore viciously under his breath, then strode into the kitchen, called Tatty, clipped her lead on and went out without a word.

So that was it. His reaction, in a nutshell, reduced to a few choice words.

Well, what had she expected? Delight? No. Of course not, because he obviously wasn't ready, didn't want children yet, and maybe never with her. He certainly hadn't wanted Grace, although her death had hurt him deeply, and it looked like he didn't want this baby, either.

Her hand slid down over her still flat abdomen, and she squeezed her eyes shut to hold back the tears.

Please be all right. Let my baby be all right. That's all that matters.

She'd be OK. She'd go back to her own house, and Ryan could make his own arrangements for the puppies. Maybe the foster lady could take them now, they were nearly six weeks old.

Not your problem.

She went into his bedroom, found all her things and stuffed them into her bag and a couple of carrier bags she found in the kitchen. Her wash things went in, but there was something else, something much more important.

She went into his study, and there on the desk was Grace's heart, but it was sitting on a sheet of paper with Ryan's writing on it, and as she reached out she saw the word 'Grace'.

She picked it up, her heart pounding, and sat down on the chair as if her strings had been cut.

My darling Grace,
I don't know what to say to you, except to tell you that I love you more than I could ever have thought possible.

I've lost so much. Your first tooth, your first word, your first step. Taking you to school, taking you to your first dance, walking you down the aisle. All gone.

I've never known what it means to be a father, I never had that chance, and I don't know if I'll ever have the chance to find out because, although I love her deeply, I think your mother is afraid to try again, and so am I.

But I want you to know that if we ever find the courage to have another child he or she will be told about you, about how much we both love you, and how very much you're missed, every single day.

Sleep tight, my beloved angel.

Daddy xxx

The words swam in front of her eyes, and she put the letter down carefully on the desk under Grace's heart, and stood up, her legs trembling.

She had to find him, and she knew just exactly where he'd be...

He didn't know what to do.

This was his fault. It had to be. He'd thought he'd been so careful, and he couldn't remember a single time when he hadn't used a condom, and he'd *seen* Beth taking her pills, because they were in the bedside table and it was the first thing she did every morning without fail, right under his nose.

And yet regardless of that, she was pregnant, but how?

He'd consciously kept using the condoms. He knew the Pill wasn't always reliable. Belt and braces? Maybe, but he'd felt that was better than an unwanted pregnancy—he knew that would devastate her.

Yet here they were. He'd seen the fear in her eyes,

the dread of facing what she'd faced with Grace all over again, and it tore his heart to pieces because it had to have been his fault.

But how? When?

Unless…

The night of the wedding, the anniversary of Grace's death.

Of course. They'd made love then, and it had been so unexpected, so emotional, so moving, that contraception was the last thing on their minds. They'd fallen asleep in each other's arms, and he hadn't left the bed until he'd been woken by Tatty whimpering. And at that point, Beth had only just started taking the Pill again, and it wouldn't have had time to work.

Idiot! How could he have been so stupid?

He stared out over the river, Tatty lying by his side, her head on his lap as he absently fondled her ears.

How could he make this right? What possible thing could he do to make it better? Nothing, except go back to her and tell her what he now knew, and apologise with all his heart for putting her in this position.

He heard footsteps behind him on the river path, and he braced himself for a cheerful 'Good evening!', but there was nothing, just silence as the footsteps stopped.

Tatty got to her feet, tail wagging, and he saw shoes appear beside him. Beth's shoes.

'I found your letter.'

Letter? Realisation struck, and he closed his eyes.

His letter to Grace. He'd written it the day of the wedding, on Grace's anniversary, and he'd put the silver heart on top of the letter on his desk, meaning to show it to Beth if and when the time was right, but the puppies had intervened, and he'd forgotten it in the chaos. Another thing he'd overlooked. *Idiot.*

The shoes moved, and she sat down beside him, leaning against him, tucking her hand in his arm, her head on his shoulder.

'I'm so sorry, Ry. I have no idea how I got pregnant—'

'I have,' he said gruffly. 'It was the night of the wedding. I didn't use a condom. I didn't even think about it. All I could think about was you, how you were feeling, how sad you were, and I just wanted to make it better, to hold you, to love you, to take away the pain. Only I haven't, I've made it ten times worse. A hundred times worse. And I'm so, so sorry—'

His voice cracked, and he looked away, staring out across the river at the boats swinging lazily at their moorings.

'You said you love me, in the letter. Why didn't you tell me? I needed to know that, Ryan.'

That took him by surprise and he turned to stare at her. 'Of course I love you, but I didn't think you'd want to know. I didn't want to put you under pressure.'

'Under pressure?'

'Yes. Pressure to return my love.'

'But I do, you know that. I'd already told you I love you.'

'Only jokingly.'

She shook her head, her eyes tender. 'I wasn't joking, Ry. Of course I love you. I've loved you since you kissed me here, by the stile, and I've never stopped. All I've done is learn to love you more.'

He studied her face, searching to see if it was true, and he could read it in her eyes, those beautiful eyes that were so very revealing today. Maybe he'd learn how to read them better if he kept on trying. All he needed was a chance…

His eyes were brighter than she'd ever seen them, and he reached out and cupped her cheek in his hand, his fingers trembling slightly.

'I love you,' he said quietly. 'I love you so much, more than I have words to say, and if you give me the chance, I'll tell you every day of our lives together. Marry me, Beth, and let's be a family. You, me, Grace, Tatty—and the baby, if the fates have finished playing with us.'

Her heart hitched in her chest and she felt her eyes well. 'You said Grace.'

'Of course. She'll always be a part of our family, Beth. She's our first child. That will never change.'

His face swam in front of her eyes, and she bit her lips and nodded wordlessly.

'Thank you. For saying that. And yes. Yes, Ry, I'll marry you, and I'll try really hard not to be too scared, but if I am, and if it all goes wrong, just—be there for me, please, like you were before? Because I can't do this without you—'

His arms came round her, crushing her against his chest. 'Never. You'll never be without me, no matter what, so long as I'm alive. I'll never leave you again, I promise you.' He let her go, bent his head and kissed her, his lips lingering on hers to seal the promise, and then he straightened up and smiled into her eyes.

'Come on. Tatty's getting hungry, and I bet the puppies are, too. Let's go home.'

Home.

She smiled back at him and got to her feet, tugging him up.

'That sounds like a wonderful idea,' she said, and with his arm around her shoulders and the dog at their side, they walked back along the river path, pausing for a moment at the stile to share another tender, lingering kiss where it had all begun.

He lifted his head and stared down into her eyes, and smiled. 'I love you,' he said. 'Just so you know.'

She smiled back. 'I think I do know now. And I love you, too. Don't ever forget it.'

'I won't.'

Then he put his arm around her shoulders again, tucked her in against his side and walked her home…

EPILOGUE

'HERE?'

He watched as Beth settled the baby in Reg's arms and walked over to where he was standing poised with a spade. She frowned thoughtfully at the rose they'd found in a garden centre. It was named Grace, and of course they'd had to have it. Now he was waiting for Beth to say where.

'Right a bit, I think. Reg, what do you think?'

The old man smiled. 'It'll be quite a big rose. Maybe a bit more to the right, and back a bit? That's it, Ryan. Perfect. That'll give it room to grow.'

'Like everything else round here,' Beth said with a smile. 'Look at how big Muddle's got, considering how tiny she was to start with. I can't believe we nearly lost her.'

Ryan grunted and glared at the pup, now a year old and full of nonsense. 'Muddle, no! Get out of the hole, I don't need help digging it!'

He pushed her out of the way, told her to sit and went back to his digging, while she sat poised, riveted by what he was doing, desperate to join in but waiting for the treat she knew was in his pocket.

Tatty was lying on her back in the sun, playing with a raggy toy, and Ryan lifted his head and glanced back at his family.

His wife, their three-month-old baby boy, and Reg, surrogate grandfather to Raoul, named after the boy he still felt he'd failed, the boy whose face he saw in his dreams, but not as often now.

They'd been married ten months, and since then they'd extended the house, making a beautiful kitchen/dining/living space that opened to the garden but with spectacular views from the front of the river and the stile where he'd kissed her at the start of their journey.

They'd added another bedroom, to allow for their family to grow, and although they'd rehomed three of the puppies, one to Ed and Annie, one to James and Connie, and another to the farmer whose black Lab, his gun dog, had turned out to be the father, they'd kept Muddle, the puppy they'd nearly lost, and of course Tatty, who'd brought them all together.

He gave both the dogs a treat, settled the rose into the hole he'd dug for it, and stood back.

'How's that?'

'Perfect,' Beth and Reg said in unison, and he smiled.

'I thought so, too. Better fill it in, then, before Muddle digs it up again.'

He knelt down, pressed the soil in around the root ball and touched the tiny bud just starting to form with the tip of his earthy finger. 'There you go, Grace,' he murmured softly. 'You can grow now. Happy birthday.'

He straightened up, dusted off his hands and went over to Beth, putting an arm around her and the baby. 'OK?'

She nodded. 'Lovely. Look, Raoul. Daddy's planted a rose for Grace. It's going to be so pretty.'

The baby gave her a gummy smile, and she dropped a kiss on his head.

'Happy?' he murmured.

She looked up at him, her eyes a little bright, and nodded.

'Very. Thank you. For everything.'

'Don't thank me. Just having you and Raoul here with me is all I need, all I'll ever need.'

'And Reg and the dogs.'

He smiled. 'Of course. That goes without saying— Muddle, no! Leave it!'

He dived at the dog, and behind him he heard Beth and Reg laughing, the happy sound filling the garden with joy.

He turned back to them with a rueful grin. 'Well, maybe not the dogs…!'

* * * * *

MELTING THE TRAUMA DOC'S HEART

ALISON ROBERTS

MILLS & BOON

CHAPTER ONE

OH, MAN...

He shouldn't have done that.

Isaac Cameron stared at the phone in his hand. He could hear the echoes of that angry edge in his own voice. Should he ring back and leave another voice-mail to apologise? To admit that it was actually none of his business?

He thought about that for a moment as he tipped his head back and took a deep breath of the clean, crisp air around him. The snow-covered, craggy peaks of the mountains that bordered this small, Central Otago township in New Zealand caught his gaze and held it as he opened his eyes again. It hadn't got old yet, this view, despite the fact that he'd been living and working here for nearly a year. If anything, it had got into his blood. And, okay, he might have come here as a last resort, to lie low and find out if there was anything left of the man he used to be, but it didn't feel like an escape any more.

He cared about this place. About the hardworking farming community that surrounded Cutler's Creek.

About the small, rural hospital he worked in. About Don Donaldson—the man who'd kept this hospital up and running for decades, like his father before him, in the face of repeated threats of closure.

That was why he'd made that call.

And he wasn't going to call back and apologise. Because he wasn't sorry.

Because tapping back into the ability to care again was precisely the reason Isaac had come to this quiet corner of the world in the first place. Not to care too much, mind you, because he knew only too well how that could leave devastation and burn-out in its wake. But caring enough for something to really matter—like the situation that had prompted him to make that phone call—was part of what made a life meaningful, wasn't it? It was making Isaac feel human again. To hope, albeit cautiously, for a future that could provide contentment, if not happiness.

He slipped the phone into the pocket of the unbuttoned white coat he was wearing over his jeans and open-necked shirt. Would the woman he'd never met respond to that message? Did *she* care about any of the things that had become important to him in the last year? Probably not, so maybe it would do her good to hear what he had said. Everybody needed a wake-up call once in a while, didn't they? Like the one he'd had that had prompted him to apply for the rural hospital job he'd found advertised in a tiny country at the bottom of the world that he'd barely heard about.

The senior doctor and medical director of Cutler's

Creek Hospital hadn't been that pleased to see him when he'd turned up, mind you.

'You're over-qualified. Why the hell would we need a trauma surgeon with your kind of experience in a place like this? Why would you even want to live here? You'll be bored stiff.'

'I'm over big cities and war zones. I need a break from patching people up when what's wrong with them wouldn't have happened if people could be a bit kinder to each other. I can do general medicine along with trauma. I've been in plenty of situations where there's been nobody but me to provide what's needed.'

Maybe it had been due to the remnants of that kind of autonomy that had prompted him to take matters into his own hands and make that regrettable phone call. Well, it was too late to worry about any repercussions now and it was time he headed back inside. There was a chill in the air that suggested the forecasters hadn't been wrong in predicting a storm that would usher in the first of the winter weather.

Isaac turned back towards the rambling, low-slung, wooden building that was Cutler's Creek Community Hospital. They had a ten-bed capacity here, including maternity and geriatrics, an outpatients' department, a main operating theatre that hadn't been used for years, and a smaller one that was used for minor procedures and as their equivalent of an emergency department where they could assess and deal with accidents and medical emergencies with resources like ultrasound, ECG, X-ray and ventilation equipment. It was by no means a large hospital but it was more than enough to keep two doctors busy as the medical hub for a community of several thousand people.

The man who had kept this hospital going—thriving even, given that the community had raised the funds for their new ultrasound equipment only recently—was walking towards Isaac as he headed back inside. Don Donaldson was scowling but that was nothing new. He'd been scowling just like this the first day Isaac had met him when he couldn't understand why he'd even applied for the job here. He knew a lot more about his boss now and, like everybody else, he accepted that this man's heart of gold was well covered by grumpiness that could border on being plain rude, but who could blame him, given the cards that life had already dealt? He'd never remarried after his wife had walked out on him decades ago, taking his only child with her to the other side of the globe. He'd come home to find his father was terminally ill and there was nothing he could do to help, had then devoted his life—often single-handedly—to giving Cutler's Creek a medical service to be proud of and now…

Well, now things might have just become a whole lot worse. It seemed that history was about to repeat itself.

'Zac… Good. You're still here.'

'I wasn't planning on heading home any time soon. I'm going to do another ward round while I'm waiting for Faye Morris to come in. Sounds like it's not a false alarm for her labour this time. Debbie's coming in with her so I'll just be available if she needs backup. Given her experience and skills as a midwife, I'll probably just be catching up on some reading.'

'Right…' The older man cleared his throat. 'Well, I just wanted to make sure you're not going to say anything. To anyone. You know how fast word gets around in a place this size and I do not want my mother upset—especially not now when she's got a big celebration coming up. This is nobody's business but mine and it's up to me who I tell. And when.'

Too late, Isaac thought. He lifted his gaze to the mountains to avoid eye contact that might reveal his discomfort over the fact that he'd already betrayed what he'd known was a confidence, even if it hadn't been stipulated as such at the time.

'I still don't agree with you, Don. You can't just diagnose yourself with something like pancreatic cancer and then give up. Have you even thought about a differential diagnosis? You wouldn't treat your patients like this so why do it to yourself?'

'Because I watched my own father do exactly what you think I should do. He went and got a formal diagnosis. He got persuaded to get the surgery, and chemo and radiation and, okay, maybe he got a few extra months from that but what good were they to anyone, especially him? He was mostly bedridden and suffering, dying by inches…' Don cleared his throat again but his voice still sounded raw, even after all these years. 'I'm not going like that, thanks very much. I've got unfinished business here and I intend to do whatever I can for as long as I can.'

'But you don't even know that you're right. Let me have a look at you and run a few tests. At the very least, let me do an ultrasound.'

'I've got exactly the same symptoms my dad had. You know as well as I do that inherited gene mutations can get passed from parent to child. That as many as ten percent of pancreatic cancers are genetic. Look… I just *know*, okay? I've known for quite a while now. I've been diagnosing illnesses for the best part of half a century. Are you trying to tell me I'm no good at my job?'

'Of course not.' Zac suppressed a sigh. 'And I'll support you in whatever way I can, you know that.'

He wasn't about to give up on this but he knew that continuing to push right now would only lead to Don shutting himself off completely. He was a private man and Zac could respect that better than most people, given that he was one himself.

'I just need to know that you'll keep this to yourself. I shouldn't have said anything. I wouldn't have, if you hadn't come barging into my office like that. Without the courtesy of even knocking…'

'Hmm…' A sideways glance showed him that Don was now the one avoiding eye contact and he understood why. He still felt uncomfortable that he'd seen too much. He'd be just as embarrassed as his boss if the tables had been turned.

'You caught me in a low moment, that's all it was. It won't happen again.'

A low moment? The man had been in tears. Trying to cover that up in the face of Zac's unexpected appearance, he had dropped the archive filing box that he had been stretching to replace on a high shelf. Despite being told to get out, Zac had automatically stooped to help pick up the contents of the box, which appeared to be a collection of unopened letters and parcels. *Not Known at This Address* and *Return to Sender* had been stamped all over them in red ink.

'Who's Olivia Donaldson?'

'Nobody. Just get out, Zac.'

'Not until you tell me what's going on. She's your daughter, isn't she?'

'Was...'

'She's dead?'

'As good as... We haven't had contact in more than twenty years. It doesn't matter now, anyway... Or it won't soon enough...'

The power of the internet meant that it had taken very little time to track down the woman who'd never opened those parcels or letters. A call to someone he knew in Auckland had given him access to a personal phone number. And, okay, he shouldn't have made that last call but what was done was done and it was highly unlikely that this Olivia Donaldson would take the slightest notice of what he'd said.

'Let's get back inside, Don. This wind feels like it's coming straight off the top of one of those mountains.'

'Yep...there's a storm brewing, all right.'

Isaac shook off the double meaning in those words that only he was aware of. It was a waste of energy to try crossing bridges before they were even visible. He had learned long ago to live in the present and deal with whatever came at you from left field. And he might be more than a bit of a lone wolf, but he was also definitely a survivor. He wasn't worried...

* * *

Stiletto heels made a very satisfying clicking sound on the gleaming floors of one of Auckland's most prestigious private hospitals. Along with the sleek, fitted skirt and matching jacket and the equally sleek hairstyle Olivia Donaldson had perfected long ago, she knew she looked the part of an up-and-coming plastic surgeon who was well on the way to being exactly where she wanted to be—at the top of the field in reconstructive microsurgery.

She'd had doubts about the value of providing cosmetic surgery to people who were wealthy enough to chase the illusion of perfection but she'd decided to view purely aesthetic surgery a stepping stone when she'd decided to apply for this job. Elective procedures like a facelift needed the same skills as reconstructive microsurgery and the hours and pay of this new job gave Olivia the freedom to do any further postgraduate study she would need.

Auckland's Plastic Surgery Institute had its own ward in this private hospital and Olivia's patients had had their surgery this morning. She had been pushed to get through all her cases today and they had all been breasts. A breast lift and augmentation for a mother of three in her forties, a breast lift and reduction for a woman in her fifties, and an implant removal for someone the same age as Olivia, who'd experienced hardened scar tissue from silicone material leaking from her implants. The lift and augmentation had been her first case this morning and Olivia could see no reason for her not to go home now.

'Sleep as upright as possible for the next forty-eight hours,' she advised. 'Prop yourself up on lots of pillows, or use a recliner chair if you've got one.'

'It hurts more than I expected.'

'We'll give you something for that but you can expect your breasts to be swollen and sore for the next few days, I'm afraid.'

'This instruction sheet says I have to avoid any strenuous activity for two to three weeks. That's not going to be easy when I've got three small children, is it?'

Olivia made an effort to keep her smile sympathetic. 'I'm sure it won't be, but it is very important. Especially not to lift them. You'll risk tearing stitches and other problems if you do.'

At least her breast reduction patient was more thrilled with the new shape of her body beneath the support bandaging and surgical bra.

'I can't think why I didn't do this years ago. I just wish I'd got you to do a tummy tuck at the same time, Dr Donaldson.'

'We can talk about that another time. It wasn't a minor procedure that you had today, you know. How's the pain level now?'

'I've been too excited to notice it much. How soon can I go back to work and show it all off?'

'Once you no longer need your prescription pain medication. In a week or so, I expect, but we can let you know when you come for your first outpatient appointment at the Institute in a few days.'

'Will I be seeing you then?'

'Of course.' Olivia's smile felt slightly forced. A lot

of her time these days was spent in the luxurious consultation rooms of the Plastic Surgery Institute. Initial consultations to discuss desired procedures. Assessment and detailed planning in conjunction with the patients and then the follow-up appointments to track recovery and deal with any complications. And, even during the six months that Olivia had become immersed in the world of private cosmetic surgery, she was already seeing patients returning for their next procedure. It was flattering that they demanded to see her but it was a little disturbing, as well.

People getting addicted to cosmetic surgery in the hope of making their lives perfect was no myth and body dysmorphic disorder—where people became obsessed with a slight or even imagined defect in their appearance—was something Olivia intended to research more thoroughly in the near future.

The mental state of the last patient she checked on before discharging from the initial post-operative care was also a bit of a worry.

'I'm confident we managed to get all the scar tissue out,' Olivia assured her. 'You should find a dramatic improvement in any discomfort you were having after you recover from the surgery.'

Her patient was in tears. 'I can't look. I'm going to look worse than I did before I had the implants, aren't I? Nobody's going to want to even look at me. I'll be flat-chested again and now I'll have all these scars, as well. I can't believe I was stupid enough to do something like this in my twenties. Why does *anybody* do it?'

'Don't beat yourself up, Janie.' Olivia took extra time

to try and reassure this patient and let her know that there were counselling services available through the Institute that she might find helpful. She was running a little late for her six o'clock appointment by the time she left.

'You're so lucky, you know,' Janie said by way of farewell. 'You're never going to need to even think of having any plastic surgery.'

It was walking distance from the hospital to the Plastic Surgery Institute, which was one of many buildings devoted to private health care in this prestigious suburb of Auckland, some of which were converted mansions on either side of the tree-lined streets. Normally Olivia would have enjoyed the swirl of autumn leaves drifting down around her but she was trying to pinpoint why her day was feeling as if it had been somewhat unsatisfactory. The surgeries had all gone smoothly and theatre staff had been complimentary about her skills. She'd had plenty of practice in breast surgery during her training, though, and she'd taken great pride in doing the best job she could in breast reconstruction for women who'd had cancer surgery. Now that *had* been satisfying...

The waiting room of the Institute was full, which wasn't unusual. Any private clinic had to cater for clients who wanted an appointment after normal working hours. Olivia didn't have a clinic to run this evening, however.

'I'm just popping in for that six p.m. meeting,' she told the receptionist. 'I believe Simon wanted to see me?'

'He's waiting for you.'

Olivia couldn't miss the knowing hint in the look she was receiving. Had someone in the administrative staff started a rumour that something was going on between her and her boss? Maybe they all thought it was only a matter of time before something happened. She was single, after all, and who could resist the charms of one of the most eligible bachelors in Auckland's A-list society?

Olivia could, that's who. She held the receptionist's gaze until the young woman looked away, flushing slightly.

'Can you let him know his next client is here already?'

Simon's office had an enormous desk, leather chairs and a glass display case of antique surgical instruments.

'Sharon told me to tell you that your next client is here already.'

'She can wait for a minute or two. Oh, wait... I think it's a "he". Our new campaign to persuade men that aesthetic surgery is not just for women is starting to pay off. Literally...'

Olivia heard an echo of that slightly bitter compliment her last patient of the day had given her—that she was lucky that she wouldn't have to think about surgical enhancement of any kind. Simon was the male equivalent, wasn't he? Every feature perfectly symmetrical and his grooming and taste in clothes contributing to make him look years younger than forty-five. Even those grey streaks in that immaculate haircut could have been put there just to make him look more attractive.

As he stood up from his desk and put his jacket back

on, she thought he looked as though he'd just stepped out of a magazine page—from an advertisement for luxury Italian suits, perhaps.

'So… Did you get my message?'

'Um…'

'You forgot to switch your phone back on after being in Theatre, didn't you?'

Olivia groaned. 'Sorry… It's been a long day. What was the message?'

'A last-minute invitation to a charity gala tomorrow night. The guest speaker is a London doctor who rang here this morning asking after you. He knew your mother well, he said, and he wanted to arrange a chance to pass on his personal condolences. He was out of the country on a sabbatical at the time of her funeral, he said, and by the time he got back, you'd already made the move here.'

Anybody who was anybody in London had known Olivia's mother, Janice, thanks to her position as one of the city's leading cardiologists and her thriving Harley Street practice. That spotlight had extended to Olivia, as her daughter, as well, bringing with it a pressure that had never felt comfortable. Escaping that spotlight was one of the reasons she had chosen to come back to New Zealand.

'I'm not sure, Simon.' Olivia knew she was frowning. 'I've never liked being in a crowd of people I don't know and any formal dresses I own are still in storage until I find an apartment I want to buy.'

'But you've got a day off tomorrow, haven't you? You

could go shopping for a new dress. And this is how you get to know people. The important people.'

Attending functions like charity galas had been pretty much her mother's only social life. It had been at a charity event she had attended with her mother that she'd met Patrick, in fact—the man everybody, including herself, had expected her to marry. That breakup had been the other, even bigger reason she had decided to come back to the country of her birth to make a fresh start in her life. Olivia knew that her mother would have shrugged off the failed relationship as no more than an inconvenience. She also knew what she would have said about going to this event.

Go, Olivia. It's important to be seen. This is your career. The most important thing in your life. The only thing you can really count on…

'You don't have to go alone,' Simon added with an encouraging smile. 'I'll be there. I'll look after you, I promise.'

Olivia couldn't help glancing at the door as if looking for an escape route. Simon couldn't possibly know how much of a nerve he was stepping on. That he was reminding her of exactly how her relationship with Patrick had started—and its disastrous ending not that long after her mother's death—when he'd moved on to someone who offered an even better step up the social ladder.

Simon had followed her glance. 'You're right,' he said. 'I'd better get on with seeing my next patient.' He went to open the door for Olivia. 'Let me know what you decide. Maybe we can meet up for a drink before the event and that way you won't have to go in by yourself.'

Olivia fished her phone out of her pocket and turned it on as she left the building. It really was a very bad habit to turn her phone off but she knew that a staff member could easily find her if there was a problem on theatre days and she hated even the possibility of distractions when she was operating. Hearing the chime of an incoming message, she glanced at the screen, expecting it to be the message Simon had left about the invitation to the gala tomorrow, but it wasn't. It was a voicemail that had been left a couple of hours ago. From an unknown number.

Curious, Olivia keyed in her code as soon as she was sitting behind the wheel of her car, turning on the ignition as the message started to play.

'My name is Isaac Cameron,' a male voice said. There was a hint of an accent there. An Irish lilt, maybe? 'I'm a doctor at Cutler's Creek Hospital.'

Olivia gasped. Hearing the name of that small Central Otago township was disturbing, to say the least. She had a sudden urge to cut the call and delete the message but it was too late. She had been captured by the sound of the stranger's voice.

'I don't suppose you want to hear this, Olivia Donaldson, but—you know what? I'm going to tell you anyway.'

She could hear the indrawn breath, as if the caller was about to start a lengthy story. And there was something about his tone that sent a shiver down Olivia's spine. Without thinking, she turned off the engine of her car and slowly leaned back into her seat, touching the speakerphone icon on the screen. She had no idea what this was about but it felt like it was going to be something significant. Potentially life-changing?

'I thought you should know that your father's dying,' the voice continued. 'He's got pancreatic cancer, which is what killed *his* father about twenty years ago. Not that that bothered you, from what I hear, seeing as you apparently refused to come to your grandfather's funeral.'

She could hear a judgemental note in his voice and that put her back up. *For heaven's sake*, Olivia thought, *I was only thirteen years old. I'd never even met my grandfather that I could remember. I hadn't seen my father since he'd walked out on his family. Why would anyone think I was expected to travel from the other side of the world to go to a funeral for a stranger?*

'I wouldn't have known anything about you,' Isaac was saying now, 'but I found your father crying over a box of old letters. And parcels. All the things that you'd sent back to him over the years without even bothering to open them.'

Olivia's jaw dropped. He was accusing her of something she knew nothing about. Letters? Parcels? She'd never seen anything from her father. He'd never even made a phone call. She could remember being in floods of tears that first Christmas after he'd gone and her mother trying to comfort her.

'I know it's difficult, Olivia, but you wouldn't want to grow up in a place like Cutler's Creek, believe me. I don't think there's even a proper school there. My new job in London is going to give us both the most amazing

opportunities, you just wait and see. We can even think about getting you that pony you've always wanted.'

Did her mother know something about that mail? Had she thought that cutting any links Olivia had to a small country town would help her embrace a new life in a huge city? She could imagine her mother being that determined. Convincing herself that she was doing the best thing for her daughter, even.

She tuned back into the continuing voicemail. 'He loves you. He wants the chance to tell you that before he dies. I have no idea how long he's got but I imagine it's not that long because he's refusing to seek treatment.'

Why would he do that? Olivia could feel the frown line between her eyes deepen. Pancreatic cancer could kill in a matter of weeks in some cases if nothing was done. Why didn't he want to fight? Did he not have people in his life who could persuade him it was worth fighting?

As if to answer her question, Isaac was talking at the same time. There was a rising note of something like anger behind his words now.

'You probably don't know and maybe you don't even care but there's a whole community here in Cutler's Creek that thinks a great deal of your father. He's a good man and I think it's a crying shame that you turned your back on him.'

'I *didn't,*' Olivia said, her tone shocking her with both its volume and the outrage it contained. 'It was totally the opposite…'

'Maybe the past shouldn't matter now,' Isaac said, and it almost felt as if they were having a real conversation. 'If the people around here knew about this, they'd move heaven and earth to grant any last wish he might have but your father doesn't want anyone to know and, anyway, there's only one person who can do that, and that's *you*. You could stop him dying with that regret on his mind.'

There was a long moment's silence, then, as if the speaker was taking a long breath. Trying to control his emotional outburst, perhaps? Yes…when he spoke again, it was at a much slower pace. In a much quieter tone.

'I don't know you, Dr Olivia Donaldson,' he said. 'And I'm not sure I'd want to know someone who could turn their back on someone who loves them that much but I thought you should know. Before it's too late. Because…because if you've inherited even a fraction of the compassion for others that your father has, you wouldn't want to refuse to give him the one thing that would mean so much to him.'

Olivia could hear a breath being released as a sigh. 'You never know…one day it might be *your* dying regret. That you never gave him a chance…'

The click told her the call was ended. Another voice was giving her the automatic options of saving, deleting or listening to the message again. Olivia simply turned her phone off and, for the longest time, she sat there without moving a muscle. She was stunned. Shaking, even.

It shouldn't matter this much. It was ancient history. Maybe she was just feeling angry that a stranger was blaming her so unfairly. Telling her that it was *her* behaviour that had caused someone grief. Enough grief that, after all these years—decades, in fact—this father that she hadn't seen since she was a young girl had been *crying*? She tried to shake off the unpleasant knot that was trying to form in her stomach. She didn't care about this man. She hated him, in fact. He'd walked out on her without a backward glance.

Or had he?

Was it true? About the mail? What had been in those parcels? Books, maybe. The thought slid into her head uninvited. Unwelcome. Her father had always given her books. He'd been the one to read the bedtime stories when she was too young to read for herself. She could remember the way he'd lounged on the edge of her bed, his elbow propped on her pillow so that she could snuggle into the crook of his arm as she listened.

Olivia closed her eyes tightly. She recognised that prickly sensation that was tears trying to form. She hadn't shed any tears over her father for longer than she could remember. But remembering him reading to her had unlocked so many things that she'd buried. There had been a time when she'd missed him *so* much... She'd missed his hugs, that gleam in his eye that told her he was proud of her, that rich chuckle that was his laughter and...and even his smell, which came from that old-fashioned aftershave he insisted on using.

That knot in her stomach was tightening enough to be painful. Olivia felt like she was being attacked on all sorts of emotional fronts. She'd only lost her mother a matter of months ago and she was going to become an orphan now? With no close family at all? There was a possibility that her mother had betrayed her long ago but even if that was the case, why hadn't her father tried harder? How unfair was it that he had given up and then blamed *her*? Okay, she had refused to go to her grandfather's funeral when her mother had passed on the information and message from her father and she had written a response telling him that she never wanted to hear from him again but she'd only been a teenager. A kid. He'd been the adult. If he'd really cared that much, he would have tried again.

And, on top of all that, here was this complete stranger judging her and deciding she wasn't a person worth knowing. It was so unfair that it couldn't be allowed to go unanswered. Olivia flicked her phone on. She was going to return that call and tell this Isaac Cameron exactly what she thought of someone who could attack someone they knew nothing about.

Maybe she would write another letter to her father as well and put things straight about who had turned their back on whom. Or…her finger was still a little shaky as she poised it over the icons on the screen of her phone…she could do it face to face. Like an adult instead of a petulant teenager. Because, if she did that, she'd know for sure what the truth actually was. And maybe she needed to know the truth.

The icon that she chose to press instead was a browser. Just to find out how hard it might be to get to Cutler's Creek. Dunedin was the nearest city but there was an airport in Queenstown, as well. With a rental car it wouldn't take too long to get deeper into the centre of the South Island. If she left early enough, she could be

back in Auckland by tomorrow night. Not early enough
to attend that gala function but, to be honest, that added
to the appeal of the plan she was formulating.

By the time Olivia Donaldson pulled out of the car
park and was headed into rush-hour traffic to get to her
central city apartment, she had been online to organ-
ise every minute of her day off. She'd also sent Simon
a text message.

So sorry but I won't be able to make it tomorrow night
after all. Something's come up and I need to head
south for the day. It's a personal thing…

CHAPTER TWO

RURAL NEW ZEALAND was a lot wilder and emptier than English countryside.

Olivia Donaldson had had memories of the country's biggest city, Auckland, because she'd lived there until she was about eight years old but she'd never been to a small town like Cutler's Creek.

The main street boasted a church, community hall, petrol station and a pub. A war memorial marked the start of the more intensive commercial area that was, surprisingly, big enough to warrant a decent-sized supermarket amongst cafés and quirky-looking second-hand shops and, on the other side of town before the buildings changed from shops to houses, Olivia spotted the fire station, where an ambulance was parked alongside the fire truck.

She pulled in to stop and stretch her legs after the drive, which had taken a fair bit of concentration—especially that last winding stretch through a gorge. She needed a moment to take a deep breath, too, before she followed the yellow road sign that indicated she would have to turn right off the main road to find the local hospital. Her heels tapped on the paved footpath as she walked a few steps to have a closer look at what seemed to be a deserted emergency response station. Were there people in there, she wondered, or were the firies and ambulance officers here all volunteers who would only come in if needed? She was pretty sure that would be the case. Government funding didn't run to luxuries like paid staff for emergency services in every small town in the back of beyond. It was astonishing, in fact, that Cutler's Creek still had its own hospital.

There was an equally deserted rugby field and clubrooms between the fire station and the first of the small wooden villas that were homes to the local people who weren't farmers. Smoke curled from a chimney or two but no other signs of life. The place was dead. Eerily so, compared to Auckland's bustling inner-city streets. Oh, wait…someone was coming towards Olivia now, on the other side of the road, walking a big, black dog. A middle-aged woman, wearing gumboots and a long, oilskin raincoat, who gave Olivia a hard stare as she went past. Even the dog seemed to be staring at her and it made Olivia feel suddenly even more of a fish out of water. Why had she chosen to wear a tailored pencil skirt and its matching jacket today? Had she really thought that swapping her stilettos for shoes with a lower heel were enough of a nod to country casual?

She turned her back on the woman and lifted her gaze for a moment before she got back into the rental car. She had to admit that the scenery was quite extraordinary with that imposing skyline of snow-peaked mountains looming over the town. On top of being an object of such curiosity for a local, the natural grandeur around Olivia was making her feel rather small and insignificant.

Vulnerable, even? No. She got back into the car and took the next right-hand turn. She had every right to defend herself and she was here to take the bull by the horns, so to speak. Vulnerable people didn't do that kind of thing, did they?

The houses in this new street had big gardens. Some had empty sections beside the houses and there were animals in them. Goats on chains, a pig, a pony wearing a canvas coat to protect it from the weather. The pony Olivia had had as a child had never needed a canvas coat like that. It had lived in a warm stable, as pampered as Olivia had been herself in that exclusive, private boarding school an hour's drive out of London. She hadn't thought of that beloved pony for years and the memory, closely followed by the feeling of loss, was unwelcome—a bit like being poked with a sharp stick.

There was an older man working in a garden as Olivia turned into the grounds of Cutler's Creek Community Hospital but he stopped for a long moment to lean on his long-handled hoe and watch her drive slowly past.

'*What?*' Olivia muttered aloud. 'Do you never get unannounced visitors here?'

He was wearing gumboots, too. If he turned up on an Auckland street in that footwear, he'd get stared at, as well. Or maybe not. The bigger the city, the harder you had to work to get noticed. Her mother, Janice, had taught her that. She'd been very proud of how much notice Olivia had always garnered. Prizes in her school subjects and in the show-jumping ring at weekends or holidays, top marks at medical school, a career choice in a field as prestigious as plastic surgery and, most recently, for making such a good choice for a life partner in Patrick.

But she hadn't enjoyed the spotlight of being noticed for her own achievements any more than for being her famous mother's daughter. You got stared at when you were under any kind of spotlight and—like this place—the stares always had an element of judgement about them.

How different was this old, sprawling, wooden building that looked like an oversized villa from the gleaming modern structure that was the private hospital Olivia had been working in only yesterday? There were several parking slots designated for visitors near the front door of the hospital so she took one of them. A quick check of her lipstick in the mirror on the back of the sun flap and Olivia took another deep breath and slammed the car door shut behind her. She might be beginning to have doubts about the wisdom of doing this but she was here now so she might as well get it over with.

The grey-haired, bespectacled woman coming out from behind the desk in the large foyer looked as surprised to see Olivia as the gardener and the dog walker had but at least she wasn't wearing gumboots.

'Can I help you?' she asked.

'I hope so,' Olivia answered. 'I'm here to see Dr Donaldson. Don Donaldson.'

The woman blinked. 'Do you have an appointment?'

Olivia raised her eyebrows, summoning every ounce of confidence she could. 'Do I need one?'

'Ah…' The woman's gaze flicked over Olivia's suit. 'Are you a drug rep?'

A good part of Olivia's confidence was starting to ebb away. Did she look like a drug company representative who was here to peddle her company's drugs or medical products? A salesperson?

'My name,' she said coolly, 'is—'

'Olivia.' The deep voice coming from behind her was astonished. 'It *has* to be.'

Olivia swung around to see who had followed her in through the front door. A tall man, with rather disreputably rumpled hair and looking like he could do with a shave to get rid of that designer stubble, was wearing a white coat over…good grief…*jeans*?

He was looking at her as if she was the last person he'd expected to see standing in the foyer of this hospital. Or the last person he *wanted* to see?

'And you must be Isaac Cameron.'

The curl of one side of his mouth was nothing short of downright cheeky. Impertinent, actually. 'Spot on. How did you guess? I have to admit I had the advantage of having seen your photograph when I stalked you online yesterday.'

It was Olivia's turn to stare. It had been his voice, she realised. That accent with the hint of a Celtic lilt that was even more noticeable in real life. She'd had no idea what the owner of that voice would look like, however, and she was taken aback. More than that. She was more than a bit…gobsmacked, to be honest.

Isaac Cameron had to be *the* most attractive man she had ever seen in her entire life and, as a disconcerting thought that came from nowhere, Olivia wondered why she'd assumed that men like Simon—and Patrick, for that matter—were so good looking because of that groomed, perfect style. This Isaac Cameron was the complete opposite. He should have had a haircut weeks ago. He had curls of dark hair touching the collar of his white coat and the locks over his forehead had been pushed back, probably with his fingers rather than a comb.

'I don't imagine this hospital is big enough for more than two doctors,' she said calmly. 'And you're not my father.'

The receptionist gasped and then stepped back as if she wanted the protection of being behind her desk again. Olivia could feel an appalled stare scorching her skin. So Dr Cameron wasn't the only person who had judged her and found her to be less than a decent human being? She didn't like being here, Olivia decided. It had been a mistake to come. And, while she might have managed to sound calm, she was feeling anything but.

This was shocking, that's what it was. Or perhaps the shock was that odd tingle that was dancing somewhere deep in Olivia's gut as she made eye contact with a pair of eyes that were the colour of a very rich caramel.

Dear Lord…she was *attracted* to this man?

A whole lot more than she'd ever been attracted to any man in the past?

He clearly wasn't aware of any unwelcome chemical alchemy in the atmosphere. He broke the eye contact instantly to allow his gaze to take in her outfit and the curl of his mouth now suggested that it wasn't at all to his taste but it was exactly what he might have expected her to be wearing. He was making judgements again, wasn't he? About her clothes and her lifestyle. About the relationship she didn't have with her father. About *her*…

'Good to know you remember what he looks like.'

Olivia's breath came out in a startled huff. The hospital receptionist cleared her throat as if she was trying not to laugh. Or convey some kind of warning, perhaps, about who might be overhearing their conversation?

The voice from someone coming into the reception area from an inner corridor was annoyed.

'Ah, there you are, Zac. Where the dickens have you put Geoffrey Watkins's file? I need to see his last ECG.'

The shock wave that shot down Olivia's spine now had nothing whatsoever to do with any physical attraction. She knew this voice almost as well as she knew her own and the sound of it was like a door opening into an entire roomful of memories she didn't want to revisit. Because this man had broken her heart so badly it was never going to be the same. She could never again in her life trust that it was safe to love someone *that* much…

She turned very slowly, steeling herself to face her father.

For his part, Don Donaldson barely gave her a glance before focusing on Isaac as he walked towards them, but then his steps faltered and his gaze returned to Olivia. He went pale. For a split second Olivia felt a beat of fear that the surprise of her visit might actually do physical harm to her father and give him a heart attack or stroke or something. Oddly, the fear made it feel like she had something to lose all over again.

Don opened his mouth and his voice came out as no more than a hoarse whisper. *'Libby?'*

Oh…that hurt with an unexpected ferocity. No one had been allowed to call her that since she'd been about eight years old. *Ever…*

'My name is Olivia,' she said, pronouncing the words as if it was of great importance that they were heard clearly.

'But…but what the hell are you doing *here*?'

Olivia blinked. 'What? This was *your* idea… What *you* wanted…'

Her father was still looking pale. Shocked. Not at all as if his dying wish was being unexpectedly granted.

'Ah…' Isaac held out his hands as if he was about to start directing traffic. 'Let's take this into the staff-room, shall we? I might be able to explain.'

'My office,' Don snapped. 'I don't want any more of my private business being broadcast, thank you very much.'

The receptionist was being scowled at. She pursed her lips. 'I think you know me better than that, Dr Donaldson.'

His grunt might have been an apology but Olivia was frowning herself as she followed him. This grumpy, older man was a very different person from the father she remembered but perhaps that was a good thing. The past could be left in the past and all she needed to do now was to clear the air of any injustice and get back to where she belonged.

If Isaac Cameron had been wearing a tie, he might have felt the need to loosen it a little as he followed Don Donaldson's daughter into his boss's office. This was his fault but, in his defence, he'd never expected Olivia Donaldson to rock up to this hospital unannounced. On the very next day to him making that phone call? Man, he must have touched a nerve…

And, even though he'd seen her profile picture on the staff list of the Plastic Surgery Institute in Auckland, he'd never expected that she'd be quite so…so *stunning* in real life. Tall and slim, with that long, honey-blonde hair combed neatly back into a complicated-looking plait. Eyes that were so blue you had to wonder if they were real. He knew she was a well-respected plastic surgeon but she could have had a career as a supermodel if she'd wanted to. It wasn't just her looks, though. There was something about her voice or the way she moved or…perhaps it was her perfume. Whatever… Isaac had never for a moment expected to be attracted to this woman but his body seemed to be defying any orders from his brain right now.

Perhaps it was just an illusion. He was rattled, that's what it was. He hadn't expected her to turn up and now he was responsible for an imminent encounter that was quite likely to be awkward, if not potentially damaging to everybody involved, including himself. Sure enough, Don rounded on Isaac the moment his office door was closed behind the trio.

'You told her, didn't you? After I specifically asked you to keep the information to yourself?'

'Ah…' Technically, Zac had made the call before Don had requested confidentiality but he'd known that he shouldn't be doing it. 'Sorry, Don… I thought it was the right thing to do. That your daughter should know that…'

'That your dying wish was to see me again?' Olivia was shaking her head. 'But that's not actually true, is it?'

Don's eyebrows rose and then lowered even more as he scowled at Isaac. 'You said *that*?'

'I don't remember saying exactly that,' Zac admitted. 'I was a bit riled up on your behalf, though. After seeing all those letters that Olivia had refused to read.'

'I didn't refuse to read them.' Olivia was sounding pretty riled up herself now. 'I never received them. I'm not sure I even believe they exist.'

Zac couldn't help glancing up at the shelf where that filing box was sitting. When he looked down again, he found both Olivia and Don glaring at him and the similarity in their gazes almost made him smile. Clearly father and daughter still had things in common.

'They don't exist any more,' Don muttered. 'I put them through the shredder. But even if they were still in that box, they're just ancient history. Totally irrelevant.'

If he hadn't still been watching Olivia so closely, Zac might have missed the way she swallowed hard just then. Those letters had been important to her, hadn't they? Maybe she was telling the truth and she hadn't known they existed and maybe she'd wanted to see them. There was something about the way she was taking a breath that made him think she was struggling with this. That, despite her very put-together and poised outward appearance, she was actually feeling quite vulnerable. The shrug of her shoulders was definitely defensive.

'I really don't care,' she said. 'But I do believe that seeing me before you died wasn't something on any list of priorities you might have. After all, you've had more than twenty-five years to do something about that. The real reason I came was to tell you it's not fair...'

Yes...there was a tiny wobble in her voice that made Zac wish he'd never made that call. What right had he had to interfere in someone else's life and upset them? And Don was looking alarmingly pale, as if he could collapse at any moment. If he did, it would be entirely Zac's fault. Olivia Donaldson was looking a bit pale herself. Old wounds were being opened here. Deep wounds.

'It's not fair to let people think it was me who rejected you,' Olivia continued. 'When it was totally the other way round. What kind of father just walks out of his kid's life and never looks back?'

He was looking back yesterday, Zac wanted to say. He was looking back and *crying*... But he kept his mouth shut and said nothing. Because he'd said too much already.

'The lousy kind,' Don said. 'And I don't blame you for hating me. I just don't understand why you've bothered coming all this way to find me.'

'Because someone suggested that I might regret not

taking the last chance I'll ever have to see you.' Olivia's chin rose. 'And I decided I wanted to tell you face to face what I thought of you. It's not much, actually. Not as a father. Or as a husband, for that matter. Mum told me how little support she got from you with her career choices. I'm not sure I think much of you as a doctor, either, when you're not even getting proper medical treatment. What kind of example is that to your patients? How can anyone trust you to do what's best for them if you won't even do it for yourself?'

Zac sucked in a breath. Wow… He might have wanted to say something similar to Don himself, but he'd never have delivered it with that much…passion. There were deep feelings there that were showing themselves in anger but he could feel something very different beneath what was showing. He could almost see a small girl who was bewildered and hurt because her father had abandoned her.

What on earth had made Don do something so appalling? There was a part of him who wanted to step in and simply give Olivia a hug. But he could imagine how unwelcome that would be. He shouldn't even be in this room. This was none of his business.

Don must have been reading his mind.

'This is none of your business,' he growled. Except that he was talking to Olivia, not Zac. 'I didn't ask you to come here. You shouldn't have come. You don't belong here, any more than your mother did. Why don't you just get out while the going's good?'

Oh, no… Zac found he was holding his breath. Could things get any worse?

Apparently, they could.

'Oh, don't worry.' Olivia was already turning on her heel. 'That's precisely what I'm going to do.'

Zac had to steel himself to meet Don's gaze as the door slammed behind his daughter. He knew he was going to be facing a man who had every right to be very angry with him.

Except he didn't look angry. He looked…as sad as anyone Zac had ever seen.

'You can go, too,' he said quietly. 'Just leave me alone, okay?'

Her hands were shaking so much that it took two attempts to get the rental car started. And then Olivia found that her vision was blurred by tears so she had to pull over, not far from where she'd stopped not so long ago, near the fire station. She swiped at her face and hauled in one deep breath after another as she tried to calm down. Why on earth was she so upset? Had she expected anything else from the man who'd walked out of her life when she was far too young to understand what might have driven him to do that? Had she had some deeply hidden hope that she might discover that her father did still love her, like that stranger had suggested in his phone message?

Of course he didn't. He hadn't expressed any desire to even see her before he died. That was simply a flight of fancy by someone who'd had no business interfering. Stirring up things that would have best been left alone. And, yes, it hurt but it was a pain Olivia had had plenty of practice dealing with. She'd had it nailed by the time she was in her early teens so nothing had really changed. She'd made a mistake by coming here, that was all, and the best that she could do now to repair the damage was to get away from this place as quickly as possible and try to just forget about it. At least she'd left the township behind now. There was farmland on either side of the road and she was heading towards the narrow, winding road that led through the gorge.

Not that it was going to be easy to push those stupidly intense minutes out of her head, she realised a few minutes later. It wasn't just that horrible conversation with her father, because she was already pushing that into the part of her brain where everything else to do with Donald Donaldson had been buried. No... There was another man whose image it might be even harder to erase. The troublemaker. Some kind of irresponsible bad boy who'd fallen into a forgotten corner of her life and had decided to wreak havoc.

It was quite possible she was going to be thinking about Isaac Cameron for a rather long time. Wondering why she'd never felt anything quite like that kind of tingle deep in her belly before and whether she would ever feel it again. That pull of sheer...desire that even thinking about the man could generate.

Good grief... Olivia shook her head. It wasn't just an electrical jolt she could feel in her body, she could hear a loud humming in her ears that was getting rapidly louder. So loud, she found herself looking up. And then she was stamping on the brake pedal and bringing her car to a complete halt as a single-engine light plane came from nowhere, only a short distance ahead of her, crossing the road barely above the level of her car's roof. Its engine was roaring as it gained some height and then it coughed and spluttered and the plane dipped again. What was the pilot trying to do—make an emergency landing in a farmer's field? If so, it needed to get a lot higher than it was, to clear the dense macrocarpa pine trees in the windbreak and how was it going to do that if its engine was dying?

Olivia watched in horror as the plane's wheels dragged through a treetop and then its wings tipped one way and then the other as it got rapidly closer to the ground, sheep scattering to get away from the overhead intrusion. It bounced as a wheel touched the ground but then the small aircraft rolled, nosedived and finally came to a shockingly abrupt halt upside down. Olivia sat there, frozen, for a moment and then jumped out of her car, her phone in her hand. She punched in the three-digit code for the emergency services.

'Where is your emergency?'

'I'm on State Highway One. About ten minutes out of Cutler's Creek, heading towards Dunedin.'

'What's happened?'

'It's a plane. It's crashed into a paddock. Small plane, a Cessna, maybe.'

'Do you have any idea of how many people are involved?'

'No… I couldn't see inside when it went over me.'

'What can you see now?'

'Um…' There was a puff of smoke coming from where the plane had crashed but Olivia was too far away to see whether there was any movement inside or around the plane. 'I can't see anything.' She needed to get closer but there was a barbed-wire fence and a ditch she would need to cross.

'Stay on the line,' she was told. 'Help's on its way.'

Olivia was looking up and down the road. How long was it going to take for that help to arrive? Surely someone would come past and be able to assist her with a first response? From the direction she'd come from, she could hear the faint wail of a civil defence siren. Were the local volunteer fire brigade and ambulance officers being summoned to the station?

Even if they were, it was going to take them at least several minutes to get here. Possibly crucial minutes if there were lives that were hanging in the balance. Someone with an arterial bleed, perhaps. Or now trapped upside down in a position that was occluding their airway. Olivia was a doctor—she couldn't stand here and do nothing, even though the prospect of being first on this scene was actually rather terrifying. She'd worked in emergency departments with all the equipment and staff available to back up or take over an attempt to save a life but here…here she was entirely on her own and in a huge space with those towering mountains in the background that were still making her feel insignificant and she had nothing and nobody to help and…

It was possibly the first time in her life that Olivia Donaldson had to rely entirely on herself and her own judgement and to act so fast it had to be based on instinct as well as any skills she had learned over the years. Those skills didn't include getting over a fence with barbed wire on the top but Olivia pulled apart two strands lower down on the fence, put her head through and then one leg and somehow the rest of her body followed easily enough, although she could feel the side seam of her narrow skirt catch and rip a little. She set off across the uneven grassed land at a run and all she was thinking about as she got closer to the plane was how she was going to try and get the doors open and how badly hurt the occupants might be and how on earth she was going to get them out and look after them with nothing more than her bare hands.

Slowing down as she got close to the plane wasn't just to catch her breath. Long ago, at medical school, Olivia had attended an interesting workshop that paramedics had given about being first on the scene at any emergency. Snippets were drifting back into her head and she knew that the first thing she had to do was to assess the scene for any dangers to herself and any other rescuers that would be arriving. Things like broken glass or leaking fuel that could present a fire hazard or power lines that were down. A glance back towards the road confirmed that nearby power lines seemed to still be intact.

It also showed Olivia that a vehicle with a flashing light on its roof had come through the gate of this huge paddock further down the road. It wasn't a fire truck or an ambulance. It looked like an SUV and the light was one of those magnetic temporary ones. Someone was driving rapidly towards her. It should have been far too far away to recognise the driver but Olivia had no doubt at all about who it was.

Isaac Cameron.

It didn't matter that it was the person who had just stirred up a part of her past that should have been left well alone. She had never been so pleased at the prospect of seeing anyone in her whole life.

She wasn't facing this alone, after all.

CHAPTER THREE

ISAAC CAMERON HAD never expected to see this woman again.

She wouldn't have been his first choice to work with in an emergency situation, either, but—fair play—when he'd arrived, he'd seen how hard she'd been running across this paddock with the obvious intention of helping whoever was in this plane. As he pulled his vehicle to a halt and leapt out to get his medical pack from the back, part of his brain registered that she must have ripped that tight skirt of her power suit getting past the barbed wire on the fence and she probably wouldn't appreciate the fact that her careful hairstyle was coming a little unravelled and that she was now well splattered with animal manure but, in this moment, her appearance was totally irrelevant to either of them.

'Did you see it come down?' Zac dropped his pack near a wingtip and bent to get beneath the diagonal strut that connected the wing to the fuselage of the small aircraft.

'Yes. It went right in front of my car.'

'So it was trying to land?' Zac could see the slumped figure of a man in the cockpit.

'I think so. It sounded like there was something wrong with the engine. The wheels got caught in the trees. It flipped over right at the last second and there was a bang when it stopped so suddenly.'

Zac wasn't surprised. The propeller had dug itself deep into the soil. The Plexiglas of the windshield was broken, too, and there were splatters of blood on it. He leaned to look in further.

'I can't see any passengers. I think it's just the pilot.' He rapped on the side window. 'Hello…can you hear me? I'm a doctor. We're here to help you.'

'Is…is he still alive?'

She sounded as if she really cared.

'He's not responding.' He tried the door. It opened an inch or two but then stuck. He braced his back against the strut and wrenched harder. With a third attempt and the screech of metal against metal he shifted the door enough to reach the victim. He eased him back, upright enough to ensure that his airway was open, keeping hold of his head to protect his neck. A trickle of blood rolled down the man's forehead from an injury hidden in his hair. That could be where the blood on the windscreen had come from, which meant there was a potential head injury to be concerned about. The man groaned loudly as he was moved.

'What's hurting, mate?' The man wasn't local, which was a relief. In a small place like Cutler's Creek, an accident scene often meant they were treating someone they knew well and Isaac knew exactly how devastating that could be—like that time their local police officer had arrived at a car accident involving his own son.

On a personal level for Zac, any emergency scene carried the threat of a flashback, along with a memory of Mia. It was no wonder he'd been able to start shutting down the ability to care too much after that—a skill that might have ended up being too well honed but was still useful in some situations, like when he'd had to work on Bruce's son, but it was always easier when the patient was a stranger. And the really disturbing flashbacks had stopped long ago.

'My back…' the man groaned. 'And my leg…'

'Are you having any trouble breathing?'

'Hurts…'

Zac could hear that his breathing was rapid and shallow but it was too cramped to try and assess anything in here.

'What's your name?'

'Dave…Wilson.' He groaned again and tried to roll his head away from Zac's grip. He tightened his hold to limit the movement.

'Do you know where you are?'

'I… It's… Oh, God…what's happened?'

'You've been in an accident. Try not to move, Dave,' Zac told him. 'We're going to get you out of here, okay?' He turned his head to meet a wide-eyed gaze from Olivia. She looked scared, he thought, and he could understand why. Used to the clean environment of first-world hospitals and a team around her, she was a long way out of her comfort zone right now. But her determination was obvious in the way she pulled back a tress of her hair that the wind had caught and shoved it behind one ear as she raised her chin. She wasn't about to let any nerves get in the way of what needed to be done.

'There's a cervical collar clipped to the side of my pack, there. Could you pass it to me, please?'

'Sure.'

He had the plastic and foam collar in his hands seconds later and he carefully slipped it into place and fastened the Velcro straps.

'Ow...'

'Sorry, mate. I know it's not comfortable but we need to protect your neck. We'll get you something for the pain as soon as we get you out.'

We...

As if they were a team? Zac knew the local first response would be on their way already. He could hear voice traffic on the radio that was clipped to the dashboard of his vehicle but he couldn't hear what was being said. He needed to update the emergency services as soon as he could to make sure a rescue helicopter had been dispatched but, yes...for the moment, he and Don Donaldson's daughter felt like a team.

Still keeping a protective hand on the man's forehead, he reached for the fastening of the safety harness with his other hand.

'Dammit...'

'What is it?'

'I can't reach the catch.'

'Maybe I can.' Olivia spoke before he could make the same suggestion.

She had to squeeze past him into the narrow space

he'd created. She was pressed right against his body by the time she was reaching in, trying to follow the safety harness to its catch.

'Be careful. There's sharp stuff in here.'

'He's bleeding. A lot.'

'Where from?'

'I can't see… Lower leg, maybe.'

'We need to get him out. Stat.'

'I can feel the catch but…it's not working.'

Zac saw the way her forehead furrowed with the effort she was making. And the way she caught her bottom lip between her teeth. She was pressing even harder against him, making it impossible for him to move that arm.

'My back pocket.'

'What?'

'I've got a multi-tool in the back pocket of my jeans. Get it out and we'll cut the harness.'

He felt her fingers slide into his pocket. He shouldn't have been thinking of anything but looking after his patient's cervical spine, watching any movements of his chest to try and assess just how much difficulty the pilot was having breathing, and planning ahead for the urgent assessment and treatment that would be needed the moment they could free their patient from the wreckage, but…

…but it felt as if there was no layer of denim between those fingers and the bare skin of his buttock and, just for a nanosecond, Zac was aware of…heat. Skin-scorching, spine-tingling *heat*… And it was the first time he'd felt even a hint of something like that since… Oh… *God*… It wasn't just an emergency scene that could bring back a memory of Mia, was it? He might not want to be someone who felt nothing at all but the pendulum swinging too far the other way—to huge emotions that could prove impossible to control—was just as undesirable.

'Take that cap off the side.' His command came out as a snap. 'See that V-shaped notch?'

'Yes.'

'Put the edge of the safety belt into that notch and just pull. Mind your fingers, it's sharp.'

Zac was holding onto the pilot with both hands to steady both his neck and his body as Olivia sliced through the heavy straps. Despite how nervous she'd looked when he'd arrived at this scene, she hadn't hesitated in following his instructions, he noticed, and she'd checked to see that their patient was supported before she cut the second strap. Then, in what seemed like an automatic gesture, she recapped the sharp implement and slipped it into the pocket of her jacket.

She was thorough, he thought. And pretty courageous, given the way she had virtually climbed into this wreck to help. Moments later, as Olivia took the weight of Dave's legs as Zac lifted his upper body, keeping him as straight as possible as they eased him to the ground beside the plane, he had to add an impression of surprising strength that this woman had.

There were so many things that needed to be done. The cries of pain from Dave let Zac know that his airway was still clear but he needed to be on oxygen to compensate for any breathing difficulty and he needed pain relief as soon as possible, which meant getting an IV line in. He needed to have any severe bleeding controlled and, given how agitated he was, it might well be necessary to sedate and intubate him so that they could transport him safely.

Zac could hear the siren of the first local response getting closer but while the volunteers here were well trained for fire-fighting and a basic level of first aid, he had to hope that Olivia Donaldson's clinical skills were on the same level as her courage and strength.

She'd never seen anyone work like this.

Isaac Cameron only had the contents of his pack to work with until the local ambulance arrived but you would have thought he was in a resuscitation area of a well-equipped emergency department given how smoothly he was using his resources.

Including her, along with the two ambulance officers that arrived within minutes of them getting Dave out of the wreckage of his plane. It was Olivia who was doing the most to assist, however, as the most qualified extra medic on the scene. She was the one who put an IV line into their patient's arm while Zac was busy assessing both Dave's head and chest injuries. She drew up the drugs needed for pain relief as the paramedics controlled the bleeding from an open fracture of his lower leg.

One of them looked up. 'D'you guys smell that?'

Zac unhooked his stethoscope from his ears and inhaled sharply. 'You're right, Ben. We've got a fuel leak happening somewhere.'

'At least the firies are on their way. I can hear their siren.'

'We still need to move him.' The other young man jumped to his feet. 'I'll get the scoop.'

'Move back,' Zac ordered Olivia. 'At least to the other side of the ambulance. This isn't safe.'

'It's never been safe.' She shook her head. 'And I'm not going anywhere.' She leaned towards Dave's head. 'Are you allergic to any medicine you know of, Dave?'

'Don't think so… Oh, *God*…it still hurts…'

'I know. I'm about to give you something for that. It might make you feel a bit woozy.' Olivia flicked the syringe and then pressed the plunger to expel any air, removing the needle and attaching the syringe to the Luer plug but glancing up before she actually injected the drug. She knew Zac was watching her and it was polite to get his permission before going any further. As bizarre as this situation was, it was *his* territory and he was in charge here.

He held her gaze for the split second it took for him to nod and she could see something more than permission to administer the drugs in that look. Respect, perhaps? Whatever it was, it felt good enough for any residual nerves at having to work in such unusual circumstances to dissipate almost entirely.

The paramedics had a bright orange, plastic stretcher that was separated into two pieces.

'We're going to roll him to each side and slip the

stretcher together underneath to clip together,' Zac told her. 'We need to be careful to keep spinal alignment, okay? I've got his head. You take his upper arm and the guys will do the rest. Ready? On the count of three. One…two…*three*…'

Carefully, but swiftly, they log-rolled the pilot to one side enough to get half the stretcher in place and then they repeated the procedure on the other side. Olivia had to scramble to her feet, then, as the three men, working as a well-oiled team, lifted the stretcher and shifted it rapidly to a safer area of the paddock. Olivia gathered up as much of the gear as she could and ran after them. She could see the fire engine coming into the paddock but then she heard the *whoosh* of fuel igniting behind them, felt the instant blast of heat from the flames and she missed her footing and fell.

No…she hadn't tripped, she realised a split second later. She'd been grabbed and pushed and she still had a pair of strong, male arms around her body. A body virtually on top of hers, in fact, but that wasn't as startling as the eyes that were so close to her own. Caramel-coloured eyes that had such an intense expression that Olivia's heart skipped a beat. Was it *fear* she was seeing?

Whatever it was, it was gone in another heartbeat. Zac scrambled to his feet and offered her a hand to get up.

'Sorry about that. I wasn't sure how close we were to that explosion, that's all.'

So he'd thrown himself on top of her to protect her?

Wow… Olivia felt the need to suck in a deep breath.

'You're not hurt, are you?' The query was concerned

but she could see that Isaac's head was turning towards where their patient had been placed.

'No. I just got a bit of a fright, that's all.' A glance at the flames engulfing the wreckage of the plane made Olivia realise that she was still rather nervous but she remembered how little Isaac had thought of her when he'd left that voicemail on her phone and she didn't want him to think she was pathetic, as well.

Except he didn't seem to. There was understanding in his gaze now. And more of what she'd seen before that had given her so much confidence. That look that made her think he might actually be impressed.

'It's okay. Our firies will get that sorted. We're safe here.'

Sure enough, the fire engine had reached the plane wreckage now and there were people running and shouting as they readied their gear to deal with the fire. The gate to the paddock had been left open behind them, Olivia noticed, and a mob of panicked sheep was now streaming out onto the main road. Perhaps their patient was aware of the chaos around him because he had suddenly become more agitated as Zac and Olivia reached him.

'Dave? Can you hear me?' Ben was speaking loudly. 'Don't move... *Dave?*'

'He's not responding.' Zac seemed oblivious to anything else that was going on around them as he turned swiftly back to lean over the stretcher and check Dave's level of consciousness. Olivia could see that he wasn't opening his eyes and his speech had become no more than incoherent groaning.

Zac had asked one of the paramedics to radio for an update. 'How far away is the chopper?'

'Ten to fifteen minutes,' Ben told him.

'I'm going to do a rapid sequence intubation,' Zac said. 'His LOC is dropping and he's not going to be safe to transport if he's this agitated.'

The young paramedic reached for a plastic pouch in the pack beside her. He glanced at Zac, who nodded in Olivia's direction.

'You happy to assist me with an RSI?' he asked.

'Of course.' Olivia held her hands out to take the pouch that she could see contained the drugs and instruments that would be needed for the procedure. Having enjoyed her training in anaesthetics so much as a junior doctor, she was very familiar with every aspect of the use of strong drugs to sedate a patient and then the sometimes tricky task of easing a tube into the trachea to protect an airway and take over someone's breathing. She had only ever done it in the anteroom of a sterile operating theatre, mind you, with any number of staff and all the equipment that might be needed if something went wrong. The thought of doing it in the middle of a paddock, with smouldering plane wreckage in the background and people yelling from the road where they were trying to deal with the mob of sheep now causing a traffic hazard was…well, it was actually rather exciting.

Thrilling, even, Olivia decided minutes later as she injected the drug that was going to paralyse Dave and watched Zac as he knelt behind the pilot's head and focused on the procedure, ready to assist with whatever else he needed her to do, like putting pressure on the cricoid cartilage at the front of the neck to aid tube placement. He had to use both hands, one manipulating the laryngoscope and the other inserting the endotracheal tube, and it felt like only seconds later that he was attaching the bag mask and holding that with one hand to provide ventilation as he used his stethoscope with his other hand to listen to breath sounds and check that the tube placement was correct. The whole procedure had been so swift and smooth that Olivia could feel her jaw dropping.

Wow… How clever were this man's hands? And how confident was he?

The rescue helicopter was coming in to land by the time they had secured the tube and made sure that all the measurements they were monitoring were acceptable. A smaller helicopter was not far behind it.

'News crew,' someone said. 'National TV.'

The air rescue aircraft landed well away from where they were working but Olivia could feel the chop of the rotors beating in her own body. They didn't shut down the engine because the crew knew their patient had already been stabilised and they would be able to take off again within minutes. They also seemed to know Zac well and he got waves and thumbs-up signals before the doors were shut and the aircraft took off again. The news crew was hovering nearby, clearly filming the accident scene and the final moments of the pilot's rescue, before swinging away.

The beat of rotors increased as the air rescue chopper lifted off and Zac turned as his hand dropped from the wave he'd been returning. His gaze caught Olivia's as they both turned to begin walking back to where his vehicle was parked near the ambulance, and maybe he was feeling the same kind of adrenaline rush that she was at being part of this extraordinary incident, because he smiled at her. A kind of lop-sided, almost grin that lit up his face and somehow coalesced with the vibration of the sound from the helicopter into something that Olivia could feel right down to her bones and then radiating out in an intensified version of the tingle she'd been aware of when she'd first set eyes on this man. It wasn't just this crazy situation or the rush of having worked to try and save someone's life that was thrilling, was it?

There was something about Isaac Cameron that was threatening to become the most memorable aspect of this brief, unexpected interruption to Olivia's life, and that was disturbing enough to make her break the eye contact without returning that smile. She glanced at her watch as if knowing the time of day was of the utmost importance. Which, of course, it was.

'Oh…*no*…'

'Problem?' Zac wasn't smiling any more.

'I haven't got a hope of getting back to Dunedin in time to catch my flight.'

A hint of that smile made one side of his mouth twitch and Olivia glared at him. He was finding this amusing? But Zac was oblivious to her glare because he wasn't looking at her face. How rude was that, to be eyeing her body up and down like some cheeky teenaged boy?

'Don't suppose you brought a change of clothes with you?'

'What?' Olivia hadn't given a thought to what state she was in but Zac's comment gave her a vague recollection of ripping her skirt on that barbed-wire fence. She looked down and then closed her eyes for a heartbeat as she groaned aloud. Her clothes weren't just ripped— they were filthy, with streaks of dirt and blood and… good grief…sheep manure? Those shoes would never be the same.

The paramedics were loading the last of their gear back into the ambulance.

'We put your pack in the back of your car, Zac,' Ben called.

'Thanks, mate.'

'See you soon, yeah? Training session tomorrow night?'

'Sure thing—as long as the weather doesn't get too gnarly.'

'True. If that storm gets here early we might be busy rescuing people, not training. Either way, we'll be seeing you soon.'

The firies were also packing up their gear, preparing to leave, as Olivia and Zac neared his SUV. A police car coming into the paddock slowed and then stopped as it got close. The driver's window rolled down.

'Hey, Zac… Bit of excitement for you, I hear?'

'Yep. If you need a statement, though, Dr Donaldson here is your woman, Bruce. She witnessed the crash.'

'Dr Donaldson?' The older man blinked but then collected himself. 'Yes, a statement would be great. I'm going to be on site until the Civil Aviation investigators arrive. They'll want to talk to her as well, I expect.' He shifted his gaze to Olivia. 'You staying for a while?'

'No. I'm on my way back to Auckland. That's my car out there...' Olivia pointed to the road. She could only see the roof of her car because it was surrounded by sheep.

'It would be helpful if you could stay long enough to give a statement.'

'And you might want to have a shower and get your clothes washed before you go anywhere,' Zac added. 'Come back to the hospital with me and we'll get you sorted.'

'No *way*.' Olivia was not going near Cutler's Creek Community Hospital again. Ever. She could still hear that dismissive tone of her father's voice telling her that she shouldn't have come in the first place. That she should get out while the going was good. She hadn't forgotten the stares of strangers, either. Curious but vaguely judgemental. Like the look on this police officer's face right now as he took a notebook from his shirt pocket.

'Be a good idea to stay in town for a few hours,' he advised. 'Perhaps you can give me your phone number so I can get in touch when the investigators get here. Hopefully it won't be too long.' He wrote down the number that Olivia recited and then nodded at Zac before driving closer to the plane wreckage.

'Keep me posted,' was all he said.

Zac raised an eyebrow at Olivia. 'How 'bout my place, instead? Not so far from here. Far enough away from town. I've got to head back to work but you'd be welcome to use my shower. And I've got a washing machine.' The corner of his mouth quirked again, making her think that this man was far too easily amused. 'I've even got Wi-Fi. You might be able to change your ticket and get a later plane tonight. And you won't be running from the law without providing your statement. Not that I expect you'd ever do anything remotely illegal…'

There was something confusing about this man, Olivia realised. At times he seemed completely laid-back and confident. At other times, he was judgemental and aloof. Arrogant, even, like he had been when he'd left that voicemail on her phone? But there'd been that moment after the plane wreckage had exploded and she could have sworn she'd seen what had looked like fear in his eyes. Or horror, even. What had that been about?

She had to admit she was curious but she was also busy weighing up her options. She couldn't simply drive off into the sunset. Quite apart from being obliged to speak to the people who would be investigating this crash, there was no way she could go anywhere looking like this. There might be a shop in town that would sell clothing but she'd already had enough of people staring at her. Besides, she hadn't realised until now how cold the wind was and the thought of a hot shower in the not-too-distant future was more than appealing. Even if there was a motel available in this small town, it would take time to find it. Isaac Cameron was offering her by far the best possible solution, she realised. And maybe she could justify her willingness to accept as a case of better the devil you knew?

'Fine,' she said ungraciously. 'I could use your place. As long as you won't be there.' Both Zac's eyebrows were raised now and Olivia suddenly felt ashamed of herself. 'Thanks,' she muttered. 'I appreciate the offer.'

'Least I can do,' Zac said calmly. 'I appreciated your help here. Reckon we might have saved that guy's life, don't you?'

Olivia caught her bottom lip between her teeth. She didn't want Zac to know how proud it made her feel that he'd found her assistance helpful. Or that potentially saving a life was the most satisfying thing she had done medically in rather a long time. She made a vague sound of agreement, however, as she turned her head to look again at the hundreds of sheep milling around her rental car.

'How am I going to get to my car?'

He was grinning. 'You're a real city girl, aren't you?'

Actually, no, Olivia wanted to tell him. I got sent away to boarding school when I was only five and it was out in the country. There were plenty of sheep around there. And then my mother found me another boarding school in the countryside in England and I even had my own pony, but you know what? I'd rather have been a city girl. Living with my own family…

But it wasn't any of his business and she wasn't about to tell him something that he might relate to her father—the man who had probably been happy to agree with her mother and send her away in the first place—so Olivia said nothing.

Zac's grin faded and then he shrugged. 'The sheep won't bother you, I promise. Someone will round them

up and get them back in here as soon as we've gone.
Jump in…' He held the passenger door of his SUV open.
'I'll get you back to your car and then you can just fol-
low me.'

Thank goodness he'd done a bit of housework over the
last few days. The kitchen bench wasn't piled with its
usual collection of used pots and plates and there were
clean towels available. Zac led the way into a hallway,
opened a cupboard and handed two of the towels to
Olivia.

'Bathroom's down the end of the hall. There's plenty
of stuff like shampoo. Probably not what you're used to
but it'll do the job. If you need something to wear while
you wash your stuff, try the bottom drawer of the tall-
boy in my bedroom. There's a bunch of old track pants
and jeans and sweatshirts that I only use for training
days. They'll be a bit big but they're all clean and they
should keep you warm.' He didn't want to think about
what Olivia might or might not be wearing under any
borrowed clothes. He didn't want to think about her
standing in his shower, either. Totally naked…

The sooner he got back to the hospital, the better. 'I'll
throw a couple of new logs in the pot belly stove in the
kitchen. I don't have a dryer but if you put your clothes
on the rack above the stove, they'll dry in no time.'

'Thanks.' Olivia was following him as he went to
poke the fire back into life. 'Do you have a code for
your Wi-Fi?'

'Yep. It's pinned to that corkboard there.'

'Do you want to me to lock up when I leave?'

'I never bother. Pretty safe place, Cutler's Creek.' Zac closed the door of the stove after putting more fuel into it. Maybe it was the lick of new flames he could see that were making him feel so on edge again. They were reminders of both unexpected heat and potentially dangerous explosions.

Yeah…he was a lot more rattled than he wanted to think about. 'Right, then… I'd better go. I'll let Bruce know where he can find you when they're ready for that statement.'

'I'd better get on with cleaning myself up.' Unexpectedly, she smiled at him. 'Thanks again, Zac.'

Oh, wow…it was the first time he'd seen any hint of a smile on her face and it was some smile. Generous and warm and it made her lips curve into the most enchanting shape ever. He'd already realised that Olivia Donaldson was quite possibly the most beautiful woman he'd ever met in real life but that smile just took the package to a whole new level and that was even more disturbing than whatever heat and fear had been flickering along with those flames.

His mouth went dry as he turned away, so he didn't say anything by way of a farewell, just raised his hand as he left. It was a good thing that she wouldn't be here by the time he got home again in a few hours' time. It was going to take some time and effort to get past the ripples of disturbance this woman had been a part of today. Zac had the feeling he could well be haunted by echoes that were unlikely to fade any time soon.

If ever…

CHAPTER FOUR

TO SEE THAT small red rental car still parked outside his barn when he drove home was a surprise, to say the least.

Zac was trying to decide whether his heart rate had picked up because the surprise was a pleasant one, rather than a potential problem, when he walked inside his house to find Olivia in his kitchen, wearing a pair of his ancient track pants and a sweatshirt with the sleeves rolled up. This was even more disconcerting, especially when the scent of the shampoo and soap she had used was so familiar it made it seem like she belonged here. She had not only washed her hair, which was hanging in loose waves down her back, she had also washed off any makeup she'd been wearing. She should have looked a lot less attractive but, in fact, the opposite was true. Olivia Donaldson not only still looked impossibly gorgeous but now seemed far more approachable—with a girl-next-door vibe instead of a supermodel pretending to be a private surgeon.

So, okay…maybe the surprise *was* pleasant. Especially given that Zac had recovered from the rattled sensation he'd had after that accident scene and that Olivia's antagonism seemed to have worn off for the time being.

'Sorry,' she said to him by way of a greeting. 'I meant to be gone long ago but I was waiting for the wash cycle to finish and then those people from the crash investigation turned up and I forgot to take things out to put on the rack…' Her nose crinkled to give her an apologetic expression. '…and I'm still here…'

'So I see.' Zac had been caught by that nose crinkling thing, which had offered a glimpse of a very different side to the sophisticated woman who had turned up in his hospital earlier this afternoon. 'No problem. Did you manage to change your flight?'

'Yes, but I couldn't get another one till early afternoon tomorrow. I've been online trying to find a motel nearby but the only place within a hundred miles or so seems to be the pub, is that right?'

'Yeah…' Should he warn her that word had got out that Don Donaldson's daughter had turned up to visit him only to storm off again, slamming the door behind her like a spoilt child, and that the community of Cutler's Creek wasn't exactly impressed? That he was thinking it wasn't such a good idea for her to stay at the pub must have shown in his face because Olivia shook her head and her breath came out in a tiny snort.

'I was wondering about that. They're not going to welcome the prodigal daughter, right? Guess I'll hit the road and find a motel in Dunedin, then.'

'It's getting dark. I wouldn't advise driving through that gorge when you're not familiar with the road. Especially with this wind picking up.'

'Oh…'

She was looking slightly anxious now and, along with that uncontrolled hair and the way that no makeup made her look years younger, it gave the impression of a vulnerability that tugged at something deep within Zac. And then something else blindsided him completely. She might look like this first thing in the morning, he thought, when she was waking up all rumpled from sleep in a strange bed after the first night of passionate sex with a new lover. Out of her comfort zone and wondering about the best way to handle things? *Oh*… Zac actually felt slightly weak at the knees. Imagine being that man. That lucky, *lucky* man…

Was it his imagination or did Olivia's pupils suddenly dilate to make her eyes look an even darker shade of blue? The way the tip of her tongue came out to moisten her lips was certainly not a figment of his imagination and it had an instant effect on his body that had nothing to do with his knees. So did that husky note in her voice. Was it possible that Olivia was just as aware of the sudden sexual tension in the atmosphere as he was?

'What *would* you advise, then?'

For a crazy few seconds, ludicrous things that Zac would very much have liked to suggest bounced around inside his skull. Not in words so much as an urge to simply pull this woman into his arms and cover her lips with his own to see if it was possible that she tasted as good as she looked. He wanted to kiss her senseless. To pick her up and carry her off to his bedroom, like some sort of caveman. Of course, he wasn't going to do any of those things. That would be a huge mistake.

It wasn't that he'd lived like a monk since he'd lost Mia. Far from it. But this felt different. For one thing, Olivia Donaldson was the daughter of his boss—a man he respected a great deal. For another, sex for Zac for years now had been a connection that was nothing more than something physical. And transient. This woman was making him feel things that were too intense to be comfortable and that made her...dangerous?

No. Zac had this under control. He even managed to keep his tone perfectly casual as he deliberately turned away to peer out of the kitchen window.

'I'm sure we can think of something by the time your clothes are dry. If the worst comes to the worst, there's a spare bed here.'

Dear Lord...the way he had *looked* at her even though it had only been for a matter of a second. Two, tops. But nobody had ever looked at her like that. As if nothing else in the world existed. As if he wanted to drag her off by her hair and have his wicked way with her.

Oh, *my*...

Olivia could feel colour flooding into her cheeks. Thank goodness she was looking at Zac's back now as he looked out of the window. Her heart rate had picked up so much it felt like he would have been able to see it making her chest jump despite the generous covering of the oversized sweatshirt and surely nobody could have missed that blush.

She couldn't possibly stay in the same house as this man because she knew what could very well happen. And that couldn't be allowed to happen because random sexual encounters with complete strangers had never, ever been acceptable to Olivia and she wasn't about to start breaking her own moral code now. She hadn't even slept with Patrick until he'd made it very clear that he was serious about a significant relationship with her.

But…there was a tiny voice in the back of her head telling her that Patrick had never looked at her like that. That no man had. That maybe she would never find anyone else who would. And she couldn't deny that there was a strong sense of curiosity, as well. If a man could do that to you, just with his eyes, what could he be capable of doing with his hands? Or his tongue…or…or…

'You might be right about the drive…' Olivia had to clear her throat. How embarrassing was that—to sound so husky? 'But… I can't stay here.'

Of course she could, that little voice insisted. It would only be one night of her life and nobody else ever needed to know about it. Besides…maybe nothing would happen. Maybe she had imagined that look.

'Up to you.' Zac turned away from the window. 'You've got a bit of time to think about it while your clothes are drying, anyway. I'll be outside for a bit. I need to go and see Chloe.'

'Chloe?' Olivia blinked. Was there another woman around here somewhere? A neighbour perhaps…or a girlfriend? And how ridiculous was it that the thought was so disappointing?

'You haven't noticed the biggest horse in the world in the back garden?' Zac opened the fridge and took out a handful of carrots. As he closed the door, there was a gentle clinking sound from wine bottles stored in a rack on top of the fridge. 'Feel free to open one of those, if you like,' he added. 'You'll find the corkscrew in the drawer by the sink.'

A combination of the emotional upheaval of that encounter with her father and then the adrenaline rush of helping with the emergency response at the accident scene on top of the fatigue of a very early start for all that travelling made the prospect of a glass of wine irresistible. Not that Olivia was about to admit it, even to herself, but there was also the bonus that if she had a glass of wine or two, the decision of whether or not she needed to stay off the road for the night would be made for her.

Putting the corkscrew back into the drawer after dealing with a cork, Olivia glanced out the window to see Zac with the carrots in one hand and a biscuit of hay under his other arm, walking towards a wooden gate beneath an archway of hedge that made a perfect frame for the horse that was standing there. With the background of snow-peaked mountains, the image looked like a postcard and there was something about the beauty of it that actually brought a lump to her throat. Gusts of wind were stealing wisps of the hay and she could hear the welcoming sounds the horse was making as it saw food and company arriving. That sound was enough to make Olivia have to blink away a sudden prickle behind her eyes.

It was another memory that had been long locked away. That soft nicker of equine pleasure and the joy that was contagious. She could almost feel the warmth of her beloved pony Koko and smell the distinctive scent that had always been there as she'd wrapped her arms around his neck and buried her face against his skin. It was a memory that tugged at her heartstrings enough to be painful.

Rather like the memories she'd already fielded earlier today that were connected to the father she'd remembered. A man who didn't seem to exist any more. Maybe her memories weren't actually real. Had she, in fact, created memories of the kind of man any child would have wanted her father to have been?

Olivia took a huge gulp of the glass of wine she had just poured as she continued staring out the window. Zac had opened the gate and the horse was rubbing its huge head on his arm. It *was* a huge horse. Zac had to be at least a few inches over six feet tall but his head didn't reach Chloe's shoulder. Daylight was fading fast but that only made the horse's fluffy white feet and the blaze on her nose more obvious.

'Is Chloe a Clydesdale?' she asked when Zac came back into the kitchen.

'Not purebred, I was told, but close enough.'

'Do you ride her?'

Zac laughed. 'Are you kidding? I'd need a ladder to get on board. And it would be a long way to fall off. Besides…she might be pregnant. Apparently.'

'Apparently?'

'She came with the house. The guy who owns this place is overseas and he wanted someone to look after things, including the hens and his horse, but I've been here for nearly a year and there's no sign of any baby so

I think he's going to be disappointed.' Zac was looking at her empty glass. 'Want a refill?'

'Um…' This was decision time. A second glass would mean she wasn't going to be driving anywhere. She opened her mouth to say something but the words that emerged were unplanned. 'Not if I'm drinking alone…'

And there it was again…that *look*…

'Just the one, then,' Zac murmured. 'It's not my night on call but…you never know what might happen, do you?'

Olivia didn't say anything. She couldn't. That lilt in his voice seemed to be a lot more noticeable when he spoke softly and it tickled her ears deliciously. The innuendo in his words had also been more than enough to silence her. He wasn't really talking about potential medical emergencies, was he?

The atmosphere in this room suddenly felt different—as if all her senses were strangely heightened. Olivia watched the rich red of the wine tumbling into the clear glass. She could hear the gurgle of the liquid but she could also hear the sound of Zac's breath. She caught the faint waft of Chloe coming from his clothing but, beneath that, she could catch the scent of the man himself and she could swear she was aware of the actual heat of his skin. It might very well be a mistake to stay here but there was probably nothing on earth that could have persuaded her to leave.

Oh, man. What did he think he was doing, playing with fire like this?

Was he just trying to prove to himself how in control

he was? Yeah…maybe that was it. Olivia followed his lead and sat down at the old wooden kitchen table but she seemed to be avoiding looking at him for a minute by letting her gaze drift around the room, taking in copper pots hanging beneath a high shelf and the wooden rack with her clothes draped over it above the pot belly stove inside a brick chimney.

'This is nice,' she said. 'Rustic.'

'I like it,' Zac agreed. 'Reminds me a bit of the farmhouse I grew up in. In County Cork in Ireland.'

'I thought it was an Irish accent.'

The expression in those blue eyes suggested that Olivia could quite happily sit here and just listen to him talking. And that maybe his accent wasn't the only thing she liked about him. He liked it that he had her attention like this, he realised. He liked it rather a lot.

'So what brought you all the way down under to one of New Zealand's smallest towns?'

'I guess it was one of the few countries I hadn't been to. And I needed a change from big cities.'

'So you've travelled a lot?'

'Aye… I think I was born an adrenaline junkie. Always been on the hunt for adventure and excitement, me. It's no wonder my poor mother went grey so early.'

'What made you choose medicine for a career, then? Instead of being, oh, I don't know…a helicopter pilot?'

'You'd be surprised how often doctors get to go in helicopters. Especially if they put their hand up to work in war zones. Or as part of a trauma team in a major hospital like Chicago or Boston.'

Her eyes had widened. 'War zones? Really?'

'It was where I headed as soon as I was qualified enough. It's not something you can do forever, though. It's…tough…'

'I can't begin to imagine what it's like,' Olivia said quietly. She was holding his gaze and this time Zac could see respect in her eyes. And something more. Concern? Empathy, even? 'But that explains why you reacted so fast when that plane exploded. And why you looked so…'

'So…what?' Zac swallowed a mouthful of his wine but he didn't break the eye contact with Olivia. What had she seen? And why did she care?

'So… I don't know. Kind of haunted. As if something terrible was happening. Or had happened.'

'It's a long time ago now,' Zac said slowly. 'And I thought it was well behind me but I guess explosions don't happen that often and they're certainly a trigger for things I'd rather forget. It took me a while to get past the flashbacks.'

Olivia didn't say anything but her gaze told him that she was listening. Really listening. Maybe that was why he gave in to the impulse to tell her something he'd never told anybody. Or maybe he was just pushing some personal boundaries because he'd been rattled today but he'd coped perfectly well. Could he risk poking an old wound to see if it might actually be completely healed?

'I had an army medic friend,' he told her. 'Mia. A very good friend. More than a friend, in fact—we were planning to get married after that tour of duty. She was walking ahead of me one day and she stepped on a landmine.' He could do this, Zac realised. He could say the words and still keep enough distance. It felt like he was describing something he'd seen in a movie, perhaps. 'It took both her legs off and she died within a couple of minutes.'

About as long as it had taken for him to get to her and hold her in his arms, but even letting that thought surface seemed to be okay. There was no sense that some kind of mental dam was about to burst and drown him in emotion. He didn't dare take the final step, though, and admit that it had been his fault. That Mia wouldn't have even been there if he hadn't persuaded her to stay on until he was due to leave.

Olivia had her hand pressed against her mouth. She looked so shocked, Zac thought. How much more shocked would she be, though, if he told her that losing Mia like that had taught him to build barriers and protect himself by not caring too much? That it was even worse to get so good at keeping his distance that it was possible to witness a death—even that of a child—and feel absolutely nothing? That that had been the point at which he'd thought he might have to walk away from medicine forever.

No. He wasn't going to say anything more. He shouldn't have said anything in the first place but this was turning out to be a very strange day. He hadn't expected Olivia Donaldson to crash into his life. Or a plane to crash, for that matter. They were both in the category of once-in-a-lifetime events.

'Anyway…that was probably a lot more information than you wanted but it's part of the reason I ended up here. I needed some time out, I guess.' He wanted to change the subject now. 'I'd rather talk about *you*, Olivia Donaldson. I'm curious about why it only took a phone call for you to turn up in Cutler's Creek. And I'm wondering why your father never made a call like that years ago.'

Olivia shrugged. 'I guess you'll have to ask him that.'

'Don't you want to know?'

'I'm not sure I do. Like you, there are things I think I'd rather forget.'

'Fair enough.' Zac was still pushing away what he hadn't told Olivia about. Would he ever be able to forget holding that small, dying child and not feeling as if his heart was breaking? Not being able to feel anything at all? Needing something physical to do to distract himself, he eyed the receding level of wine in Olivia's glass. 'Top-up?'

'It is very nice wine.'

It was probably an unconscious action for Olivia to run her tongue slowly over her lower lip but Zac couldn't look away. If she looked up and caught his gaze right now and there was any hint of what he'd thought he'd seen in her eyes before, there would be no turning back. Hurriedly, he pushed back his chair and stood up, heading for the wine bottle on the kitchen bench.

It was completely dark outside now. The wind was picking up enough to rattle the glass in its pane and there was no question of Olivia driving anywhere after a second glass of wine. Knowing that they were going to be under the same roof for the night was…well… Zac looked over his shoulder, as if looking at her might give him whatever word he was searching for. But Olivia wasn't sitting at the table now. She'd brought her glass over and was standing right behind him.

For a long, long moment they simply stared at each other and it was a silent acknowledgement of an over-whelming sexual attraction. One that carried no strings whatsoever because it was highly unlikely that they would ever see each other again after tonight but one that meant something because they'd been through some things today that had given them an insight into each other that he suspected was probably hidden to anyone else in their lives. He had been able to see that Olivia was still affected by what she perceived as abandon-ment by her father. And Zac had just shared something incredibly personal because he knew that Olivia had so easily seen past the laid-back image that was his pro-tective shield.

It was that feeling of connection that made Zac re-linquish the tight hold he had on his self-control. If this was a mistake, he'd deal with any repercussions tomor-row because the temptation to lose himself for a brief moment in time was irresistible and he was quite sure that Olivia Donaldson wanted this as much as he did. Slowly, deliberately, he reached to take the wine glass out of her hand, put it down on the bench and turned back to her.

The ground was shifting beneath Olivia's feet.

She was falling. Tilting forward, anyway. Could just a couple of glasses of wine on an empty stomach have been enough to have an effect like that? No…this wasn't something you could find in a bottle. This was something that most people never found in a lifetime—an attraction to someone that was intense enough to be completely overwhelming. When it was coming from both sides, the collision was inevitable and there must have been an explosion of some kind because all oxygen in this room seemed to have vanished. Not that Olivia felt any need to breathe in this instant. All she could possibly need was…*this*…

The touch of Zac's lips on her own. The glide of his tongue dancing with hers. The searing warmth of his hands as they slid beneath that baggy sweatshirt. The silk of *his* skin as she let her own hands roam.

There was a moment when they could have both stopped. When they had to pause for breath and she saw Zac glance at the door and then back to her—a silent invitation to take this somewhere more comfortable. Like his bed…

'I don't…' Olivia had to pull in a new breath. She could hardly say she didn't want this and sound sincere. 'I mean, this isn't something I usually… I don't want you to think that…'

'I'm not thinking anything.' Zac's voice was a low growl. 'Except that you are amazing. That we happen to be together and will be for the night, but after that we're probably never going to see each other again, are we?'

She shook her head very slowly. She'd had a similar thought herself, although everything felt hazy now. One thing was very clear, though. She couldn't stop. The pull of desire was threatening to drown her.

Something banged overhead, as if a gust of wind had lifted a sheet of the corrugated-iron roof and then let it

slam down again. The startling sound was instantly followed by the brief rattle of heavy rain and it felt like a
drumbeat that was adding to the intensity of what was
happening here. Olivia knew she might never feel passion like this again in her lifetime and she had to know
what it would be like.

Just once…

CHAPTER FIVE

IT WAS THE rumble of distant thunder that woke Olivia the next morning.

For a minute or two she didn't open her eyes. She wanted to snuggle a little deeper beneath the soft duvet and bask in the warmth of this bed. She knew she was alone and that was okay. She could take her time to stretch her limbs just enough to wake up her muscles and skin. To let her mind drift and sift through the memories of a night she was never going to forget.

A sexual fantasy that she'd made the most of because she knew it was never going to happen again. She'd had no idea that sex could ever be that good. That someone could tease her to the brink of something so huge, hold her there until she was begging for release and then take her even further before letting her fall off the edge of bliss. And the things she'd wanted to do to him… She'd never imagined that she could feel comfortable enough with anyone to be so uninhibited. She could actually feel herself blushing a little as she remembered.

Okay…maybe that was enough sifting for now. Olivia opened her eyes and moved to get herself up. It was no real surprise that she'd slept through Zac leaving this bed. He'd warned her that he would probably be gone by the time she woke up and she'd been deeply asleep because it can't have been very long ago that they'd finally found themselves too sated to begin making love yet again. She could feel her still-weary body protesting as she pulled the duvet with her to use as a cover when she rolled out of bed. What time was it? She had to get on the road and drive to the airport. She had to leave this fantasy behind and head straight back into her real life.

'Zac?'

Her call echoed down the hallway of the cottage and Olivia knew that he was gone. It wasn't simply because there was no response, it was because the air felt flat. The charged atmosphere that their mutual attraction had created was merely a memory. Like a fragment of a dream that had no relevance in real life. Padding through the house in her bare feet after a quick shower, Olivia retrieved her clothes from the rack above the stove in the kitchen. They were going to look appalling and that rip in her skirt was barely decent but it couldn't be helped.

There had to be some shop at the airport where she could purchase something else to travel in. She didn't have her hair straightener with her so it wasn't possible to give her hair its normal sleek look but she twisted it into a loose braid that would, at least, keep it out of her face. Thank goodness she always carried a basic makeup kit in her large shoulder bag.

The kitchen was a bit of a mess. She'd almost forgotten that they'd found themselves starving in the earliest hours of the new day and had come in here to make fried-egg sandwiches with thick slices of bread and a layer of onion jam. She'd been wearing nothing but Zac's T-shirt that was big enough to be almost decent. He'd been wearing the tracksuit pants that she'd borrowed earlier. They'd polished off that bottle of wine, too, and it had been the most delicious meal Olivia had ever eaten. Should she take the time to wash the frying pan and plates that were cluttering the sink now and give herself the luxury of sinking into the memory of that meal and what had happened again as soon as they'd finished it?

No. She might still have plenty of time to get to the airport but she needed to allow extra to drive as carefully as possible through that gorge. Especially with the weather still deteriorating. There had been intermittent rain squalls during the night but apparently there was a real storm on the way and that rumble of thunder that had woken Olivia had been a warning that it was nearly here. Through the window above the sink, she looked up at an ominous steel-grey sky where billowing clouds had an eerie light to their edges. A flicker of lightning near the mountains made her turn away. The sooner she hit the road, the better.

But… Her head swung back as what she'd caught in her peripheral vision registered. Yes. The gate to that paddock beyond the garden hedge was open. And… Olivia leaned over the sink to see more and her heart sank. Yes…there was Chloe the horse, standing to one side of a vegetable garden. She might not have any obligation to deal with dirty dishes before she left Zac's house but she couldn't leave his horse somewhere unsafe. What if she got out onto the road and was hit by a truck?

Olivia found the last of the carrots in the fridge in case she needed an incentive to persuade Chloe to return to her paddock but when she went out the back door into the garden there was no nicker of appreciation for any treats. Chloe's head was hanging low and she had a strangely hunched look to her back. By the time Olivia had walked the short distance to reach the horse, Chloe had crumpled to the ground and was stretched out flat on her side.

'Oh, my God...' Olivia crouched by Chloe's huge head. 'What's wrong?' She patted her neck. 'Don't worry. I'll go and call Zac. He'll know what to do.'

She didn't have his phone number, she realised as she ran back into the house, but she could look up contact details for the hospital and get hold of him that way. Except that as she was searching online, the power on her phone died and it was at that point that she remembered that she'd hadn't thought it was necessary to bring her charger. Because she'd expected to be back in Auckland well before it was needed.

This was turning into a nightmare. Could she leave Chloe and drive to the hospital to find Zac? Olivia took a deep breath and went out to see if anything had changed. The horse was still lying on its side and Olivia could hear loud grunting noises. She could also see what looked like a white balloon expanding under Chloe's tail. It took only seconds to realise what was happening. The pregnancy *had* been genuine and Chloe's baby was about to be born. Had the mare broken through that wooden gate looking for help as her contractions started? Olivia crouched to stroke Chloe's neck again.

'It's okay,' she told the horse. 'You're going to be fine. I'll be here to help.'

She had to be. However long this took and however difficult any consequences might be, there was no way Olivia could drive away now. She had to wait to make sure the foal arrived safely and she would also have to get them both into shelter, preferably before this storm broke. Leaving Chloe for a few minutes, she went to check the barn to one side of the cottage and was relieved to find it empty apart from a water trough in a penned-off area and a stack of bales, both straw and hay. Pulling the twine from a bale of straw, she scattered it over the cobbled floor of the pen. Then it was back to Chloe to find that the balloon now contained the front hooves and the head of the foal pressed against the legs.

'You're doing so well,' she told Chloe. 'Keep going... Big push...'

The mare's grunts and groans sounded almost human and the whole of her enormous body was moving with the intensity of her contractions. Olivia had no idea how long she was there, trying to encourage and reassure Chloe with her voice and touch as she watched what was happening. Was it too slow? What was she going to do if a vet was needed? Finally, with an even bigger contraction, the foal's body slid onto the ground, still encased in that thick white membrane.

Olivia knew what she needed to do now. She stepped around Chloe's huge, fluffy feet to reach the foal and she broke the membrane and pulled it back so that the baby could take its first breath. Chloe lifted her head and then curled her front legs in and pushed herself to her feet, breaking the umbilical cord as she did so. She came to sniff the foal cautiously as Olivia pulled more of the membrane away. The foal tried but failed to lift its head. It would be some time before it was strong enough to be on its feet, Olivia realised, and she didn't need the chill of a wind gust bringing a splatter of rain to remind her that she couldn't leave either of these animals out in this weather.

The foal was not small and it took an enormous effort for Olivia to lift and then half carry, half drag it to safety. At least Chloe didn't object to her intervention and followed her into the barn. There, Olivia could start rubbing the foal with handfuls of straw and its mother started to lick its face thoroughly. The foal made a stronger effort to move and managed to keep its head up this time.

'There you go…' She could feel a smile that just kept getting wider, but oddly she had tears on her face at the same time. 'You know what to do, don't you, Chloe? And look…isn't your baby just gorgeous?'

Having made sure the water trough was full, Olivia stood for several minutes and watched the mother and baby get to know each other and the foal make new attempts to get to its feet. It was adorably wobbly but the determination was there and it wouldn't be long before it could get the milk it needed. Long enough for Olivia to go back into the house and change her clothes. Her suit was really ruined this time, so she had no choice but to get back into the clothes Zac had provided yesterday.

She also had no choice but to drive back into Cutler's Creek when she was finally satisfied that the animals were safe. She might have vowed never to set foot in this community hospital again but Zac needed to know about the new arrival. It was only going to add an extra twenty minutes to her journey and, with a bit of luck, she might actually still get to the airport in time.

Or perhaps a lot of luck. The flash of lightning as she turned her car onto the road was almost blinding and the crack of thunder followed so fast she knew that the storm was right on top of them. Even with her windscreen wipers on the highest speed, visibility was poor in the torrential rain that began only minutes later.

Olivia could only grit her teeth and keep going. What was it about this place? Nobody was going to believe the series of extraordinary events the last twenty-four hours had provided. On the plus side, it would make for entertaining dinner-party conversations in years to come, wouldn't it? Being first on the scene at a plane crash. Delivering a Clydesdale horse's foal. Driving through an apocalyptic storm. Fantasy sex with the most gorgeous man in existence…

No. That could never come up in conversation with anyone.

It was something totally private that belonged only to her. And Isaac Cameron.

'Look at that, baby George.' Zac held Faye Morris's two-day-old baby up to the window. 'That's one heck of a storm you're going to go home in.'

He turned back to where Faye was packing her small

suitcase. Debbie, her midwife, was folding some baby clothes. 'You sure you don't want to wait it out?'

He wondered if Olivia had got past the gorge already on her journey north. He hoped so because it would be a tricky drive in conditions like this and he certainly wouldn't want her involved in any kind of accident.

'I'd rather be at home on the farm,' Faye said. 'With our log burner going full tilt and a pot of soup on the stove. Besides, George's older brother is running his father ragged. Jamie's hit the "terrible twos" with a flying start.' She came to look out of the window and had to grimace. 'It does look a bit nasty. We'll have to make a dash for the truck.' She rubbed at where her breath had misted up the glass. 'Speaking of dashing…who's that coming in so fast?'

Zac could feel the hairs on the back of his neck prickle. Nobody skidded to a halt like that outside the doors of a hospital unless someone was in trouble. He pressed the bundle of baby he was holding back into Faye's arms and headed out of her room at a near run, with Debbie hot on his heels. He got to the main reception area at the same time the occupants of the car came through the doors but he had been able to hear screams from the other end of the corridor.

He knew the tall man who was carrying the screaming girl. Mike was one of the local firemen who'd been at the crash scene yesterday. It had to be his youngest daughter he had in his arms and she was clutching at a blood-soaked towel wrapped around her head and face.

'Come this way, Mike…' Zac led the way to their

minor procedures room, which doubled as their emergency department. 'What's happened?'

'Shayna was heading out to catch the school bus. She got hit by a piece of iron. Must've come off one of the dog kennels in that wind, I reckon.'

Debbie was still right behind him. 'What do you need, Zac?'

'A dressing kit for now, thanks. And saline.'

Sixteen-year-old Shayna was still screaming as Zac helped Mike to put her on the bed. 'It's okay, Shayna,' he said. 'We're going to look after you. Try and take a deep breath for me and calm down. I need you to tell me what's happening for you.' He glanced up at her father. 'Was she knocked out?'

'Don't think so. Knocked over, but I saw her from the house and she got straight back up. Came in with blood pouring everywhere so I grabbed the first clean thing I could find to put some pressure on the cut.'

'Good job.' Zac was easing the towel away from Shayna's head. 'The bleeding's stopped, which is great.' What wasn't great was that it was a deep wound that had carved out a V of flesh that was hanging just above Shayna's eye.

'It's my eye,' Shayna sobbed. 'I'm blind...'

Carefully, Zac lifted the flap of skin and held a sterile gauze pad over it to keep it in place. Although the eyebrow was involved, her eyelid seemed to be uninjured.

'You've got your eyes closed, sweetheart,' he told Shayna. 'I think you'll find you can see if you open them.'

'I can't. They'll be all full of blood.'

'I promise they won't be. Look, I'm going to put a bandage around to keep this dressing in place and make sure it doesn't start bleeding again. And then we're going to check you out properly.'

A thorough neurological check came next, along with making sure there were no other injuries that had been missed. He took Mike out of the room to talk to him while Debbie began to sponge dried blood off the girl's face and hands.

'She's okay,' he told the worried father. 'It's a deep laceration but there's no evidence of an underlying head injury or nerve damage, which is good news.'

'She'll need stitches, though, won't she?'

'Yes. The wound is too large and deep not to be stitched and, because it's on her face, it needs to be done by an expert to minimise scarring. I'm thinking we should transfer her to Dunedin and get a referral to a plastic surgeon.'

Plastic surgeon… How many times was he going to be thinking about Olivia Donaldson today? Even as he pushed that awareness out of his mind, he could feel the tingle of sensation that ran through his limbs to pool somewhere deep in his belly.

Man, that had been a night to remember last night, hadn't it?

'She won't be going anywhere in a hurry,' Mike told him. 'Nobody will be flying in this and Bruce is even thinking of closing the gorge road. That wind is getting dangerous. I was already getting calls to the station for things like roof damage before I brought Shayna in. Which reminds me…reception is lousy at the moment with this weather, and I need to let them know where I am. Where's your nearest landline?'

'Reception. Come with me.'

He might need to make some calls himself, Zac decided. To bring in some extra staff because it looked as though Cutler's Creek was in for a rough day. How many other storm-related injuries could come in?

'Where's Don, Jill?' he asked the receptionist as Mike called the fire station.

'On his way. He had to go and check that his mother was okay. Some windows of her house blew in. Oh...' She turned her head. 'That's probably him arriving now.'

Except it wasn't.

It was his daughter and, if anything, Olivia Donaldson looked more of a mess than she had in the wake of helping with that accident scene yesterday. There were strands of hair that had escaped from a plait and glued themselves to her face. She was streaked with what looked like mud and... Why was she still wearing his clothes?

'It's your horse,' she told Zac. 'Chloe. She's just had her baby...'

'No way...' He knew he was staring. Not at how dishevelled she was or the dirt she had on her face. He was holding those extraordinary eyes because it was hard not to feel like they were the only two people in this space. In the world, even, for just a heartbeat. 'Is... is everything okay?'

Olivia nodded. Smiled, in fact. 'I stayed with her. I

got them both into the barn and there's clean straw and hay and water. I just thought you should know. And... and my phone had died.' She looked at Mike, who was still using the phone on the reception desk. 'I don't suppose I could use your landline? I need to check the status of my flight.'

Mike put the phone down. He'd overheard Olivia's last comment. 'Dunedin airport is closed,' he told her. 'So's Queenstown. And Invercargill. You won't be driving anywhere, either, because the police have just closed the gorge road. There's been a slip.'

'But... I *have* to... I can't stay here.'

Zac saw the way Olivia's gaze raked the area—as if she was afraid she might see her father again at any moment. It was just as well the person coming in from the corridor was Debbie.

'Shayna's asking for you,' she told Mike. 'And she wants to know when her mum is getting here.' Her voice trailed off as she stared at Olivia.

Everybody was staring at Olivia and Zac felt the sudden need to protect her. Of course she didn't want to be here. He'd had the privilege of getting to know this woman on a very intimate level last night and he knew that she was a very different person from the one he'd thought he'd been leaving that voicemail for. Olivia Donaldson had an intelligence to match her beauty and she was passionate and generous but had an edge of vulnerability that he guessed had its roots in what must have been a difficult childhood. He'd been judgemental without knowing the truth. He owed her more than an apology for his assumptions.

He stepped closer to Olivia and caught her gaze, trying to convey the silent message that he was going to make this awkward situation better for her if it was at all possible. Then he turned to the other people around them.

'This is Olivia Donaldson,' he told them. 'Another Dr Donaldson—and, yes, she's our Dr Donaldson's daughter but that's none of our business. Through no fault of her own, she's stuck here until the road's open again so let's make her feel welcome. Debbie, perhaps you could find Olivia a set of scrubs, please?'

'Of course. Come with me, Dr Donaldson.'

Zac lowered his voice as he leaned closer to Olivia. 'Sorry about this but there's really nothing we can do other than make the best of it, yes?'

As if to applaud his attitude, there was another huge crack of thunder outside and then the lights flickered and went out around them. Even though it was daytime, it felt as if they'd been plunged into late evening.

'Oh, no… Shayna…' Debbie turned towards the doors. 'I'd better get back to her.'

'It's okay,' Zac said. 'The generator will kick in very soon.'

Mike looked torn. 'I need to get to the fire station,' he said. 'But I don't want to leave Shayna until her mum gets here.'

'We'll look after her,' Zac promised. 'And you know what? It's actually a real stroke of luck that Dr Donaldson's been trapped here with us.'

'Why's that?' Mike sounded even more suspicious than Olivia was looking.

'Olivia's a plastic surgeon,' Zac told him. 'She has the perfect qualifications to tell us the best way to manage Shayna's injury.' He turned back to Olivia. 'We've got a young girl with a serious facial laceration,' he explained. 'Could I trouble you for a specialist consultation, please?'

He liked the way he could see Olivia straighten her back. She was standing in possibly the last place in the world she wanted to be and she was being forced to stay here by circumstances that she couldn't possibly control. She was also dishevelled and dirty, which was obviously not the way she would want to present herself anywhere, but here she was drawing on some inner strength and turning into a professional person before his very eyes. A person who was confident of the skills she might have to offer. Proud of them, in fact.

'Certainly, Dr Cameron.' She nodded. 'Just show me where to find those scrubs and give me five minutes to clean up.'

Zac's smile of appreciation barely had time to touch his lips before the front doors of the hospital slid open beside them to let in a blast of icy wind and rain.

'Oh...no...' Olivia's barely audible reaction was so heartfelt that Zac took a step closer. As he turned, he could feel his shoulder touching Olivia's and it felt as if she was glad of the contact. As if she was leaning closer rather than moving away.

Her father had just come in, his arm supporting a much older woman. The umbrella he had in his hand had turned inside out and he looked windblown and damp. He also looked completely shocked to see Olivia.

'You're still *here*?'

Zac could feel the tension in Olivia's body increase and it felt like she was still tapping into whatever professional mode she had accessed when he'd asked her for a consultation. She intended to cope with this situation, no matter how difficult it might be, and Zac… Well, he was proud of her, that's what he was.

The older woman was small and plump. She peered over her glasses at the people in front of her.

'Well…' she said. 'This is a turn-up for the books, isn't it?' She nodded at Zac. 'Don insisted I come in with him,' she apologised. 'I had a bit of a fall, trying to get away from my broken window. He seems to think I might need an X-ray of my wrist.'

Olivia's father had an odd look on his face. It was obvious that Olivia was the last person he had expected—or *wanted*—to see but he didn't look angry. He looked nervous, she thought. Scared, even?

'No problem, Mabel,' Zac said. 'I'll look after that for you very soon.'

She gave him a bright smile and then turned her head, her gaze zeroing in on Olivia with such focus it sent a shiver down her spine.

'You must be Olivia,' she said. 'I heard you'd been in town and I'm so happy you haven't left just yet.'

'Oh?' Olivia felt an urge to step back as the elderly woman walked towards her but she found she couldn't move. There were creases in this Mabel's face that had nothing to do with age lines. They suggested a warmth that came from smiling often and they deepened visibly as she smiled at Olivia. She really was happy to see her.

'I'm Mabel Donaldson. I'm your grandmother.'

CHAPTER SIX

THE LIGHTS FLICKERED back into life around them as Mabel Donaldson reached up to touch Olivia's cheek.

'I can't tell you how thrilled I am to meet you, darling. And I can't wait for us to have a proper chat.'

It was a total surprise to find she had another member of her family in Cutler's Creek. Her grandfather had died so long ago that it hadn't occurred to Olivia that his wife might still be here decades later. To feel as if finally meeting her was the best thing that could have happened for her grandmother was just as astonishing. Nobody had ever called Olivia "darling". Not her parents. Not even Patrick.

The phone on Jill's desk was ringing. 'Cutler's Creek Community Hospital,' she said when she answered the call. 'How can I help you?' She held out the phone a few seconds later.

'It's for you, Dr Donaldson,' she said.

Don Donaldson moved towards the desk but Jill shook her head. 'No…the other Dr Donaldson. It's someone called Simon Ellis.'

'Who the heck is Simon Ellis?' Zac asked.

Olivia swallowed. 'My boss.' She was a little nervous about speaking to Simon. She suspected he would have been disappointed that she'd chosen not to go to that gala. Now she had to tell him that she wasn't even going to be at work anytime soon. But he didn't sound angry.

'Thank goodness you're all right,' he said. 'I've been trying to call you all morning.'

'Sorry. I didn't bring my charger. I wasn't expecting to have to stay but there was an accident—'

'I know… I saw you on the news. Way to go, Olivia. I've made sure that the media knows you're employed by the Plastic Surgery Institute. It's great publicity for us. Plastic surgeons are *real* doctors, too. Pure gold.'

Olivia could hear an approving smile in his voice but found it disturbing. Would he be so happy if she hadn't inadvertently given the private clinic some free publicity? Having a spotlight on her that was better than being seen at some charity event?

'I'm stuck here now because of the storm,' she told him. 'The airports are closed. So's the road.'

'Don't worry about a thing. We've got all your patients covered. It's not a problem.'

'Thanks, Simon. I appreciate that.'

People were moving around her. Mike the fireman was leaving, going out the front doors. Her father and grandmother were heading in the opposite direction, into the hospital—the direction that the nurse, Debbie, had taken when the power had cut out. Zac was still here, though. Watching her. She could feel that gaze on her skin like a physical touch…

'I've got to go,' she said. 'I've got a patient waiting for me.'

'What? You don't need to go overboard, you know. Don't take on something that might turn into a problem.'

And cause adverse publicity? Olivia gave her head a tiny shake. 'I'll be in touch, Simon, when I know where I am.'

Zac had clearly been waiting for her to finish the call. 'I'll show you our storage area and bathroom,' he said. 'And where to find me when you're ready for action.'

His smile was barely there but Olivia could feel a warmth that felt almost as welcoming as her grandmother's and that lilt in his voice seemed even more charming after listening to Simon's crisply enunciated vowels. She actually wanted to be here, Olivia realised as she changed into the scrubs Zac had provided and used the bathroom facilities to clean up and tidy her hair. Much more than she wanted to be in Auckland. And, okay, she wouldn't have chosen to be here and her father certainly wasn't happy that she hadn't disappeared yet but... Zac wanted her to be here. Plus, she had a grandmother who had been genuinely delighted to see her.

Who had called her "darling".

It wasn't just how long the storm would take to blow over that would enable Olivia to tell Simon where she was in terms of returning to her work and her normal life. It felt like the foundations of her world were still shifting beneath her feet and this time she couldn't run away. She would have to face everything head on. Starting with a young girl who might need her help if she wasn't going to end up being scarred for life. She had been shown the direction to take to find the minor procedures room but Olivia found an obstacle around the first corner.

A human obstacle.

And her father still looked, inexplicably, nervous.

'Ah… Lib—Olivia. Could I have a word?'

He was standing right in front of her. She could step around him, given that there was no one else in sight, but Olivia's feet had stopped without any conscious direction.

'I…um… I think I should apologise. I was rather rude yesterday.'

Olivia couldn't argue with that. She said nothing and, for a long moment, they simply stared at each other.

Don cleared his throat. 'I didn't expect you to still be here.'

'No. I didn't expect it, either.' That feeling of having old wounds opened up increased. 'Don't worry, I'll be leaving as soon as I can.'

'My mother…your grandmother is going to want to talk to you.'

'So it seems.' And part of Olivia wanted that. She hadn't had any grandparents on her mother's side. Or not that she knew of, but there were doubts waiting to surface about all sorts of things concerning her mother now, weren't there?

'She doesn't know.' There was an urgent note in her father's voice. 'About me. About…about the cancer and…and I'd be grateful if you didn't say anything.'

Olivia could feel her jaw dropping. He wasn't going to tell his own mother that he was dying?

'It's just that it's her ninetieth birthday in a couple of weeks. The whole community is planning to celebrate and I really don't want to spoil that for her. I'll tell her afterwards but…it would be better for everybody if that party wasn't spoiled in any way.'

At least he cared about his mother, Olivia thought, but she could feel a wash of bitterness lacing itself into the pain of those old wounds.

'As you said yourself,' she muttered, 'it's not really any of my business, is it?' But it felt like it was. Or that she wanted it to be.

'Thank you. And I…' He seemed to catch his breath as a look of pain crossed his face. 'I'm…sorry. For everything.'

Was that physical or emotional pain he was experiencing? It certainly looked real and Olivia felt a beat of concern. But that apology?

'You think that makes everything all right? That you can just say sorry for everything you did? Or should that be everything you *didn't* do?'

'You don't know what I tried—and unfortunately failed—to do.'

'I know that you failed to be a good husband. Or a good father.'

'Marriages fail, Olivia. Sometimes people just want different things from life. And they want them so badly that they are prepared to hurt others to make sure they get what they want.'

'What are you talking about? That you wanted to come back here so much that your family didn't matter any more?'

'I was always going to come back here. Your mother said she was happy about that but she was a city girl through and through and she had no idea what she was signing up for. In the end, she couldn't do it. And she wasn't going to let you be taken to live in a place like this. She said it had nothing to offer you and she was going to make sure you only got the best of everything.'

Olivia had to brush away an echo of that memory of her mother telling her that Cutler's Creek didn't even have a proper school. And Zac's voice telling her that she was such a city girl, but he didn't know her, did he? She hadn't thought of herself as being like her mother and she was less sure than she had been, even a day or two ago, that she wanted to be focused on her career more than anything else in life.

But surely that wasn't entirely her mother's fault?

'You couldn't make the effort to stay in touch,' she accused her father. 'Have you any idea what that was like for *me*?'

Again, Don closed his eyes tightly and seemed to be holding his breath, waiting for a wave of pain to pass. When he spoke, his voice was ragged. 'I know an apology will never be enough but that's all I've got to offer.'

No. It could never be enough. Except that Olivia's gaze was locked on her father's face. On dark blue eyes that were a mirror image of her own and she could see something very genuine in those eyes. Worse, she caught a whiff of the aftershave he was wearing and it was like she'd stepped into a time machine. She hadn't invented those memories of what her father had once been like. They were all real and she was a child again and all she wanted to do was hurl herself into her daddy's arms and feel them folding her into a bear hug. She *wanted* that apology to be enough. For there to be a way back…

'Liv?'

Zac's call was more than welcome. It offered an escape from a confusion that Olivia didn't want anything to do with. She could even forgive him for using the short version of her name that her friends used because, right now, he felt like a friend. He was rescuing her from the emotional minefield that being with her father represented.

'I'm ready.' Olivia turned her back on her father and moved swiftly. 'Let's see what we've got and whether there's anything I can do to help.'

It was an enormous relief to have something clinical to focus on and satisfying to know that she had the skills to make a real difference. Zac took her aside to discuss the case after her assessment, leaving Debbie keeping Shayna company for a minute. Debbie was also a midwife, Olivia had learned, and both she and Shayna had been easy to find a rapport with as she'd told them all about the foal's delivery while she had examined her patient carefully.

'So what do you think?' Zac was trusting her judgement here. That felt good, too.

'The frontal branch of the facial nerve is intact but it's a deep wound and the capillary refill at the edges isn't great. If it's just stitched as it is, it could leave a scar that will need more surgery in the future.'

'Can you manage it?'

'Of course, but how well I can do depends what you've got available. A magnifying headset with a light? Good range of sutures and surgical instruments?'

'Yes. I'm sure we have everything you could need. Your dad has always had enormous community support to ensure we're very well equipped.'

'I can use a supraorbital nerve block for anaesthesia without the tissue distortion that injecting local could create but, given how anxious Shayna is, I think she'll need a good level of sedation. Ideally, I'd want to do this under a general anaesthetic but I don't suppose that's an option here?'

'We do actually have an operating theatre and all the gear but it's been many years since it was used. It would have to be a life-or-death emergency to justify the risk.'

'Sedation it is, then. But I'll need you to monitor her.'

'I'm all yours.' Zac's smile was warm. 'Thanks, Liv. I really appreciate this.'

This time, the short version of her name sounded perfectly natural coming from Zac. As if they'd been friends forever. His smile felt equally familiar and it had the effect of making something deep inside Olivia feel like it was melting.

But she couldn't allow herself to acknowledge that reaction, let alone wonder what it meant. She had a job to do. Zac might have been in charge at the accident scene yesterday but the spotlight was firmly on her this time and she was going to do her absolute best.

For Shayna.

And for Zac.

* * *

Wow…

Just wow…

Zac had been watching Olivia Donaldson very closely for some minutes and he was blown away by her skills. And her confidence. He was learning stuff here. They were alone in the room with Shayna because her mother had arrived and Debbie had gone to make her a cup of tea and keep her company while the stitching was being done.

'See that blue tinge?' She had pressed the edges of the wound with a haemostat. 'No capillary refill. That tissue's not going to make it.'

'What's the answer? To trim the edges first?'

'Trick I learned years ago. Watch this.'

Olivia picked up a suture from the sterile tray she had prepared while Zac had been putting an IV line into Shayna's arm and giving her the drugs that would keep her asleep for a short time.

'I'm putting in a whip stitch, taking the smallest possible bites to bring the edges together. You don't even think about trimming, or what's going on with the deeper structures.' Then she reached for a scalpel. 'Now I'm going to cut down one side of the stitch and then the other.'

Her hands were absolutely steady as she made cuts so close together they almost looked as if they were in the same line, but then she picked up the line of suture material with forceps and lifted it clear.

'See that? Nice, smooth, healthy edges to put together, which will give us better closure and therefore a better scar. Now we do the deep dermal tissue absorbable sutures.'

She worked at an impressive speed, the curved needle taking a bite from one side of the wound and then the other, the knot being tied so fast it would have been impossible to see what she was doing if he didn't know the procedure so well himself.

'You're good,' Zac murmured. 'And I know. I've done my fair share of stitching over the years.'

'I love it. I've still got room to improve, though. With some more postgraduate training I might be able to do more reconstructive work. The kind that can make a real difference to people's lives.'

'That's what you want to do?'

'It's something I'm definitely interested in. I certainly want to do more than appearance medicine, anyway.'

So she wasn't just a private cosmetic surgeon pandering to people wealthy enough to change their appearance. But he'd known that already, hadn't he? He felt like he knew a lot about this woman, even though she hadn't intentionally revealed it. Like that look of being totally lost on her face when he'd found her talking to her father earlier. Then she'd looked genuinely pleased to see *him* and he'd felt something he hadn't felt in… well, it felt like forever. Since Mia, and that was years ago now. A need to be with someone. A desire to be as close as possible to that someone. And an urge to do whatever it might take to achieve that.

The kind of feeling that meant you cared. A lot. The kind of feeling that, if it was allowed to grow, could mean that even falling in love was a possibility. In a way, it was a relief to know that he was still capable of feeling like that about someone if he chose to let it happen but, on the other hand, it was a warning that couldn't be ignored. Get involved and you got hurt. Get hurt often enough and you lose faith in humanity and even in yourself.

It was much safer being a lone wolf and Zac knew exactly how to respond to that warning because he'd done it often enough in recent years. You moved on. You found new places to roam and people who were no more than strangers. Where you could care enough to make sure that you provided the best possible medical care but you never crossed that line.

You never got so close to someone that you simply wanted to be there. To watch them breathe…

'Almost done,' Olivia murmured. Shayna made a tiny sound that could have been expressing relief and Olivia smiled. 'It looks like the sedation is wearing off. That's good timing.'

'It is. What do you need for a dressing?'

'Some antibiotic cream and just some dry gauze for the first day. She can look after herself after that, washing it with gentle soap and water. She'll need to sleep with an extra pillow for a few days and avoid any bending or heavy lifting. I'll have a chat to her mother about that.'

'I'll send her in. I need to go and do that X-ray of your grandmother's wrist. I hope she's not going to be in a cast for her birthday party.' Zac was watching Olivia's face closely as she cut her last suture. How did she feel about that chance meeting? 'It might make her dangerous on the dance floor.'

Yes...he could see the flicker of surprise—or possibly interest—in the way her gaze flicked up to meet his. And then he could see the shutters come down. She didn't want to talk about her estranged family.

It was safe to leave Shayna now, as the sedation wore off. 'I'll ask Debbie to show you where the staffroom is,' Zac added. 'Help yourself to some coffee and biscuits. You never know, I might need your help again before we're out of this storm.'

You never know.

It seemed to be a favourite thing for Isaac Cameron to say. He'd said he would only have one glass of wine last night because you never knew what might happen.

Well...they knew now...

And Olivia couldn't stop thinking about it, especially after she'd been sitting in this empty staffroom for over an hour. Every crack of thunder that made this old wooden building vibrate seemed to reignite the tingling in every cell of her body that still hadn't worn off. She'd known that it might well be a once-in-a-lifetime experience and she'd been fine with that so why did it now feel like nothing else was ever going to get close enough to make it seem worthwhile or even desirable?

It was bad enough that it was so easy to remember every touch from Zac. Every kiss. The tenderness that had gone hand in hand with that unbelievable passion. That instead of being an experience that she could file away as a magic memory, which was what had been intended, Olivia couldn't deny that the desire to do it again was unexpectedly strong. Or that when Zac walked into the staffroom and smiled at her, it was fierce enough to make it feel like her heart stopped for a moment. Her breathing certainly did. Or maybe there just wasn't enough oxygen in here, like that lack she'd noticed in his kitchen last night.

'That's some storm out there, isn't it?'

'Mmm…' Olivia's response sounded a bit strangled but Zac didn't seem to notice. He was helping himself to coffee from the cafetière.

'Your grandma's wrist is only sprained.'

'Oh…that's good.'

'I should warn you that she's planning to give you an invitation to her birthday party. She's insisted on being taken home to fetch one, along with something else she wants to show you but I have no idea what that might be.'

Olivia shrugged. 'I doubt very much that I'll be coming back here anytime soon for a party. Coming back ever, for that matter.'

Zac turned to face Olivia, his coffee mug in his hands. 'Funny… Apparently that's pretty much what your mother said the only time she ever came here.' His breath came out in a soft snort. 'Mabel's been telling me all about her. She said, "And she always got what she wanted, that one. I've never met anyone so driven."'

'I don't need to hear the local gossip about my mother, thanks very much.'

Zac's gaze was steady. 'Even if it explains why your father gave up trying to contact you?'

Olivia was silent. She couldn't look away. Her voice came out as a whisper. 'What are you talking about?'

'Your parents agreed to separate. Your dad had to come back here to help his father or the hospital would have been closed. He didn't agree to you being taken out of the country but that's what your mother did and then she used lawyers to make it impossible for him to get access unless he wanted a huge legal battle. He tried ringing but your mother wouldn't let him talk to you. She said you were having enough trouble settling in a new place and that if he cared about you, he would wait. So he waited. And waited. He sent you cards and letters and gifts but they all got sent back, and every time it broke his heart. And then you finally sent *him* a letter—asking him never to contact you again.'

Olivia closed her eyes for a long moment. She could remember having that "trouble settling" only too well. So many tears because she'd missed her father so much.

Had her mother been so "driven" that she'd really believed that she was setting up the best future she could for her daughter by making sure nothing would hold her back from success and a stellar career? Had she sent those letters and parcels back so as not to have her message diluted?

Olivia could remember sending that letter to her father, too, with her mother helping her with the wording. She could remember how angry she'd been because it had been easier to cope with anger than any more grief. It had made her feel as if she was in control finally. That she could not let it affect her life any more than it already had.

'You okay?'

She hadn't realised that Zac had put his mug down and come towards her. Or that she had put her head in her hands because of the way it was spinning. The way Zac took her hand in his and then put his other hand over the top of it had the effect of stopping that spinning. It felt like an anchor.

She looked up. 'Do you believe that?'

'I only know what I've seen. That your grandmother was perfectly sincere and she's not actually one to gossip. And that your father *was* crying when he was looking at those old letters.'

Olivia swallowed hard. Her mother had been at the top of her field. Ambitious. Success had always been the yardstick of acceptability and the only way Olivia could find the approval that made it feel as though she was loved.

'Even if it is true,' she muttered finally, 'it's too late. It can't change anything.'

'No?' Zac gave her hand a squeeze and then let go. 'He's not a bad man, your dad, Liv. Quite the opposite. Sometimes...' His breath came out in a sigh this time. 'Sometimes you have to shut yourself off from something that hurts too much because, if you don't, it can destroy you. It *will* destroy you.'

He went to pick up his mug of coffee but he didn't drink any more of it. He took it to the sink and emptied it out. Then he turned on the tap to rinse it.

Olivia was staring at his back. He'd sounded as if he knew what he was talking about. As if he'd had to do exactly that and shut himself off because something had hurt him too much. Her hand felt cold now that it was no longer between Zac's. She wanted that touch again. She wanted to somehow help him get past the things that haunted him. How heartbreaking must it have been for him to lose the woman he loved in such a horrific way? And he'd said that Mia's death was only part of the reason he'd come to the most isolated part of the world he could find. How much else had Zac had to deal with? He'd mentioned flashbacks. It would be no surprise that the traumatic things he'd witnessed had affected him badly.

She wanted to walk over to him and wrap her arms around him. To tell him that she understood. She wanted to tell him that she cared. That she wanted, if it was at all possible, to make it better for him somehow. The power of how much she wanted all those things stole her breath away.

How could you feel that strongly about someone who'd been a complete stranger only twenty-four hours ago? But the thought of Zac being a stranger was also weird. It was as if she'd been unknowingly searching for something for her entire life and she had finally found it. No—not some*thing*. Some*one*.

But Oliva didn't believe in soul mates. Or love at first sight. Because they were based on emotional reactions that couldn't be trusted to last. Like you couldn't trust that the people you loved the most were actually going to stay in your life. Over-the-top emotions were not acceptable because they messed with your head and made you vulnerable. Like Zac had just said himself, if you cared too much, it could destroy you.

For a heartbeat, Olivia felt something like fear. That something important could be in imminent danger of being destroyed?

Did she care too much already? Fate was forcing her to stay in a place where there was a pull that seemed to be dragging her in. A pull towards a past where she'd had a father she'd adored who'd loved her just as much. Towards a grandmother she'd never met but who seemed ready to welcome her with open arms.

Towards an extraordinary man that—just maybe— she'd been waiting her entire life to meet?

CHAPTER SEVEN

THE STORM CONTINUED to batter the small town of Cutler's Creek.

Mabel Donaldson had not yet arrived back at the hospital with whatever it was she wanted to show Olivia but a lunch of toasted cheese sandwiches and a delicious vegetable soup was being provided by a lovely woman called Betty who was in charge of the hospital's kitchen and laundry. Everybody seemed to be welcome in her kitchen, whether they worked in this hospital or not, and they all seemed to know when lunch was being served.

Zac came in and announced to no one in particular that he'd finished a check on all the inpatients and that they were now all enjoying their lunch. He happily accepted a large mug of soup from Betty and helped himself to a sandwich from the pile on the platter.

Bruce, the local police officer, arrived. 'I went past your place a while ago,' he told Zac. 'Your roof's still on and the barn's secure. Just as well that foal's out of the weather, that's for sure.'

'Thanks to Liv,' Zac told him.

'Didn't realise you'd stayed on.' Olivia wasn't absolutely sure but there was a distinct possibility that Bruce had winked at her. 'Not the first time you've been in the right place at the right time, then?'

Olivia concentrated on her soup and hoped that the hot food might provide a reason for any extra colour in her cheeks. The locals had already been talking about her. Now they would be able to embellish their stories with the knowledge that she'd stayed overnight and had just happened to be at Isaac Cameron's property when his horse had unexpectedly foaled the next morning.

That was something else about country towns, wasn't it? Everybody knew everybody else's business. She'd never want to live in a place like this. She could forgive her mother for having been appalled at the prospect. There was a lesson there, wasn't there? If you wanted a life partner, you found someone compatible and attractive who wanted the same kind of things out of life as you did and then you built a relationship that would hopefully be solid enough to last a lifetime. And, okay, she'd chosen the wrong person with Patrick but how much worse would it have been if she'd been completely in love with him? If she'd felt the kind of intense emotions that Zac was making her feel?

Ben, the paramedic, came in a few minutes later. 'Thought I could smell your soup, Betty.'

'Grab a mug, lad. There's plenty. Want a toastie?'

'Wouldn't say no.'

'You haven't been out on an ambulance call, have you?' Zac asked. 'I didn't get paged.'

'I've been cruising,' Ben told him. 'Thought I'd check in on Bert and remind him to use his spray instead of just calling us when the cold weather makes his angina worse.'

'He is one of our frequent flyers.' Zac grinned. 'Good on you for checking.'

'No worries. He lives next door to Rob, anyway, and I've put the word out that our training session for tonight is postponed until further notice.'

'I hope we can do it soon. I want to improve my abseiling techniques.'

'Abseiling?' Olivia blinked. 'I thought you were doing medical training for the local ambulance officers.'

'We swap,' Ben told her. 'Zac teaches us stuff and we teach him. Most of us are also part of the local mountain rescue team. We don't get called out that often but when we do, it can be full on.'

Debbie joined the group in the kitchen. 'Shayna and her mum got home safely. She rang to ask me to say thank you to Dr Donaldson again. She wasn't sure if she'd let her know how grateful she was that we happened to have a plastic surgeon available.'

Olivia ducked her head. 'It was a pleasure. And call me Liv. It'll save confusion if…' Her voice trailed into silence. It felt too weird to call the other Dr Donaldson her father in public.

A few looks got exchanged around the room.

'Where *is* Don?' someone asked.

Betty clicked her tongue. 'He'll be working in his office, I expect. He never looks after himself properly, that man. Someone should go and tell him to come and have some lunch.'

'I think he took his mother home,' Zac said. 'There

was something she wanted to get for Liv. I imagine he'll be back very soon.'

'I heard she had a fall.' Bruce picked up another sandwich. 'I had a chat to Mike a while back and the boys had been around to board up that broken window at her place. Is she okay?'

Almost as he asked the question Mabel Donaldson appeared in the doorway of the kitchen, and Olivia wasn't the only person who was shocked by how she looked—because it was a very long way from okay. The smiling, confident woman she'd met earlier this morning was gone. Mabel looked every one of her almost ninety years right now. She also looked pale and... frightened?

'I need some help,' she said, her voice shaking. 'It's Don. He's...he's not very well...'

'Where is he?'

'In Reception.'

Zac moved first. And fast. But Olivia was right on his heels.

Jill, the receptionist, was kneeling beside the crumpled figure on the floor. She had taken off her cardigan to use as a small blanket. Zac dropped to his knees and put his hand on Don's wrist.

'What's going on?' he asked. 'What's happened?'

He looked extremely pale, Olivia noted. There were beads of sweat on his forehead and he had a bright smear of blood across his face. Zac was frowning, as if he wasn't happy with what he could feel beneath his fingers.

'Tachycardic?' she asked.

Zac nodded. 'And it's a very faint pulse. I think he's hypotensive.'

'Where's that blood come from?'

Don rubbed at his face. 'It's nothing,' he muttered. 'Just give me a hand up, will you?' He looked past Zac and Olivia and she realised that everybody else had followed them from the kitchen. They were all looking extremely anxious. Betty had her arm around Mabel.

'He had a terrible pain,' Mabel told them. 'In his stomach. He almost couldn't get out of the car. And then he was sick everywhere and…and…' She had to gulp in a deep breath. 'I've never *seen* so much blood…'

Zac caught Olivia's gaze. They both knew how serious this was. Don was showing the symptoms of hypovolaemic shock from potentially dangerous blood loss.

'Bruce? Ben?' Zac sounded calm. 'Help me carry Don into the procedures room.'

'I can walk,' Don protested. 'Stop making such a fuss.'

'Stop arguing,' Zac told him. 'This time we're in charge. Me and Liv. Okay?'

Olivia was watching her father's face so she felt the instant he made eye contact with her. He looked scared, which was understandable because he would be well aware of the significance of vomiting blood like that. He also looked as if there was a lot he wanted to say to her and she could read a plea in his expression. Was that a plea to help him survive? Or that he would have the opportunity to say whatever it was on his mind? Or…

it could have been just a plea to stay close. To let her know that he wanted her to be with him.

It didn't matter.

Olivia wasn't going anywhere.

This mattered.

Not just because any life-or-death situation mattered. Or that this patient was a colleague he'd come to respect and like very much. It mattered because he'd seen the fear in Olivia's eyes. She might not be ready to forgive her father but she was most definitely not ready to lose him, either. She might be conflicted but she cared a lot more than she wanted to admit.

It was Zac who examined Don while Olivia was inserting an IV line and putting up a bag of fluids to start managing his low blood pressure. Debbie put an oxygen mask on their reluctant patient and then some ECG dots to attach him to the monitor.

'Sharp scratch,' Olivia warned when she had cleaned the skin above his vein with an alcohol wipe. 'There we go... Now, don't move while I get this cannula taped down.'

'Didn't feel a thing,' Don told her.

He could certainly feel Zac's hand on his abdomen. 'That hurts, doesn't it?'

Don couldn't hide the fact that he was in pain. 'Of course it does. It's been hurting for some time. It's only to be expected with this disease I've got.'

Debbie looked shocked. 'What disease?' she asked.

Zac gave his head a single shake. 'Nothing's been confirmed,' he told Debbie. Then he looked back at

Don. 'And as far as I know, sudden onset abdominal pain along with vomiting a large amount of blood is not a symptom of pancreatic cancer. It's far more likely to be a perforated peptic ulcer.'

Don just grunted as Zac palpated another quadrant of his abdomen. 'Your blood pressure is in your boots and you're showing other signs of hypovolaemic shock. You must have lost a significant amount of blood.'

'He's still tachycardic at one twenty.' Olivia was watching the ECG trace on the monitor screen. 'And his blood pressure's dropped even further. Systolic's down to ninety. How far away is the nearest blood bank?'

'Too far,' Zac admitted. 'But we do keep a limited supply of blood products here. Some O-negative packed red cells and some plasma. They're in the second fridge in the staffroom. Debbie, could you go and get a bag of the PRC, please?' He caught Olivia's gaze as Debbie left the room and they both acknowledged the real problem they had here. They weren't going to be able to transport her father to a larger hospital any time soon and they weren't going to be able to get more blood products delivered. If this was a perforated ulcer Don could still be losing a potentially dangerous amount of blood. Right now it didn't matter that his self-diagnosis might have been completely wrong because this could still prove to be fatal and even more rapidly.

'We could do with a CT scan,' he added. 'But we'll have to make do with what we've got. An ultrasound and then an upright chest X-ray. If we see any free air under the diaphragm on X-ray then we can be a lot more sure of a perforation.'

And then what?

Surgery?

In an operating theatre that hadn't been used in a very long time?

Don gave a strangled groan and then tried to turn onto his side. Electrodes popped off his chest and an alarm began to sound on the monitor. Olivia grabbed her father's shoulders.

'What's going on? What's wrong, Dad?'

Zac barely registered what she had called Don as they both dealt with another vomiting episode. Another several hundred mils of blood lost. But he remembered as they reassessed Don's condition to find that his level of consciousness was dropping sharply and they worked together to put a central line in so that they could deliver more fluids and the blood products that were obviously needed urgently. It was undoubtedly the first time she had called her father "Dad" since she'd been a small child. There was nothing like a crisis to make it obvious what was really important, was there? Olivia's anger at her father for her apparent abandonment was irrelevant when she was face to face with the possibility of watching him die.

Surgery was needed urgently if that wasn't going to happen.

'How are you with giving a general anaesthetic?' he asked Olivia quietly a short time later when they had stabilised Don well enough to do the tests that increased Zac's confidence in his diagnosis.

'I did a six-month rotation in anaesthetics. It was near the top of my list for a chosen speciality.' She held his gaze. 'You said you worked in war zones and on trauma teams but did that include any surgical experience?'

'I qualified as a specialist trauma surgeon before I went anywhere near a war zone. I've worked in major hospitals in the UK and the USA since then and my last position was Chief of Trauma Surgery in the biggest hospital in Chicago.' He wasn't telling her his credentials to try and impress her. He simply wanted to reassure Olivia enough for that fear in her eyes to lessen.

'We can do this,' he told her. 'As long as we do it together.'

He saw the way her chin came up and it was a familiar gesture already. A sign that she was gathering her courage and that she was prepared to face a situation she really didn't want to be in. Once again, he felt proud of her but this time there was also a wash of a much stronger feeling. Of caring. Of feeling as invested in a successful outcome here as she was because the alternative of Olivia being hurt again was unacceptable.

Sterile drapes were rolled around surgical instruments that were kept sterilised so that they could be available in an emergency but no one had ever expected that Cutler's Creek Hospital would have to deal with trying to save the life of the doctor who'd kept this hospital going almost single-handedly against the risk of closure. The son of the man who'd devoted *his* entire life to the medical needs of this community.

Don Donaldson was under general anaesthetic now and it was his daughter who was monitoring his vital signs, the blood transfusion and the medications being administered. She nodded in response to Zac's silent question. They were good to go.

Zac was scrubbed and gowned. So was Debbie, who'd come into Theatre with them to assist.

'I'm not sure I remember what the names of some of the instruments are,' Debbie said anxiously. 'It's a long time since I did any theatre training.'

'You'll be fine,' Zac told her. 'I'll tell you which ones and what to do as we go along. The first thing I need is easy. A scalpel, please.'

There was only one goal on his mind as he made his midline incision and then started a thorough examination of the abdominal cavity, and that was to stop whatever bleeding was going on. Don Donaldson might well have to be taken back to Theatre once he reached an expert in the field at a main hospital but if whatever blood vessel had ruptured wasn't taken care of right now, he would never get that far.

Zac had to resist the urge to work too swiftly, which could mean he might miss what he was looking for. He had to coach Debbie in assisting him, to find the instruments he needed and how to manage the suction. He also had another part of his brain that needed managing and that was his awareness of Olivia at the head of the bed, watching over her father and watching *him*...

And he was too aware of her.

Their roles were reversed this time but he was strongly reminded of when he'd been the spectator, watching Olivia's skill in suturing Shayna's facial laceration. When he'd realised that somehow Olivia Donaldson had almost instantly got past any protective barriers he had in place to prevent himself caring too much about other people. Barriers that had been added to and added to until they were too big and too strong and he'd feared that he would never truly care about anything again.

'There it is.'

'A perforation?'

'Yep. The bleeding's coming from the gastroduodenal artery.' Zac adjusted the tilt of the powerful light above them, swabbed the area he had identified and watched the blood well swiftly back into the space. 'Okay… I need a suture now, Debbie. Yes…that one at the top of the tray. And a needle holder. And then I need you to help keep things visible by using the swabs and suction. How're things looking at your end, Liv?'

'Blood pressure's still on the low side. I'm going to hang that second bag of packed red cells. He's throwing off a few ectopic beats, too. The sooner you can stop that bleeding the better, Zac.'

'I'm on it.'

He was. He'd be able to stop this life-threatening blood loss within seconds. With the curved suture needles secure in the holder, Zac moved to ligate the artery before repairing the perforation by excising the ulcer that had created it.

And that's when it happened.

His hand shook.

Just for a heartbeat, and it was probably imperceptible to those watching what he was doing but it felt huge to Zac and he froze for another heartbeat because he knew why it was happening. There was too much resting on the outcome of what he was about to do. This wasn't a purely clinical challenge that needed only the best of the abilities he knew he had. Not only did he care a great deal about the man on this operating table, he was desperate to do whatever it took to protect his patient's daughter.

He cared *that* much about Olivia Donaldson.

And it felt too much like love…

Too much like the overwhelming emotion he'd felt for Mia and a reminder of the devastation and guilt that had come so close to destroying him. And, while it was a good thing that he had healed from the dead space he'd been in emotionally when he first came to Cutler's Creek, he'd only wanted to open windows in that barrier that protected his heart—this felt like a door was opening.

One that he might actually want to step through.

He didn't. He couldn't. He had to slam that door shut.

Maybe it had only affected him for a split second but that was enough. Zac used every ounce of his determination to get past that blip and focus completely on what he was doing. There would be time later to reflect on the fact that he'd faced his worst fear—that caring too much really would make it impossible to do his job to the best of his ability—and, even though he could get past it, he'd been right to fear it because maybe next time it would be worse. When it was appropriate to think about that, he would take the time and action that was needed to regain control and make sure it never happened again.

But not yet.

'Gotcha…' There was huge satisfaction to be found in lifting that swab and seeing no new blood loss. Now he could turn his focus to cleaning out the abdominal cavity as thoroughly as possible before closing up and starting Don on antibiotics. Then they would just need to monitor him and manage anything else until he could be evacuated for more definitive care, hopefully within the next few hours.

'Blood pressure's coming up already… Good job, Zac.'

He didn't look up from what he was doing. He didn't want to see respect or gratitude or anything else in Olivia's gaze. He didn't want to see those extraordinary eyes again right now or feel the connection that he knew would kick him right in the gut. The sooner this was over the better. Not just this emergency surgery but his time with Olivia.

If only he'd known…

He would never have left that voicemail on her phone.

How extraordinary…

They'd faced a challenge that could have gone very wrong even in a major hospital and they'd done with minimal staff and resources but they had succeeded against the odds.

No wonder the people who had gathered in the reception area of Cutler's Creek Community Hospital looked like they were collectively holding their breath as Olivia walked in to tell them the news.

'The surgery was successful,' she announced. 'Dr Donaldson is stable for now and we'll be able to transfer him to Dunedin as soon as the weather allows for a chopper to get here.'

'Shouldn't be too far away,' Bruce said. 'The storm's blowing through faster than expected and the wind's started dropping already. I'll get a road crew out straight away to start dealing with that slip in the gorge, too, in case we need a Plan B to go by road.' He cleared his throat and sounded as though emotions were doing their best to break through his professional focus. 'This is… this is such *great* news…'

Mabel Donaldson was wiping her eyes with a handful of tissues as she came towards Olivia.

'Oh, my dear…thank you. I was *so* worried…'

'I know. He's still not completely out of the woods, but we've stopped the bleeding and that was the critical thing to do.'

Mabel opened the clasp of the old-fashioned handbag she was clutching. 'This is for you, Olivia.' The embossed envelope she pulled out of her bag was sealed and Olivia's name was written on the front. 'It's an invitation to my birthday party. I do hope you'll be able to come. It's far enough away for Don to be back home by then, I hope.'

'I hope so, too.' Olivia accepted the envelope but didn't clarify which of those hopes she shared. There was no way she would be heading back here for a party in the near future but her grandmother was clearly a lovely woman and she didn't deserve to be rejected in public.

'There's something else, too.' Mabel had a wallet in her hands now. 'This is Don's,' she told Olivia, as she opened it and fished inside a small pocket. 'And this is what he's carried with him for the last thirty years.'

It was a small photograph of a young girl. A photograph of Olivia taken when she'd been about four or five years old. Golden curls, big blue eyes and the happiest smile ever. Had it been her father who'd taken the photograph? The one who had been on the receiving end of that smile?

'There's so much I want to tell you,' Mabel said quietly. 'But it'll have to wait until another time. Bruce is taking me home so I can pack a bag for Don and for myself, if they'll let me go with him, and get back here before the helicopter arrives, but…could you give him his wallet, please?' She tucked the photograph back into its pocket. 'He'll want to have this with him now, I expect.'

Olivia took the wallet. She had no choice when it was being pressed into her hand like this. How could she refuse when Mabel was looking up at her so trustingly? So lovingly…

'He loves you, darling,' her grandmother said. 'And so do I. We're family, even though it might not feel like it quite yet. You'll always have a home here, you know, if you ever need a new one.'

Olivia opened her mouth to say she already had a new home and it was in the country's biggest city about as far away as you could get from a place like Cutler's Creek but the words got stuck somewhere in her throat. It might be an unwelcome connection but she had ties to this place that she would be aware of for the rest of her life. Mabel was right about her having family here.

And Zac was here, as well.

He was in the room with her father when she went in with his wallet. Debbie and Ben had wheeled a comfortable hospital bed into the procedures room and Don was lying propped up on soft pillows, surrounded by the machine monitoring his heart rhythm and blood pressure, the IV poles and lines that were still providing fluids, blood products and medication, and the oxygen tank that was attached to the mask he was wearing. He looked drowsy but his eyelids flickered open as Oliva entered the room and she knew he was watching her.

Zac was also watching her and he held her gaze for a heartbeat before his lips curved into a smile. A tiny moment of time that was enough for Olivia to realise how fierce the connection between the two of them had become in such a very short time.

'Everything's stable,' he told her. 'But could you stay with your dad for a few minutes, please? I need to write up as detailed a report of the surgery as I can for the team he's going to be transferred to.'

'Sure.'

'I'll be in my office if you need me. That's next door to your dad's office, if you remember where that is?'

Olivia gave a single nod. She hadn't forgotten where she'd had that horribly awkward meeting with her father for the first time in decades. Her hand tightened around the shape of the wallet she was holding. So many years and he'd been carrying a photograph of her in his wallet for that entire time?

'I'll be in Theatre for a bit,' Debbie said. 'I need to start cleaning up in there.' She tilted her head at Ben as if encouraging him to leave the room, as well.

'I'd better make sure the ambulance is ready,' he said hurriedly. 'Just in case we need to meet land transport for Dr Donaldson halfway or something—if a chopper can't get here.'

If they'd agreed on a plan to try and leave Olivia alone with her father, it had worked remarkably well.

'Your…um… Mabel gave me this to give to you.' She put the wallet on the table beside the bed. 'She's gone to get a bag packed for you to take to hospital but she thought you might want to keep this with you.'

Don reached for the wallet. The movement was clearly painful and he couldn't reach. Olivia picked the wallet up and put it close enough to his hand for him to take it but Don's hand closed around hers instead. With his other hand, he pulled the oxygen mask away from his face.

'Thank you,' he said softly. 'Zac said he couldn't have done this without you.'

'Oh, I don't know about that.' Olivia was trying to keep her tone light as she extracted her hand. It was too much to cope with right now, knowing that that photograph was caught up in the middle of that physical contact. An image of herself, before she'd been betrayed by the man she'd loved so much. 'But we did make a good team.'

'I'm very lucky you were here, though. Not just because you saved my life.'

Olivia had to look away from what she could see in her father's eyes. A gleam of something that looked like real joy. She had to clear her throat to get rid of the lump.

'This should never have happened, you know,' she told her father. 'Peptic ulcer disease is very easy to manage these days.'

'I know.' Don held the mask up to his face again and closed his eyes as he took a couple of deep breaths. 'I was stupid. Not for the first time.'

'And it didn't look like there was anything at all wrong with your pancreas when Zac did that ultrasound examination. By the time you've had a good check-up in hospital, I think you'll find you're not going to die anytime soon.'

Her voice wobbled at that point. She didn't want to lose her father. To her dismay, a single tear escaped and rolled down the side of her nose just as Don opened his eyes again.

'Oh, *Libby...*'

It wasn't just the use of that old nickname, it was the wealth of love in his tone. Olivia wasn't sure who reached out first, but the end result was that her father had his arms wrapped around her and she was back in an embrace she hadn't felt since she was a child. And it felt...as if it could be as comforting as it had always been if she could just allow herself to trust it. And it felt as if it was really going to be possible to trust it and that just made her tears fall so fast she had to extract herself and pull a handful of tissues from the box on the bedside table.

'So...' she said into the silence that followed. 'There you go. I'm glad you're not about to die.'

Don's smile was fleeting. 'I was sorry to hear about

Janice's death,' he said slowly. 'It must have been hard on you, losing your mum.'

'Yeah…it's never easy losing a parent. Even if you're not that close…'

It was possible that Don would interpret that statement as applying to himself but it didn't. Looking back on her relationship with her mother, Olivia realised how distant they'd really been. That it had been a complicated dance of trying to win approval and affection. Her mother had never glowed with the kind of unconditional welcome that her newly found grandmother had displayed in the first minutes of meeting Olivia. Or spoken her name with the kind of love her father had when he'd called her "Libby" again.

'It was a tragedy that she died so young. I hope… I hope that she was happy in her life in London, though…'

'She was successful. A big name in a big city,' Olivia told him. 'And that made her happy, I think.'

Don simply nodded. He wasn't about to criticise her mother, Olivia realised. Or say anything that might be unwelcome. Maybe this was actually an unspoken agreement between them to try and leave the past in the past and move on and, for a beat, Olivia could feel sorry for her mother, in fact. How sad was it that she wouldn't have even recognised the rewards that could come from being part of a community like this because they were so different from the status and success that came from being the top of your field in a huge city? Had she really been happy with her life?

Was Olivia in danger of making the same kind of mistakes?

'I wanted to contact you when I heard she'd died,' Don added. 'I picked up the phone. I started writing you another letter but… I wasn't sure you would want to hear from me. I thought that it might be far too late. That you hated me…'

'I don't hate you,' Olivia whispered.

Not any more. She had at one point, though, when that bewildered and sad child had grown into an angry teenager. It had been a relief to leave those teenage years and the anger behind and find a much emptier space that could keep her safe if she stayed within its boundaries. Hate and love were both intense emotions and they were more closely related than people realised. It was safer to stay in that safe space away from anything too intense and Olivia had managed to do exactly that, until she'd driven into this small town.

'And it was about then that I noticed the first symptoms of the cancer I was sure I had.' Don's breath came out in a soft groan.

'Are you in pain?'

'A bit.'

'On a scale of one to ten?'

'About a seven. Maybe eight.'

'I'll top up your analgesia.' It was a relief to have something medical to do for a few minutes. To check her patient and make sure it was safe to give him a higher dose of pain medication. To spend a minute making sure that she recorded everything on the paperwork that would go with him to the hospital.

The extra medication was enough to let Don sink

back against his pillows with a sigh of relief. He closed his eyes.

'They're still there,' he said, his words a little slurred. 'The letters. In that box. Take them with you, if you want.'

Don appeared to have fallen asleep as he finished speaking because he didn't stir when Olivia gently pulled his oxygen mask back into place. Her fingers touched his cheek as she did so and she found she had to swallow past another huge lump in her throat.

She had never stopped loving her father—she had just buried those feelings long enough to make them disappear. Was it really possible to tap back into the love that had been there in her earliest years? To make up for all those years that had been lost, even? An almost desperate longing was being balanced by fear, however. She would have to step out of her safe space and that would be taking a huge risk.

Was she brave enough to do that? If she went and got that box of letters, would she be brave enough to read them?

'Liv?' Her gaze flicked up to find Zac was standing in the door. 'The chopper's on its way. It'll be here in thirty minutes. Can I borrow you for a bit? Debbie's coming in to watch Don and I need your notes on his anaesthetic for the transfer report.'

'Of course.' But Olivia let her gaze rest on him for another beat before she moved.

Zac was still wearing the scrubs that he'd had on

under his Theatre gown. He still had a line across his forehead where the elastic of his cap had been a little too tight and he must have fluffed up his hair to have it as rumpled as it was again now. He wasn't smiling but there was a warmth in those gorgeous caramel-brown eyes that Olivia could feel right into her bones and it came with a tingle of the kind of excitement and joy she hadn't felt since she'd been very young.

She had assumed that not feeling things this intensely was simply a part of growing up and becoming a sensible adult and it was a complete revelation that it could still happen. But it was also as scary and wonderful and confusing as the beginnings of reconnecting with her father. The only thing Olivia could be absolutely sure of in this moment was just how far she had already stepped out of any safe place.

There was no going back.

CHAPTER EIGHT

'PROBLEM?'

'No, not at all.' Olivia eased herself into the seat behind the desk in Zac's office. She had no problem with complying with the request to add to the report he was making on her father's surgery. She'd just been a little disconcerted to sink into a seat that felt like it was still holding the warmth of Zac's body because it was doing odd things to her own body, like making her heart speed up and her breath feel like it was catching as that warmth in her belly became that distinctive tingle of desire.

'I'll just need five minutes,' she added, taking a folded piece of paper from her pocket. 'I've got my record of all the drugs I used during the anaesthetic and my monitoring of his vital signs.'

'I'll come back in a few minutes, then. Hit "print" when you're finished. I'll just check that Debbie's still okay monitoring Don and that Bruce knows to clear any debris from the car park before the helicopter comes in to land. There must be quite a lot of broken branches after the winds we've had today. You planning to fly with him?'

'No.' Olivia shook her head. 'I'll keep in touch with his progress, of course, but Mabel will be going with him. I was only supposed to be away for a day so I'm already very late getting back to Auckland and it's not as though I can just abandon my rental car here in the back of beyond.'

There was something odd in Zac's expression but he turned away too quickly for Olivia to try and interpret it.

'Of course not,' was all he said as he left the office.

Writing a succinct medical report was easy enough to be almost automatic. The focus required still allowed for a part of Olivia's brain to be trying to process other things. Like the confusion she'd been grappling with as she'd followed Zac to his office to do this task. That tumble of emotions that was undermining her ability to think straight. Joy. Fear. Excitement. Relief. Trust. They all felt too new and fragile. Bubbles of sensation that might pop if she tried to catch them to see if they were real. And that confusion that had just ramped up a little in the aftermath of that look on Zac's face when she'd said she was already too late in getting back to Auckland.

There was an echo of Mabel's voice in there somewhere, too.

You'll always have a home here, you know, if you ever need a new one.

But Cutler's Creek was the last place she belonged in. Wasn't it?

She hadn't wanted to be here this long. So why did she feel as if she wasn't ready to leave yet? Why did she feel as if all she wanted to do right now was go over to where that leather jacket was hanging on a hook on the back of the door? To put her cheek against the lining of that jacket perhaps and inhale deeply to find out whether there was any lingering scent of the man who'd been wearing it?

She had her chance to do that when she went over to the printer to see why the report hadn't emerged, despite the sound of the machine working. A red light was flashing on the control panel and it appeared that the printer had run out of paper. Olivia was looking around to see where a new ream might be stored when the door opened right beside her and Zac stepped in so swiftly he almost collided with her.

'Oh…sorry. I didn't see you.'

'No worries… I'm…ah…looking for some more paper for the printer.'

'It's there.' Zac pushed the door shut behind him, nodding towards a shelf that had been partially hidden by the door. 'I can do that.'

But they both moved at the same time, ending up even closer to each other, and, for the longest moment, it felt like time stood still. Olivia's mouth went dry as she held her breath, remembering how they'd both moved together at the same time yesterday evening and ended up this close to each other. She was reliving that thrill of sensation she'd had when Zac had taken her wine glass out of her hand and that look in his eyes had told her exactly what was going to happen in the next few seconds. She just hadn't known that that kiss would be the first move of a kind of lovemaking so amazing she would never have believed she would ever experience it.

The pull towards this man was so astonishingly powerful it was scrambling her brain completely. Like giving in to a human magnet, Olivia just wanted to press herself against his body. To lift her face and look into his eyes so that he knew just how much she wanted to kiss him. No…make that throw her arms around his neck and pull his head down so that she didn't have to wait a second longer to feel his lips touching hers. To feel that heat and a taste that she would never, ever be able to get enough of…

But Zac made a strangled sound that could have been interpreted as irritation and Olivia froze as he moved around her to pick up the ream of paper and tear the wrapping open.

'Bruce tells me that they've got one lane open in the gorge now.' His voice sounded slightly hoarse, which was probably why Zac cleared his throat. 'It'll be a slow trip but you should be able to make it back to Dunedin today. Unless…'

Olivia's heart skipped a beat. What was he going to suggest? That she might want to stay a bit longer?

He wasn't looking at her as he opened a drawer of the printer and slotted the new supply of paper into place. 'Unless you want to do something to really help your dad recuperate,' he added.

'How do you mean?'

'We'll probably need a locum if it's going to take a while until he's back on his feet properly.' Zac still wasn't turning to meet her gaze. 'I thought maybe you'd like a chance to get to know your gran. Stay for her birthday party, maybe. You left your invitation in the procedures room, by the way.'

It felt like he was asking more than whether she would like a chance to get to know her grandmother. Was he offering Olivia the opportunity to get to know *him* better? Was Zac feeling something like the overwhelming connection to her that she had found with him? Was he afraid that the person he might have been destined to share his life with was about to walk out, never to be seen again?

'I…*can't*…' The words came out as a whisper. It felt as if they were being dragged out because something was fighting that conviction.

You don't really want to leave, a tiny voice was insisting in her head. Or was it her heart? *You might think this is the back of beyond, and that you'd never want to live in a rural town, but that's not true, is it? That sense of space that the mountains and land give you here doesn't really make you feel intimidated, does it? It makes you feel free. You don't need a crumpled photograph to convince you that your father has never really stopped loving you. Part of you has always wanted to believe that—you were just too scared to take the risk of finding out you might be wrong. And what about Zac? You don't still believe there's no such thing as love at first sight, do you?*

Talk about having your head messed with. This was too powerful. It couldn't be trusted. Or…maybe that was exactly what she needed to do.

Trust it.

She should have trusted her father more. Maybe she could trust Zac as well?

She wanted him to step closer. To take her into his arms and tell her that Auckland was not the right place for her. To persuade her to stay here, at least long enough to find out for sure whether there was something real about this fantasy she'd stepped into with Zac.

But he turned to collect the printed pages that were appearing in the tray so she opened her mouth to speak herself. To say that she'd need a couple of days to sort things out in Auckland but that she would come back just as soon as she could—if he wanted her to.

It was Zac who spoke first, however.

'Don't let what happened last night put you off,' he said. 'I can promise it wouldn't happen again.'

Olivia froze. Why not? Could he dismiss last night *that* easily? Did he not even have the slightest desire for it to happen again?

'Besides,' Zac added, 'I won't be here much longer myself.'

He'd hurt her by being so dismissive.

Maybe it had been inevitable that she was going to be hurt but there was no relief to be found in the sudden distance Zac could feel between them. The way Olivia had been looking at him when he'd come into this office had made him doubt his ability to control what was going on in his head. He still wanted to drop this sheaf of papers he had in his hands and grab Olivia's shoulders. To close the physical distance between them and dip his head—to breathe in the scent of her hair and skin. To kiss her and then kiss her again and never bother coming up for air. To take her home and shut the door and make everything and everyone else in the world irrelevant for as long as possible.

The desire to do exactly that was just as bad as that momentary wobble he'd experienced in Theatre today. Or the way he'd acted so instinctively to protect Olivia when that plane wreckage had exploded. They were all signs that he was starting to feel things too much again. It wasn't simply that he was risking opening the doors to flashbacks that could be terrifying in their intensity. He wanted to keep Olivia close. To say something that would persuade her to stay in Cutler's Creek. The way he had persuaded Mia to stay for those extra few weeks? The extra weeks that had taken her life? He couldn't live with that kind of guilt again. He knew what he had to do but, dear Lord, it was hard.

'You've reminded me that there's a lot more to life than an isolated place like this,' he carried on. 'I only ever came here on a temporary basis and I'm ready to get back to the real world. It's time to move on. Another war zone, perhaps. They're always short of volunteers and things don't get any more real than that.'

He was thinking out loud, really, so it didn't matter if no one else heard him but the silence coming from Olivia was so profound that Zac had to look up to make sure that she hadn't somehow slipped out the office while he'd been collecting the printout of that report.

And then he wished he hadn't looked up.

Those eyes…

For a horrible instant, Zac had a glimpse of what he could imagine Olivia had looked like as a child. When she'd believed that her father had walked out on her life without a backward glance. She looked lost. Bewildered. As vulnerable as it was possible for anyone to look. She'd look like that if she was being dumped. How crazy was it to feel like that was exactly what he *was* doing? But it had to be done. And done convincingly enough to make sure it was really done, for both their sakes. Giving in to the disturbingly intense emotional reaction he was having to this woman might only end up hurting her more. What if she stayed here because of him and she became unhappy? Or, worse, that something terrible happened to her? He couldn't do it. It was too big. And it was too destructive when it went wrong.

The best way to be convincing was to be honest, wasn't it?

'I'm sorry,' he said quietly. 'But it's who I am now. I can't get attached. To places. Or people.'

'You can't just walk away from your responsibilities here.' Her voice was tight. 'You'd leave Cutler's Creek without a doctor. The hospital will get closed down.'

'I'll advertise for a locum, unless you want to change your mind about staying?'

She avoided his glance. 'And you'll stay until you find one?'

'If I can. Your dad managed pretty well by himself for a long time before I came here. It takes a special kind of person to want to live in a place like this, I guess. Maybe this time we can try and find a couple of married doctors who like the idea of running their own hospital and bringing their kids up in a pretty magical part of the world. That way, Don could retire any time he wants to.'

'You can't do that. He might think that he's not wanted any more. This is *his* hospital.'

Zac almost smiled. 'You sound like you care,' he said quietly. He was reminded again for a moment about the assumptions he'd made about Olivia when he'd left that voicemail—that she was someone who could simply walk away from someone that loved her. That she had no compassion for others.

How wrong had he been? She'd been in there, boots and all, to help save that pilot's life. She'd helped deliver Chloe's foal and had missed her chance to get away from Cutler's Creek because she'd taken the time to retrace her steps to tell him about the birth so he could make sure the foal was kept safe. And she'd been so afraid that she might lose her father today. How ironic was that when the only reason she'd come here in the first place had been because she had believed he was about to die and wanted to tell him how little she thought of him? From the atmosphere he'd felt in the room between father and daughter when he'd gone in to find Olivia, something huge had changed for the better.

Life could change in an instant, couldn't it?

Things you had come to believe were absolute truths could be thrown into doubt. Like being able to fall in love again? It was confusing. Alarming.

Olivia was staring at him. 'Why wouldn't I care? My grandfather worked here. I expect my father will work here again as soon as he's back on his feet because I don't think he's anywhere near ready to retire. His mother's about to have a significant birthday and knowing that the hospital might be closed would not be a great way to celebrate that occasion, would it?'

'And you think that's *my* responsibility? It's your family, Olivia.'

'You can't tell me you don't care. Well, you can and you did and maybe you even believe it yourself but I saw how hard it was for you to operate on someone you care about but you did it, Zac. You saved my dad's life. And I don't believe that you're going to let him lose what matters most to him.'

Oh, God…she'd seen that momentary hesitation in Theatre. Of course she had. She'd seen the flashback he'd had when that plane had exploded and she'd known exactly how significant that had been. Had she also known why that tiny wobble had happened? That it hadn't just been the respect he had for her father that had made it matter so much but how he was feeling about Olivia herself? He couldn't say anything. Because…

Because he didn't dare admit—to himself, let alone someone else—that he cared that much.

Because caring that much was something he simply couldn't allow himself to do again. He knew where that led to. That dark space. Where it was too real and too raw to pretend it was any kind of a movie. He'd learned how to control his mind. And his heart—in the same way he'd finally gained control of those flashbacks after Mia had died. Sure, he'd come here to try and balance that control because not feeling anything was just as bad as feeling too much, but the seesaw was teetering too much right now. The holes in that protective wall were getting too big. If he didn't take control he might lose himself and that couldn't be allowed to happen. It was very obvious what the first step in taking that control back needed to be. To get far enough away from this woman who was messing with his head. And his life.

'I already told you what matters most to your dad,' he said as he stepped past Olivia to get to the door. 'But that wasn't enough to make you want to stay, was it?'

Nothing could have made Olivia stay a minute longer than she absolutely had to so she was in that rental car heading back to the airport in Dunedin almost as soon as the helicopter evacuating her father had disappeared in the same direction.

She'd said goodbye. She'd told her father and grand-mother that she would be calling the hospital regularly to get updated on his progress and that she would be in touch as soon as she'd had time to get her head around everything.

She was still wearing hospital scrubs under her coat because that had been preferable to putting Zac's bor-rowed clothes back on. If she didn't find something new at the airport, she'd just fly back to Auckland like this because she was that desperate to try and find the solid foundations of the life she had chosen for herself again. She'd told Zac that she'd post the scrubs back as soon as she'd had them laundered.

'Don't bother,' he'd said. *'They're no great loss.'*

He wasn't bothered that she was leaving, either. He'd

just told her to drive carefully and then raised a hand in farewell as he'd walked back inside the hospital without a backward glance.

It was still raining but the damaging winds had lessened and she'd been assured that the road was passable as long as she took enough care.

'Not that we're chasing you out of town or anything,' Bruce said after updating her on road conditions in the gorge. 'And we're all hoping you'll be back real soon now that you and your dad have reconnected. When the doc gets out of hospital, maybe?'

'Yes, of course. But I'm not sure how soon that will be.'

All she wanted was to get going and put as many miles as possible between herself and Cutler's Creek.

Between herself and Isaac Cameron.

There was no pause to swipe away tears near the rugby field this time. It was tempting for a moment to stop at Zac's house and go and have a peep at Chloe and her foal but Olivia knew she couldn't afford the time and it would only make it more difficult to settle the confused emotions that kept ambushing her. At least there was no chance of a plane crashing to bring her journey to an unexpected halt this time and no irresistibly attractive doctor with an Irish accent to ply her with wine and make her break so many of her own rules.

Well, she'd learned her lesson, that was for sure.

Olivia might not have been crying as she drove away from both old and new memories but she'd never felt so…hollow.

Empty.

Crushed, even.

And how stupid was that? She barely knew Zac. It shouldn't matter that he had so little interest in her that he couldn't wait to get out of the country and head back into some war zone. It really, really shouldn't make her feel like she'd been dumped, let alone that she'd been abandoned. That she had been prepared to take the risk to trust someone and that trust had been broken—again. It was casting a shadow on the hope that she and her father could rebuild their relationship. Feeding into a fear that Olivia had always had—that, deep down, maybe there was something wrong with her that made men not want to stay around…

Oh, let it go, Olivia told herself sternly. *You knew all along that over-the-top emotional reactions can never be trusted. That disappointment was the best outcome you could hope for and that devastation was the real risk.* Her mother had taught her, by example, that staying in control and true to your ambitions was the key to success in life and you could only stay in control if you didn't give in to emotions that probably wouldn't last very long anyway.

Was that why she'd been sent to boarding school at such a young age?

Why her mother might have felt quite justified in changing her mind about going to work in a country hospital with the man she must have loved enough to marry?

Why she might have tried to teach her daughter that a career was more important than relationships with people?

Was Olivia like her mother because she had inherited

her personality traits or was it due to the way she'd been brought up? No. She *wasn't* like her mother. Not at all. If she ever had a child, she'd make sure it knew it was loved. She wouldn't send it away to boarding schools and she would call it "darling" at every possible opportunity. She knew that from now on her father was going to be a part of her life—she just didn't know how big a part that would be.

That small box of letters and parcels was on the back seat of this car. But there were still echoes of her mother's voice there, too. Warning her not to throw away the belief that her career was the most important thing in her life. It was too hard to keep a coherent thread of thought going so Olivia knew she had to give up and just let things settle in her head.

She wasn't going to think about it any more right now. She could see the flashing lights ahead that were a warning of the road crew that were clearing the slide of mud and rocks on the narrow gorge road. She needed to focus completely on her driving from now on and make sure she reached the airport safely.

Hopefully, there would be a late plane she could take to Auckland. A shop that was open for some form of clothing. And a phone charger. She needed to ring the hospital and find out how her father was doing because, once she knew that he was going to be fine, she could draw a line under this extraordinary couple of days and normal life could resume.

Nothing felt normal.

When the rain had stopped a few hours after Don had

been evacuated Zac had made a late round to check on the few inpatients at Cutler's Creek Community Hospital. He had phoned Shayna's mother to remind her that extra pillows were needed for tonight to help any facial swelling to go down and he'd spoken to Faye Morris to check that all was well now that she was at home, coping with her toddler as well as her newborn baby.

Now *he* was at home, too, and there was a newborn baby in the barn. The foal had astonishingly long, gangly legs that were already fluffy, and Chloe rubbed her head up and down Zac's arm as if nodding in response to being told how clever she was to produce such a beautiful baby. It was warm and cosy in the barn and there was a lovely smell that was a mixture of sweet straw and hay and horse but eventually Zac had to go inside the house and he knew the minute he walked in that he'd had good reason to be dreading this moment.

There were dishes piled up in the sink. There was the frying pan he'd used to cook the eggs in the middle of last night and plates that were still smeared with the onion jam they'd put into those sandwiches. The room felt so empty that Zac had the weird impression that he was catching a glimpse of Olivia from the corner of his eye. A ghostlike image that was felt rather than seen and it made his skin prickle. It was going to be worse in the bedroom. Even if those rumpled sheets didn't still hold an echo of her scent, he wouldn't be able to lie there without reliving every single moment of the most astonishing night of his life.

Well…he could fix that. He just needed something else to think about, didn't he? Dealing with the dishes in the sink was a good start. He'd change the sheets on his bed as well, but not just yet. Taking his laptop from his bag, Zac sat down and logged onto a website he had used many times before.

There would be more than one place in the world where Doctors without Borders would be currently more than welcome. Like Afghanistan and Yemen. Bangladesh, Bolivia and Myanmar. Sadly, there were more than seventy countries in the world that were in need of the humanitarian assistance Zac was more than qualified to provide.

He just needed to decide where in the world he wanted to go next.

CHAPTER NINE

THE OVAL WINDOW of the plane framed a very familiar cityscape with the needle point of the Sky Tower amongst high-rise buildings and the gorgeous backdrop of the rising sun on a sparkling blue sea and scattered islands. Olivia let out her breath in a heartfelt sigh as the plane banked to head away from the central city towards the airport.

'Gorgeous, isn't it?' The man in the seat next to her was leaning to see out of the window, as well. 'It's no wonder that Auckland gets rated every year as one of the top cities in the world for quality of life. I certainly wouldn't want to live anywhere else.'

'Me neither,' Olivia murmured, stamping on any tiny voice in the back of her head that might try arguing with that.

'Been away on holiday?'

'Not exactly.' She offered a wry smile to her fellow passenger on this red-eye flight from Dunedin. 'It was supposed to be a day trip but I got caught out by a storm in Central Otago.'

'Oh… I think I saw something about that on TV. Or was it a plane crash or something?'

Olivia made a noncommittal sound and was grateful for the announcement about putting away tray tables and making sure her seat was in the upright position for landing. She wasn't about to start telling a stranger about her unexpected adventures. She could feel her lips curling into another almost-smile as she imagined the questions that would have come her way if she had still been wearing the scrubs she had borrowed from Cutler's Creek Hospital.

It had been a blessing in disguise that there'd been no late-evening flights from Dunedin last night. The five-star hotel she had chosen had not only offered a luxurious room and range of beauty products but there was also a boutique clothing shop that they were only too happy to open for her to choose a new outfit—the kind of skirt and jacket that was entirely appropriate for her position as a private surgeon.

The two-hour direct flight had left Dunedin before dawn and she was going straight to the Plastic Surgery Institute. She would hopefully be able to step seamlessly back into her work and her real life would fold itself around her. Surely she only needed to be back where she belonged to know that everything was going to be okay? She agreed wholeheartedly with her neighbour's sentiments about this city and she could feel her spirits lifting noticeably as the plane's wheels bumped onto the tarmac. She wouldn't want to live anywhere else in the world. This was where she had been born. This was home.

More than an hour later, Olivia was still in the back of a taxi, caught up in a traffic jam on Auckland's motorway system because there had been an accident somewhere miles ahead of her. Sitting there in four lanes of bumper-to-bumper traffic was bad enough but then it started to rain. Watching the drops splatter onto the windows and then trickle down the glass made it impossible not to get dragged back into memories from the last couple of days.

Like the splatter of rain on a tin roof that had made being in Isaac Cameron's bed even more cosy.

Feeling the rain on her skin as she'd carried that huge foal into the barn.

And...*oh*... Zac's touch on her skin...

The ringtone of her phone was a jerk back to reality and Olivia snatched it from her bag. Part of her brain was still letting go of what had just been on her mind with such startling clarity, however, so she actually thought it might be Zac calling her and her heart rate accelerated as she looked at the screen, expecting the call to be from an unknown number. It wasn't. It was her boss.

'Simon... I'm so sorry. I thought I'd be at the Institute a lot sooner than this.' Would Simon notice that her tone was artificially bright? 'That bad weather seems to have followed me up the country and I'm stuck on the motorway now.'

'Not to worry. Your first appointment's not till eleven. I'm sure you'll get here by then.'

'I certainly hope so. I can't believe how bad this traffic is.' Olivia looked out of the window as she spoke.

How different was this from driving on a country road with a backdrop of a mountain range? The closest thing she'd seen to a traffic jam around Cutler's Creek had been that mob of sheep that had escaped when they had been rescuing the pilot of that small plane.

'The downside of living in the biggest city of a small country.' Simon didn't sound upset that she was late yet again. 'Let's catch up tomorrow. I'm tied up with an out-of-town consultation for the rest of today. I can't say much yet but you'll hear all about it soon.' Simon was sounding very pleased. 'It's celebrity stuff. International... Could be the start of something big. New Zealand is the perfect place to come and hide away from the media if you want to get some work done and then recuperate in privacy.'

She should be interested, Olivia thought. As excited as Simon even, but she wasn't. 'Are you near your computer?' she asked. 'Could you tell me if my eleven o'clock is a new patient or someone I know?'

She needed to get her head into the right space to be ready for what the rest of this day was going to bring because Olivia had the horrible feeling that it was not going to be as easy as she'd hoped. On a par with actually getting into work, judging by how slowly this taxi was inching forward in the traffic jam.

'Someone you know,' Simon said a moment later. She could hear the smile in his voice. 'Someone we all know rather well. How 'bout that? Peggy Eglington has asked for you specifically.'

Peggy was famous for her charity work in Auckland. She was also famous for the amount of plastic surgery she'd had over the years. Had it only been a few days ago that Olivia had reminded herself that she needed to do some more research into body dysmorphic disorder? Peggy was a prime example of the condition. She was probably due to have more filler injected into any tiny lines she was noticing. Or that she had a new bump on her nose and she couldn't believe that she had only just spotted it.

But no…arriving just in time for her first appointment, Olivia discovered that it was something else that was distressing Peggy.

'Can't you see it? I can't bear to look in a mirror. I haven't let anyone photograph me since I noticed.'

'I think you look wonderful, Peggy. You always do.'

'But…*look*…my eyes are completely different sizes. Even my eyebrows aren't even. It's that brow lift I had years ago, isn't it? Before I started coming here. Oh… I knew that was a mistake. I should make a complaint. Sue them, perhaps?'

'It was a long time ago. Things do change over time.' Olivia was having to work hard to sound sympathetic. Her patient was well into her seventies. Surely she would have to accept ageing a little more gracefully soon? Her grandmother had it nailed, she thought. About to celebrate being ninety and what you noticed about her was that the deepest creases on her face were the ones that accompanied that warm and welcoming smile.

Peggy put down the hand mirror she had been peering into so that she could show Olivia exactly what she was worried about.

'You can fix it, though, can't you? Redo the brow lift? Would that work?'

'It would be another general anaesthetic for you, Peggy. We do need to consider your problems with your blood pressure and your heart when thinking about a more major procedure like that. I wouldn't recommend it.'

'But would it work? Without leaving a visible scar?'

The mention of a scar made Olivia instantly wonder how Shayna was today and whether she had followed all the instructions to help her injury heal swiftly. She'd love to be there when the stitches came out to see whether she was justified in feeling as satisfied as she did with that work. Right now, however, she had to think about creating scars that were totally unnecessary rather than helping someone get past what could have been a disfiguring accident.

'The scars for a brow lift are hidden by the hair,' she told Peggy. 'It could certainly address the unevenness you're aware of but, as I said, there are risks—'

'No.' Peggy's head shake was firm. 'No "buts". You're not going to talk me out of it, Dr Donaldson. Book me in, please. As soon as possible.' She stood up. 'I know you're going to insist that I have all sorts of tests first but I like that about you. You're careful and that's how I know I'm in safe hands. Just call me, dear, when you've got a date for me.'

Olivia did pick up the phone later that afternoon but it wasn't to call Peggy Eglington with an admission date to the Plastic Surgery Institute's ward in the private hospital. It was a call to a hospital at the other end of the country.

'His name's Don Donaldson,' she told the operator. 'He was brought in by helicopter yesterday afternoon from Central Otago. I imagine he's in Intensive Care?'

'Who's calling, please?'

'I'm his daughter. Olivia Donaldson.'

It didn't feel weird to say that now. It felt important. A ticket to being given some information that she was anxious to have and it was very reassuring to have her call passed to one of the doctors in the ICU.

'He's doing very well,' she was told. 'He went for endoscopy first thing this morning to see if any further surgery was needed but…' There was an incredulous huff of sound on the other end of the line as if this doctor was shaking her head. 'I can't believe that somebody could operate in a country hospital that hasn't been used for surgery for years and do such a good job. That doctor your father works with is a bit of a hero, I'd say. Cutler's Creek is lucky to have him.'

Olivia could feel a lump forming in her throat as she thought back to watching Zac performing that surgery. She felt so…proud of him? Cutler's Creek wasn't going to have him for much longer, though. She wondered if her father knew about that yet.

'If it's all good, how come he still needs to be in Intensive Care?'

'It's just a precaution. He lost a lot of blood so we'll keep a close eye on him for at least the rest of today. Oh…he's just had an MRI as well and you'll be happy to know that there's nothing obviously wrong with his pancreas at all. I think we've been able to reassure him completely that he's not about to follow in *his* father's footsteps.'

A corner of Olivia's mouth curved up. Zac would no doubt be delighted to know he'd been right about that. She could just imagine the gleam in those gorgeous brown eyes. How good would it have been to be the one to tell him that news? And that the specialists from a major centre had been so impressed with his skills in operating. Olivia could imagine exactly what it would be like to be holding that gaze. She was never going to forget doing exactly that when he'd taken that wine glass out of her hand. When they'd both known what was about to happen. Oh, *help*…

The wrench back to reality came like a physical slap.

Zac hadn't felt like that. He'd had no lingering desire to spend more time with her. He'd rather leave the country and find an exciting war zone to be in and the last image she would ever have of him was the way he had been walking away from her with one hand in the air. Without looking back.

It was weird how you could have thoughts and such powerful emotions that could overpower your mind and your soul in the space of just a heartbeat or two. Olivia tuned back into what the person on the other end of the line was telling her, having only missed a few words.

'…so we've started him on the standard triple treatment antibiotics for peptic ulcer disease, which was confirmed with the biopsy taken during the endoscopy. And he'll need to take proton pump inhibiters to reduce stomach acid but I would expect that he'll go to a ward by tomorrow morning and we're talking about transferring him back to Cutler's Creek hospital for a recuperation period by the end of the week. Now...would you like to talk to him? Or your grandmother, perhaps? I can give them this phone. Your grandmother's been telling me that you were the one to do the anaesthetic for Don. She's very proud of you.'

'Oh...?' That lump was back again at the thought of someone being genuinely proud of her. Someone who had called her "darling" as if it was the most natural thing in the world to do. 'I can't at the moment because I've got a patient waiting but I'll call again as soon as I can.'

'That's not a small cliff.'

'Don't worry, Zac. We're not about to let you fall.' Ben was grinning. 'Let's have a look at that Prusik knot you've tied and see if you remembered how to do it.'

'Bit easier doing it at home in front of the fire than out here with half-frozen fingers.'

'Looks good, though.' It was Mike, the fireman, who checked Zac's knot-tying. 'Okay...put a loop of your rope through the belay plate and then into the carabiner and screw it shut.'

Zac followed instructions and soon had both the rope and the Prusik loop attached to his harness.

'Check to make sure the loop grabs the rope if you let go. And remember to always keep your hand on the rope in front of the loop. Okay...you're good to go. Climb over the edge but don't weight the rope until you're holding onto it.'

Zac had done this before but not on a cliff anywhere near as rugged or high as this one. He was determined to learn to abseil well, though. He didn't want to have to wait until others could bring an injured climber up to him on a rescue mission. He wanted to get down the cliff and start treating them so that by the time they got the stretcher to the top, they wouldn't be wasting any more time in evacuating someone.

Not that it should still be a priority, mind you. It was several days since Zac had made the decision to move on from Cutler's Creek and it was unlikely that he would find himself a mountain rescue team to join in whatever part of the planet he landed in next.

It was also several days since Olivia Donaldson had gone back to her real life so he shouldn't even be thinking about her any more. Thinking that maybe she'd be into something as physical as this mountain rescue or abseiling, judging by the way she'd clambered around that crashed plane, determined to do whatever it took to save that pilot. Who wouldn't have been impressed by that?

'Adjust your harness if you need to,' Ben said. 'You want to make sure it's comfortable before you start the descent.'

Being about to trust his life to some ropes and belay devices should have been enough to focus Zac's thoughts completely on what he was doing at this moment but, somehow, moving his legs to feel how the straps of his harness were gripping the top of his thighs sent his mind fleetingly in another direction that also involved Olivia, and he gave his head a slight shake to get rid of the unwanted distraction. That it was so annoying to have intrusive thoughts like this was a reminder of just how much a couple of days with Olivia had unsettled him, and the amount of effort it was taking to gain control back.

'I'm good to go.' He had his feet wide apart and was leaning back into the harness. Getting safely down this cliff was only the first part of this training exercise. There were other members of the team who were already at the bottom, along with a stretcher and a mannequin that represented the injured climber they were going to have to get back up the cliff and then carry down to their transport vehicle, which was a good hike away.

By the time the group of men were on the track leading back to where they'd parked, they were all a little weary and ready to enjoy the aftermath of a very physical session.

'So who's coming to the pub for a beer after this, then?'

'I'll come to the pub,' Zac said. 'But it's no beer for me at the moment, being the only doctor in these parts.'

'When's Don getting home?' Bruce was in front of Zac.

'Tomorrow. He's done really well.'

'He's lucky to be alive,' Ben said. 'Wouldn't be if you hadn't been there.'

'It wasn't just me.' Zac adjusted his grip on the handle of the plastic stretcher they were carrying, which was loaded with both the mannequin and all their climbing gear. 'It was a team effort.'

'Yeah…' Mike sounded thoughtful. 'Not just for Doc Donaldson, either. My Shayna was pretty lucky that there happened to be a plastic surgeon in town that day.'

Ben threw a grin over his shoulder. 'Not the only lucky one, from what I've heard. She stayed with you the night before, didn't she, Zac?'

Zac shook his head. 'Who told you that?'

'Not me,' Bruce said.

'Could have been Debbie,' Mike suggested. 'Or my missus. She put two and two together when Shayna was telling her all about how Doc Donaldson's daughter delivered that foal of yours on the morning of the storm.'

'Not *my* foal,' Zac muttered. 'I'm just babysitting till Steve gets back from his mid-life crisis world cruise.'

'He's not coming back, didn't you hear? He's fallen head over heels for someone he met on the cruise and he's planning to sell up and go and live in…where was it, Bruce?'

'Can't remember. Iceland?'

'Nah… I think it was England. Hey, maybe you want to buy the place, Doc.'

'I never own property,' Zac told them.

'Why not?'

'Because I never stay in one place that long. I get itchy feet after a year or so.'

A silence fell amongst the group. They all knew how long he'd been in Cutler's Creek and that meant they were all acknowledging that Zac might not be here for much longer, but no one wanted to say anything aloud, including Zac. He was one of them now. How could he tell them that he had to go somewhere else because he liked being with them too much? That he couldn't allow himself to get too attached to people. Or places. And especially not to any particular person, no matter how profoundly they might have disrupted his world.

It was Mike who finally broke the silence, as they slowed to negotiate a steep part of the track.

'I hope Don will be on his feet well enough for his mum's party. Sounds like it's going to be a right knees-up. My missus is in the Women's Institute and they're doing the catering.'

'I helped shift about a hundred hay bales into the old McDrury barn last weekend,' Ben added. 'They'd started some of the decorations and it looked awesome.'

'I've heard they've got the best bluegrass band in the South Island, too,' Bruce put in. 'Three fiddles and a caller. People are going to be dancing all night.'

'Mabel will be, that's for sure.'

'I have no idea what to wear,' Bruce said, as their laughter faded. 'Why the heck is it a fifties theme, any-way?'

'I guess that's the era when Mabel was a young woman and out on the town.'

'It's all right for the women to want to dress up but there's nothing for blokes.'

'Oh, I dunno.' Zac was enjoying this distraction.

'Think James Dean or the Fonz. You know, jeans and white T-shirts and a black leather jacket.'

'You're sorted then,' Ben said. 'You've got the jacket.'

'And then there's the gangster look with braces and one of those hats.'

'Reckon I've got a pair of braces somewhere.' Bruce sounded happier. 'In a box of my dad's stuff.'

'She'll have to come back for that, won't she?'

'Who?' But Zac knew exactly who they were talking about and his enjoyment of the conversation evaporated instantly.

'Doc Donaldson's daughter.'

'Nah.' They were back at the parking area now and he helped slide the stretcher onto the back of the ute. 'She didn't bother taking her invitation with her.'

He'd found it that day, on the bedside table in the procedures room, minutes after she'd driven away from Cutler's Creek. And he'd felt guilty about that. He was the one who'd pushed her away, wasn't he? Had he pushed so hard she wasn't even going to consider coming back to her grandmother's birthday party?

'So I don't think she wants to come back,' he added. Not while he was in town, anyway.

Bruce slammed the tailgate of the ute shut. He slapped his hand on Zac's shoulder as he walked past to get into the driver's seat.

'Maybe you should post it to her,' he said quietly. 'Could be that she left it behind by mistake.'

'Olivia?'

'Yes?' Olivia paused as she walked through the reception area of the Plastic Surgery Institute.

'There's mail for you. A really odd-looking letter.'

'Oh?'

Olivia knew what it was as soon as the embossed envelope was held out to her but she was puzzled about

its arrival here at work. During one of her phone conversations with her father in the last few days she had
promised to try and come to the party, but who had
posted this invitation that she'd left behind at Cutler's
Creek Hospital?

Someone who had found it and wanted to make sure
she didn't forget the date? *Zac...?*

She didn't open it until she was in the privacy of her
consulting room with some time to spare before Peggy
Eglington arrived for another appointment to discuss
the surgery she was still determined to have.

There was nothing to suggest that it had been Zac
who had forwarded the invitation but he was still on her
mind as Olivia smiled at the photograph on the front
of the card—a woman wearing a polka-dot dress with
a circular skirt and cap sleeves, with a big bow on a
sweetheart neckline. Quintessential fifties style. The
woman was dancing and the skirt was as wide as the
smile on her face.

Olivia peered more closely at the image. Was that
her grandmother? Kicking up her heels way back when
she had been just a young woman? Opening the card
confirmed her guess.

Mabel's never stopped dancing!
Come and join us to celebrate her 90th year
of making the most of life.
Classic night of fun
to be held in the McDrury barn
See you there...

It was something on the other side of the card's interior that caught her gaze then. A personal note that had been written beneath a small photograph held in place by a piece of tape.

The note wasn't from Zac. Of course it wasn't, Olivia growled at herself. Why on earth had she thought it might be? Mabel had written it.

I borrowed this from the frame on your dad's bedside table. Maybe you can return it when you come to my party?

It was another picture of Olivia. She'd been a bit older when this one had been taken. Almost eight— just before her world had fallen apart when her father had disappeared from her life. It had been taken at her boarding school and she could remember the moment with absolute clarity, possibly because it was her favourite photo ever and she had exactly the same one in a small heart-shaped silver frame on her own bedside table.

It had been taken in the stables at her boarding school at the end of a weekend show-jumping event and both Olivia and Koko had been exhausted. The first-place ribbon had been discarded in a puddle of red silk on the straw in the corner of the stable. Koko was also on the straw, half–asleep, and Olivia had curled up between his legs, her arms just reaching around his neck and her cheek pressed against his shoulder. She had filthy jodhpurs, mucky boots and bits of straw in her hair, but to her it was an image of the happiest moment in her life. She only had to look at the photo to remember the warmth of being so close to another living being that she loved so much. The feeling of being in the only place in the world that she wanted to be.

Olivia had tears running down her cheeks as she took the photo from the card and held it in her hand. It wasn't simply the extra evidence of how much her father had always loved her that was her undoing. It was realising that she'd only ever once had that kind of feeling again that she'd had when this photo had been taken, and that had been those moments in Zac's arms—between their lovemaking and finally falling into that dreamless sleep.

It was crazy to miss someone so intensely when she had only known him for such a short time but there it was. Isaac Cameron had rocked her world and it was never going to be the same. She wanted to tell Zac that. Even if he didn't feel the same way and even if he believed he could never get attached to anyone again because of whatever tragedy he'd been through, maybe he should know that he had changed someone else's life for the better.

Maybe it might make a difference if he knew that he was loved. It might even change Zac's life for the better and he deserved that, didn't he?

Olivia dried her eyes and straightened her back, opening her phone to find that voicemail message that had changed her life. The number was still tagged as "unknown". How crazy was that? It felt like she had known Isaac Cameron forever.

It was going to take courage to tap that link and, in that moment of hesitation, Olivia remembered the last time she had been about to do exactly this. She had been going to return the call and tell this stranger what she thought of him. And then she had decided that she would tell her father what she thought of *him* but, in the end, she had chosen to say what she needed to say face to face.

There was even more reason to have this conversation face to face. It would be so much easier to keep the truth hidden when you were on the other end of a phone call. And Olivia really, really needed to know if what was simmering behind all this—somewhere between a longing and a belief—might be true. That you couldn't feel the kind of connection with someone that she had found with Zac if it was totally one-sided.

Simon wasn't going to be too impressed by her leaving town again so soon but, perhaps because Peggy Eglington was the next patient she was due to see, something else was suddenly very clear to Olivia.

This wasn't the place she belonged and it was time she did something about that.

Peggy was in the waiting room as Olivia walked out of the Plastic Surgery Institute after she'd been to talk to Simon.

'I'm so sorry,' she told her client. 'But Simon will be delighted to see you today. I can't stay, I'm afraid. It's a personal thing…'

CHAPTER TEN

No…

It couldn't be. Zac took a second look at the car pulling in to one of the visitors' parks in front of Cutler's Creek Community Hospital. His breath caught as he peered through the window to see the figure climbing out of the driver's seat.

It was definitely Olivia Donaldson. Not that she looked anything like the first time he'd seen her, in that tight skirt and matching jacket. Or the last time, when she'd disappeared wearing hospital scrubs under her coat. Right now, she was wearing jeans and jodhpur-style boots and a warm jumper under an anorak. As if she was quite used to living in a place like this with its hot summers and icy winters.

This was his own fault, Zac realised as he walked towards the reception area. If he hadn't taken Bruce's advice and forwarded that party invitation, maybe Olivia wouldn't have come back here so soon—and he would have already left the area. This was unsettling, to say the least. Just when things had started to settle down properly and he was feeling completely back in control of his life.

On the other hand, maybe it could be useful. Perhaps Don Donaldson would listen to his daughter and not insist on being back at work when he was only just getting back on his feet. "Light duties" he was calling it but really he should be at home for at least a few more days.

He reached the entrance to Reception just as Olivia was coming in through the front doors and his steps almost faltered as he realised just how unsettling this actually was. It wasn't just that Jill wasn't behind the desk that made it feel as if he and Olivia were the only people on the planet right then. It was a flashback to when she'd come here to tell him about Chloe's foal being born. When he had still been dazed from what had gone on between them the night before and when he'd been aware of a connection that had made the rest of the world seem irrelevant. His senses were suddenly heightened to the point that tiny details were leaping out at him. How could he have forgotten how incredibly blue her eyes were and surely he couldn't actually be aware of the scent of her skin when he wasn't even within touching distance? And, oh…man…he had completely blocked the memory of what that smile was like, hadn't he?

Yep. This was unsettling all right. So why did it feel good at the same time? As if something at a cellular level was coming alive all over again?

Olivia's smile was faltering. Because he wasn't smiling back?

'You're still here,' Olivia said.

'You thought I wouldn't be?' Had she hoped he wouldn't still be here?

'You said you were planning to leave.'

'I am.' This was better. Talking about future plans was a good way to regain control. 'It's not that easy to find a locum, though. It's always been hard to find any-one who wants to come and live in a one-horse town like Cutler's Creek.'

'I might know someone,' Olivia said. 'Though she might need a refresher course in general medicine and whatever other training is available to work in a rural hospital.'

Zac blinked slowly. '*You?* But… I thought it was the last place you'd want to be.'

'So did I,' Olivia said quietly. 'But I was wrong. I'm starting to think that this might be the place I really be-long. And that's thanks to you.'

'Oh?' A prickle of something like premonition made Zac rub the back of his neck. 'How's that?'

'You told me about those letters. And the parcels. I took them back to Auckland with me and…and maybe my mother had some idea what was in them because if I'd opened them and read those books I might have dreamed of coming here a very long time ago. I might never have even gone to medical school and she would have been so disappointed by that. She would have thought I was throwing my life away.'

'What sort of books?'

'Pony stories. Books about Central Otago with the most amazing photographs. And there were stories in Dad's letters. About the people who lived here and what the mountains were like. I could understand why my parents' marriage could never have worked and why my mother might have thought she was protecting me by cutting me off from my dad. But there was so much about how much he missed me and hoped that I would come and visit. So, here I am. For a long visit, I hope…'

Zac was trying to find the words to tell her what good news this was. Because her father and her grandmother would be thrilled. Because it meant that he would be free to leave anytime he wanted. For some reason, however, the words were hard to find and in the slightly awkward silence he became aware of something else. A sound he was very familiar with.

Olivia knew what it was, as well. 'That's the civil defence siren,' she said. 'That means there's an emergency somewhere, doesn't it?'

'Aye.' Zac was reaching for the phone he had in the pocket of his white coat. 'It does.' He activated a rapid-dial number. 'Bruce? What's happening?'

Olivia was watching Zac's face as he made a phone call. She had, in fact, been watching his face very closely from the moment she'd walked in here. He'd felt it, she knew he had. He'd felt that connection between them that might have started as nothing more than a powerful sexual attraction but it had become something far more significant during those intense hours they'd shared since then. Taking it further was a risk, of course. Loving anybody was a risk and maybe Zac wasn't ready to take that risk yet. She could still hear an echo of what he'd said to her that day.

'Sometimes you have to shut yourself off from something that hurts too much because, if you don't, it can destroy you. It will *destroy you.'*

Olivia could understand that. He'd loved and lost someone and it would be a huge leap of faith for him to risk doing that again. This was pretty scary for her, as well. She'd come here to offer her heart to him and it was going to be devastating if he didn't want to accept it. He'd said he was still planning to leave Cutler's Creek. And he hadn't even smiled at her.

He certainly wasn't smiling now.

'What...? Oh, no...'

Zac had gone noticeably pale, and for a horrible moment Olivia was reminded of the expression on his face when that plane wreck had caught fire behind them. As if, for a heartbeat, he was somewhere else. Somewhere soul-destroying. From the corner of her eye she saw Jill coming back into Reception, and walking slowly beside her was Don.

'Okay,' Zac said. 'Tell Ben and Tony to take the ambulance. I'll meet you at the farm...'

'Libby...' Don was smiling at her. 'I didn't tell anyone that you were coming. It's still going to be a surprise for your gran's party tomorrow.' He turned to Zac as he ended his call. 'What's going on?' he asked. 'I heard the siren.'

'Gavin Morris had an accident on his quad bike up in one of his higher paddocks. He might have broken his ankle by the sound of it, getting himself out from under the bike, and he lost his phone so he had to drag himself down to the road to flag down some help.'

'You going to pick him up, then?'

'Yes. And no. There's something else and I don't know where I'll be needed more.'

Olivia could see how still Zac was holding himself. This was something huge, she realised. Something painful…

'He'd taken Jamie out on the bike with him to give Faye a chance to have a sleep while the baby was sleeping.'

'Oh, no…' Don's face creased. 'Jamie's been hurt? He's just a wee lad—two years old now?'

'We don't know if he's hurt,' Zac said. 'He ran off while Gavin was getting out from under the bike and he's vanished. He's somewhere on the side of that mountain and we've got to find him.'

'I'll come, too,' Don said.

'Don't be daft, man. You're in no fit state. What you can do is be here. I might need to send Gavin to you in the ambulance if he needs treatment.' Zac was already heading for the door. 'Maybe you could stay and help your dad, Liv.'

'No.' There was no way Olivia could let Zac walk out that door alone, looking like that. 'I'm coming with you.'

'Yes, go…' Don nodded. 'I can manage here.'

Olivia was shoulder to shoulder with Zac as the doors opened. He turned his head as they walked through them and, this time, as his gaze met hers, that feeling of connection was even stronger. She knew, without a doubt, that Zac wanted her beside him for whatever they were about to face.

He needed her.

* * *

There was an unsealed road that led well up into the Morris family's high country farm and a paddock was being used for vehicles to park. Zac's SUV with its magnetic light on the roof was one of the first to arrive, along with the ambulance Ben was driving and Bruce in his police car. Mike and his colleagues from the volunteer fire service arrived a short time later as Zac was assessing Gavin's injury, and then more and more people that Olivia had never met were turning up. One of Cutler's Creek's people was in trouble and the community was gathering to do whatever it could to help. Under Bruce's direction, they were fanning out over the tussock- and rock-covered land, starting to search for a small boy. His helmet had been found, not far from where the quad bike had rolled, but there was no sign of Jamie.

Olivia had helped Zac splint Gavin's ankle.

'It could well be broken given how painful it is,' Zac said. 'But it's not displaced and your limb baselines are all okay for the moment. I'll get Ben to take you in to the hospital and Doc Donaldson can X-ray it for you. You'll need to go to town to get it plastered if it is broken, though.'

'I'm not going anywhere until Jamie gets found. Just give me something for the pain. I've got to help search.'

'Where's Faye?'

'Someone's gone to get her. And the baby.' Gavin covered his face as he groaned. 'What if…? Oh… God…this is unbearable.'

'I know.' Zac gripped his shoulder. 'We'll give you

something for the pain and you can stay here for now, in the ambulance. We'll get someone to keep an eye on you but if things get worse, we'll have to take you in to the hospital, okay?'

Gavin scrubbed at his face as he looked up at both Zac and Olivia. 'Can you go and help?' he begged. 'Please… I just need someone to find my son.'

How far could a two-year-old boy go?

The search had been going for an hour. And then another. People were searching in pairs and moving further and further out from where the accident had happened. Olivia was climbing around some big rocks, peering into gaps that could be large enough for a small body to have squeezed into.

'Jamie?' she called. 'Where are you, sweetheart?'

In the silence that followed her call she came to stand beside Zac, following his example to shade her eyes against the lowering sun to look down the slope of this paddock.

'Have you had an update on Gavin?'

'Nothing's changed and his pain's under control. He's got his wife and their new baby in the ambulance with him and they're being well looked after.'

'They must be frantic. I know I would be. That caravan wasn't there before, was it?'

'I think it belongs to the Women's Institute. They'll be providing hot drinks and food for everybody involved in this search. I imagine your gran is down there in the thick of it. She's been running that club forever.'

'She's an amazing woman,' Olivia said. 'I'm really

looking forward to getting to know her. And... I can't believe how everybody is here helping. They...they really care, don't they?'

She looked up at Zac and he could see tears shining in her eyes. It was an effort to pull in a breath because of the squeeze he could feel in his own chest.

'Who wouldn't?' he said, a little more sharply than he'd intended. 'This is a two-year-old kid. It's...' He turned away. 'Come on...we've got to keep looking. Let's head for those trees in the gully.'

He strode ahead but Olivia was keeping up with him. She touched his arm. 'What is it, Zac? Tell me...please?'

He walked a few more paces before saying anything. He'd held back from telling her this once before but maybe she needed to know the worst about him. Maybe *that* would keep him safe?

'It was the reason I came here in the first place,' he said. 'A kid of about the same age.'

'He got lost?'

'No. He got beaten up by his stepfather. Drug addict mother didn't even come into ED with him. There was nothing we could do and there was nobody who cared enough to be there with him. Or to hold him while he died.'

Olivia caught his hand in hers. 'What did you do?'

'I held him.'

The squeeze on his hand was sympathetic. 'I can understand why you needed to get away,' she said. 'How heartbreaking that must have been.'

'No, you don't get it.' Zac pulled his hand free from hers. 'That was when I thought I should walk away from medicine completely. Because, after Mia died, I'd taught myself not to care too much. Not to get attached to anything. Or anyone. I thought it was the only way I could keep doing the kind of work I thought I wanted to do for the rest of my life.'

He could still feel the horror of that moment. 'I got to the point where I could hold a dying child and not feel anything but numb and I just wanted to hide. I realised that I had no idea who I was any more and I didn't like the person I'd become. Not caring at all is actually worse than caring too much because it takes any meaning out of life. That's why I came here. To hide. To see if I actually still existed.'

'You *do* care, Zac. You know you do. *I* know you do. It's one of the things I love about you.'

Her words skated past his brain. He knew she was right. He did care again. He could feel the pain of it pressing down on him. He could still take control, though. He knew how to push it away and slam the lid down on the pain that caring so much could bring.

Olivia was slightly ahead of him as they reached the edge of a gully where the ground dropped sharply. She stopped so abruptly that Zac almost walked into her and he had to catch her shoulders to stop her falling down the steep slope.

And then he looked to see what had made her stop and he froze, as well. The last tree he could see was on such a steep part of the slope that it was growing out at a ninety-degree angle with its canopy hanging over a cliff edge and its twisted, exposed roots clinging to the rocky slope. Curled up in a gap between those huge tree roots was a small boy who was wearing gumboots and a warm coat with a hood. He had his eyes closed and he was so still that Zac could feel his own heart stop for a beat. He could feel it cracking. Was Jamie asleep? Unconscious? Or had the worst happened?

'No...'

Olivia slid out of his grasp and took a step onto the slope. She started to slide instantly and only prevented the momentum of her fall becoming uncontrolled by catching the branches of another small tree.

And something snapped inside Zac as that crack burst wide open.

This was *his* fault. He had persuaded Olivia to be here. By making that phone call in the first place and now by having sent that party invitation. She was here because of him and now she was in danger herself. And there was a small child who was also in danger. Was history trying to repeat itself by creating a combination of the worst moments of Zac's life?

He was sliding down that slope himself before he'd given it any real thought. He had to get to Olivia and make sure she was safe.

'Don't move,' he said, as soon as he could touch her. 'We don't have any idea how high that cliff is. We need to wait for the right equipment.'

'We can't wait,' Olivia said. 'If Jamie wakes up and climbs over those roots, then he's going to fall.'

'I'll go.' Zac still hadn't let go of Olivia. 'This is my fault. I'm going to deal with it.'

'Don't be daft. How on earth is this your fault?'

'You're only here because of me. You said so yourself. I couldn't live with myself if you got hurt. *Please*, Liv…stay here… For me…'

He didn't give her time to argue. Carefully, he let go of both Olivia and the tree that was their anchor to let himself slide down to the next safe point he could see, which was a large rock. Another slide took him close to the tree roots and it was then that he saw Jamie move. The little boy opened his eyes just as Zac reached out to touch him.

'Where's Mummy?' he asked. 'I'm hungry.'

Zac had to swallow past the constriction in his throat to try and make his voice sound normal. 'We're going to go and find Mummy,' he told Jamie. 'Are you okay? Is there anything that hurts?'

Jamie shook his head. He held out his arms. 'Up,' he said. 'My legs are tired.'

Holding Jamie tightly against his body with one arm, Zac started to climb, using his other arm to catch the branches and rocks he needed to keep them safe from sliding towards that cliff. Olivia was waiting to help as they reached the final part of the climb and she took Jamie into her own arms as they finally got back onto safe ground. It was only then that Zac realised he had tears rolling down his face.

He cleared his throat as he hit the speed-dial number on his phone.

'We've found him, Bruce. He's fine. We're heading back…'

His voice cracked on his last word. He looked down at Olivia and Jamie and he had to put his arms around both of them.

'It's okay,' Olivia said softly. 'Everything's going to be okay.' Her sniff suggested that she was crying, as well. 'And it's true that I'm here because of you, Zac, but it's *my* choice to be here and, whatever happens, it's the only place I'm going to want to be. It's not your fault. You've blamed yourself for too many things that weren't your fault.'

And it was only then that Zac remembered what else Olivia had said.

That she loved him…

He had that strange internal cracking sensation again but this time it was the opposite side of fear and pain. This was joy.

This was love.

The door in that protective barrier was swinging wide open and the pull to step through it was too powerful to resist. This was what being alive was all about. He didn't need to shut feelings like this away. Not when he was with the one person who had brought him back to life. Who was giving him the strength to believe in important things again. Things like life. And love…

Zac needed to hold Olivia even closer. To press his forehead against hers. He still didn't have any words but it felt as though he could communicate anyway. Just for another heartbeat, before they took Jamie back to his family, he wanted to soak in that touch of his skin against hers. That incredible feeling of connection that was so strong you could believe that you would never feel alone again. And that you could cope with anything at all because it would be shared. He wanted to feel love—both given and received—because, in the end, that was all that really mattered, wasn't it?

He knew Olivia didn't want to break that connection, either, because she kept so close to him as they walked back across the paddock. Zac was carrying Jamie who had fallen asleep again in his arms. People were gathering below them and they were all watching. They knew the search was over but they wanted to witness every moment of its joyful conclusion.

'I think we've got the whole of Cutler's Creek watching us,' Zac said.

'I'd better stop hanging on to your arm, then.' Olivia grinned. 'Or the rumours will start.'

'They already have. Everybody knows you stayed with me that night.'

'They don't know that anything happened.'

Zac caught Olivia's gaze and he could see the reflection of exactly what he was acknowledging. That what had happened had been the most amazing thing possible.

'I'm in love with you, Liv. Is that crazy when we hardly know each other?'

'I feel like I've known you forever,' she said. 'And I'm totally in love with you. It feels like I've been looking for you forever.'

'That's it, exactly. For me, too. Even though I didn't know I was looking for you.'

They were almost at the fence of this paddock. People were coming to join them now, needing to be close enough to see for themselves that the fear for one small boy was really over.

Zac slowed his steps so that he could have just another moment of privacy with Olivia.

'And that's how long I want to be with you,' he added. 'Forever.'

'And a day.' She was smiling up at him, tears of joy in her eyes. 'Don't forget about that extra day,' she said. 'There's always an extra day.'

It took a moment before Zac could trust his voice not to crack. 'Absolutely,' he murmured. 'Forever *and* a day.'

EPILOGUE

One year later...

'It still fits.'

The dress Olivia was wearing was the same one she'd worn to Mabel Donaldson's fifties-themed ninetieth birthday party a year ago. It was a plain dark blue with gores in the skirt that had tiny white polka dots on the blue background and the same spotted fabric peeped out from beneath the heart-shaped neckline. She had left her hair loose but had a silk scarf in a matching blue that she wound around her head and tied in a bow at one side, pulling out enough hair at the front to give herself a boofy fringe, and she was smiling widely as she did a twirl in front of her husband.

'It's not going to fit for much longer. You'll start showing soon.' The smile they shared acknowledged the secret they'd been keeping for quite a few weeks now. It also acknowledged that life was about to change again in the not-too-distant future but they were more than ready for the coming changes. They couldn't wait, in fact. They'd only waited this long to start a family because Olivia had wanted to get her new postgraduate courses finished and then to settle into her new position as the next generation Dr Donaldson at Cutler's Creek Community Hospital.

Oh, yeah…there'd been the small matter of that glorious summer wedding that they'd held outside with the backdrop of the mountains she now loved so much. The whole town had been invited and the celebration in the community hall afterwards had rivalled Mabel's birthday party as one to remember.

Olivia wanted to do another little twirl to let her skirts billow. She had never dreamed that she would ever be this happy but maybe it took knowing that you were finally living in the place you truly belonged. No, it was more about the people you belonged with than a place, wasn't it? Or one person in particular. She had her soulmate right beside her and she had more family and a whole community around her, as well. It was home and family and forever, all wrapped up together, and it felt just as solid as those mountains she got to admire every day. Blinking back happy tears, she held her hand out to Zac in an invitation to dance with her.

He was wearing faded denim jeans and a close-fitting white T-shirt under a leather jacket. His hair was slicked back, although his curls were already trying to break free of the product and he looked just as gorgeous as he had the first time Olivia had ever set eyes on him. No… More gorgeous, she decided as he caught her in his arms and twirled her around in the kitchen. Then he stopped, pulled her closer and kissed her. Olivia wound her arms around his neck and kissed him back. Somewhere, in the back of her mind, she realised that this was exactly the same place they'd shared their very first kiss. They owned this cottage now and the biggest horse in the world still lived in the paddock they could see from the kitchen window, along with her baby, who was doing his best to grow just as tall.

Finally, they had to break their kiss and come up for air. Reluctantly, Olivia pulled out of Zac's arms, as well.

'I'd better get those sausage rolls out of the oven before that flaky pastry burns to a crisp.' Putting oven gloves on, she pulled out the savoury rolls and wrapped foil and then a towel around the oven tray so they could carry it out to the car. 'Don't forget the tomato sauce,' she reminded Zac.

'Will they have those square cakes again this time? The pink ones with the coconut on the outside?'

'Lamingtons? Of course. It has to be a classic Kiwi supper.' Olivia smiled. 'I'm so glad Gran decided to have another fifties party this year. It was all a bit of a blur last time, what with so much happening in such a short space of time. And it was all so new for me.'

'You'll get used to it. Mabel told me the other day that she was going to have this party again every year from now on,' Zac told her. 'That every year after ninety was a bonus that needs celebrating and you can't beat the fifties for a party.'

'At least this year Dad will be well enough to dance.'

'He'll be showing us all up on the dance floor, from what I've heard.'

'I know. He and Jill have been going to rock 'n' roll dance classes for months now.'

'Do you think there's something going on there?'

'I hope so.'

'Maybe they'll announce something at the party to-night.'

'Maybe *we* should announce something.'

They shared another smile. 'Maybe we should.'

It was time that Mabel Donaldson stopped dancing.

Just long enough to catch her breath, mind you. And to find where she'd left her glass of champagne.

She paused for a moment beside a stack of hay bales and looked around her party. The music was loud and almost everyone was still on the dance floor. She could see Don and that lovely Jill, who was about to take over Mabel's presidency of the Women's Institute. My word, those two could dance now. And Don looked so happy. Happier than he had ever looked. Mabel knew that had a lot to do with his daughter coming back into his life. Into all their lives.

Including that lovely young man Isaac Cameron, who was not only going to stay in Cutler's Creek forever but was also now part of her very own family. Married to her gorgeous granddaughter. They were dancing, too, and they looked for all the world as if they were on their very own dance floor. Staring into each other's eyes as if they were even more in love than ever.

Last year's birthday, when she'd turned ninety, had been very special, of course. The surprise that Olivia had come back in time for her party had been the best gift possible. But this year's surprise—learning that she would be meeting her first great-grandchild in about six months' time—well…could life get any better?

Now…where *had* she left that glass of champagne?

* * * * *

COMING SOON!

We really hope you enjoyed reading this book. If you're looking for more romance, be sure to head to the shops when new books are available on

Thursday 31st October

To see which titles are coming soon, please visit

millsandboon.co.uk/nextmonth

MILLS & BOON

Coming next month

HIGHLAND DOC'S CHRISTMAS RESCUE
Susan Carlisle

Cass picked up her other shoes and placed them in the box while Lyle held it. She met his gaze. "By the way, what's your favorite color?"

"Green." His eyes didn't waver. "I'm particularly fond of the shade of green of your eyes."

Her breath caught. "Are you flirting with me?"

"What if I am?" He took the box and set it on the bench. "I've been thinking about that kiss."

A tingle ran through her. "You shouldn't."

"What? Think about it or think about doing it again?"

"Both," she squeaked.

"Why?" His voice turned gravelly, went soft. Lyle stepped toward her.

Because she was damaged. Because she was scared. Because she couldn't handle caring about anything or anyone again. "Because I'm leaving soon."

"Cass, we can share an interest in each other without it becoming a lifelong commitment. I'd like to get to know you better. Couldn't we be friends? Enjoy each other's company while you're here?"

Put that way, it sounded reasonable. Lyle moved so close that his heat warmed her. Why was it so hard to breathe? She simmered with anticipation. His hands came to rest at her waist as his mouth lowered to hers.

She didn't want his kiss. That wasn't true. Until that

moment she'd had no idea how desperately she did want Lyle's lips on hers. Her breath caught as his mouth made a light brush over hers. He pulled away. Cass ran her tongue over her bottom lip, tasting him.

Lyle groaned and pulled her tight against his chest. His lips firmly settled over hers. Cass grabbed his shoulders to steady herself. Slowly she went up on her toes, her desire drawing her nearer to him. Sweet heat curled and twisted through her center and seeped into her every cell. She'd found her cozy fire in a winter storm.

The sound of the door opening brought both their heads up. Their gazes locked with each other's.

Continue reading
HIGHLAND DOC'S CHRISTMAS RESCUE
Susan Carlisle

Available next month
www.millsandboon.co.uk

LET'S TALK

Romance

For exclusive extracts, competitions
and special offers, find us online:

[f] facebook.com/millsandboon

[twitter] @MillsandBoon

[instagram] @MillsandBoonUK

Get in touch on 01413 063232

For all the latest titles coming soon, visit

millsandboon.co.uk/nextmonth